AT THE CROSSROADS

AT THE CROSSROADS

Frankie Schelly

PRAISE FOR FRANKIE SCHELLY'S
AT THE CROSSROADS

…The nuns have not been sheltered from events and issues of the larger world. Their spirituality has not been an escape from it, but is a guide and resource for dealing with the tough choices they face. This spirituality gives an added dimension to the treatment of the contemporary issues. The nuns are not feminists in the familiar or stereotypical way, but rather their actions disclose new shades of involvement, concern, and also effectiveness, with respect to circumstances and events of contemporary life facing thoughtful persons. The reader becomes absorbed in following the characters as they struggle to make up their minds about what to do in their changing circumstances.

—Henry Berry, *The Small Press Book Review*

… As each woman struggles with individual crises, they must pull together to find the strength to survive the end of life as they know it. The depictions of sex are more graphic than usually found in Christian fiction, but Schelly's first novel grapples with topics of current interest in much the say that Bambola's *Tears in a Bottle* does. A strong contribution for most [library] collections.

—Melanie C. Duncan, *Library Journal*

I cried; I laughed. The struggles of these four nuns are the struggles of all women. I liked the humorous touches.

—Ellie Zitin, history department chair

... a fascinating picture of convent life and how it has changed. Beautifully crafted in superb style and elegantly simple language. I cared about the characters and wanted to find out what happened.

—Linda Coppens, author of *What American Women Did, 1789-1920.*

... cleverly woven individual, family, societal, and religious systems collide and push well-drawn characters into "ready or not" life decisions. Issues core to being human and how the past impacts the present are masterfully handled.

—Sharon Renfro, family therapist

... the stories of four strong women, connected by faith and vows, as each confronts her own fears and is challenged and embraced by the others. This realistic portrayal of their personal and communal struggles offers a touching glimpse of humanity's vulnerability and power, courage and compassion.

—Sandra Smith, M. Div., co-founder and director of Holy Ground Retreat Ministry

Dedicated to the single, largest,

most educated group of

successful career women in the world.

ACKNOWLEDGMENTS

Gratitude goes first to my mother, Frances Frank, who came to the United States via Ellis Island, and who, with great sacrifice and devotion, saw to it that my brothers and I had the kind of education she had so wished for herself. To Sister Paschal Marie, OSF, who in fifth grade ignited my love for learning. To Sister Mary Helen Rappenecker, CHM, who asked that fateful question: "Frankie, did you ever consider becoming a writer?"

I thank members of the Charlotte Writers' group, members of the Western North Carolina Writers' Guild, Erwin McIver Hinson for sharing so much of her music knowledge, and readers Shirley Blue, Peggy Ryan, and author Jack R. Pyle—who, whenever I grew discouraged, insisted on the importance of this novel, and to Donna Jansen, Robin Smith, and Susan Snowden for insightful editorial and marketing assistance. Oprah Winfrey must be included for all the readers she has turned on to worthy writing.

Gratitude also belongs to my children, Lin, Phil, and Tom, for their endurance and support, and to my husband, Cy, who came up with the title and worked tirelessly when asked, and who gave me the solitude and time necessary to breathe life into the characters that live on these pages.

Ill habits gather by unseen degrees,

As brooks make rivers, rivers run to seas.

Dryden, 1700

CHAPTER ONE

The floor-to-ceiling, white marble altar looked like an overfrosted wedding cake. In the central niche stood the statue of St. Anthony, the saint to whom you prayed to find what was lost, while Matthew, Mark, Luke, and John upheld gospel truth from the four overfrosted outer reaches. In the front pew, Vivian Tiamet nervously shifted her weight.

She was a slender, small-boned woman with angular features in her mid-forties. She felt hot and heady with her navy blue woolen coat over her gray woolen suit. Though PTA mothers teased her about her virgin-blue eyes and her graceful gestures, in this moment she felt no grace. Father Rupert had given yet another homily on: In marriage avoid the sins of sex. Irritated, anxious to exit, Vivian edged toward the aisle. The scent of stale incense made it hard to breathe. The priest turned to the congregation, raised his hand and blessed them, making the sign of the cross, saying, "Go in peace."

Vivian moved into the aisle, nodded a token bow toward the altar, and hurried toward the door. She felt nauseous. She reached up and pushed back the right side of her blunt-cut hair, should never have agreed to a cut that hid some of her view, even if the style suggested that her gray streak belonged there.

Whatever did Father mean when he said, "Purity of intention renders the conception of a child holier"? She gripped and squeezed the figure of Christ on the pectoral cross hanging between her breasts. *Not once did he mention pleasure. Not once.* Caught up among others now, she moved more slowly. Surely the

13

priest knew that kind of sermon put struggles in the minds of wives and mothers. They brought them to Vivian's principal's office and expected her to come up with solutions. He had actually encouraged couples to deny sexual pleasure in marriage. Lest anyone ask her opinion of the homily and she betray her disdain, Vivian kept custody of the eyes, kept her eyes downcast.

Outside it was predawn, still dark. She stepped gingerly over a thinly iced puddle and off the curb into the street. Behind her, a woman screamed. Brakes screeched. A car horn blared. Vivian found herself illuminated in the beam of headlights, hands clutching her ears. *What on earth?* The car's radiator blasted heat and looked like a confessional grill.

Rankled—she could have been killed—Vivian chopped a hand behind her at those watching, to say, "I'm all right," and waved the driver on. Once safe and shuddering on the other side of the street, she drew her lips into a thin, pinched line, and strode, determined to hold her own against the priest's ignorance. She trembled at her near miss as she passed the school, moving toward the house that was their convent. Despite tremors, her thoughts invaded. *Imagine a wife saying to her husband in that most intimate of moments, "Darling, remember, self-denial!" If sexual pleasure doesn't compensate for all those wakeful nights with a colicky baby, for all those times when a mother sets a child firmly on the moral path, what does?*

How convenient for Father Rupert if she had landed in the hospital or ... worse. Her heart pounded. As she approached the back door of the convent, she realized how much it would upset Sister Dominic to see her this way and turned and paced on the asphalt playground between the convent and the school.

From day one Rupert had scotched every visionary plan she proposed until his dumb decisions brought them to the brink of their current financial troubles. He meddled, couldn't seem to remember that she answered to him only in parish matters, that the other three sisters answered to her, and she to Reverend Mother Philip Neri, who lived in SIHM's motherhouse, in Sisters of the Immaculate Heart of Mary headquarters in Brandenburg, Indiana. Mother's lack of support disappointed her. Men believed in control; priests were men. That was the nub of it. Why in the world had Mother ever sent her here to Sleeder, Illinois, to save St. Anthony School if it couldn't be done?

Damn. Sometimes couples marry to avoid the sin of sex. They do.

If Vivian had known her life would become as spiritually and financially bankrupt as the lives of the women who confided in her, never would she have entered the convent in the first place, not that she had felt she had had much choice back then. She fumbled in her pocket for her key, drew a deep breath of cold air, and opened their back door.

The kitchen's bright fluorescence always reminded

Vivian of the transfiguration. Sister Dominic looked up from the batter she was mixing in the stainless steel bowl and smiled. Vivian nodded and hung her coat on the coat tree beside the sewing machine in the corner. Like many sisters after Vatican II in the late sixties urged religious orders to modernize, their housekeeper chose to keep wearing her black habit, and to keep her sister title. Sister Dominic said, "There will be no ankle showing or jewelry wearing for me."

"What was the commotion I heard?" the old woman asked, pushing her trifocals higher from the bridge of her nose. Before her shoulders bent, Sister Dominic had stood a shy five feet. The corners of her mouth perpetually turned upward as if she had just grasped some delightful cosmic joke. People said they experienced awe in her presence.

Vivian touched the spot in her chin where her old starched guimpe had dented it so deeply she thought it would never go away, but it had. Unnerved, not wanting to admit her own stupidity, Vivian said, "Someone didn't look before entering the street. The fool could have been killed," she muttered. "Thankfully the car stopped in time."

She entered the ill-placed bathroom they had added near the back door after climbing stairs had become too difficult for Sister Dominic's arthritic knees. Though inconvenient, the plumber claimed it the most economical location. For modesty the bathroom had two doors. When the second one closed, the vacuum between the two sounded a grand *phuff*, calling attention to you when you least wanted it. By the time Vivian came out she had breathed herself into some calm. The red light on the waffle iron glowed.

"You have a visitor."

"Who?"

"Mrs. Suges and her daughter."

"Jennifer? Jennifer Suges?"

The girl had graduated from Vivian's eighth-grade class two years earlier. "I wonder what she wants. That priest," Vivian said, seeking comfort. "Picking up his psychological litter makes me feel like a wife picking up a husband's dirty socks." They exchanged conspiratorial smiles. Vivian sighed. She loved this dear woman whom she could count on for comfort, wisdom, balance.

Sister Dominic pushed her trifocals higher, said, "Kimberly's staying in church a bit."

"Well," Vivian smiled suggesting Kimberly could use a bit of extra prayer. She tugged the hem of her jacket and straightened her cross, wanted to say, *I love you*, but, of course, couldn't; tradition discouraged any show of affection. "I'll see what the Sugeses want. Thanks for the waffles. My spirit could use a lift."

"I can tell."

Vivian moved through the hall, past the small telephone table, past the closed door of the reception room they had turned into a bedroom for Sister Dominic, and arrived in the entry hall. Behind the closed music room door, Mary Ruth was playing Bach on the piano. The room had been a formal dining room before they sealed off the archway to the kitchen and turned it into the piano lesson room. If only Kimberly were as malleable as Mary Ruth. Her task of coaching this only child of a doctor and his socialite wife into manners and behavior becoming to a religious would be easier. Vivian lightly tapped her plain gold wedding band on the parlor door and opened it.

Mrs. Suges rose. "Sister, I hope you don't mind us dropping by." Mrs. Suges was one of few parishioners who refused to drop the sister title. "Sister, I been threatening to bring Jennifer for some time. You're the only one Jennifer ever listened to."

"No. No. Of course not." Vivian said, closing the door, not liking the idea of being used as a threat. Tension between the mother and daughter was palpable. The woman's pudgy knuckles whitened on her clutch purse. Dark puffy crescents under Mrs. Suges' eyes suggested the woman carried germs of worry there. The problem must be serious.

The girl wore a yellow sweatshirt with rhinestones on it and her hair had been died a brassy strawberry color. Dark eyeliner exaggerated her eyes like a doll's. Underneath all that eyeliner Vivian could tell Jennifer's eyes were red and swollen from crying.

Vivian said, "It's nice to see you, Jennifer," and offered a warm smile.

The girl turned her gaze away.

"Please sit down. What can I do for you?"

"She don't come home, won't listen, won't mind, stays out too late." The woman sat on the edge of one of the two Queen Anne chairs, drumming her fingers on her purse.

Vivian wanted to help. Humbled by their confidence, needing to pull out the problem, she turned to Jennifer and tried a tactic that worked in the classroom. "That doesn't sound like you, Jennifer, not like the young woman who stayed home and cooked for farmhands when your mother had pneumonia, and then worked doubly hard to make up lessons. Not the Jennifer who nursed the new calf for nearly fifty hours after everyone else had given up on it."

The girl peeked at her mother, seeking approval. Not receiving it, she slid one soiled sneaker over the other and stared at her toes.

Vivian wanted to reach out and squeeze the girl's hand, say something reassuring, but she dared not take sides. She waited. When the girl said nothing more Vivian turned to Mrs. Suges and said, kindly, "Maybe Jennifer doesn't want my assistance."

"She doesn't listen! Somebody's got to help!"

"My brothers stay out all night."

"They're not girls!"

Trying to persuade Mr. Suges would be like going up against the old Soviet Union—a cold war. At least Mrs. Suges was trying to confront whatever it was. Vivian's own family had settled squabbles by not acknowledging them. What would possibly make Jennifer so inconsolable? Vivian experienced a sudden visceral dread followed by a drain of energy. Her heart dissolved into fear. *That* problem still ruined a girl's life. Her hand moved to her abdomen. She swallowed.

Jennifer muttered, "S'ster, my dad's mad 'cause of geometry. That's all."

Vivian wanted to reach out and hug Jennifer. She softly signaled the girl with her hand to say, Save this conversation until we're alone. She could hold her. The girl blinked understanding. This pact happened so instantly that Vivian questioned whether it had even occurred. She became aware of eyes in the portrait of the founder of their order, the eyes of Mother Mary Gertrude, watching, and felt the weight of authority. *Jennifer doesn't need self-righteousness*, her mind protested, *Jennifer needs compassion.* Vivian fairly brimmed with it.

She drew in a quivering breath, turned, and addressed Mrs. Suges in an overly light tone. "Mrs. Suges—Clara, Jennifer wouldn't be the first student stumped by geometry. If you like, if *she* likes," she said, smiling then addressing the girl, "I'll tutor you."

Jennifer peered into Vivian's eyes, then away. She shrank into what looked like shame, pulled her mouth to one side, bit on her lower lip.

In a small farming town of twenty-five thousand like Sleeder, Protestants outnumbered Catholics two-to-one. Everyone knew everyone else's business. Protestants never failed to point out when a Catholic teenager got pregnant. It would be difficult for Jennifer; she wanted so much to be popular. *Maybe I'm wrong,* Vivian told herself. *Please, God, let me be wrong.*

Mrs. Suges raised her purse and set it firmly on her lap as if sealing some agreement.

"It's a start. A start," she said.

Vivian experienced the same kind of betrayal she had felt when her mother acted as if Sister Rosella, her eighth-grade teacher, were all knowing and *she* no-count. Jennifer's toe traced the blue geometric border of the rug.

Vivian rested her hand on the girl's and said, "If that's what you want. Only if that's what you want."

"Okay," Jennifer breathed. "Okay."

Mrs. Suges stood. Vivian and Jennifer followed suit. The woman said, "You're too good to the children, Sister. Too good. We wish you could be here forever. We, my husband and me, we want you to know we are grateful."

The decision was made. Vivian tried to smile and extended her hand. Mrs. Suges held on and patted it.

"You're welcome," Vivian said, feeling a tinge of guilt for her complicity with the girl against her mother. As they walked to the door, Vivian put her arm around Jennifer's shoulders and tried to draw her close, but Jennifer tensed and resisted. Vivian knew full well the girl's awful anxiety.

"Dear, when would be a good time?" Vivian asked.

Without looking at her, Jennifer said, "I have to check my schedule. I'll phone," and shrugged free.

Will you? "I hope you will." Don't let the problem grow." *Terrible choice of words.* "I mean, it's better to deal early with any problem."

Jennifer looked into Vivian's eyes. Vivian sensed Jennifer knew that she knew.

Now shame engulfed Vivian. *How will I ever keep my own guilt and shame out of this?*

She took the girl firmly by the shoulders, and said, "Trust me. It'll be okay, Jennifer. It will." Mary Ruth was playing *Clair de Lune.* Vivian turned to Mrs. Suges and said, "We'll do whatever Jennifer needs, whatever she wants. That's a promise," she said, turning to Jennifer. To both of them, she said, "Thank you for your confidence."

Through the shaved head of St. Anthony in the stained glass panel in the door, Vivian watched them get into their rusty green station wagon and drive away. "Call. Please, call," she said to the empty parking space. When Sister Dominic rang the breakfast bell, Vivian was still standing there with her hand on her abdomen, praying, *St. Jude, patron of the impossible, help me here.*

20

CHAPTER TWO

Vivian continued to pray as she moved to the kitchen. Lord, make me an instrument of your peace. Set aside the problem until you know more. Mary, mother out of wedlock, make me sensitive and caring; don't let me give Jennifer away. She tried to detach, lest she forget and say too much. As soon as she entered the kitchen, Vivian spotted Kimberly's mismatched pumps, identical, except one was black, the other navy blue.

The young woman carried a platter of bacon in one hand and a small bowl of Sister Dominic's homemade chokecherry jam in the other. She set them on the mahogany pedestal table that had been set the night before with their gold-rimmed, Limoges china, one of many donations willed to them.

Vivian caught Sister Dominic's eye, then sent her gaze down to Kim's shoes, covering her amusement behind the back of her hand. They exchanged knowing looks. "Praised be Jesus Christ," Vivian said, offering their traditional greeting.

"Praised be Jesus Christ," they responded.

Kimberly said, "Mary Ruth must not have heard the bell."

Kimberly's high energy made her seem taller than Mary Ruth, though she wasn't. Actually, Vivian was the tallest.

Vivian chuckled, said, "Perhaps you'll fetch her in your magic shoes."

Kimberly's soft brown eyebrows raised in question over her hazel eyes. She exclaimed, "Nummers!" She flexed her toes and laughed, reached up and slid the silver barrette higher in her naturally curly hair. "Look, Sister Dominic! I dressed in the dark."

"Easy mistake," Vivian said, smiling, moving to the stove and turning on the flame under the percolator. She envied how comfortable Kimberly seemed to own mistakes and how relaxed she was "in the world." She wished she knew as much about her own family history as Kimberly knew about hers.

"I could say I was saving electricity," Kimberly said, playing Sister Dominic like a pro.

Sister Dominic unplugged the waffle iron and beckoned the girl. "You could," she said, taking and leaning on Kimberly's arm for support as she hobbled to the table. The old woman walked as if her feet were in two narrow ditches; today her limp seemed more pronounced. Vivian reminded herself to ask Sister Dominic if she wanted to visit the doctor.

Kimberly wore a red, possibly silk, dress Vivian hadn't seen before. SIHMs, like all orders, lacked young applicants. The motherhouse used to train young women before sending them out to teach. Now aspirants arrived on mission with little spiritual or emotional preparation, with clothes they already owned, which in Kimberly's case meant rich fabrics in bright colors, and expensive jewelry. Though twenty-seven, Kimberly still fairly bristled with teenage unpredictability. Vivian was supposed to develop the spirit of contemplation in the girl. No easy task.

"If I wore these mismatched shoes to class, Sister Dominic, what do you think my first-graders would say?"

"They would giggle and point behind your back. It's more fun that way."

Kimberly tended the old woman with great kindness. In return Sister Dominic overprotected the girl for whom temporary vows were still two years away, permanent ones, three if she ever got that far. Vivian wasn't supposed to lose an applicant; she didn't know if she could keep this one. She sighed and slid her hands up her forearms, the way she would have hidden them inside her sleeves had she been wearing a habit, and reminded herself, *At Kimberly's age, I did dumb things, too.*

"In the old days," Vivian said, pouring coffee around the table, "we shaved our heads against vanity."

Kimberly said, "I'll get Mary Ruth," clearly wanting to escape hearing about the good old days.

Vivian looked after her, shook her head, said, "The other day she suggested God might be a woman."

Sister Dominic smiled the same way Vivian's grandmother had smiled gently when reprimanding her mother. "Worse things could happen," she said.

"I didn't hear the bell," Mary Ruth said breathlessly, pulling the tape recorder earphones from her head. She recorded lessons to review a student's progress.

"Look." Kimberly pointed to her shoes.

Mary Ruth's deep-set dark brown eyes, her finest feature, sparkled with amusement. "That's unique." Mary Ruth wore a white blazer over a white blouse, a forest green skirt. She often wore white or cream in contrast with her olive coloring and glided gracefully, as if listening to sacred music. Though a decade older than Kimberly, Mary Ruth could easily be taken for the same age. Unlike Kimberly's unruly curls, Mary Ruth's dark hair clung close to her head.

"Sorry," Mary Ruth said. "I'll wash my hands."

"Vanity is still around," Sister Dominic said.

"We could still shave our heads against it," Kimberly said with irony. "Or whiplash each other before sleep or wear ashes on our foreheads and insist the pope take no more whirlwind tours, tell him to, 'Stay home.'"

They laughed.

"Straightaway," Mary Ruth said, meaning she was ready now. She had grown up in England and South Africa and spoke with a slight British accent. Sometimes she called sausages "bangers."

In the old days one earned a veil only by keeping their order's rule as tight as skin.

"The waffles are getting cold," Sister Dominic said. "Bless us O Lord—"

As senior, not according to age, but according to who first entered the convent it was her role to say grace. Seniority determined who gave permission to leave a room, to speak, to precede whom in line. Seniority determined everything; it made Kimberly "the baby." Vivian, as superior, however, prevailed in matters of obedience. Vivian pulled her napkin from the ring she had brought with her as part of the prescribed dowry.

"Prunes," Kimberly said, crinkling her nose at them. "Maybe we could have kiwis sometime. Did you believe that sermon?"

"Put me in a bad mood," Vivian muttered.

Kimberly paused, holding the small pitcher of syrup, and looked up in surprise.

While they were well aware of Vivian's power struggles with Father Rupert, criticizing him only set a bad example. The man had been right about lay teachers' salaries pushing their budget to the brink; she had to give him that. If he had heeded her plan for a Catholic high school, if Jennifer had attended one, the girl's plight might be different. *Trying to revive a dying school or trying to provide for an unexpected baby challenged the soul, the spirit.*

Sister Dominic said, "I miss peeking into your classrooms now and again." She added a dollop of jam to her waffle. "Tell me what you're teaching."

You can't be sure about Jennifer, Vivian told herself, *or about Sister Dominic's condition, about anything. Don't project.*

Kimberly said, "I'm teaching the 'God made me' lesson. First I'll have to come up with a way to stop their preoccupation with Babe."

They laughed. That pig movie star had invaded all of their classrooms.

"My kids were caught up with 'Mr. Holland's Opus,' " Mary Ruth said. "I wish there were more uplifting movies like that. We're on sentence diagramming, not fifth-graders' favorite, but when they grasp it, composition improves. Please pass the butter. When that happens—" she sang, "Al-le-lu-ia."

Vivian smiled. Her movie pick of the year was "Dead Man Walking." Not often did a sister's ministry take center stage, and Susan Sarandon had insisted on making the movie, which didn't ridicule or distort convent life the way so many others before it had.

Vivian said, "Church History. Tomorrow, it's the no-meat on Friday lesson," *the outcome of which usually determines whether or not I stay in control of my class for the rest of the year.* Back when students addressed her as "Sister," the title lent authority, an aura long gone. First thing each morning, she assessed which students had arrived as stable adults and which were fighting raging hormones, then proceeded accordingly. This daily tally she believed made her successful both as a teacher and a confidante. She really worked at befriending her students because she wanted them to know, like Jennifer, that they could always return for help.

Kimberly said, "Teaching kids how to think is so rewarding."

If Kimberly taught eighth grade, she would no doubt discuss birth control and God knew what else. The girl was a product of public high school. Vivian hoped to convince this novice to question Rome less; however, both children and parents loved Kimberly, which proved her a worthy teacher.

"What prompted you to enter?" Vivian asked Kimberly.

25

"I wanted to help others. You know, do something meaningful. Not like marching in a crusade or becoming a martyr. Living and working in a religious community seemed, well, I don't know ... "

"Safe?" Sister Dominic asked.

"That, too, I suppose. SIHMs taught me in elementary school, so choosing this order came naturally enough. I never expected to teach first grade though."

Vivian asked, "What did you expect?"

The girl's cheeks flushed. She rested her spoon on a prune pit. "I had some juvenile notion of, you know, like getting inside the power structure, affecting major changes."

She wants to be a priest!

Kimberly's eyes flitted from Sister Dominic's down to a strip of crisp bacon in the woman's gnarled fingers, then to Mary Ruth, seeking what? Support?

Kimberly asked, "What brought you all the way from South Africa?"

Mary Ruth said, "I was there with my father. Actually, he started out in the military; then when apartheid became an international issue, he transferred to government. It bothered me that we lived so well surrounded by people in real poverty. When my grandmother, my mother's mother, was dying, I returned to the States. That's when I opted for a life richer in music than in goods."

"Hm," Kimberly said. "What about you, Vivian?"

Careful. Be truthful, but brief, Vivian told herself, stiffening. "I ... knew I didn't want to be a wife ... or mother. I mean, I didn't like the idea of being pulled between husband and children like so many women I saw. I needed—wanted time—and energy for spiritual growth. I wanted a career. Entering seemed a good way to do that."

"The convent was your GI Bill!"

Vivian had not thought of it that way.

26

Sister Dominic jumped in and saved her. "In my time, entering was just what some women did. That first Christmas away from home was the hardest. I've never been sorry."

Vivian remembered being homesick. Back then they couldn't visit family; now they visited annually and during times of particular stress, like illness. Over time, convent traditions became special, too.

"Nothing compares to a child's Christmas," Kimberly said, sounding wistful.

Vivian couldn't help but think of Jennifer. *Are Jennifer's childhood joys over?* The girl was an odd mixture of adult seriousness and teenage foolishness. One Halloween, dared by her brother, Jennifer thrust a skunk-scented newspaper into the town bonfire. That ended the party!

Mary Ruth said, "I have good news. The assistant coach at Sleeder High has scheduled"—she pronounced it shed-u-eled—"a lesson. He plays by ear and wants to learn correct technique to advance. When he asked around for the name of a good teacher, he said mine kept coming up."

"That's a real compliment," Kimberly said.

Vivian said, "You've earned it. I hope it works out." Ever since parents found rising tuition costs harder to meet, Mary Ruth's piano income had become increasingly important to them.

Mary Ruth pressed her lips together in an effort to conceal her pleasure.

"That'll be a nice change," said Sister Dominic. Occasionally the old woman complained about having to listen to the same mistakes year after year.

Mary Ruth said, "I think it will be satisfying."

They were quiet.

Vivian broke the long silence, surprised herself, by saying, "That sermon made me want to vomit."

CHAPTER THREE

Before bedtime, Vivian buffed snow salt stains from the toes of her pumps with her elbow, one-two, one-two, and examined her conscience. She faulted herself for belittling Father Rupert. She should not have spoken out against his homily. *If I hadn't been preoccupied with Jennifer—Mary, clear me of agitation. Help me help Jennifer.* She slipped her arms into the sleeves of her worn black flannel robe. She looked at the crucifix on the wall above her twin-sized bed. A sick-call crucifix, it contained a vial of holy oil and a pair of small candles for a priest to use for administering the last rites.

She never looked at the crucifix without wondering why those daily tending the sick couldn't give the last sacrament. Why did a priest have to be the one? He might not even know the sick person. *Mary, release me from my obsession with Father Rupert's attitude. Discipline will set me free. Bring me to obedience and good cheer. Let it go, let it go.*

She layered her clothes over the back of the chair for morning, tried to take comfort in routine: beige tweed jacket, brown skirt, cream blouse, pantyhose. She set her freshly polished, dark brown slip-on shoes under the chair. She wondered why it had bothered her when Kimberly asked why she had entered the convent. It was a natural question. *Guilt.* Vivian swallowed. Did the girl even believe in the one, true, objective, and universal Church? Kimberly might not belong in SIHMs or in any convent.

Having a room of my own leads to too much thinking. The post Vatican II change Vivian valued most was having her own room. She had never mastered dressing and undressing under the tent of her robe. She hung her white cotton panties on one rung of the chair, her cotton bra on the other. She supposed Kimberly's undergarments were made of silky fabrics. She folded the white cotton spread into neat thirds and rested it over the footboard. *To Kimberly truth is like Silly Putty that can be shaped any way she wants.*

There were times, though, when Vivian agreed with the girl. Like, the Holy Father couldn't possibly understand what terrible moral suffering a young woman endured, often while still a child, trying to decide between birth and adoption. *You don't know what Jennifer's problem is, not for certain. Why carry on?*

Steam coated the bathroom medicine chest mirror, their only one, because the convent had originally been built as someone's home. Vivian couldn't justify the cost of removing the chest and repairing the wall, and she hadn't found a medicine chest without a mirror. Now that they dressed like everyone else covering it seemed excessive and impractical. An oversweet scent hovered in the air.

She turned on the tub tap and, because she was supposed to follow up on such matters, rummaged through items on Kimberly's shelf. Sure enough, at the bottom of the girl's sanitary napkin box her fingers located translucent purple beads. Unsure of what they were, Vivian stopped the sink, turned on the faucet, and tossed one in. Bubbles foamed smelling to high heaven. She had smelled the scent somewhere before—in preconvent days. *Jasmine?*

Her fingers touched tiny rainbows in the bubbles, bursting them here, there. Tweaking them made her feel playful, soft, feminine, sensual. The water in the tub gurgled into the safety drain. Feeling like a snoop she turned off the tap and rinsed away the foam in the sink.

Once bathed and in her nightgown, Vivian poked her head out in the hall and looked both ways, before using the door as a fan to expunge the scent. Kimberly had probably done exactly the same. She smiled. Pretty humorous.

Vivian's brush with humor didn't last long; it had been a trying day. She knelt beside her bed with her breviary open at her bookmark. Under her thumb lay the image on the holy card, King Solomon sitting on his throne, listening to two women plead for custody of the baby lying on a blanket near his sandals.

Holy cards depicted saints or Christ or some religious event. They were given to a sister on her birthday, which was celebrated on the anniversary of her entrance day, given in memory of the deceased to those attending a requiem mass, and to children for good classroom performance. Or, like this holy card, kept as a reminder of something one must never forget. The pleading mothers made Vivian long for her unborn child.

Outside, the twin clocks on the church spires struck ten. *Mary,* Vivian prayed, *remove my bitterness. Purify me. Bring me inner peace.* Oh, how she wanted to feel forgiven. The clock chimed ten-fifteen. Vivian turned off the lamp and crawled into bed.

She smelled the scent on her fingers. *Must talk to Kimberly.*

Ten-thirty.

Jennifer.

Vivian rolled onto her stomach, covered her head with her pillow.

Eleven.

A shadowy, ominous figure advanced toward her. Vivian took the crucifix from above her bed and struck and struck at the figure until her bloodstained hands suggested she was blessed with stigmata.

Twelve.

The cock crowed thrice.

Vivian felt along an impenetrable stone wall, searching for some way out. Desperate, she stepped back and bumped into someone standing in shadow, a man; she shivered with fright. But then Rob emerged from behind the shrub, smiled, and beckoned her. Her teenage self approached. He parted the bushes to show her the plaid blanket he had laid in the secluded grassy area. She heard children's voices cheering on others playing games at their annual church picnic. She smelled spring flowers and lamb roasting on spits being turned by the old men of the parish.

"You're beautiful," Rob said softly, taking her hand and kissing it, exactly what her sixteen-year-old heart had waited so long to hear. They lay down on the blanket. "Beautiful," he repeated. Against her palm his cheek felt like fine sandpaper. Such a romantic setting, one as risky as a scene in a romance novel, better than she had dreamed.

She had pursued this college man all summer and now, before he left again for school, finally they were alone. She pushed her fingers through Rob's thick, dark hair, drew him to kiss her as she had so often imagined. They wouldn't go all the way, just enough for her to guess how going all the way would feel. Rob nuzzled her neck, her ears. His blue-gray eyes softened with desire. Her throat parched.

"Vivi, do you know what we're doing? Are you sure?"

"I do," she said, sounding just like a bride. Once, just this once she would feel like a woman.

At her answer his eyes leapt the space between them, entered her soul, traveled deep inside her. Softly, gently, he kissed her shoulders, her ears, her eyes. His touch, velvet. Velvet. Gently he removed her tee shirt, her bra, her shorts. He fondled her breasts, explored the outlines of her hips. His kisses made her lips swell, her nipples sing.

"Vivi," he whispered, sucking them.

At the sound of her name, her breathing quickened. Parts of her she didn't even know existed, opened ... yielded. So many new sensations. Parts of her ached and burned—her mouth, her ears, her swollen nipples. Between her legs a moist fire blazed.

"Ooooooooouu," she whispered when he stroked her there. Soon they would have to stop, but not yet, not before she knew more of the mystery. He flitted his tongue faster and faster around her nipples, creating sensations beyond anything she could have imagined.

"Lovely," he said. "Lovely. You're so beautiful."

Rob trailed kisses down her thighs, her ankles and up behind her knees, between her thighs, then ... she FLEWWWWW, holding onto his mane, arching her back, giving every part of herself into molten fire.

"Don't—stop, don't—stop, don't—stop. DON'T stop!"

He took her hand then and placed it on himself. He felt hard, hot, wanted her, only her. She peered into his hungry, distant eyes.

"A minute," he said, his eyes hard, his hands kneading her thighs. "I need a minute." He moved her on top of him, gripped her buttocks and drew her tongue into his mouth, his tongue, thrusting, twirling around hers. That's when his fingers found her secret spot.

Oh, God, oh, God, oh God. When she thought she couldn't breathe, he paused just long enough to let her catch her breath, then rolled her over and gently slid his penis across her moist opening, pressing, gently pressing, sliding, pressing, pulling back.

How she pulsed for him to enter her. Vivi pulled hard on his shoulders. Still he slid, pressed, retreated, slid, pressed, retreated, slid, pressed, pushed, retreated, pushed in further, retreated, raising her anticipation so much she thought she would scream.

"Shhh," he said, thrusting his tongue into her mouth. She felt a ping of pain, then opened, opened to receive him. Pleasure sent her up, up, up, higher, pitch-pitch-PITCHING her UP into molten golden red heat, liquid fire. Her nails dug into his shoulders. He rode her into the blinding sun. Fireworks burst inside her. Everywhere sparks! Sparks! Gasping, drowning on the thinnest, wispiest cushion of air—she wanted this to last forever—forever lost in bliss.

Treetops swayed. Down she floated, down. Contractions inside.

The tips of her breasts tingled and cooled, she burned between her legs. Deep inside, throbbing fueled glowing embers. She kissed his hand and drew two of his fingers into her mouth; they tasted of her. She tried to imagine what it would be like to be married, allowed to do this all day, everyday.

She opened her eyes, saw the blanket folded over her, Rob, dressed, standing a few feet away with his back to her, one shoulder pressed against the oak. Beyond the shrubs, voices sounded low and even now. Rob turned, saw her gaze, came and knelt beside her. He seemed pale.

"Are you all right?" he whispered.

She stroked his sandpaper cheek. "Why wouldn't I be?"

He raised an eyebrow, slipped a clean, folded handkerchief into her hand and stood and turned his back. A touch of pink mixed with the secretions on the handkerchief.

She dressed and smoothed her hair with her hands, said, "Okay."

Rob turned and swallowed. "Uh," he said, not looking at her, "we can't do this again."

"Oh, no," she said. "Definitely not. I'll return your hanky when it's washed."

"No!" He took it, giving her the strangest look, then tossed it onto the blanket and rolled it up, and put it under his arm, then disappeared without even a good-bye kiss.

The morning Angelus tolled like a delayed SOS, *bong, bong, bong,* followed by three beats of silence, then *bong, bong, bong.* Vivian bolted, clutched the covers to her chin. On her fingers she smelled what she had done. *God, no!* She rolled out of bed onto her knees and kissed the floor. She slid her arms into her robe and her feet into her fleece-lined slippers, and took her sexual anguish to the chapel.

There before the communion rail she stood with her arms out like Christ's on the cross. *I've kept my promise. I have. All these years to the best of my ability. Still you elude me, you tempt me. I feel betrayed. Why can I not remain pure?* An image of shameful Jennifer came to her; she brimmed with her own shame. Once again she repeated the promise she had made so long ago: *I'll join the Sisters of the Immaculate Heart of Mary and atone every day of my life. I'll love other's children. I'll teach other's children. Just, please, please, don't let my parents find out.*

She had struck and kept that bargain. Now an image of her unborn baby, the one she had voluntarily aborted, appeared—pink, swaddled, wailing. *Jennifer is a test; Jennifer wants to be saved.* Vivian drew a deep, quivering breath and slowly exhaled it. *I want to help her. I will. Show me what to do. Jennifer will do the right thing.*

CHAPTER FOUR

"Caboose, caboose," the first-graders giggled and pointed at Kimberly.

"Who me?" she asked, feigning disbelief.

"Yes, Miss McCall. Yes."

Kim smiled at Brenda Sullivan, Sherry's mother, her only Protestant mother and longtime friend, who had brought this morning's cookies and decided to stay for the lesson. At the back of the room Brenda's big frame scrunched into a small-sized chair, ankles out, the hem of her pinstriped suit skirt above her together knees.

"Oh, oh," Kimberly said, "I see books and papers, but not on Sherry Sullivan's desk. *Muchachos*, what's—?"

"Next to godliness," they called out, a few scurried to clear the tops of their desks.

Kim felt a rush of heat on her cheeks, her hazel eyes bright from being involved. She wore tan chino slacks and a white cotton blouse, washable clothes, because she would be crawling. The kids plopped about, forming a train. She couldn't resist performing for her friend, hummed a few bars of the "Mariachi Suite." The women smiled at each other.

Brenda's eyes were the color of the orchid crayon, the same color as her blouse. Brenda knew more about her than her own parents did. Brenda knew Kim didn't know how not to be involved. Kim felt a tug on her sleeve and bent and gave Steffanie permission to leave the room.

She watched the girl leave, thinking about how she and Brenda had worked beside their fiancés helping illegal aliens, who hoped for asylum, enter the States. After arrests and pressure from the US government they had had to go underground. Brenda knew Kim when Kim wrote brochures for Planned Parenthood— "The Pap Smear and What It Can Do for You," "Practicing Safe Sex," "Nine Months Is Not a Lifetime. Or Is It?"

Later when Kim accompanied Guillermo into Guatemala, not knowing how long they would be gone, she took several months' supply of birth control pills. She should have listened to her parents, never have gone to Guatemala, never been involved in Guillermo's south-of-the-border activities. She turned to look at her friend. Back then Brenda's hair had been dark; now it was ash blond and coiled in a chic French roll. Being part of a couple seemed part of another lifetime.

Steffanie waddled in with the hem of her dress caught in the waistband of her panties. Kids snickered. Kimberly turned and glared at them; the giggles stopped. The children hurried to link themselves into boxcars.

Kim went to the girl and freed the dress without the girl noticing. "Honey, we waited for you," she said. "You may be any car you like."

Steffanie pranced happily and wedged in behind the coal car.

They said teachers were most like the age group they taught. If that were true—well. Kim left her shoes in the corner and took her place at the end of the train.

"All aboard, *muchachos*. Urrrk-urrrrk. Eeeek," Kim sounded the rusty wheels of the caboose connecting. Jon Ben and Davey punched each other over the coal car position. "Settle," she told them. "Okay, *muchachos*, listen inside yourself for what's right, what's wrong. You know."

Brenda covered her eyes with her hand and shook her head as if to say, I can't believe your patience.

"Full steam ahead, *chug-chug*. Go!"

Scotty raised the striped engineer's hat high, bucked, *chug-chug-chugged*, and the train moved. "Choo-choo," he said. "God made me."

"Why did God make you?" called the caboose.

"Woo-wooo. God made me to be the engineer."

"That's cheating," Lizabeth said.

"Choo-choo," said the coal car.

"Why did God make you?" The caboose.

"Wooo-wooo," Steffanie said. "God made me to be like him."

In that instant, Kim heard Guillermo's voice said, *God made me to become who I am*, not *God made me to know, love, and serve him in this world and to be happy with him in the next. "De corazone nuevo nace la paz."* From a new heart peace is born. Guillermo's favorite saying. Guillermo had always known God's purpose for himself and now God had taken him, and Kim needed to find a new purpose for herself.

"Choo-choo. Why did God make you?"

"To be beautiful." Thin-voiced Meagan.

Kim hurried to say, "Oh, Meagan, you *are* beautiful. Each of us has a special beauty that no one else has. Notice, everyone, how together we can pull a bigger load than any of us could pull alone. Notice how we depend on each other and how together we can make bigger things happen. *That's* beautiful."

She wondered, *Will I ever find God's purpose for me?*

"God made me to blast your heads."

"Adam Hill!"

Cars collided.

"I'm hungry, Miss McCall," whined Adam.

"I'd rather be a dinosaur than a dumb ole boxcar," Jon Ben said.

Living in a religious order stuck in the Middle Ages made Kim feel like a dinosaur. She had failed to do necessary homework;

37

only after entering did she realize that orders ran the gamut from conservative to liberal.

Kim sighed and leaned on her haunches. "I'm hungry, too," she said. "Anyone else?"

Hands raised.

"Are we done?"

The children giggled and tumbled, called "no," and pointed at her.

"Okay, *muchachos.* Okay." Kim stood with her hands on her hips and crossed her eyes at them. She reached up and tugged on the imaginary chain. "Woo-woooo! God made me to ... become-the-best-person-I-know-how-to-be."

They clapped and straggled to their desks.

Kim glanced at her friend. She and the other sisters were supposed to be family, yet they lived like separate boxcars that came together only if an accident caused a chain reaction. With Brenda she felt she belonged; she felt safe. If it weren't for kids, for play—

"No hitting on the playground," she called after the departing children. "Be good for Mrs. Flanagan."

Scotty climbed onto the banister and slid down it.

Brenda came up beside her. "You really have the touch," she said.

"Thanks. I try. Sherry's doing really well. You and Mike must be proud of her."

"She's spoiled."

"How could you do otherwise?" Kim said, smiling, stacking the books on her desk. She set *The New York Times* on top. If Brenda had been Catholic, Sherry might never have been born by way of *in vitro* fertilization. Kim had consoled her friend over the many months she and Mike were trying to conceive. "You and Mike worked so hard to have her."

Brenda nodded, smiled softly, asked, "How are *you*?" Her eyes brimmed with concern.

Kim experienced a tinge of guilt. She should never have told Brenda how adrift she felt in a life of nos and don'ts when she had expected it to be spiritually rich. She must change the subject.

"Maybe it's appropriate that Vivian worries about money and mustard seeds. Thanks for the cookies. The kids really liked them."

"Credit my favorite bakery. You avoided my question."

Kim felt in her pocket for the slip of paper on which she had written the eight hundred phone number for the *Newsletter of Leadership Conference of Women Religious.* When Vivian was out of her office, she would use Vivian's phone and her mother's Sprint and VISA cards, neither of which Vivian knew she had, and subscribe to the nuns' liberal newsletter in Mother Philip Neri's name. Anonymously, of course. She hoped it would inspire Mother to nudge SIHMs in the liberal direction.

Brenda said, "I'm waiting."

Kim looked at her friend and nodded and sighed and rolled her eyes upward. "Mary Ruth sings and gets this spiritual glow like a halo. Sister Dominic, bless her, has this direct line to heaven's throne. I can't believe either of them ever played hide 'n seek with God the way I am. The other day Vivian asked me what saint's name Kimberly comes from." At baptism one was supposed to be acquire a saint's name. "I didn't know."

Brenda chuckled. "We ran into that when we baptized Sherry." She was silent for a few beats, then asked softly, "Do you think about him?"

Kim immediately saw Guillermo's sparkling, dark velvet eyes full of love shining on her, saw his strong, chiseled features, his soft, sensual lips and neatly trimmed mustache. She smelled his bay rum aftershave. She said, "I never see you without thinking of him."

"When I see you my mind flashes images from that night."

39

Once again Kim experienced the cold, the tension, the fear, and shivered. That night pulsed with the urgency of life and death. Coyotes, guides paid to escort people safely into the States, fearing the border would be closed, had been taking foolish risks. The INS, the Immigration Naturalization Service, added more helicopters and searchlights, and robbers attacked more frequently.

Brenda's hand covered Kim's for a moment and squeezed.

Kim said, "I still pray for Consuelo."

"Me, too."

The coyotes were late, not a good sign. She and Brenda had parked the camouflaged SUV near Guillermo and Mike's forward watch and moved back. Twice, helicopters had crisscrossed in front of them. The half moon might help or expose them. Quiet, tense, they breathed, waited.

"Listen." Kim straightened her spine.

Brenda pulled her down. They heard shouting in Spanish, women screaming, sounds of skirmish for ... several minutes. The quiet that followed seemed to last forever. Guillermo signaled the animal night sound saying he and Mike were venturing forth. Kim and Brenda held onto each other. The air stood still. Kim counted her breaths. Before long she saw Guillermo's silhouette carrying a body toward them. The women ran to the SUV. The back seat was protected against bloodstains with a plastic cover. Brenda turned on the ignition. Kim opened the back door. Helicopters approached.

Guillermo said, "*Pronto, pronto.* A girl. Not conscious." Kim smelled blood. He lay her in the back seat. "Most are dead. Mike's still checking. Go. The planes." He left, dragging a cloth behind him to cover his tracks.

Brenda drove slowly to avoid stirring up sand. Blood soaked the girl's skirt. Kim knew what she had to do. Bandits seized whatever they considered property. She packed cloth between the girl's legs.

"Mary mother of God," she said, crossing the girl's ankles. "When you can gun it."

Brenda phoned the coded message to the safe house. As soon as the 'copters passed, they moved. Once in town they took back streets and alleys. The garage door to the safe house opened automatically. The man, in his forties, gray hair at his temples, scooped up the girl who appeared to be twelve, thirteen. The woman led them to the attic, saying, "The doctor's scrubbed."

The doctor waited masked and ready at the table. Brenda's scissors cut away the girl's clothes. Kim swabbed her wrist, inserted the needle, and started the IV. The girl's genitals looked like fresh cut raw meat. Kim turned her face away, resisted the urge to upchuck.

The doctor said, "We're going to need blood."

Kim ran down to the refrigerator for type O—universal donor blood. When she returned the woman assisted the doctor, handing instruments. Brenda was examining the girl's clothes for identification. Kim started the transfusion and ferried boiled water. The man of the house was scrubbing down the SUV. Each worked like a robot steeled against emotion.

"Name's Consuelo," Brenda said.

The girl was a child, a mere child. Her pain would be unbearable.

Kim asked, "Will she live?"

"Can't tell," the doctor said.

The woman asked, "Children?"

He shook his head.

Depression flooded Kim. Dogs were kinder to each other than humans were. She knelt beside the waiting twin bed, pressed her forehead against one of its posts, closed her eyes, and prayed for this girl who might not live, who, if she did, could never have children and surely would never ever enjoy sex. *Have we really done her a favor? Have we?*

Later when Guillermo tried to comfort her, Kim whispered, "I can't do this anymore."

"*Mi amor*," he said, embracing her tightly.

Later he said, "You're right. It has become too dangerous."

Brenda said, "The kids love you."

Kim looked blankly at her friend in the classroom. If she and Guillermo hadn't gone back to rescue his brother, Juan, Guillermo would be alive now and she would be his wife. Brenda was right. She should appreciate what she had.

"How long do you plan to torture yourself?"

Kim winced, had the odd sensation that Brenda knew something she didn't, but of course that was her imagination. When you searched for meaning, clues were everywhere. She said, "It's an unbelievable gift to help shape such sweet souls."

Brenda said, "In Third World countries the Church stands up for its people. In a First World country, you have to stand up for yourself. Kim, you said it earlier. Settle. Listen to yourself."

If only it were that simple. Kim hugged her friend. "Thanks," she said. *What am I ever going to do?*

CHAPTER FIVE

"Miss Vangaard, I never saw diagramming on television Arvid Allan said.

"Perhaps because no one rapped it," Mary Ruth answered.

Arvid Allan pretended to be Coolio and rapped a line from "Gangsta's Paradise." Everyone laughed.

Mary Ruth stood at the side of the room with her grammar text open on her palms. She waited for Arvid Allan and Betty Lou Wesley, African-American twins, to diagram the sentence each had copied on the blackboard from their English text: A novena consists of nine consecutive recitations of prayer, whether said in nine successive hours, days, or weeks, and is expected by the devout to bring results for an explicit, special intention.

She said, "Diagramming is like learning Latin. It teaches you how to think critically."

"You're not going to make us learn Latin!"

"No, Mary Beth, I'm not. *Ego amo te.* Look up what that means and come back and tell us."

The Baptist Wesleys needed no definition of novena. Like many black parents, the Wesleys sent their children to Catholic school, hoping for an equal education. More than once Mary Ruth had asked herself what it would feel like to be a black person in a white world.

She was four when she first experienced discrimination and still felt the spurn of it. Her father had just told her that her mother wasn't going to join them, that her mother would stay in Kentucky.

Life drained away inside her like water spinning down a drain. She stood on her tiptoes and peered over the sill out the window of their new London flat, a three-story narrow stone affair attached to others just like it, watching children she didn't know kicking a ball in a game she'd never seen. What terrible thing had she done that her mother would abandon her? Finally she worked up the courage to ask her father.

Instead of answering, he said, "They'll be delighted to meet you. You'll pass. Go out and play. Despite how she was feeling she obeyed, but as soon as she opened her mouth, the children mocked her southern drawl. In that moment the black guardian angel to whom she still prayed, came to life.

Mary Ruth peered out at the falling snow, at the twin clocks on the church spires. That incident occurred before she understood what her father had meant by passing, that having a white father and a black mother was not only atypical, but, for many, unconscionable.

This was not the only time her father had deliberately deceived her. Still, while she learned to distrust what he said, she tried very hard to please him. She often felt isolated inside her own skin. Did all mulatto children feel this way? Black children? White children? Raised as a white person, how could she possibly know any other view? She sensed something essential was missing from her life, but what?

Silence told her the children were waiting for her. Mary Ruth smiled at them and glided to the blackboard.

"Straightaway," she said, urging the twins. At times like this she often felt some kind of rebuff as if she had wronged them. She didn't want to think about that.

Arvid Allen and Betty Lou glanced furtively at each other, feigned with the chalk, not wanting her to know they didn't know. Instead of hugging them as she wanted to—children who knew they were colored contended with enough without adding teacher's

44

pet to their list—Mary Ruth sent them back to their seats. "You did fine," she said. "Just fine. Let's give someone else a chance, shall we? Okay, Kristopher. Give it a go."

She saw Father Rupert come out of the rectory and fling his scarf around his neck and move down the steps. Priests were such mysterious creatures. Did they have fun, experience the same kind of joy she did when she played music? It was music that instilled passion into life. The hands on the clocks on the church spires moved simultaneously to three-quarters past the hour. Mary Ruth breathed in the sound of the chimes, the knell of tradition, the very meter of life. She intoned the prayer they said every fifteen minutes, "All for the honor and glory of God ... "

"And for the poor souls in purgatory. Forever and ever. Amen," the children responded.

"Who wants a stab at this sentence? Maren."

Children responded more enthusiastically after Mary Ruth changed her habit to ordinary clothes, at least she thought they did. Children fathomed strange ideas, like sisters dressed in habits had no legs, no unmentionable body parts.

Maren passed the chalk to Andrew. Andrew separated phrases into sections as neat as parts of a crossword puzzle.

Music patterns wired your brain and became second nature sure as a line of melody that you learned as a child. For some reason, an old Catholic joke came to her, the one about a child who went to the hospital to visit his teacher, but found there only a little old man in bed. On the chair lay an empty habit. Non-Catholics never got it. Without the habit, a sister possessed neither life nor gender and had to disappear or turn into a withered old man. Feeling a wave of sudden discomfort she did not understand, Mary Ruth snapped her book closed.

"Okay," she said. "That's it." She pointed out each part of speech and its structural role. Like her, the children were relieved when the boring, necessary lesson was over.

"Books away," she said.

She sat and folded her hands on top of her desk. The children followed her example. They waited for the chimes to strike noon. She hummed softly, found herself salivating for a bowl of sherry-sauced mushrooms, probably because she had been thinking of England. Mostly she needed to urinate. When children were present, sisters couldn't use the school bathrooms. *Chimes* marked time passing. She intoned, "All for the honor and glory of God ... "

"And for the poor souls in purgatory. Forever and ever. Amen."

CHAPTER SIX

"Miss Tiamet, you mean on one Friday you could eat meat, die, and go to hell forever in mortal sin, and the next Friday you could eat meat and that was *okay?"* Stevie's acne-speckled face crumpled in disbelief.

Outside, a light snow drifted across the rose window in the church choir loft. Given her preoccupation with Jennifer, Vivian should have delayed this lesson; she lacked the required patience. She tried to soften, said, "Intention is everything. If you ate meat on Thursday thinking it was Friday, intention would make that a sin; if you ate meat on Friday thinking it was Thursday, it would not be a sin. The Church—"

"Foul," protested Stevie. "If the pope's infallible, how can he change his mind?"

Vivian felt naked without her veil. She reached up and moved hair from her view. "He's infallible only when he speaks as head of the Church on matters of faith and morals. Only then."

They groaned and argued among themselves.

She fiddled with a button on her beige suit jacket. Watching TV, that's what produced these doubting Thomases. In the early sixties when jolly, overweight John XXIII called the Vatican II Council, he asked Catholics to embrace a more ecumenical attitude. No one knew exactly what that meant. By the late sixties when the council ended, that ecumenical attitude remained a mystery like that snowflake clinging to the window. Well. Hoping to end the fracas, Vivian erased the board. She said, "For years St.

Augustine and St. Thomas Aquinas fought to be heard. Now, what they had to say forms the basic structure of everything we believe." She brushed chalk dust from her hands. "Let's light the Advent candle and—"

Marta Vilnius interrupted her. "You know, about that meat on Friday thing? My dad's mad forever."

Helen Pzsinski said, "We *still* don't eat meat on Friday. Miss Tiamet, if I eat one more tuna casserole—" The girl did breaststrokes, puffed her mouth like a fish's, said, "I'll die."

She has a silver earring on her tongue! Vivian thought she couldn't be shocked anymore by rebellious signs, but at this she was. Calling attention to it would only make matters worse.

"Quick," Vivian said, capitalizing on their laughter. "Let's clone you, just in case."

Someone said, "We better clone the whole class."

"Oh, spare me," Vivian said, teasing. "Maybe you'd rather eat my mother's dreaded Friday dish—creamed hard-boiled eggs on toast."

They groaned.

George Hyduk stuck his index finger in his mouth and mimed gagging.

They were always ahead of her and their outdated textbook. These kids surfed the Net, calculated farm futures, were sharper than she was. Fifty percent of eighth-grade classrooms already accessed the Net with another fifteen percent forecast for next year. *Jennifer's not ahead of the times, though; Jennifer's stuck where some young women always got stuck.* Vivian shuddered at the realization she was a living fossil, switched the subject to the Christmas Eve midnight mass procession.

"We're not going to wear those *gross* angel robes," protested Hank Lucky. "If St. Joseph took a DNA test, Miss Tiamet," he said, sneaking a peek at Charlene Melrose's ample breasts, "he couldn't pass. Then what?"

Charlene's outgrown jumper pulled like stretched taffy across her breasts. Vivian flipped hair out of her view. The girl, hair plaited in cornrows, slid lower in her seat. Mrs. Melrose apparently intended to make the girl's uniform jumper last until graduation. The boys liked to stare at Charlene's taffy. Vivian wanted to say: Forget sex; just forget about it. Instead, she opted for comic effect, said, "Without one of those robes, Hank, how would I ever recognize you as an angel?"

At the sound of the lunch bell Vivian's students lurched from the room. Her boys claimed it took one bull row to pollinate eight rows of female corn. When it came to sex, that's what her boys talked about, corn.

She set out her lesson plans for the afternoon.

For Jennifer, life has moved beyond pollen wafting from golden tassels into the breeze in search of a mate. What if one day, like eating meat on Friday, the Church annuls this sin?

If the Church eliminated the need for the bargain she had struck— Vivian's body stiffened into ramrod armor. This question always lay just beneath her consciousness, refusing burial, forever and ever, amen.

Jennifer, why haven't you called? We must— Vivian shook her head to free it of thoughts. She moved soundlessly, sedately, down the stairs, carrying intact the eleventh commandment she had learned early and held onto like a rigid buoy tossing recklessly on a raging sea: Neither question nor doubt.

CHAPTER SEVEN

From the kitchen Sister Dominic pulled aside the curtain on the door with her blue-veined hand and watched Vivian as she wove among children crossing the playground to the convent. The kids tugged on Vivian's skirt, her sleeve, seeking a glance or a smile, a sign of love.

Vivian, bless her, always took time for them. Love chalked up souls for God. If only those engaged in ethnic cleansing in the Balkans would remember that. When on the news she saw animals starving in the Sarajevo zoo and felt more sorrow for them than for the refugees, her heart filled with sadness. If starving animals provoked more of a response than desperate people did, desensitization had numbed us beyond feeling.

Sister Dominic turned away from the window. Her slippers *flip-flopped* as she made her way to the sink where a jar of her homemade dill pickles waited. *How lucky I am to be here and not there.* She prayed a quick prayer for troops going over, rested one hand on the counter, pushed her trifocals higher, and drew a deep breath. I need my energy right here, right now, she reminded herself, grateful that her heavy serge skirt hid her misshapen knees.

Seventy-seven years old and vanity remained her nemesis, though her Minnie Mouse shape had tempered that some. Dear John XXIII, who died too soon after taking reign, proved you were never too old to make your mark. Every day Sister Dominic asked God, *What's my mark? What are you waiting for me to do?* So far, God hadn't answered.

Vivian's entrance let in a cold draught of air. After their customary greeting, Sister Dominic looked up from the pickle she was slicing and pointed to the Monte Cristo sandwiches on the cookie sheet, sourdough bread dipped in egg batter sautéed on one side and filled with thin slices of ham and turkey and three different cheeses. "Would you put those in the oven for me, please?"

"Sure."

The bathroom doors *phuffed*.

The others were doing too much of her work. Though Dr. Milde had advised a knee replacement operation, Sister Dominic had not told Vivian. This breach of obedience bothered her, but if the mend didn't take Mother would send her to the Brandenburg infirmary. While sisters tended to live longer than the rest of the population, Sister Dominic wasn't counting on any centennial birthday. If Ross Perot could come out of nowhere and run for president, why couldn't she keep the position she had always held? Mr. Perot intended to serve through the end of his days and so did she.

"Stevie," Vivian said, coming out of the bathroom, "and Hank Lucky teamed up to undo me. How many minutes?" she asked, fingers on the timer.

"Twenty or so. There are fruit salads in the refrigerator, jam, sour cream."

"I resorted to humor. Oh. Sister, I keep forgetting to ask. Would you be willing to try letting out the underarm seams of Charlene Melrose's jumper?"

"I'll take a look-see."

Mary Ruth arrived. The bathroom doors *phuffed*.

"Those boys." Vivian clucked her tongue. "I'll check the answering machine."

As a child Sister Dominic believed sisters did not go to the bathroom, that sisters had no hair anywhere on their bodies, and were capable of only pure thoughts. Despite growing up on a farm where she saw animals mating, living, and dying, she had believed such nonsense.

Vivian reappeared. "No messages," she said, her expression crumpled with concern.

"I didn't hear it ring. Set the pickles in front of Kimberly's place. Were you expecting a call?"

"Yes and no."

"What may I do?" Mary Ruth asked.

"I'll help," Vivian said.

"Fifteen minutes," Sister Dominic said, keeping conversation to a minimum. They conversed freely during their noon meal, called dinner because it was their main meal, during community hour after supper, and during Sunday breakfast. Contemplation required quiet time.

Mary Ruth picked up her breviary, said, "I'll be in the chapel," and left humming. The breviary prayerbook contained daily hours to be read from the divine office. Hours was an inaccurate term because each hour took fifteen to twenty minutes to read. Teachers, nurses, priests, those with an active work schedule, read the daily office at will. Cloistered sisters and priests still chanted hours at the prescribed time of day: Lauds at dawn, a prayer of praise, followed by Prime to ask blessings on the day; after breakfast Terce celebrated the coming of the Holy Spirit; before lunch Sext offered reflection; in mid-afternoon None commemorated Christ's death; evening Vespers recalled night sacrifices in Jerusalem's temple; and at the end of the day Compline set the contemplative tone for the Grand Silence that lasted until after breakfast the next day.

Kimberly's coat was caught in the door. She had to open and close the door three times to free it. Then she dropped her books and newspaper. Sister Dominic and Vivian exchanged smiles as Kimberly bumbled on the floor for her belongings.

"What's for dessert?" she asked. "Oh. Praised be Jesus Christ."

"Praised be." Vivian chuckled.

Sister Dominic took hold of Vivian's arm and they moved to the table.

Sister Dominic said, "Sponge cake with almond glaze."

"Yum."

Phuff.

Vivian asked, "How are you feeling?"

"I'm cutting my pain pills in half; that's a good sign." *Half a truth's better than a lie.*

Late last summer when Vivian asked if she might not be more comfortable in the infirmary, Sister Dominic quickly changed the subject. Since then, however, trifles like making a sponge cake had taken on greater importance. Besides prayer, cooking remained her only pleasure. She was grateful that Vivian indulged her requests for ingredients. Despite poverty, she made lemon dill salmon, *coq au vin,* beef *bourguinon.* Still, age took its toll.

Some days her body reminded her of her father's old tractor; after replacing so many parts so many times, he just abandoned it in the south pasture where it stood like a tombstone. No doubt about it, her body had put her on eviction notice.

"Sister, are you in pain?"

"The pills slow me down too much," she said, gripping the back of her chair. She felt her eyes take on distance.

"You're thinking of Yvette."

"Yes."

For over a year now her dearest friend, Sister Yvette, lay dying in the infirmary. God had abandoned Yvette like an old tractor, like a tombstone over an undug grave.

Kimberly emerged from the bathroom smoothing lotion into her hands. "David brought in Pokemon stuff his uncle sent him from Japan. His uncle predicts Pokemon will come to the States and be a big hit. The kids thought I was dumb when I didn't know about

Ninja Turtles. Babe was funny, but this was too distracting. I had to confiscate all of it."

Vivian said, "Don't start. We're not going to get cable. Would you ring for Mary Ruth?"

Kimberly stood on her tiptoes to snatch the bell from the top of the refrigerator. Vivian waited for her to leave. "Sister, I'm worried about you."

Sister Dominic waved a dismissing hand. "Don't fret," she said. "It's nothing. I shouldn't feel sorry for myself."

"You're entitled!"

Maybe so, maybe no. "Tell me," she said, "if we could afford to renew cable, would you sign us up?"

"We have better things to do."

That's what I thought. Vivian feared becoming obsolete. *Don't we all?*

The women gathered around the table. Sister Dominic said grace. Determined to raise her spirits, she asked, "How did the lessons go?"

"Killed by Pokemon whatever he, she, it is. Looks like a retarded alien, a changeling. Pickles!" Kimberly plucked a slice from the dish with her fingers.

"Did the piano tuner come? Super, as always, Sister Dominic. Super. I've got jolly good singers this year."

"He did."

"Good. I'm keen on rehearsing the Christmas music."

"Baby Divine Sleep," Mary Ruth's own composition and her favorite carol required the vocal range of a diva.

"If SIHMs gave out chef's blue ribbons, Sister Dominic, your pickles would win every year."

Sister Dominic felt pleased and sad at the same time. "It's a joy to watch you."

Come spring, she knew there would be no garden; a garden had become more than she could endure. Vivian still wore that troubled frown.

Sister Dominic asked her softly, "What's bothering you?"

"Oh, just the no-meat-on-Friday thing. I can't get it to make sense for them."

"Maybe because it doesn't," Kimberly said. "How many turnabouts have there been? It's confusing. Even simple things like a man used to have to take off his hat in church while a woman was supposed to put one on."

The girl had this way of making custom and theology sound ridiculous. It irritated Vivian to no end. Vivian narrowed her eyes at Kimberly's *New York Times* on the sideboard as if she might be thinking of forbidding her from reading it. Vivian, who had grown up in Chicago, claimed big city living exposed young people to choices about crime and drugs long before their morals were lashed in tight enough to resist.

"December 5, 1968," Mary Ruth said, "that's when we started eating meat on Friday. I remember my father saying,'Now, now, Missy,'—that's what he called me when he instructed— 'Now, now, Missy, not eating meat didn't hurt you and neither will eating it.'"

Kimberly said, "That's such a minor thing. Up through the middle of the 1800s not one word about abortion. Now it's become part of: Thou shalt not kill. Vivian, I'll bet your Church history text doesn't mention the tenth-century popes who were sons of priests or how fathers donated girls—Hildegarde de Bingen for one—to convents as early as age eight."

Vivian choked.

Sister Dominic slapped her on the back.

Kimberly said, "Rome's the original ice palace. Vivian, are you okay?"

When Vivian finally caught her breath, she glanced up, seeking Sister Dominic's advice. Sister Dominic pressed her lips together and barely shook her head, suggesting Vivian let Kimberly's remark go. Vivian stared at her in disbelief, finally sputtered, "Th-thank you."

Their dear novice needed to learn when to keep quiet, when to speak up.

Kimberly said, "I think each of us should pull our own weight, like boxcars. We women make a difference. Sisters tended soldiers during the Civil War and made a difference in killing prejudice against Catholics. Poor women started labor unions and made a difference for all workers. When Mrs. Robinson became the first woman president of Ireland, she said, 'The hand that rocks the cradle rocks the system.' "

Vivian winced. Her face flushed.

"I intend to make a difference."

Sister Dominic covered her smile with her napkin. Kimberly's tone had implied, *Do you?* Sometimes the girl hit the bull's eye without even knowing she had picked up the bow. Vivian would feel a whole lot better if she could tell Father Rupert to mind his own business and make it stick.

Acting as Vivian's spiritual director allowed Sister Dominic to glean such insights. Vivian had troubles: Father Rupert's meddling; Reverend Mother's failure to respond to her concerns; fear of inadequacy, especially when it came to turning Kimberly into the kind of religious that would make Vivian proud of her own efforts. That girl, God love her, ranked right up there in pioneer pluck and determination.

Sister Dominic said, "It's a gift, faith. Much has to be taken on faith."

"Tell that to *my* kids!" Vivian said.

"What happens," Mary Ruth asked, "between the time they pass through my classroom, through Mr. Meriwether's and into yours, Vivian?"

Mary Ruth's tone neither judged nor accused; it was an honest question.

Vivian twisted her wedding band and didn't look at Mary Ruth. "I wonder sometimes if we had a Catholic high school, if St. Anthony's might not be in this fix. I just don't know."

"I don't think that has anything to do with it," Kimberly said, her brow furrowed in thought. "Kids understand what's going on. I explain the health hazards of smoking, my first-graders get it. I explain the earth's dwindling resources, they get it. I explain the power struggles of the Sanctuary Movement, they—"

"You're not teaching them to challenge authority!"

Kimberly blanched. "No. I wouldn't describe it that way. Vivian, no. What I'm doing is teaching them to think for themselves!"

Sister Dominic lowered her gaze and pursed her lips against smiling. The dear girl wouldn't last three weeks in an order like the Good Shepherds, whose aspirants were limited to reading spiritual material for the first seven years. Oh, to be so young and full of zest, to still have wings to fly!

CHAPTER EIGHT

"Vivian," Father Rupert commanded urgently over the phone, "I need to see you. Now."

"Yes, yes, of course, Father."

Vivian hurried across the street to the rectory, wondering what the emergency was.

"Yes?" she said, one hand flat on her chest as she tried to catch her breath.

"Sister—"

Vivian stiffened. When he called her Sister he usually wanted something she didn't want to give him.

" … how are plans for the Christmas procession?"

She blinked. *This is emergency!*

He offered his Play Doh smile.

"Fine, Father. Just fine," she said steeling herself against whatever was coming. Two handmade calendars were tacked up on the pair of bulletin boards behind him, one on either side of the picture of St. Anthony. Written on one: Baptisms, first communions, weddings; on the other, color of the vestment for that day's liturgy, appointments. Friday, a week: Bishop Marduk.

He said. "I'd like you to make it a procession to remember."

"Father, I always make it a procession to remember," she said, forcing her voice even. She didn't want to engage in a contest of wills, peered through the gauzy curtain at the convent's old red Ford parked in their driveway; it needed an oil change. If they were trading favors, she would ask for a better car.

Grinning, clearly sensing her miffed, he asked, "Who's bringing the hay for the manger?"

She knew the pattern: He cried wolf then baited her into anger. Sometimes he took so long to get to the point she got defensive before he stated it. To keep from blowing up, she set her mind on how remarkable it was that they had joined forces and helped achieve public funding for textbooks, for science equipment, for school busing. When Pius XI declared parents could not send their kids to public schools under pain of sin, the pope couldn't have guessed the current steep decline in religious vocations nor the spike in tuition to over two thousand dollars a year.

Vivian wanted to be objective, to be charitable.

Despite his messy office, Rupert, Father Rupert, was always well groomed—spotless Franciscan cassock, belted just so by the white cord with three knots that represented poverty, chastity, and obedience, slicked down dark hair. Discounting neatness were his shifty green eyes and that hair in the mole on his chin that she'd like to yank out with tweezers, that patronizing grin she'd like to smack off his face.

She said, "It's always a procession to remember, Father. Who can't recall those scrubbed cherub faces raised in song at midnight? The bright poinsettias? The smells of tallow and incense? The children's bright eyes and sleepy nods?"

The man liked to pick something insignificant and gradually eke his way into matters of increasing importance. He had crossed the line on an insignificant matter into her turf; if she gave in, he'd cross another and another until—his grin seemed pasted on. She said, "I'm not prepared to say who's bringing the hay. We draw straws—no pun intended—we draw straws on the Friday before rose Sunday."

There, she got in a jab. She had voted against buying that rose vestment. Worn only twice a year, she considered it a luxury. What had the school done without in order for him to have it?

"That way," she explained, "children associate opening the manger with the rose vestment, making it a memorable event."

"Memorable," he said, tapping the eraser end of a pencil on his desk. His crooked smile suggested she was about to find out what he really wanted. He asked, "What additional ideas have you come up with for cutting expenses?"

You haven't asked for any. "Father, you know where every penny goes. Without computers St. Anthony is not competitive. We have to have them. You must be kidding about making more cuts. *You're not kidding.*"

He twirled the end of the cord he wore around his waist. She twisted her ring. How could she have known when she vowed to obey that she would be subject to such a devious man?

"Contributions are down," he said, dropping the cord and leaning forward. "Parishioners are losing farms."

"Maybe contributions are down, Father, because parents are not getting what they're paying for. We're teaching moral values but we're failing to teach computer literacy."

"Are you computer literate, Sister?"

I. Will. Not. Become. Hysterical. He will point at me and call me irrational and unreasonable. Even the mothers recognized this as his favorite ploy.

She said, "Without a computer one does not become computer literate."

"Vivian," he said, sounding impatient, "I'm not asking for an accounting."

Oh yes you are. What about you? Have you removed liquor from your cabinets? Have you stopped going out to dinner? Do you spend parish money foolishly? Do you keep celibacy? Vivian's spirit drooped. Once again, she could not win.

She cleared her throat, said crisply, "I'll consider what might be done."

"I knew you would!" He raised his hand, blessed, and dismissed her with a wave.

Indignant that the priest reduced her to the kind of pettiness she attributed to him, afraid now of what she might say or do, Vivian left. It infuriated her that he used sacred duty as a power ploy, just infuriated her.

Crossing the street, her mind raced: *When my dress needs mending, I fix it. If his needs mending, we fix it or he gets a new one!* Kimberly was descending the convent steps. Heart thumping, nerves on edge, Vivian said, "I want to speak with you."

"I was just going for a walk."

"Do I smell something sweet?" Vivian sniffed the air.

"I don't know. Do you?"

It took an act of will for her to resist slapping the girl. "That business about the Sanctuary Movement has no place in first grade. No place." She cast the girl a look that would instant-freeze fire and moved into the convent and closed and locked the door behind her. *Stop it!* she told herself, *before you make a total fool of yourself.*

CHAPTER NINE

Vivian flung her coat over the banister, picked up the phone, and punched in numbers.

"I want to speak with Reverend Mother. It's urgent." Strains of childlike Kabelevsky rose from behind the closed door of the music room.

The answering sister said, "It's not long distance hours."

Have I control over nothing? Vivian repeated, "It's urgent." She heard the woman breathe in, then a series of clicks paging Reverend Mother.

"Praised be Jesus Christ. This is Reverend Mother Philip Neri."

"Mother, you won't believe what I have to—"

"To whom am I speaking?" The shortness of breath in the low-timbered voice disclosed the woman's obesity.

"Oh. Vivian Louise Tiamet. St. Anthony's, Reverend Mother."

"I have seven St. Anthonys."

"Sleeder, Illinois, Reverend Mother. St. Anthony in Sleeder, Illinois. The one in financial peril!"

"Vivian, all my convents are in financial peril. Tell me. Who is on mission with you?"

Vivian ticked off facts Mother should know. "Kimberly McCall, novice, first grade. Mary Ruth Vangaard, music, fifth grade. Sister Dominic Ozretich, housekeeper, the one who's seventy-seven and crippling with arthritis, who I think belongs in the infirmary."

"Mary Ruth. Mary Ruth?"

Vivian's anger deflated into defeat. She resorted to Mary Ruth's sister name, the one Mary Ruth had used before resuming her birth name. "Sister Martin de Porres."

"Oh, the sister who composed 'Baby Divine Sleep!'"

"Yes."

"Impossible to sing that song."

Strains of early Mozart, "Twinkle, Twinkle, Little Star," played inside the music room. Vivian pictured Mother, feet up on her needlepoint stool. She tried to breathe in the innocence of the melody. She wanted to keep her cool.

"The infirmary," Mother said in an authoritative tone, "maintains five hundred sisters in a wing designed for two hundred. It's unfortunate but we need every functional sister in the field. Doesn't Sister Dominic take in sewing?"

"Yes, Mother, but she *deserves*—" Vivian stopped protesting; old training clicked in. She responded, "Embroidery, French cutwork, gold and silver embellishment of vestments."

"I remember. Exquisite work. She's earning her keep then, isn't she?"

Vivian hated the idea of one minute without Sister Dominic's reassuring presence and wisdom. Still, fair was fair; Sister Dominic needed and deserved care. She must try. "Mother, pain pills give Sister Dominic temporary relief at best. She's on her feet and alone all day. She *needs* to be off her feet. She's earned the right to have someone waiting on her for a change."

Vivian waited through a prolonged silence, thinking, *Did I cross the line? Plead too much?* She hoped for thoughtful consideration.

Finally Mother said, "We wish to keep Sister Dominic ... there."

At the use of the imperial "we" Vivian's vision blurred with tears. Mary Ruth and her student were playing Chopsticks, the duet that signaled the end of the lesson.

"Mother, please," she whispered, wiping tears away, lest she be caught crying.

"Vivian, dear, we know you're trying hard and doing your best and have every confidence in you. Our prayers are with you."

Finding no alternative, Vivian said, "Praised be Jesus Christ," and hung up. She hadn't even mentioned the reason for her call. Left with the paradoxical combination of depression and anger, she blew her nose, dried her eyes, and moved into the kitchen, hoping that a smile from Sister Dominic would help her regain some measure of deportment. Sister Dominic was not alone.

Charlene Melrose's cheeks flushed with embarrassment as Sister Dominic felt inside the armhole of the girl's jumper to learn if the seam were generous enough to let out. The poor girl carried shame like a butterfly on her forehead.

Seeing Vivian, "Miss Tiamet," she whispered.

Vivian nodded to them, said, "I forgot you were coming." She smiled to put the girl, who might die of adolescence, at ease. "I'm glad you're here."

Sister Dominic reached into her pocket and pulled out a heart-shaped pincushion attached to a black shoestring. "Hold this," she said, handing it to Vivian. She extracted pins and held them between her lips.

Vivian, eager to forget her own troubles, said, "You used to be able to tell what a sister did by what she pulled out of her pockets. Scissors, a gym whistle. Sister Dominic used to carry a Swiss Army knife to dig up young dandelions for salad."

Sister Dominic removed the pins from her mouth, said, "Sometimes a screwdriver. Turn a bit now. Miss Vangaard toted her pitch pipe."

Charlene asked, "How could you carry such big, clumsy things and not have them show?"

"The skirt openings were just slits," Vivian explained. "Inside were two deep patch pockets attached to a waistband that buttoned on."

"It's close. I think I can do it."

"Good," Vivian said. "Items like this pincushion were tied onto the waistband by the shoestring. The skirt was so full, nothing showed." How Vivian missed those pockets; without them, hiding tampons often became a challenge. Sometimes tampons determined what she wore.

"That'll do," Sister Dominic said, patting Charlene's arm. "You can change now, dear."

Vivian remembered a time at about Charlene's age, when she was kneeling at the communion rail with her tongue out to receive the round holy communion wafer, when the priest unwittingly dropped it down the front of her jumper. In that awful moment they both realized only he of consecrated fingers could retrieve it. The altar boy, who had failed to catch the host on the gold paten, turned crimson.

Vivian slid the side of her hand up the front of her jumper to tip the lining toward the priest. Without touching any part of her, he reached with his thumb and forefinger and retrieved the host and placed it on her tongue. She returned to her pew wondering who had seen, and felt faint.

Even though she knew Charlene wasn't Catholic, every child deserved an invitation to God's table. Vivian said, "You may pick up your jumper after mass on Sunday." Maybe this time Charlene would accept the invitation.

CHAPTER TEN

Vivian looked at the closed door through which Sister Dominic had passed more than an hour and a half ago. This was the second time Sister had asked to see the doctor alone. Why?

A woman among a clique of pregnant women was telling a story about getting stuck in her husband's reclining chair, that she had to call him home from work to pull her out of it. It didn't seem funny but the others huddled over their baby-full middles laughing.

Vivian looked at her watch and at the door again. Custom taught they should see the doctor in pairs. What was taking so long? Four days had passed since Vivian's visit with the Sugeses. If Jennifer hadn't called by the end of Sunday, she would risk calling her.

Vivian flipped pages past photos of food in a gourmet magazine Sister Dominic had been looking at. Soon she would have to cut Sister's food budget. She set down the magazine, blindly picked up another. A pretty young woman on a glossy page anticipated a happy outcome from a do-it-yourself pregnancy test. Such information should not be so readily available. Vivian closed the magazine. Had Jennifer taken this test? Did the girl know for sure? Vivian crossed her legs and swung her foot. Why did she feel so little joy for these mothers-to-be?

Ads for pregnancy tests, Planned Parenthood, sanitary napkins, douches, spermicides, coils, condoms, anyone could see them. In her grandmother's generation pregnant women did not appear in public. Now the pregnant women were discussing morning sickness. *What would it feel like to carry a child to term, to give birth and hold your own baby?* Canon law, Church law, once prohibited women from assisting in the health care of a pregnant woman, assisting at childbirth, or in cases treating adult males.

Maybe Stevie was right. Vivian looked at the closed door. She should have insisted on being with Sister Dominic. Like worry beads, she moved her rosary beads between her fingers. Seeing a doctor alone could be terrifying.

"You must be contemplating something mighty important."

"Oh," Vivian startled, stood, and bumped the table. Magazines fell and scattered. She stooped and gathered them, thinking herself as clumsy as Kimberly. She set them in place, asked, "What did Dr. Milde say?"

Sister Dominic waved a slip of paper. "We have to pick up a prescription. He gave me a gold shot," she said, taking Vivian's arm. "Sorry. It's got to be expensive. Gold."

"Don't even mention money, Sister Dominic. Whatever will help, whatever's best." Vivian helped her into the car. "Listen," Vivian said, waiting for the engine to warm up. "Sister Dominic, listen. How many hundreds of yards of gold thread have you embroidered into vestments? We used to give a priest a gold chalice when he was ordained. Isn't it time you had some of your own gold?"

The woman couldn't help but smile.

They drove past winter fields manicured into squares and rectangles, past neat fallow land barren as a childless woman. Nothing was the same anymore. Thieves robbed churches for drug money. Pottery chalices replaced gold ones. Family farms broke up. Newspapers reported tragedy after tragedy.

They, she and the sisters were lucky to live in a time-warped, small town. She glanced at pensive Sister Dominic, wanted to reassure her, but hesitated to intrude on the woman's privacy. Appearances could be misconstrued. Sisters had practiced detachment against any kind of overture that might suspiciously lean toward lesbianism.

"You know what Father Rupert wanted?" Vivian mimicked him, "More suggestions for cutting expenses."

"Sister Dominic sighed, said, "I suppose what's good for the goose should be good for the gander."

Vivian looked at her. When had the light in the old woman's eyes gone out? Disturbed, hoping to raise the old woman out of her doldrums, she said, "I wonder what Kimberly will do next to test my patience?"

"I suppose you'll be cutting the food budget."

Sister Dominic had already given up so much; Vivian did not want to take even more pleasure away. Inconsistent with what she had been thinking only minutes before, she said, "Not yet." They crossed over the Vermilion River. Vivian said, "The Melroses live on the banks of the river. I wonder if they fish." The old woman paled. "Sister, are you all right?"

"I'm here."

Are you?

Sister Dominic wilted like a flower folding in its crimped, dark edges. It hurt to see her this way. If Sister Dominic didn't want Vivian to know why she wanted to see Dr. Milde alone, she should respect that. Vivian turned the car onto Elm, their street, and drove past rows of post-World War II crackerbox houses.

"Sister?"

"All that dressing and undressing made me tired."

"Of course it did. Soon as we get home, I'll tuck you in for a nap."

When Vivian saw the closed door to the parlor her heart skipped a beat. *Jennifer's here!*

She settled Sister Dominic in her room, then tapped her ring on the parlor door. The textbook rep stood. Her disappointment showed.

CHAPTER ELEVEN

Late the following Sunday Jennifer slid through the convent's front door as secretively as a note passed in Vivian's classroom. The girl wore a pink sweatshirt with *Go For It* written across her breasts and jeans tight as skin. Jennifer's eyes appeared glassy and bloodshot; she had been crying.

Vivian said, "I'm glad you're here. I was going to call you."

Light filtered through the Belgian lace curtains and ricocheted off the crystals of the chandelier. Sunspots sparked prisms on the white wall. Lace patterns played on the rug.

Jennifer popped her gum then removed it from her mouth and wrapped it in a small piece of foil she took from her pocket. She sat on her hands and looked toward the window. Tufts of prematurely green grass pushed up, the result of an untimely December thaw. It was a long way to spring. Slush would give way to more snow. The girl wound hair around her finger.

Tentatively, Vivian said, "I sensed your discomfort, also your mother's, when you were here. I hope you didn't feel slighted."

"S'ster, it's all right. Everyone slights me."

Vivian winced. She wanted to hug Jennifer, but resisted; the girl needed to do for herself what she could. Jennifer needed to be strong.

Vivian softened. "You don't have to call me 'Sister.' I'll do my best to help you with whatever it is. I promise not to judge you. You can trust me."

"My mother would kill me if I didn't call you 'Sister.' " The girl bent over and hugged her middle. Not looking at Vivian, she said, barely above a whisper, "I want an abortion."

Suddenly Vivian felt cramping deep inside, the response to the saline solution aborting her child before she had even felt life. To quell the urge to upchuck, she pressed two fingers against her lips and inhaled a long, slow breath. "Jennifer," she said kindly, "that would only trouble your soul more."

"I don't think so."

"Please. Look at me." Vivian peered into the girl's eyes. "No matter how awful you feel now, one day, Jennifer, this ... episode ... will be but only a small part of your past. Pregnancy doesn't make you a bad person. It doesn't."

The girl buried her face in her hands. Her shoulders shook. Vivian stooped beside her and stroked her back, vowing to God, *I'll help you the way I wanted to be helped.*

"You must feel so alone," she said, offering her handkerchief. "It's okay. Shhhh, shhh. It's okay." She rocked the girl in her arms. "God forgives, Jennifer. He forgives. He does."

"Wh-what am I going to do?" Jennifer sputtered. "What am I going to *do*?"

"First you need to talk to someone and I'm here. I won't tell anyone, not without your permission."

Streaks of mascara made the girl's face as grotesque as she must feel. How dreadful to be so needy, so frightened and helpless.

"You're not alone. We all make mistakes. Big ones."

Jennifer pinched her sweatshirt between two fingers, pulled it out, let it go. The back of her hand wiped her eyes and her cheeks. Vivian drew her chair close and took one of the girl's hands in hers. "Jennifer, the young man, does he know?"

"No! I don't want him to either!"

"Would you like a glass of water?"

"What I want, Sister, is an abortion."

Always the first thought, the quick fix that haunts you forever.
"Are you sure? Have you seen a doctor?"
"What doctor? Everyone in town knows everyone else."
True. "Your parents?"
"I could never tell my father. My mother tells him *every*thing."
The girl sobbed.
Vivian stroked her back. She said, "Are you sure? Young women miss periods all the time."
The girl's torrent ran its course. She looked up at Vivian.
Vivian said, "You know I keep my promises. I'll stand by you. That's a promise. First, let's see a doctor. Then, if we have to, we'll plan. Do I have your permission to find a doctor? Someone who won't lecture you?"
"W-will you go with me?"
"Of course." Vivian smoothed back a wisp of the girl's hair.
"S'ster, wh-when I grow up, I want to be just like you."
Shame churned inside Vivian. She tipped up Jennifer's chin, said, "You give me much more credit than I deserve. I—uh, have to ask some questions. This is important, no time to be embarrassed, okay?"
The girl sniffed, nodded.
"When was your last period?"
Jennifer reddened to the roots of her hair. "I don't know," she whimpered. "I don't know."
"Before or after Thanksgiving? Before or after Halloween?"
Jennifer's toe traced the pattern in the rug. "After Halloween. Before Thanksgiving."
"Good. Good." *Isn't it too soon to tell?*
Jennifer said, "I feel different. I don't know any other way to explain it. I just feel different."
Sin makes you feel different. It does.
"We must find out. I wasn't kidding; going to confession will comfort your soul." The girl wouldn't risk Father Rupert

recognizing her. "Maybe your boyfriend could drive you to LaSalle or Peru, some other town."

When Jennifer didn't comment, Vivian reached out and embraced her and held her for what seemed a very long time. "If we're agreed that finding out is the next step," Vivian said, "let's turn it over to God, just set it aside for now. Come to the kitchen and say hello to Sister Dominic. She's embroidering. She doesn't get many visitors and loves young people. I'll tell you a secret. She fasts during Advent, but if you have ice cream," Vivian said conspiratorially, "she'll use it as an excuse to enjoy a gooey banana split."

Jennifer almost smiled, popped her gum into her mouth, and nodded. She preceded Vivian from the parlor. As fate would have it, Kimberly was bounding down the stairs without looking ahead and nearly crashed into Jennifer. The girl's bubble burst across her face. Vivian remembered catching Kimberly tossing water-filled balloons from the choir loft window—what the novice explained as rehearsal for a class demonstration on Galileo. Imagine considering letting those little ones lean out of a choir loft window!

"I'm sorry," Kimberly said, watching the girl peel gum off her face.

Vivian introduced them.

Kimberly said, "I used to get bubble gum all over my face, too."

In a manner of speaking, she still did.

"Not as bad as the egg that's on it right now, though," Kimberly said, glancing at Vivian. "Nice to meet you, Jennifer. Sorry," she repeated, escaping out the front door.

"Would you like an ice cube?"

"Thanks. I think I've got it all."

"Looks like you do."

"Sister Dominic, remember Jennifer Suges? Her mother makes those potato dumplings you like."

"Gnocchi. What a nice surprise." Sister Dominic set her embroidery hoop on the table, saw that the girl had been crying and looked to Vivian.

Vivian shook her head.

"How would you like a dish of ice cream?" Sister Dominic asked.

"I'm on a diet." Then, remembering, Jennifer glanced at Vivian and said, "Maybe a little."

"Don't mind if I do," Sister Dominic said. "We have bananas," she said to Vivian.

Vivian patted the back of a chair telling Jennifer to sit in it and went to the cupboard. She said, "We have marshmallow, caramel, chocolate, and strawberry toppings."

"Nuts, but no cherries," Sister Dominic said, pulling the cord of the large magnifying glass she wore up over her head.

"No thanks."

Vivian held up the pickle dish in one hand and a custard cup in the other. "This? Or this?" she said.

Jennifer pointed to the custard cup then turned and examined the tiny embroidered flowers.

"It's a baptismal dress for Mrs. Pzsinski's grandchild. Due in Mary's month."

Jennifer dropped the garment as if it had ignited.

"I'll just move this so it doesn't get soiled," Vivian said, setting down the dishes and taking the needlework to the sewing machine. "I've offered to help Jennifer with geometry," she said.

"I hate geometry." Jennifer took one taste of the ice cream and put the dish on the table.

"Is something wrong? Don't you like it?" asked Sister Dominic.

"My stomach's a little upset, that's all." Jennifer turned to Vivian, said, "My mother doesn't know where I am."

Vivian nodded. "Can you stay until Sister Dominic finishes hers?" she asked.

"Guess so."

Vivian didn't feel much like eating hers either. She dutifully nibbled, made small talk.

"Next time," Vivian said, escorting Jennifer, "you might want to use this back door. Mary Ruth's piano students come and go in the front."

Guilt slashed across Jennifer's face. The girl nodded and scampered away, running from herself as fast as she could, not realizing she would carry the weight of shame forever and ever.

CHAPTER TWELVE

On the playground the children seemed particularly noisy. Mary Ruth responded to a tug on her coat sleeve.

Kimberly said, "I'm worried about Vivian."

"What do you mean?"

"Don't you think she's acting a bit ... bonkers?"

Mary Ruth couldn't believe this. She stepped back.

"I know stress when I see it," Kimberly said, closing the gap between them. "Maybe she needs time off. She could go on retreat, be quiet, pray awhile."

"I cannot be party to this conversation," Mary Ruth said and walked away.

As he did every Tuesday Father Rupert arrived to teach Marriage and the Family to Mary Ruth's fifth-grade class, a course reserved for the priest. She promptly scuttled over to the convent where she nodded a quick "praised be" to Sister Dominic in the kitchen and moved up to her room. There, Mary Ruth slipped a new cassette into her tape recorder and adjusted the volume to high. She set the recorder on her dresser and pulled the straight chair over and thought a few moments before beginning.

She had begun asking her mother questions about her parents' relationship. Neither of her parents would speak of it. She knew they met when her father was stationed at Fort Knox, Kentucky, where her mother had worked in the PX. To hear Granny Mae tell it, her mother's curvaceous figure had a way of "gluing men's eyes to it."

Mary Ruth reached out and started the whirring cassette and spoke in her soft, clear voice:

> *"Dear Mum,*
> *Advent is in full glory now with the littlest ones anticipating Baby Jesus as if Christmas were their very own birthday, or that of a new baby sister or brother. They delight in discovering their mums and dads already know the carols they're learning. At home, they sing along and tell me it makes them feel grownup. If only they could recite Bible stories the way they remember 'Rudolph' and 'The Grinch.'"*

Her mother had read the lilting, rhythmic words of the *Bible* to her.

> *"Parents seem to have precious little time to spend with their children, except when the children work alongside them. Most mums work on the home place. If the farm does not fare well, tuition payments lag behind."*

It was hard for Mary Ruth to know what came from her father, what from her mother. Her father pretended that only his blood ran in her veins. With so much divisiveness, she lacked a sense of heritage, longed to know more, but needed to be subtle in how she asked.

> *"When you were little, did you hoe tobacco fields? Climb the rafters, hang leaves? Was it working the soil that shaped your body so beautifully? I remember the*

*tobacco smell on your hands, the brown stains. Maybe
that's why I like the smell of tobacco. Besides beauty,
do you know what drew father to you?"*

It certainly was not money. Her mother's family was cash poor,
but owned land.

*"Vivian is edgy about finances; Father Rupert must
be pressing her again. Vivian says her eighth-grade
children identify with the shepherds; they want to stay
out all night!"*

Mary Ruth couldn't imagine wanting to stay out all night. She
had been overprotected to the point of being almost paranoid about
safety.

*"Sister Dominic seems increasingly preoccupied.
Though she seldom complains, I think her joints ache
more. I'm growing to like Kimberly, but she still, as you
would say, 'stirs up the hive.' Sometimes Vivian leaves
the room to chill down after an exchange with her. This
amuses Sister Dominic. Father Rupert provides all of
us with enough trauma and drama without Kimberly
adding to it. Vivian likes everything in its place and
Kimberly's a young woman who makes up plans as she
executes them."*

Maybe Kimberly would leave the convent, go back to a world
of boyfriends.

*"The motherhouse reported two more sisters
dispensed from vows. When that happens, we're
depressed for a few days. It used to happen only every*

77

other year or so; now it happens as easily as divorce. I don't know what has happened to commitment to vows.

"I'm glad I don't have to wrestle such a problem. Maybe there are too many opportunities for young people today that take away from the idea of dedication to a spiritual way of life. Of course, celibacy is harder for some than for others. Oh. One piece of good news. Widows are applying. Imagine! Maybe when one gets older, spiritual life takes on more meaning.

"More good news. Remember how the Winkle boy used to hold everyone back because his parents wouldn't consider sending him to a special school? Well, Terry Winkle's doing just fine in his new school. It's unfortunate that his parents didn't act sooner. With his presence the children learned a bit about overcoming prejudice of the handicapped. My heart went out to him. Nevertheless, it is a relief to conduct class without his constant interruption.

"As Arvid Allan and Betty Lou blend in more, the children's racism breaks down. Sometimes a racist remark comes from a child from whom I'd least expect it. I'm giving an assignment I hope will cure them. The children are going to draw a family tree and name contributions each family member makes. That should shake a few skeletons loose."

Mary Ruth pictured her mother rocking in front of the hearth, listening to this tape. One day she must tell her mother in person how much she loved her.

"Mum, I appreciate all you have done for me. I know how hard separation must have been for you. Sometimes when I see Sister Dominic squinting at

78

white-on-white embroidery on which she has worked
too long, I remember you and Granny Mae stitching
that quilt in front of the fireplace. I hear Granny
ooooh-ing and aaaah-ing over your ten-to-an-inch
stitches, which she said she would teach me to do."

Of course, Granny died before she could do that and Mary Ruth
would have no children through whom she could pass along their
quilting tradition. Mary Ruth's body shuddered. She said, "Those
were warm, safe times.

"I almost forgot to mention my new piano student!
Mr. Johnson teaches physical education at Sleeder
High and plays by ear."

She paused, wondered if she should mention he was African-
American, decided not to.

"Imagine, teaching an adult, someone who already
knows the keyboard!
"Mum, I've been trying to remember how you
constructed those folded paper mangers. I was thinking
of making them to extend holiday wishes to the other
sisters. I'm giving them coupons for time and labor that
I could slip inside the paper mangers. That is, if you
can explain how to make them. Can you send me a
sample? All thumbs, I've wasted a lot of paper trying."

Mary Ruth glanced at her watch. Father Rupert would soon be
finished. She had to conclude.

"I hope the sow has recovered. After such a medical
investment it would be a shame to lose her. Often I

79

think I might understand my children's lives better if I had tended the farm with you."

Sometimes she fretted over what might have been. One day she hoped to be able to release all that.

"It was thoughtful of Moss to come calling, surely more than for a glass of cider. I trust Uncle Wilbur has set enough wood by for the whole winter. Next week, instead of Father Rupert taking my class, I will be rehearsing the Christmas procession, so I will not be able to make a tape for you. Mum, don't forget to rewind before you speak into it. Greetings to all I love. With prayers and hugs. Your loving daughter, Mary Ruth."

CHAPTER THIRTEEN

Vivian lugged the stepladder up to the second floor and placed it under the hallway attic trapdoor. She removed her suit jacket and rolled up the sleeves of her blouse and ascended it slowly. Whenever she stuck her head through the ceiling opening she thought of prairie dogs peeking out of their earthy holes as if, like her, they needed to be alert and ready to hide in an instant.

The sisters' trunks stood on rafters, eerie versions of Stonehenge. Vivian crawled into the attic, stood, and pulled the string to the overhead light. Gingerly, she stepped from rafter to rafter until she arrived at her archaic metal trunk.

The hinges squeaked. Back when she entered the convent this trunk held her required trousseau: twelve pairs of black cotton stockings; twelve white cotton slips, six cotton undershirts, six cotton brassieres; six nightgowns, two nightcaps, two black cardigans, one cotton, one wool; one black robe (cotton or wool); four pairs of oxfords and two pairs of slippers; one black shawl. An applicant's financial dowry varied with family circumstances. Vivian removed her neatly folded summer-weight items and set them to one side.

Her trousseau had lasted through her degree at Catholic University, through her master's at Georgetown, and parts of it even into her first years of teaching at Our Lady of Conception School in Charlotte, North Carolina. When she matriculated at Loyola for her doctorate she purchased new undergarments.

Vivian wondered from time to time about Reverend Mother's arrangement with Mary Ruth's father not to compromise Mary Ruth's heritage, which meant Mother had promised to do nothing that might trigger interest in Mary Ruth's black ancestry, let alone reveal it. At best, the arrangement seemed strange.

Vivian's fingers probed and rummaged under old, unstarched guimpes at the bottom until she felt the satin cover she sought. Her heartbeat quickened. She glanced furtively at the trapdoor. She had astonished Mary Ruth and Kimberly by suggesting they go window-shopping, even gave them money for dessert and coffee. Down in the kitchen Sister Dominic clanged a lid on a pot. Vivian turned back to the trunk and withdrew the diary she had kept by claiming it was her spiritual journal. The bright red cover had become the hue of dried blood. She rested it on top of Mary Ruth's trunk and replaced items in a tidy manner.

Despite the unlikelihood of Sister Dominic coming upstairs, Vivian remained fearful of being caught; she closed the trapdoor and descended the ladder in a rush. Trying too hard to be quiet, her elbow bumped the smoke detector. Fumbling, she caught it before it thumped to the floor. That's when her diary fell and thudded. *Jesus, God protect me; guilt betrays me.*

She managed to rehang the smoke detector on its screw. Once down, she rested the ladder against the wall, snatched her hand towel from the bathroom, and wrapped the diary in it, then moved stealthily down the stairs. In the front hall she put on her coat and hid the diary wrapped in the towel inside it, then moved through the kitchen, pausing only long enough to say with a quiver of betrayal, "I'll be in my office."

The school smelled of chalk and Lysol. Once in her office, Vivian leaned her back against the locked door and tried to still her runaway breathing. She was attempting foolishness, but needed to try; she wanted a doctor whose discretion she could rely on and this physician had proved trustworthy, even if so long ago. She knew firsthand how fright turned a young pregnant girl to desperate thoughts, whether or not she would go through with them. Vivian felt underneath her top desk drawer for the key taped there. She tried to calm down, to reason; too many years had passed; the doctor could be dead. *How could I ever get Jennifer to Chicago?*

In this moment she was less concerned with practical matters than with finding a discreet physician. She located the number in her youthful scrawl camouflaged inside a circle of red hearts and dialed it. A recorded voice said the call could not be completed as dialed. *Jesus, Mary and Joseph* she prayed and tried again and heard the same recording. *It's not the end of the world. Stay calm. Think.*

Ever since she had agreed to help Jennifer, guilt followed her with vengeance like the headless horseman pursuing Icabod Crane. She might be walking across the street or standing in front of her class when a wave of guilt overtook her with a vengeance. Her overwrought psyche was as vulnerable as an infant's crown, that sacred place through which, her mother said, God's grace entered. Sneaking around this way, Vivian experienced the dreadful fear of exposure, the same kind of nakedness she felt when the nurse set her bare feet in cold stirrups, pushed her knees apart, and motioned her closer to the edge. She remembered the heat of the gooseneck lamp shining on her genitals. The brittle sepia page crackled.

Given holiday rehearsals, it would not be easy to get away with Jennifer. If only her idea had worked. She retaped the key under her drawer, then stared at the phone as if it would ring and magically produce the solution she wanted. Last night she dreamed of being in labor so painful and intense that today she actually felt tender inside. Unconsciously her hand stroked her abdomen. *Jennifer is not alone; Jennifer has me.* Without thinking, Vivian picked up the phone and dialed the one woman who, in spite of everything, might comfort her.

"Mom?"

"Vivi, what a nice surprise! How are you?" When she failed to answer, her mother said, "Honey, you're not sick, are you?"

"No. I was just in the school and thought I'd call."

After her father died, her mother had moved from Chicago to Tomball, Texas, north of Houston, along with Vivian's sister Chris and her family, though her mother had since purchased her own home.

"Vivi, you sound depressed. Don't make me ferret it out of you. Drives your sister and me nuts, the way we have to pull things out of you."

It occurred to Vivian that it would probably help Kimberly if she could turn the novice's spiritual direction over to her mother. She couldn't help but smile at the thought.

She said, "Nothing new. Just wrestling to run the convent on a shoestring, that's all."

"Poor times were some of the best your father and I had, bless his soul. We didn't think so then." Her mother chuckled. "Not that I believe you're Depression hard-up. But we did little things I still do, like rinsing out the laundry soapbox or the ketchup bottle, measuring out toilet paper. Thank goodness he never expected me to turn his shirt collars around the way some women did. Do you remember how Chris and I went house to house collecting coffee cans full of cooking grease in her little red wagon? Of course that was during the war."

Vaguely, Vivian did remember.

"We didn't call it recycling then, but that's what it was. We collected string and foil, too. Sometimes I siphoned some string for myself." Her mother's voice trailed. After a moment she said, "Seemed like a sin, taking that string."

It was not the kind of thing she would have guessed her mother would do.

"I confessed stealing it, Vivi. I'm not sure I would call that a sin now. God considers the situation, doesn't he? If I were ill and needed medicine to keep from dying—if we couldn't afford it— stealing wouldn't be a sin, would it? Surely God considers the situation."

"I hope so," Vivian said, thinking of herself, thinking of Jennifer. "If God isn't merciful, who is? At least since Daddy's been gone, you've been a lot easier on yourself."

"It feels good, Vivi, really good. He could be such a stickler. Should've been a priest."

He probably should have. Her father had attended mass daily and given up candy for Lent and made all of them feel guilty when they didn't follow his example. He believed Vivian's entering the convent purchased his ticket to heaven.

"Vivi. Dear, what *is* it?"

Vivian suddenly knew what she wanted—forgiveness. That's what she wanted. "The kids seem more on edge this holiday," she said. "I struggle with ... being strong, setting a good example."

Because she saw her mother only once a year, their phone conversations were often long and more intimate than they might be otherwise. Over the years they had discussed personal matters that she might never have broached in person.

"The continuing financial crunch?"

"More than that. It's ... complicated." She didn't want to reveal too much. "Sometimes it's hard to be Catholic," she heard herself say, changing the subject. "What's been hardest for you, Mom?"

"Oh. Well—"

Her mother's tone dropped, suggesting Vivian had stumbled upon something buried, but still alive.

"To be honest, Vivi, birth control."

"Birth control?"

It was an issue she herself had never faced, not directly.

"Oh, Vivi. Christine was born and so welcome, but come the Depression, times were hard. Your father and I ... abstained, or tried to. He went to mass more often and got down on his knees and struck his breast."

She could hear her mother's nervous breathing.

"Well ... it's difficult. I mean, I hate to say," her mother said.

"What? Say what?"

Catholic mothers often exchanged snide and not-so-snide remarks about children who had slipped in despite the natural rhythm method of birth control they were following that depended on determining safe days by taking their temperatures. Her mother coughed falsely. Vivian straightened. *Am I the result of a failure to abstain? Larry? Might we never have been born?*

"After you were born," her mother said, "Dr. Zelasny said we should be careful. You know I had those female troubles. We didn't have so many names for them then. The war was over and I was thirty-two. He said another pregnancy would do me in. I guess I can say it now. He said another pregnancy would kill me and probably the baby, too."

"Oh, Mom. How awful!" Vivian's hand pressed on her heart. "How have you kept this to yourself for so many years?" Larry was younger than she. His conception might have left them without a mother, without him. Vivian felt weak.

"It was a difficult pregnancy," admitted her mother, as if she had shared too much.

Vivian remembered being four and thinking that she must've done something terribly wrong because her father was stomping about the house. Instead of bouncing her on his knee and singing rhymes to her, he had taken to hunkering into long, dreary silences and snapped at her whenever she approached him. Only after Larry was born did he smile again. And then he doted so much over Larry, she came to think of this new baby brother as The Invader. She actually decided that her father no longer loved her. Today she realized his mood swings were rooted in fear for her mother's life. The love her father had lavished on Larry was gratitude to God, nothing less, certainly not a dismissal of her.

"Oh, Vivi, if we wore pantyhose back then, I probably wouldn't have gotten pregnant. They're the most natural birth control ever invented," joked her mother, clearly uneasy now. "Tell me, when will you visit?"

"I haven't thought about it. I'm not sure."

Vivian hadn't considered her parents as a couple trying to avoid the sins of marriage, not as conjugal partners. The purpose of sex was procreation and pleasure merely a byproduct. If one took Father Rupert at his word, pleasure occurred only if pleasure couldn't be avoided.

Her mother was going on about her coming for a visit.

Vivian wondered how such an unfortunate pregnancy had affected their family. Their life. She felt dizzy and put one hand on her forehead. It felt hot and cold, clammy.

"Vivi, I have the girls over for bridge. I go out to lunch. I keep appointments with Dr. Kreppit. Nothing to worry about. Routine. I'm slowing down. Can't do too much anymore. Vivi, it would be nice if you could visit. I miss you."

"Nice," repeated Vivian. She could try during Easter break, but summer was best, before or after their annual three-day retreat at the motherhouse.

"Larry rarely writes. You know what they say: A daughter's a daughter for all of her life, a son is a son 'til he takes a wife. Larry calls and talks legal trivia, bores me to death. And Christine, bless her, all those grandchildren tugging at her skirts while Loey works. I can never get a word in. It's you I want to see. It would do my heart good."

"I'll try," Vivian said, thinking, *If you really knew me, you wouldn't be so eager.* "I'll let you know."

"Oh, Vivi, that's wonderful."

"Mom, pray for me."

"Oh, I do, Vivi. Every day. I pray for you every day."

Vivian paced the school corridor as if someone she loved were about to die. Her mind bounced between finding a doctor for Jennifer and the unsettling news she had just learned. She supposed a child seldom thought of parents as sexual. Jennifer needed a home for unwed mothers, and names of doctors who would not sermonize. Vivian dialed a home for unwed mothers.

When the woman answered, Vivian experienced a rush of adrenaline. She said, "I'd like the name of an understanding obstetrician."

"Just a minute." She heard clicks, then, "This is Constance Marshall. May I help you?"

"Uh," she stammered. "This is ... Miss Tiamet." She repeated her request.

"Depending on your religious convictions, Miss Tiamet—"

"Oh, I don't have any," Vivian said, as if she had been caught sinning. She panicked. "Does religion matter? Don't you take anyone regardless of religion?"

"Yes. Of course we do. I can't actually recommend a physician, but I can refer you to any number of doctors who care for our young women."

"Please," Vivian said. She repeated the spelling of their names and phone numbers, recording them with the dedication of a child learning to write. Kaczmarek, Michael. Lovejoy, Monica, Horowitz, Samuel.

"We have a long waiting list," the woman said. "When are you due?"

"Oh, we don't know what I'm due," Vivian said, closing her eyes at her Freudian slip. "Not me. Goodness no. I'm inquiring for ... a friend, someone else."

Vivian didn't remember hanging up or what she had said, only that she had asked that an application be sent to her. She glanced at the names she had written, saw the results of all those ovals and slanted lines the mistress of novices had made her practice to turn her handwriting into penmanship becoming of a nun. A woman doctor might be especially compassionate. But one named Lovejoy? She circled Kaczmarek, the Polish name, the most likely Catholic candidate; surely such a sensitive matter required a Catholic. Frazzled—she had spent as much courage and energy on this as she could afford in one day—she ripped the page off the note pad, folded, and slid it into her pocket, and tried to collect herself.

CHAPTER FOURTEEN

That evening Vivian still felt unhinged as the sisters sat around the kitchen table enjoying community hour. Her box of buff-colored stationery lay open and untouched before her. Sister Dominic wove a darning needle in and out of a black stocking pulled over a light bulb. The two younger sisters were making Christmas cards. Vivian poised her ballpoint pen over a notepad trying to create the list Father Rupert had requested.

"What do you think?" Kimberly asked. She slid angular bits of colored construction paper into a Picasso-like collage of the three kings in front of Sister Dominic.

"Quite contemporary," Sister Dominic said, leaning forward and pushing up her glasses.

Mary Ruth crumpled paper she had tried to fold into some sort of origami creation and tossed it into the wastebasket.

Vivian had already cut expenses too much; there was nothing she wanted to add.

Kimberly said, "Maybe I'll do the halos in glitter."

"Like yours?" teased Sister Dominic.

Kimberly moved her fingertips along her imaginary halo. "Only more so," she said. She rolled a glue stick across bits of paper, said, "The goddess gave life before any notion of god existed."

"Oh, pooh," Vivian said, mocking her. "Whatever *do* you read?"

Mary Ruth tossed another wad of paper into the wastebasket.

"What *are* you doing?" Kimberly asked.

Trying to recall something I once knew. I give up." She sighed. "Sister Dominic, would you pen 'Baby Divine Sleep' in calligraphy for me? I could run it through the copier."

"I don't know as I have the time. The baptismal dress is taking longer than I expected."

Mary Ruth nodded and seemed to apply her efforts more pensively.

Vivian had written: Turn off water heater? hours/day. Yes. The old woman worked a lot slower than she used to.

Kimberly said, "Miss Frank's sister works at the Sleeder library. She locates anything I want on their computer."

Vivian moved her index fingertip across her forehead as if the pressure of her starched headpiece were still there. They said computers would soon make any library in the world available to anyone and even translate the material into English or any language.

Kimberly said, "With democracy of information, no government or Church will be able to impose control."

Could any superior maintain control? How would sisters behave? Priests? Would it really make a difference?

"Is that true?" Sister Dominic asked, dropping her darning into her lap.

"Laura Frank says it is."

Sister Dominic said, "Maybe I could learn about my heritage."

Mary Ruth had *etch-etched* a row of red treble clefs with her calligraphy pen.

Sister Dominic said children used to ridicule her in school before she lost her Croatian accent. Sadly, she had all but forgotten her native language.

Kimberly said, "I've been reading about different religious orders, about how early American bishops kept sisters in tow."

"Whatever do you mean?" Vivian asked, not sure that she wanted to hear the answer.

"Bishops issued a list of 'Thou shalt nots' longer than your arm: 'Don't teach women to read; don't teach women anything about their bodies; don't help women find jobs.' The women who wanted jobs were often single moms forced into prostitution *because* they couldn't get jobs."

"Ouch," said Sister Dominic, sucking on her fingertip.

Vivian dropped her pen.

"That's hard to believe," Mary Ruth said.

"Well," Kimberly said, sprinkling multi-colored glitter on a piece of paper, "seems the sisters were pretty good fundraisers and the bishops wanted in on it. They finagled power, appointed themselves financial advisors and treasurers of women's orders, tried to name convent superiors, and even confiscated contributions. When none of those ploys worked, they ordered priests to withhold the sacraments of communion, and confession.

"Listen to this ultimate endplay—when sisters had had enough, they moved to another diocese. Then one clever reverend mother thought of applying directly to Rome for approval of their charter and scored."

Vivian *click-click-clicked* her ballpoint pen.

Mary Ruth asked, "Is that really how orders began to report directly to Rome?"

"It is," Sister Dominic said. "Vivian, stop that clicking. It's annoying. True enough, though I didn't know all that was behind it!"

Vivian's mind calculated. At the beginning of the twentieth century there were four sisters for every priest. Sisters started and staffed schools, hospitals, missionary outposts. Now, except for administering a few of the sacraments and saying mass, sisters ran the parishes while priests like Father Rupert took full credit.

Mary Ruth started to hum.

"Course," Kimberly said, pressing her thumb down on bits of paper to help the glue hold, "sisters associated with men's orders didn't fare as well."

Agitation flowed into Vivian's bloodstream. The girl would say anything for shock value. She couldn't sit still. "I need to make a phone call," she said, turning to Sister Dominic for the required nod of permission.

"Why do you have to ask permission?" Kimberly, of course, who else?

Vivian had never questioned this formality regarding obedience. There were reasons for every rule, every custom. She said, "Sister Dominic, please explain," and left the kitchen.

Now raging with fury for every time she had asked permission to take a pencil from a cupboard or requested a bar of soap, resigning herself to accept whatever brand she was given whether she liked it or not, she yanked the phone into Sister Dominic's room and closed the door over the cord. Asking permission for such a mundane thing made her feel reduced to childhood and Kimberly's constant questioning reduced her to a fool. The phone rang on the other end. She took a deep breath. Patience, kindness was required.

"Jennifer. I was hoping you'd answer. It's Miss Tiamet."

"Don't call me *here*," whispered the girl.

Vivian felt chided. "I don't know where else to call," she said. Do you have anything ... to report? Listen." Vivian forced herself to soften. "I have the names of three doctors in Peoria. Would you like to make the appointment or shall I?"

"You do it," Jennifer said. "Only not on a Friday. Friday's football."

Vivian heard a click and pulled the receiver away from her ear and looked at it in disbelief. The girl had hung up. She hadn't even had a chance to explain what little she knew about the three doctors so Jennifer could choose.

The others watched Vivian slide uneasily into her chair. After what seemed an expectant, interminable moment, Sister Dominic turned to Mary Ruth.

"That's nice," she said, referring to a green treble clef overlapping a red one.

Kimberly said, "You're not making cards, Sister Dominic! We can make them for you, can't we, Mary Ruth?"

"Surely."

"Why, thank you," Sister Dominic said, sounding pleased. "I don't have family to send them to. Except you, so I won't need many." She smiled.

Vivian twisted her ring, flipped the corners of her stationery, *clicked* the ballpoint pen. Writing personal notes exacted the same kind of patience it had taken to hem the rolled edge of her thin, woolen veil with silk thread that tangled. Pick up one thread, skip two. Pick up one, skip two. Obedience made tangles, demanded patience, was supposed to make her feel like a grownup when she felt just the opposite.

Kimberly pressed a black face onto one of the three kings on each of three cards. "Did you know," she said, addressing no one in particular, "that there once was an order of black sisters who trained black girls to be domestics?"

"No!" exclaimed Mary Ruth.

Sister Dominic glanced at Sister Vivian, cleared her throat, said, "I loved early Christmases in the convent. As novices we were in charge of post midnight-mass activities. Once we went out and cut down the biggest tree, then wouldn't let postulants into the community room. That tree must've been twenty-five feet tall. We trimmed the lower branches off to make wreaths and centerpieces for the refectory tables and decorations in the community room. After the postulants and first-year novices left for midnight mass, we laid sprigs of evergreen tied with red ribbons on their pillows. The smells," she said, closing her eyes, breathing in.

Mary Ruth said, "French pies with the flakiest crust."

"On each plate," Sister Dominic said, addressing Kimberly, "grapefruit halves with pointed rinds and a cherry. Homemade coffee cake. Poinsettias. Candles."

"The carols," Mary Ruth said, humming a bit of "Wolcome Yole."

Kimberly clapped. "What fun."

Vivian wrapped her ankles around the legs of her chair. *What is wrong with me? Why can't I enter into the spirit of this joy?*

"Sister Yvette made the pies," Sister Dominic said, sounding wistful.

Vivian thought she saw a tear in Sister Dominic's eye.

"My class was the last class to enjoy them," Mary Ruth said.

Sister Dominic intoned, "Mary, Queen of Angels."

"Lord, help Sister Yvette," they responded.

Sadness filled the silence.

Lord, thought Vivian, *they pander to Kimberly and I not only get furious, but jealous!* A little too loudly, Vivian said, "We used to take the Christmas cards from the previous year, cross out the signatures, sign our own, and exchange them among ourselves."

"Isn't that taking poverty a bit far?" Kimberly crinkled her nose.

Sister Dominic jabbed her needle at the sock-covered bulb as if it were a voodoo doll. "Love," she said, "is meeting another's needs, providing what's entitled."

Vivian jumped at this reference to Sister Yvette's plight as if Sister Dominic's needle had stuck her. "Generosity of spirit *is* true poverty," she said.

"Sure," Kimberly said, "redistribute the wealth."

"No," Mary Ruth said. "I think it's more like recycling. Living with our lovely antiques I never feel poor."

Vivian wanted to take comfort in tradition: One took according to one's needs; one gave according to one's ability. Communism with a small "c." The ideal. Back when she was learning to practice poverty, using only three pairs of underpants when there were nine more pairs in her trunk made absolutely no sense to her: one pair on, one pair at the laundry for the week, the third, to be handwashed daily. She had learned to live with the most intimate kind of soil; she didn't like it then and she didn't like it now.

Kimberly said, "I'm glad we no longer wear bridal gowns and promise 'to obey.' "

Investiture had been Vivian's most sacred moment. Now a novice created her own ceremony, wrote her own vows, an extreme in the opposite direction.

Kimberly said, "Gratefully, we're beyond the veil now."

Vivian said, "If you paid as much attention to answers as you do questions, you wouldn't have so many."

"Dour and sour."

Kimberly was the kind of novice who took dogma and custom with a grain of salt, then stayed at the banquet table as if she were welcome. Sometimes coping with her tried Vivian's patience even more than Father Rupert did. There had to be an end to it. Vivian tapped her ring, signaling the Grand Silence. When they looked at her, no one was more surprised than she!

Long after Mary Ruth had assisted Sister Dominic to bed, Vivian sat waiting as Kimberly wet her fingertip on her tongue and sorted each bit of paper by color into sandwich bags. Watching, waiting, it occurred to Vivian that if her child had lived, she would be Kimberly's age. If her child failed to obey, what could she do? If she insisted— Vivian got up and left the room.

CHAPTER FIFTEEN

Vivian awoke the next morning full of regrets. She would never reach Kimberly if she discounted every observation the girl made. The young woman was right. Like their school, SIHMs was outmoded. The sisters at the motherhouse probably still ate oranges halved like grapefruit, using narrow serrated spoons. How did one eat a furry kiwi? *Lord, forgive me. I must do something nice for Kimberly, but what?*

Vivian phoned Jennifer and told her that January 2, Thursday, was the earliest doctor appointment she could obtain. Jennifer declined meeting with her before then. Vivian felt absolutely unneeded. She determined to mentally set aside the girl's pregnancy for the time being and threw herself into holiday rehearsals.

The day of the first procession, the one on rose-colored Sunday, dawned bright and clear. Effortlessly Mary Ruth's heavily chorded organ playing pulled the children through the notes of "Baby Divine Sleep." Afterward, warmed by the poignancy of the ritual, Vivian moved among the parishioners outside, expecting compliments.

"Vincent did a nice job with the straw," she said, approaching Berneta Cellini, brazenly fishing for one.

"Vivian," Berneta said, touching Vivian's sleeve to keep her there while she turned and said, "Hurry," waving her children toward the car. Berneta turned to Vivian. "Our husbands don't understand how you love our children," she said. "This procession. Music lessons. The May crowning. All the extras you work so hard to provide. Carlos! *Mama mia.* Get into the car! Sorry, Vivian, we have to leave."

It was the same with everyone Vivian approached. They were all in a hurry. *Why?* She felt unfulfilled, disappointed, like she no longer belonged to this church family.

At breakfast, Mary Ruth suggested, "Maybe there was a Knights of Columbus breakfast or something."

"Or Christmas shopping," posed Kimberly. "I could never find enough time."

Shopping would be a dreadful way to spend the Sabbath.

"The procession went well," volunteered Sister Dominic.

"It did, didn't it?" Vivian said.

"The music, too," Kimberly said, complimenting Mary Ruth. She turned to Vivian, said, sounding self-satisfied, "My kids behaved admirably."

No matter what they said, Vivian felt something just wasn't right. Something—she didn't know what—lay awry. Afterward she remained to wash the dishes.

"They did seem rushed, didn't they?" she asked Sister Dominic, who sat embroidering. "And did you notice how few men attended mass?"

Sister Dominic tugged on a French knot, testing it. "We'll probably never know," she said.

"Sister Dominic, is the gold working?"

"A fleck at a time. I'm sorry you have to help so much."

"Don't give it a second thought. You're family. We love you." Vivian hesitated. Whatever possessed her to take the risk, she didn't know. "Sister, sometimes I wonder if you wouldn't be more comfortable in our infirmary. Might your needs not be better met there?"

Sister Dominic's lips puckered and twitched. "Never."

"Never?"

Vivian had expected Sister Dominic to be happy with the idea of retirement, which was why she had insisted that Reverend Mother transfer the old woman. *Wrong again!* Vivian felt heady, dizzy at the gravity of her mistake. "I'm glad I asked," she managed to say. *How many mistakes have I made like this that have gone unnoticed?* "I'm truly sorry," she said. "I thought it would please you."

"It's easy to think we know what's best for another," Sister Dominic said.

Meaning Sister Kimberly. Vivian fairly riddled with humility. "I like to think I try with the best of intentions."

"Maybe so." Sister Dominic bent her head to the thread, twisted and severed it with her teeth. "She means well," she said.

Vivian scoured the frying pan. "Don't we all?"

Sister Dominic rested her embroidery, said, "Ambition's not necessarily a bad thing. Nor idealism. At thirteen, I dreamed of becoming a scholar the way other girls dream of Prince Charming coming on a glorious white stallion. There were few places a young woman could get schooling. I certainly loved God in a romanticized way. That's not a mistake Kimberly makes."

Hardly.

"God gave me my comeuppance when I learned my destiny."

Housekeeping, not scholarship, had proved to be her destiny. "Oh, Sister Dominic, I had no idea, no idea. How devastating for you! How awful!"

Sister Dominic moved a knuckle behind her lens and brushed under one eye. "It wasn't easy," she said. "Bending my will was supposed to bring me closer to God's will."

Back then religious life ranked first, single life second, marriage, a lowly third. When a child entered religious life, parents bragged about their chosen child.

"Sister Dominic, isn't it possible to bend too much? To break?"

"That depends on whether you're looking forward or back with hindsight. It wasn't easy, but it *has* been good." She rested her needlework, thought a bit, then pulled the cord of the magnifying glass over her head, and braced her weight with her hands on the arms of the chair and raised herself. "The body gets old and tired," she said, shuffling along an invisible path she sometimes paced when giving spiritual direction. "But, mind you, not the soul. The soul, Vivian, stays alert and young." She paused and narrowed her eyes the way she did when she intended to make an important point.

When Sister Dominic took to this mood, Vivian didn't want to miss a syllable. She dried her hands and sat down to listen.

Sister Dominic pulled up one of the large wooden beads of the rosary hanging from her waist and worried it between her fingers. "It's important," she said, "to find that spiritual light inside, and to heed where it takes you, to notice the pattern. As the smallest willow twig at the top of the tree connects to a small branch and that branch connects to a bigger branch and so on all the way down to the trunk, there's pattern. The trunk stands firm and embraces all heaven above. Underground the pattern's the same in reverse. The roots branch down and out embracing the earth, making the tree as strong as it can be. Those relationships," said Sister Dominic, gesturing, "leaf, branch, trunk, roots, are all part of the same divine pattern. There's no getting away from it, it repeats and repeats everywhere sure as a wallpaper pattern." The old woman stood still and held up a gentle parental finger. "Find and follow that inner light, Sister Vivian, and you've found your own pattern."

How far Vivian had yet to go.

"It's the way. The only way," Sister Dominic said. "I tell you there's a core of strength in Kimberly that's aligned with God's will. That girl, Vivian, will not break."

You think Kimberly's already found her light? Maybe so, but she hasn't made a really big mistake yet. It takes one big one. Then she'll learn the same way we all do.

"Mary Ruth now, there's another matter," continued Sister Dominic. "I don't know what Reverend Mother was thinking to discount truth so."

For a moment Vivian was struck dumb. *Yes. Secrets have a way of invading every waking hour of every day; they distract you and sap your energy and pitch you into despair.*

"Sister Dominic, what about me? What can you tell about me?"

The old woman's eyes seemed to leap a chasm between them toward a bull's-eye in her soul.

"Ah. You, Vivian, you must decide where to prune, where to trim, which way to grow. Maybe you will learn where your light is strongest and draw on that strength." Sister Dominic moved her needle demonstrating. "Up. Out. In. They are different directions."

Vivian lowered her gaze. Sister Dominic knew her far better than she knew herself. In exchange for scholarship, this woman had accepted obedience and freed herself from having to make a living. For her part, Vivian had struck a bargain with God and gained recognition she had both earned and, yes, *deserved.* Even in this moment of insight, pride, sinful pride, prevailed.

"Dear," Sister Dominic said kindly, "if you let go of control your soul will find and create its own pattern. Guaranteed."

CHAPTER SIXTEEN

After midnight mass the sisters returned to the convent laden with gifts.

"I've never seen so many," Vivian said, tumbling packages at the foot of their sad little tree.

"Isn't it fun?" Kimberly asked, who, prior to the procession, had moved among the first- and second-graders, forming their fingers into steeples, crossing their thumbs. Kimberly lifted Sister Dominic's legs, one, then the other, onto the couch.

Vivian said, "I'll get the champagne."

In the kitchen she removed plastic wrap from the tray of fruitcake she had sliced earlier. Given their financial difficulties, champagne seemed frivolous. *Rupert's not going to ruin my Christmas.* The procession had achieved exactly the right mix of innocence and drama. Stirring, that's what it was. Gifts had been delivered from stores, by mail, and by parishioners themselves, including a half dozen bottles of Jacques Bonet champagne.

Vivian offered the tray to Sister Dominic.

Taking a slice and putting it on a small paper plate, the old woman said, "Little Betty Pzsinski couldn't have placed the Baby Jesus more reverently, could she?"

"Perfect. Everything was perfect," Kimberly said. She sat on the floor sorting gifts into four stacks.

"So many compliments," Sister Dominic said, crinkling her nose against the tickle of champagne bubbles.

"Not that I noticed," Vivian said, smiling, setting down the tray.

"The music *was* divine," said Sister Dominic.

"My mum would have been proud," Mary Ruth agreed.

"I didn't know you had a mother," Kimberly said.

Vivian and Sister Dominic exchanged quick glances.

"Oh. I just meant—" Kimberly bent her ear to a present and shook it. "You never speak of one. So, naturally I thought—"

" 'When Blossoms Flowered Mid the Snow,' " Sister Dominic said. "'Twas smooth."

"Yes," Vivian said. "Syncopation's hard for children."

"Why did everyone keep wishing us well as if they hadn't seen us for a long time?" Sister Dominic asked.

"A toast to 1996," Kimberly said. "A blessed healthy, Happy New Year."

"Hear, hear!"

Mary Ruth said, "I've sampled all five fruitcakes. Sister Dominic, beyond a doubt, yours is the best."

"No raisins," the old woman said, revealing her secret.

Vivian said, "I'll pop the cork on another bottle. Then, unless Kimberly prefers to wait until Twelfth Night, we'll open presents."

"Oh, you," Kimberly said to her, mimicking Sister Dominic.

They laughed.

Vivian refilled their glasses. Because Sister Dominic had no living relatives, she opened gifts given to them as a community. As Vivian filled the old woman's glass she peered into wisdom's eyes and said with deep affection, "It's been a good year. Let's hope for another."

"Yes," Sister Dominic said, squeezing Vivian's hand. "We'll pray for Father Rupert."

Wasn't it just like Sister to raise the bar on charity in the face of adversity? Vivian sat on the floor and nestled her back against the couch. Opening Christmas presents was the closest they came to real family intimacy, unless one counted moments of prayer. Reverend Mother would give each of them an envelope containing this year's Nativity holy card and a medal of the Holy Family tied on a square of white cardboard with red ribbon.

"An electric keyboard!" Mary Ruth exclaimed, unwrapping a box posted in South Africa.

"Wow!" Kimberly said.

"You'll enjoy that. Fudge," Sister Dominic said, passing the tin.

"I'm holding out for Mrs. Racine's paté," Vivian said, not taking any. She wanted this moment to last forever.

Kimberly inserted one hand inside a pair of green pantyhose and held it up to the tree lights. The box on her lap held a rainbow assortment of them. Vivian twinged with dread because she had to review gifts and rule out anything inappropriate or inconsistent with poverty and the gift was either returned or donated to charity. It took relatives about three years to learn what was acceptable. Since they retired their habits the line between what was and what was not appropriate had blurred. A sister could keep what she brought when she entered until it wore out. Approval of future choices belonged to the superior.

"Food and more food," Sister Dominic said, delighted.

"Three sets of stationery, two boxes of notecards, two scarves, and *eau de toilette*," Vivian said. She had saved the gifts from family for last.

Mary Ruth extracted a nun doll from white tissue paper.

"Oh, what's it made of?" Kimberly asked, sounding envious. Kimberly had yet to open the big box from her parents, the package from Arizona.

"Dyed corn husks," Mary Ruth said, tears glistening her eyes. She touched the natural color guimpe, the coif, the skirt. She turned to Vivian.

Vivian wanted to decide quickly, to be generous. She nodded.

"How lovely," Sister Dominic said, voting.

"Thank you," Mary Ruth whispered.

"A laptop!"

"A computer?" Vivian had not anticipated such a gift.

"I can teach all of you," Kimberly said. "And a portable printer. We can go online!"

"Isn't there a fee for that?" Vivian asked.

"It's included," Kimberly said, waving the card that came with the gift. "I hope I can remember how. It should be like riding a bicycle and come back. Isn't it wonderful? The library must have those Dummy books for a refresher course."

Kimberly was the kind of enthusiastic, persistent young woman Vivian might have become. *Before Rob, if they ... if she, hadn't—*

Kimberly turned to Vivian, her anxious expression asking, May I keep it? Responsibility turned Vivian's best moments into her worst moments. Once she herself had to return a black sweater her grandmother had knitted for her because its neckline of tiny flowers was "too perky." Why did no one ever discuss how reviewing gifts affected the one who had to do it? Well, she had hoped to do something nice for Kimberly and she had wanted computers for all of them.

"It's time we learned," she said.

Kimberly whooped.

Vivian smiled, turned to Sister Dominic for approval, but the woman's mind seemed far away, her thumb moving absently over Mother's Nativity holy card.

"Here," Vivian said, picking up and offering Sister Dominic a gift. "From all of us."

Sister Dominic took the box and shook it and smiled. "A puzzle!"

Mary Ruth said, "I knew we couldn't surprise you."

"Hope it's difficult enough," Vivian said.

"The Danube," Kimberly said, as the gift came into view. "To remind you of the part of the world you came from."

"Thank you. Thank you."

Mary Ruth passed out clever, folded paper mangers. Inside each was a small piece of paper. "That's too much," Sister Dominic said, looking up in surprise. "You're going to mend my socks?"

"I will," pleased Mary Ruth said. Addressing all of them, she said, "You don't have to redeem the coupon for what it says. You may barter for whatever you like."

"Very thoughtful," Sister Dominic said. "Indeed."

Vivian thanked Mary Ruth for her most graceful, nunlike gesture. The woman was a natural nun, one to emulate.

Kimberly passed out envelopes. "I wanted to give everyone bubble bath, but since this is my first Christmas on mission, I wasn't sure about that. So," she said, "I decided to share a monetary gift I received."

Inside Kimberly's Magi card was a twenty-dollar bill. "Thank you, Kimberly," Vivian said, envious, wishing she could offer them the same. "Thank you," she repeated, very much meaning it. She didn't have the heart to take away the girl's colored pantyhose. It was time they had bit more color around anyway. Her own gift of prayers seemed wanting alongside such thoughtfulness.

Vivian passed crayon drawings from her grandnieces and nephews for all to see. She received a short terry cloth robe from her sister, Chris. She had requested it to wear from the dressing room to the hospital pool, where she often swam to restore a sense of charity and balance to her soul after stress, especially after coping with the priest. Larry, her brother, had sent a pen and pencil set, and her mother an airline voucher with a note, "I'm excited about seeing you."

They left the holiday litter where it fell and retired to the kitchen for breakfast, which started with fruit Vivian had sliced, fresh strawberries and kiwi.

"So Christmasy," Kimberly said. "I appreciate this, Sister Dominic."

"Thank Vivian," said Sister Dominic.

There was a moment when Kimberly looked at Vivian that almost brought tears to Vivian's eyes, a moment of loving gratitude.

"What do you think?" Kimberly asked.

Vivian laughed. "I thought my teeth would itch, but they don't. I like the taste."

"Great," Kimberly said.

Vivian looked around at their happy faces, wanted hugs from these women, wanted comfort with and for them, wanted not to feel so alone like puny David facing Goliath, which reminded her that Father Rupert had not yet asked to see her ledger. Maybe he had changed his mind or maybe he was just waiting to strike when her guard was down.

CHAPTER SEVENTEEN

Kimberly experienced only minor guilt at having fibbed about the Internet fee being paid because she knew her parents expected her to charge it to them. The next day, Thursday, she tucked her plaid blouse into a pair of old jeans, pulled on her bright blue cardigan, boots and coat. She took her laptop and told Vivian she was going to the library, except when she disembarked the bus, she headed straight for Brenda Sullivan's office.

"To what do I owe the honor?" Brenda asked, surprised. The woman wore a dark, pinstriped suit with a paisley bow tie at her throat and sat behind a sleek, highly polished executive desk with thick glass across its top.

"Guess I should have an appointment. Nice office. Contemporary."

Brenda smiled and touched a red fingernail to the bow. "I was able to choose what I wanted."

"Do you have time for a brief visit?"

"Sure. It's slow now. Customers are trying to figure out how they're going to repay what they've borrowed for the holidays. Jeans, not very nunlike."

Kim wrinkled her nose. "People stare and hold me to a higher standard. I get enough of that from Vivian."

Kim spotted the family photo, Brenda and Mike and Sherry, at age three or so, sitting on Mike's lap. She experienced a twinge of sadness because she would never have a photo with a child of her own.

"Sherry's not the reason I'm here," she said.

"That's a relief." The lines on Brenda's forehead knitted into puzzlement.

Vivian would spit holy cards if she knew I was doing this. Suddenly breathless, Kim said, "Vivian's always making meticulous lists of how we can cut costs. Father Rupert's never satisfied. We don't even have cable. He seems to think we should operate the school like a soup kitchen that depends on donations. At best, the bishop's annual collection for our order is a token. We sisters don't have equity or collateral. All we have is ... our personal resources."

"Vivian sent you here to ask for a loan?"

"Oh no! She doesn't know I'm here. It's just that I heard a rumor that the school's worse off than anyone's letting on. I thought maybe you might know something."

Brenda diddled her index finger on a pile of papers.

"Sisters in other orders take jobs for pay, which seems to me like an in-your-face solution to money problems." Vivian couldn't distinguish obedient acceptance from deliberate passivity.

Brenda set her elbows on her desk and interlaced her fingers, said, "I don't pretend to grasp how one reconciles a vow of poverty with earning power."

"God. Power's the right word. Vivian would turn all of us into victims. We're not using our personal power." Kim moved to the edge of her chair. "I have an idea. Maybe you can help. As a group women religious are business savvy. Principals. Hospital administrators. Running missionary outposts. We're highly educated and run multilingual international organizations in many countries. The clergy think of us as the helpful helpless. We're naturally set up for networking, but we don't."

Brenda's brow rippled into concentration the same way Sherry's did. "I understand lack of income. What do you want?"

109

"Shades of Freud, Brenda." Sisters assigned to a school or job were supposed to act like a family. Instead they were four lonely women rattling around in a cold house saving scraps of paper, keeping silent about Father Rupert's abuse of power.

"A loan requires collateral."

Kim threw up her hands in exasperation. "I don't want a loan. Today's sister is like a wife who sacrificed everything, including her dreams, to wait on her husband and kids in the sixties or seventies. Then one day when her kids are grown and her youth is gone, hubby up and leaves. Having fulfilled the terms of her marriage contract, she's left cold. What I want is money. Like this betrayed woman, sisters have two fatal flaws—gullibility and obedience. After a lifetime of caring for the Church family, we find ourselves divorced without compensation and without legal recourse. The logical answer for the betrayed bride is—get a job."

Brenda's face radiated. "This is the Kim I remember!"

"God," Kim said, banging her forehead with the heel of her hand. "You probably aren't tuned in to the power plays of Catholic politics."

"I know they're petty."

"Not in the bigger picture. The pope gives all of us a bad name. For instance, he forced Agnes Mary Mansour, a Michigan sister who headed up the state's social services, to choose between her job that included legal abortion or obedience to him." Kim paused to catch her breath.

"What did Agnes do?"

"Unfortunately, she resigned." *When it comes to sisters, priests slice themselves off from brotherly love quick as a guillotine.* "Not everyone caves in. When the pope ordered two Rhode Island sisters to resign their jobs—one was a state legislator, the other state attorney general—the women left their orders and kept their jobs. Sisters need a strong, feminist example to follow. Of course, there's a new canon law forbidding women religious from holding elective office."

Brenda remained quiet and thoughtful, studying her.

"This conversation stays between us," Kim said.

"That sounds healthy. I didn't think— Well. Is your résumé updated?"

Kim felt her conspiratorial smile. "I can hardly put on a résumé that I worked for the Sanctuary Movement when it was considered illegal. You know my skills. I coordinated and supervised volunteers, lobbied the state legislature, wrote and distributed material, much of which I later published."

"Anonymously."

To avoid danger to those seeking asylum.

"Bless Guillermo's soul, the law was after big potatoes, not me. I was just a tiny pea under piles of large, thick mattresses. What I lack in tact, I like to think I make up for in raw courage. Brenda, I can't put any of it on paper. Run interference for me; verify what I can do. Be my reference. I'd have to schedule work hours around teaching."

Brenda laughed.

"Laughter may be good for the soul, but I'm dead serious here. I'm tired of others deciding what's best for me."

"You're asking so little."

"What are friends for?"

"God, Kim."

Kim watched a range of emotions cross her friend's face.

Finally Brenda said, "I laughed because I know of an opportunity, but it's not right for you."

"Sure it is. Why not?"

"It's at Planned Parenthood, a part-time position."

A poison dart struck Kim's heart with a sudden sharp pain. She covered it with her hand. Pro-life was a euphemism the world could do without, abortion an issue that turned best friends into diehard enemies. Violation happened to both girls and women. Hadn't Consuelo landed stateside with more than sand in her vagina?

Kim's mind tried to finagle a way to take the job. "You know I'm pro-choice. Part-time doing what?"

"Newspaper releases. Updating brochures. Writing an occasional new one."

"Well, studies show Catholics are using birth control at the same rate as the rest of the population. Maybe you don't know, eighty percent of priests won't advise against it in the confessional." She was thinking out loud, running off at the mouth. Making abortion a choice between life and murder, who wouldn't choose life? Putting it in terms of what was best for the child, making abortion a choice between privacy and a woman or a girl's capacity as a parent—with the ability to provide emotionally, spiritually, physically—

"Microscopic cells divide and multiply like loaves and fishes, don't they? How can anyone possibly pinpoint the single moment when life begins? Arms and legs and nostrils and gender, hair, doesn't everything develop gradually? Who says that consciousness doesn't? Who can say with certainty when the human spirit, the soul, enters a tiny body? The moment of consciousness could be different for each of us. If science doesn't have the answers, how dare anyone play God and impose their version of truth on others? Tell Planned Parenthood I'll do a sample assignment. Free."

"I can't believe this conversation." Brenda picked up a pencil and dropped it. "You sound—manic. Are you sure?"

Kim was reconsidering. *Vivian would kick me out in a flash and prevent me from entering any other order. She could do that ... and would.*

Brenda said, "Our Planned Parenthood has a secret benefactor allowing us to refuse government funding, which means the federal gag rule doesn't apply to us. We're trying to get rid of the required parent signature before a minor can get an abortion. Think. Planned Parenthood would be a foolish risk for you."

Brenda was right and Kim knew it. She sighed with resignation. "Well," she quipped, "if I were having a baby, we'd both know what I should do."

They laughed.

Brenda said, "Well, there are possibilities now that didn't exist when I was trying to conceive. Women can sell their eggs on the Internet."

Kim smiled and shook her head. "Rome must be in fits. Do you know of anything else?"

"Not offhand. I will keep my eyes open."

"Maybe if I had prayed harder when you and Mike were trying, you would have had sextuplets!"

"Pu-lease."

I musn't leave Brenda with the wrong idea. "Brenda, I need to say that as much as I complain there's a lot I like about convent life—strong women doing important work, time for prayer and nurturing a spiritual life. If I ever choose to leave, I want it to be on my own terms, not because ... someone else decided my fate."

Brenda came around the desk and hugged her. "I know. I love you."

Kim looked into her friend's eyes. "I hate feeling powerless when I know I'm not. If only I knew what I wanted—"

Brenda's hand rested on Kim's shoulder. Kim patted it. "I love you, too. As always, you've helped more than you know."

CHAPTER EIGHTEEN

When Vivian answered the convent phone Kimberly was visiting the family of one of her students, Mary Ruth was giving a lesson, and Sister Dominic sat in the kitchen embroidering.

Father Rupert clipped, "You're needed."

"Of course," she said, later regretting how quickly she had succumbed.

Vivian drew her shawl across her shoulders, crossed the playground to her office, where she picked up the ledger and the list she had prepared. She looked both ways before crossing the street. Cold air filled her lungs. The man extended his hand toward his office without a word. There stood three parish farmers, hats in hand.

"Oh," she said, clutching the ledger to her chest.

"You won't need that," Rupert said, taking it.

"I won't?"

He rested the ledger on the windowsill. She felt disarmed, naked, crumpled the list in her hand.

"Sit, sit," the priest said. The others seemed to have lost their tongues.

Vivian slid into the chair near his desk. The others sat on folding chairs. She looked from one to the other of them.

"How are you?" overweight Mr. Novotny asked, not looking at her. He hooked his arthritic thumbs in his overall straps. When he moved his head, white creases in his sun-darkened neck showed.

Lean, taciturn Mr. Suges wore a thin, striped tie over a denim shirt. He reminded Vivian of the farmer in *American Gothic*, except Mr. Suges' eyes were troubled.

Mr. Yeuhaus, whose German work ethic thought nothing of taking his sons out of school to work in the field, asked, "Have a good holiday?"

"Yes. Yes. Thank you."

Father Rupert nodded to Mr. Novotny.

The man said, "We, the men of the parish, have been meeting to discuss—" He turned to the priest.

Why they've rehearsed!

"Condition of the parish," finished Mr. Yeuhaus.

"That's it," Mr. Suges said.

Vivian shifted with discomfort. Like the priest, Mr. Suges could offer poison with a smile. *Rupert's outnumbering me, relying on my civility. Careful. Don't be rash. Count. Reason. Use reason.*

"Plow ahead," Suges said.

"To the point," Yeuhaus said.

Apparently Mr. Novotny, the one with the sweetest temperament, was supposed to lead them. He mumbled something about having to make hard decisions.

Vivian sent a spiteful glance to the priest.

"Cut losses," Suges said. "Bite the bullet."

"What is this?" Vivian asked, addressing the priest. *A lesson in clichés?*

"Vivian, Sister," Mr. Novotny said, sitting straighter as if adding respect might help him. "We know you like teaching our children. We know you love them."

Suges said, "Cut to the chase."

"Pssst," Novotny said, silencing them. "The price of futures is through the roof, Sister. An old machine is an old machine."

Vivian's mind went blank.

"We voted to close," Yeuhaus said.

"Close," Suges repeated.

"Th-the school?"

"Before classes resume." The priest.

"But—" She pointed to her ledger.

"We've not looked forward to this," Father Rupert said.

The hell you haven't! Vivian wanted to scream. She gripped the fingers of one hand inside those of the other and pulled until she felt her fingernails bite. *How did I miss so much? Emotion will lose points. Don't lose it. Reason. Use reason.*

"The children are not morally prepared for such a quick change," she said evenly. "They'll encounter daily temptations in public school. We must prepare them for a year or two. All of us must do that."

Mr. Suges shook his head.

Don't discount me. "I understand business," she said, turning to him. "Did I not build enrollment from thirty to three-hundred?" Two years after Father Rupert came, enrollment dropped down to one hundred thirty-six. The priest was expecting her to hang herself here, as if she, and not he, were the guilty one. Her lungs worked hard as bellows. "I love every single child. I know each one's foibles and strengths, have pulled for every single one of them, and after they married, I pulled for their children."

Mr. Suges' lips parted.

Rupert held up his hand to stop him from speaking.

Oh there had been telltale signs: overfidgety children, nervous mothers' profuse compliments, too many gifts. Vivian suddenly felt weighted and like she was disappearing into wet clay, being buried alive, never to crawl out.

She summoned passion. "Let's divide and conquer," she said, in a weak appeal. "Energize benefactors. Hold a fundraiser. Mary Ruth could give a concert, we could auction antiques—" She was going to say from the convent instead said, "from the rectory."

Rupert pretended to peer out the window.

"An auction! That's it!" she said, looking from one to another of them.

The priest's hands slid through the slits of his cassock into his pants pockets. "Sister," he said, still not looking at her, "When you don't have the money, what you do is close. A done deed."

Vivian's heart thumped. This wasn't the whole country; this was one school, *her* school. She caught the farmers looking at one another. "You're being rash," she said. Her head throbbed, threatening a migraine. "Some churches encourage their youth to work. Parishioners, too. They ask for generous donations." She wasn't prepared, not for this. Overwrought, she said, "If we had to I suppose we could combine a couple of classes, double up, let one or two lay teachers go." Rude, that's what the priest was. "Certainly, Father, there are places you can cut. Where have *you* cut?"

The men sat sculpted in place. Vivian saw herself no longer in charge of anything, scrubbing floors in the infirmary or running some other downtrodden school with a priest no more interested in saving souls than this one. Where were the women? Not one of the wives was here.

Sisters' assignments no longer changed every three years to prevent attachment to a place, to people, to each other. They were attached. Vivian stood and tried to sound authoritative. "This decision also belongs to me, to Reverend Mother, and to the mothers of all St. Anthony children."

Mr. Novotny dropped his chin and appeared sheepish. Mr. Yeuhaus and Mr. Suges sneaked a peek at one another.

Vivian backed away objecting in a tone so shrill it frightened even her. "Ask the Holy Father, who lives in the largest residence in the world, to give us a loan. Closing in the middle of the year, that's preposterous! The lay teachers won't be able to get jobs! Their families depend on *this* job."

What about us? What about my future? What about Jennifer's?

"Be reasonable."

"Reason has nothing to do with this, Father Rupert." She snatched her ledger, wanted to hit him over the head with it. "It's money, always money, that root of all evil, th-that eye in the camel's needle that dictates how we live, how we dress, how we behave, who we keep, who we let go. You know what Christ did to the money-changers."

The men paled.

"I will not accept this decision. Not without Reverend Mother and me having a say. We will meet again in three days, after early mass on the first. In the meantime, I charge each of you to come up with an alternative plan, one that's not so selfish, one that's in the best interest of the children."

The men, properly contrite, hung their heads.

Father Rupert said "Sister," in a patronizing tone that suggested she should know better. Kimberly had been right labeling the man a sexist! *Kimberly would never take this. What would Kimberly do?*

"When you think you're God, you can go to the devil in style!" snapped Vivian, exiting.

CHAPTER NINETEEN

With Vivian out of the convent and her piano lesson over, Mary Ruth closed her bedroom door, slid an audiotape in the recorder, and set it on her pillow. She slipped off her shoes and lay propped on her elbows on the bed.

> *"Dear Mum,*
> *I'm going to snatch a bit of time."*

She touched the cornhusk skirt of the doll on her bedside table.

> *"Thank you for the doll! I love it! I think Vivian is envious. I've named her Sister Rose of Lima and will show her to my class. The children will appreciate what you've done with a material they know well. Such craftsmanship takes more patience than I have, as verified by my many attempts with the paper mangers. In the end they turned out all right. The sisters thought they were clever. Thank you for helping me. No one here I know uses cornhusks as an art medium. My nimble fingers at the piano must come from you.*
> *"The holidays seem to have taken a toll on Vivian. She can't relax. I trust my gift of doing four weeks of her laundry duty will help. I gave mending time to Sister Dominic, plus all the help I can manage with her garden next spring and later with canning. I enjoy*

*eating her home-canned goods as much as she likes
putting them up.*

*"Kimberly has spent many an afternoon visiting
homes over the holidays and also with a laptop
computer she received for Christmas. I offered to take
some of her playground duty. I hope I haven't
overcommitted. If everyone redeems their coupons at
the same time—"*

Mary Ruth paused, did not quite know how to proceed.

*"Thank you for telling me how you met father. It's
clear what drew him to you, your attractiveness, your
smile, your flashing eyes, and ready wit." But not your
uneducated diction.*
*"You liked his strength, his sense of order, his
willingness to take you places you had not been before.
What's not clear is what led to or ... caused ... the rift
between you. Perhaps that is too personal a question. I
was so young and, as children do, I thought I had done
something wrong, that that was the reason why you did
not want to be with me. Please help me fill in some of
the missing pieces."*

Mary Ruth wanted to enter this dark subject gently. If only she
knew her mother better— She proceeded more lightly.

*"Clyde Johnson, my adult music student, calls his
nimble fingers 'digits.' One thing about him is
refreshing: Not being Catholic, he doesn't set sisters up
on a pedestal."*

Mary Ruth smiled and rolled onto her back.

"He and I laugh a lot."

In fact she couldn't remember when she had laughed so easily or so much.

"His ready wit seems southern. I must remember to ask him where he grew up.

"Already I'm dreading the mournful Lenten music and wish someone could do it for me. It's a comedown after holiday music. I guess everything must run its cycle.

"Clyde wasn't keen on having to execute scales, but if he's going to play the kind of music he says he wants to, he must start with basics. Wouldn't we all just like to skip discipline and go straight to accomplishment?

"When it comes to classical music, Clyde lacks taste. He has no foundation in,"

she paused, was going to say music theory, said,

"lessons, yet he improvises well. That fascinates me. Perhaps he grasps it intuitively, the way you and Granny read people's hearts."

It had been too long since Mary Ruth had seen her mother. Maybe she could schedule a visit at the end of the school year. The tape whirred on, leaving a silent gap.

"Vivian and Father Rupert are once again prickling each other like cacti locked close together. He made her return our beautiful new English textbooks and is wrangling about her bookkeeping methods again. When

Father Damien was here, he said she did an exceptional job. I think this priest's interference is like someone telling me how to inscribe my own compositions. On some days, Vivian, like any of us, swallows her pride easier than on others.

"The one who knows how to handle Father Rupert is Sister Dominic. She feigns helplessness, smiles, and agrees with everything he says; then when he leaves, she does what she wanted to anyway. Once he tackled a slow leak under the kitchen sink and Sister Dominic complimented him profusely. Afterward, she shook her head and took the pipes apart and fixed the leak herself. Another time when he was trying to replace the wax seal under the commode none of us could lift—she sent him down to the basement for some nonexistent thing. While he was gone, she sealed the wax with her feet, saying she didn't want that leaking on her floor. Of course, she can no longer take things apart. Her fingers are so gnarled. I fairly stay out of the man's path. Kimberly's too low in the status scheme for him to heckle her or else he just knows better."

Mary Ruth paused to think.

I'm pleased to turn the marriage and family lesson over to him. Still, the questions the children pose afterward make me wonder what he teaches them. They often giggle and mutter secretively about what he said.

"Kimberly says when he's confronted, steam shoots from his ears. Kimberly is delightfully irreverent and perceptive at the same time, which drives Vivian to distraction."

Mary Ruth reached out and touched Rose of Lima's skirt.

"For some reason I've been recalling the Christmas when I was nine. Daddy told me if I was good, St. Nicholas would bring me a rocking chair I had admired in an antique shop. It was child-size, bentwood with an intricate cane seat. I liked it because it reminded me, of home, of you and Gran. I wanted it in the worst way. To earn it, I kept quiet when I wanted to run. I tiptoed around the house. I even volunteered to go to bed early. Then Christmas came and there was no chair. I was terribly hurt. Night after night, I drifted into sleep, feeling betrayed and angry; I told God I would steal away and join you. Then Epiphany, Twelfth Night, came and with it my rocking chair! Daddy thought this a merry joke. When I didn't laugh, he grew solemn and said, 'I suppose you'll want to save it for your children.'"

He always joked at her expense. Mary Ruth resisted the anger she felt rising inside her.

"Sometimes I wonder where that little chair is, if he still has it."

The doorbell rang. Mary Ruth popped up and slipped on her shoes.

"As usual I've lost track of time. A piano student's at the door." She *smacked* kisses. *"Say hello to Uncle Wilbur. A blessed and healthy New Year. Hugs and kisses. Mary Ruth."*

CHAPTER TWENTY

Vivian yanked the phone into Sister Dominic's room.

"This *is* urgent."

"Reverend Mother is in an important meeting and cannot be disturbed."

Vivian slammed down the receiver. She hadn't been this upset since when the doctor validated her pregnancy. She moved her handkerchief across her brow, her cheeks, her eyes. Sour notes came from the music room as she made her way to the kitchen.

How long have they been conspiring? Is it the whole parish or just Rupert and his puppets? Mr. Suges was no puppet. This is unimaginable ... unconscionable. Why did I not see this coming?

Sister Dominic set down her needlework and removed her glasses and laid them on the table and folded her hands and waited.

Vivian felt like a small vessel tossed about in a raucous sea bumping against flotsam.

"That priest," Vivian said. She pulled her chair close.

"Maybe he's eating prunes with pits. Needs cranberry juice, broiled grapefruit?"

Vivian couldn't smile. "Worse than that, Sister Dominic, much worse." Shame flowed over her the way Sister basted a turkey. The old woman had told her she needed to decide how she would grow, that Kimberly was the one who would not break. She had made a fool of herself. Vivian reached out and touched the baptismal garment on the table. She said, "I-I've lost all trace of acceptance. When I got to Father's office Paul Novotny and Eugene Yeuhaus and Evan Suges were already there. They inferred that the whole parish is behind the decision to send our children to public school."

Color drained from Sister Dominic's face. Her lips parted emitting an audible gasp. Her eyes stared at Vivian.

"I didn't think it would happen here," Vivian said, two fingers pushing at her temple. "Not like this. They've been meeting behind our backs." Her tone registered rejection.

Sister Dominic moved her quivering index finger up and pushed her glasses which weren't there, higher on the bridge of her nose, as if that would somehow help her to understand.

"Sister Dominic, where was I? Where? You'd think I would have noticed signs. Signs."

A range of emotions flickered through the old woman's eyes. Vivian reached out and touched Sister's forearm. "How insensitive. I'm sorry. I should've softened the blow."

"We've been here a long time."

"I acted stupid and stubborn, lashed out." *Does Reverend Mother know? If she does—* Vivian didn't want to think about that, withdrew her hand.

"What will we do?"

"I'd like to shoot all of them. All of them."

"What did Reverend Mother say?"

"I haven't been able to reach her."

"Mary, Mother of God— "

"Pray for us."

"Oh, Sister Dominic, it was a shock to me, too." She brushed the old woman's cheek lightly with the back of her hand. "I insisted on another meeting on the first. I'll do my best to change their minds. I will. Let's not mention this to the others. Not yet. Maybe we won't have to." Dread moistened Sister Dominic's eyes. Vivian's heart and body ached with abandonment. *My best is insufficient.* "I'll try my utmost. I will."

* * *

"Vivian, these things happen."

"Not to me, Reverend Mother, not to me." Vivian sounded short of breath.

"Closings are epidemic. Calm yourself."

Well, I haven't been inoculated.

The woman sighed heavily. "Try not to take it personally." Tentatively she said, "I'd like to ask you a question."

It was not like Mother to sound unsure.

"Vivian, do you have an opinion on ... the ordination of women?"

Stunned, Vivian failed to answer. Had she not communicated? Didn't her superior even know what they were discussing?

"Did you not understand my question?"

Vivian hedged. The question presented a minefield in which she didn't want to step. In moments of pride she had imagined herself celebrating mass on the altar relishing all the recognition she deserved. What kind of test was this? Vivian said, "I, uh, haven't given it much thought. I accept the teachings of the Church."

"What is your opinion on sisters' holding public office or accepting civil appointments?"

"Well. Citizens do have duties. I-I would need to think more about that. Rights balance responsibilities. Everyone should try to be a good citizen."

"Exactly," Mother said.

What does this have to do with anything? "Reverend Mother, did you know about the closing?"

"I knew it was inevitable, but specifically when, no." She paused. Her tone turned to empathy. "I've seen many sisters work through this, Vivian. It's hard."

"Is there nothing we can do?" Vivian thought of Sister Dominic. "This gives us no time to adjust. We need time."

"Pray. That's all we can do. Pray."

She had been praying daily for years. Wasn't this proof of the inadequacy of prayer?

Mother said, "I need to think about this, too. When I have instructions, I will call you. Praised be Jesus Christ."

Afterward Vivian sat staring at the cradled phone, wondering if Jennifer knew, if the girl was fretful about being abandoned. She wondered whether or not to phone Jennifer.

CHAPTER TWENTY-ONE

The dark stone library exterior reminded Kim of a Halloween horror house. Secrecy had never been one of her strong suits, but this one she intended to guard with her life.

She chose a secluded corner in the high-ceilinged reference section and opened her laptop, hoping she would remember how to use one. She accessed the Net easily enough and typed in gynecology + infertility and clicked on Search. Thousands of references. She needed to be more definitive. She typed in ovarian eggs + surrogate. Still too many references. She scrolled down reference titles until she spotted the term Assisted Reproduction and returned to Search and typed that in.

Bingo.

She glanced around to be sure no one she knew was there. Her emotions skipped with glee. Cyberspace to the rescue.

The ideal egg donor was in her late twenties/early thirties and could provide a detailed family health and genetic history on each family member covering three generations. That alone would stop most donors, but her father was a physician who had actually been fanatic about such information. He researched a branch of her mother's family as a gift when they were courting and he was still in medical school. One phone call should provide what she needed.

The psych and intelligence section asked for IQ and SAT/ACT scores. These were part of her convent records; she could request a copy of them. Personal interviews sought honesty and dependability to determine if the applicant would be disciplined enough to follow detailed instructions. The agency wanted applicants with integrity and ruled out women who seemed primarily motivated by money.

An interview situation might prove problematic; she tended to say more than most people wanted to hear. *I will have to be careful, very careful.* While initially the convent's need for money had been her motivation, Kim knew from Brenda and Mike's struggle that helping an infertile couple was nothing short of a sacred and noble gift. In a flash she glimpsed Guillermo's dark eyes peering into hers, heard him saying how much he wanted children, their children.

She understood Guillermo's desire more fully when he left her temporarily living with women and children in a cave outside Sanarte while he searched for his brother, Juan, who had infiltrated the fighting line. Her inability to speak Spanish made her a threat to Guillermo's safety, so during the day while the other women gathered food, she babysat the little ones. She drew pictures in the sand on the cave floor and they taught each other words. They played "Hide the Pebble" and any game that required quiet.

She learned to make tortillas and helped with sanitation. At night when the women ferried guns from one place to another, Kim told stories to the children and grew to love every single one of them. Only the children made Guillermo's absence bearable. After three weeks had passed without a word from him, she began to fear the worst. Then one night after midnight she thought she was dreaming when she heard him whisper, "*Amor mio. Mi vida,* I am here."

Kim bolted up and embraced him, pressing the sounds of her sobbing gratitude into his chest. He stroked her back, raised her chin, and touched her fingertips to his lips and kissed them. "I have been spotted," he said softly. "We leave before sunup."

"Juan?"

"I sent a message for him to meet us. It was the best I could do. God protect him. We, all of us, are meant to be together. I must rest. I love you."

"Guillermo, we are risking our entire future, even the lives of our unborn children. Please. Let's go home."

He didn't answer. Without Juan, her request was premature. Never had Kim known such fear. She moved her softness against his hardness. Soon Guillermo's breathing took on the rhythm of sleep. She prayed for their safety, for Juan's, for all those sleeping in the cave and those they loved at home.

Before her the cursor blinked-blinked-blinked.

That was then, this is now. Kim exhaled long and slow. She and Guillermo had never had the chance to discuss the number of children they wanted; however, she suspected he would want a big family, many children. She must not dwell on what would never be, on loss. She turned to the computer screen.

Typical compensation included $1865 for registration fees, $195 for legal fees and medical bills, $3500 for the actual ovarian donation.

What if Vivian finds out? Don't be rash. Think. I need a meaningful path, not foolish jeopardy. Been there, done that. An appalling question posed itself: *What if, once grown, the child decides it wants to meet its biological mother?*

Twenty-one plus years in the future when the adult child searched, DNA would provide no hiding place; Kim would be identified. Would her superiors, would Church fathers believe her when she said the child was conceived without sex? Could confidential records be opened to prove truth?

Scrupulous ninny, you're creating problems that don't even exist about a child that doesn't exist! You don't know if you'll still be in the convent. It was true that a part of her wanted out while another part of her felt she truly belonged. She was convinced that the answer to her dilemma was to find a meaningful path. Kim bent to the screen.

The sample donor profile covered hair texture, tanning ability, sexual orientation, number of teeth removed, learning disabilities, anything that might be passed genetically. Required tests included blood, urine, screening for anemia, a pelvic exam. Once chosen by a couple, the donor would take birth control pills to coincide her menstrual cycle with the recipient's. After three months or so, the donor's eggs would be extracted in a process that sounded painful. After that, hopefully, the stork arrived. If not, they would try another time or two.

Kim scrolled down to Cooperating Physicians In Your Area to IL and typed in her zip code. Peoria came up. Not too far away. She considered physicians' names, decided she would prefer a woman and there was only one: Monica Lovejoy.

CHAPTER TWENTY-TWO

Vivian dusted, dusted, dusted everything. She washed each crystal of the chandelier. She took down the parlor curtains, shook them outside, and rehung them. She even cleaned the pantry, top to bottom. She didn't know where her energy came from, only that she needed to free herself of it. She regretted dumping her anguish on Sister Dominic, who had grown sullen. Kimberly was so preoccupied with her laptop that the girl didn't notice anything amiss. Vivian tried desperately to come up with a viable plan for the meeting on the first; so far she had drawn a blank, unless one counted angst.

When the first arrived Vivian couldn't pay attention during mass; it was as if her mind had departed her body. She had come up with no alternative, no way to save grace, nothing that would work. She needed magic, a miracle. Backed now into a corner, she hoped to negotiate as long a delay as possible, which, on the outside, might be two additional school years. That's what she would fight for, two more after this one. If pushed, she hoped to be able to agree on the end of next year. If there was a homily, she missed it. Already they were at the end of mass.

Father Rupert and the two altar servers, Stevie and Danny, turned to the congregation. Father raised his hand in blessing, and said, "Go in peace." Instead of leaving the sanctuary, however, the priest bent and whispered into Stevie's ear. Stevie nodded and looked up and spotted her. Father moved into the sacristy. People rose to leave.

Stevie bent to Vivian 's ear and whispered, "Father would like you to come to the sacristy."

Her lips formed an "O." She nodded and followed Stevie.

The priest motioned her to a chair, said, "We'll wait for the boys to leave."

The two boys hurried to hang their surplices. Vivian twisted her ring. Though there was an hour between masses, the priest did not remove his vestments. The boys pointedly avoided looking at her. They said, "Happy New Year, Father. Happy New Year, Miss Tiamet," and left.

"The men are not coming."

Vivian stood. "Why not?"

"There will be no meeting. Any effort on your part would be as effective as a Band-Aid on a hemorrhage. The deal's done, Sister."

Her mind absorbed the blow. *Today commemorates the circumcision, Christ's first suffering.* Distress opened some terrible vulnerability in Vivian. She wanted to hit this man, to weep openly; she couldn't speak.

He said, "Count it as a blessing. Sister Dominic can go to the infirmary."

"She doesn't want to!"

"Perhaps Mary Ruth will get her doctorate."

"Don't meddle! For once, just don't meddle. We're attached to St. Anthony's, to the people, to the children, and we're committed to them, now and in the future."

"There is no future."

Thanks to you.

"Vivian, the bishop is *not* exactly sanguine about this; the abbot's rattling my chains."

Don't expect me to feel sorry for you!

She said, "You're hanging on while letting me go."

"There is nothing for you to hang onto. Your job doesn't exist."

Defeat descended on her, a personal Gethsemane. She had expected him to be solicitous, not to erase her life's work. Inside, she felt dead. She shook her head, covered her mouth with her hand, felt tears coming, took a hurried exit. Tears hampered her vision as she crossed the street. The parlor door was closed; the last thing she needed was a visitor. Vivian pulled the phone into Sister Dominic's room and dialed Jennifer, who had not attended mass with her parents.

"Thank God, you answered, Jennifer. I-I want you to know that I will keep your appointment with you." She heard the girl's ragged breathing. "I just wanted you to know. Any change?"

"No."

Vivian leaned her back against the wall, wanted to ask Jennifer if she had known about the closing. Of course, she did. Everyone knew except them.

"That's all I wanted to say."

"S'ster?"

"Yes?"

"I hope it works out for you."

What more was there to say?

Vivian looked toward the kitchen, wanting to seek solace in Sister Dominic, but the old woman already carried enough burden. She turned her attention to the closed parlor door, thinking *I must tell the sisters before they find out some other way.* She dabbed at her eyes and composed herself. A piano student struck discordance. Who could be calling on her? Who had a lesson on Sunday? Vivian smoothed her skirt with her hands, tugged the hem of her suit jacket, pushed hair back from her view, and put on a brave face. She took a deep breath and, tapped on the door, opened it.

Simultaneously six PTA mothers rose.

"We couldn't stop them," big-framed Gertrude Yeuhaus said. "You know how stubborn a man can be. A *Cherman* man," she said in her accent, rolling eyes upward, her tone suggesting they were the worst.

"What can we do?" begged chubby Mary Novotny. "What can we do? Pigs in the blanket," she said, extending a Dutch oven kettle.

Holding the pot, Vivian felt defenseless, fragile. *Where to put it, what to say?*

Mrs. Sullivan, Kimberly's friend, the woman who did not come to PTA and whom she had yet to meet, was here. Unlike the others, Mrs. Sullivan held no gift. The woman looked around, picked up the newspaper and spread pages over the rosewood table.

"Thank you," Vivian said, meeting eyes so blue violet they must be colored contacts.

Vivian tested the bottom of the Dutch oven and set it down.

"Kolachie's," Agnes Pzsinski said, sliding a foil-covered paper plate onto the newspaper.

"Banana bread and nut roll," Berneta Cellini said. "Still frozen, Sister, you wanna put 'em in the freezer."

"Spareribs and caraway sauerkraut," Gertrude said.

"Like a shower," muttered Mrs. Sullivan.

"What?" Vivian asked, confused by all the attention and activity.

"This reminds me of a shower, gifts for a bride or a baby. Sorry. I didn't know I should bring something. Mike said I should come."

Addled, Vivian said, "It's nice to finally meet you." After such a big letdown this was much too much stimulation. Ears of husked corn drooped over the top of Leila Flahaut's brown grocery bag. Leila always explained that her one-syllable last name rhymed with how. Elizabeth Lucky's bag held cabbage and potatoes still mottled with dirt.

"Thank you for all of this," Vivian said, setting the bags on the floor beside the table. "Thank you for coming. I ... uh, haven't told the other sisters yet. They'll be distressed. I had hoped for some some recourse, another chance."

The women settled uneasily into a semicircle of chairs and avoided looking at one another, and at Mrs. Sullivan whom they considered alien, probably because she was beautiful and sophisticated, not to mention gainfully employed and Protestant. Sadly, no one picked up on Vivian's hope.

Agnes said, "They've been plotting for months."

"Gestapo!" Gertrude said. "KGB."

Berneta raised her right fist and struck her elbow in an up-yours gesture.

"Really," Mrs. Sullivan said.

"I'm so disheartened," Vivian said.

"We got to bring the kids to CCD?" Mary asked.

"CCD?" Mrs. Sullivan.

"Confraternity of Christian Doctrine," Leila and Elizabeth said in unison. Those two stuck together like Siamese twins.

Vivian hadn't thought about CCD. The sound of the piano had stopped. "Catechism classes," she explained for Mrs. Sullivan's benefit. "Children who attend public school attend catechism classes. Listen," Vivian said, twisting her wedding band. "All of this happened so fast. Is there nothing we can do?"

They appeared glum, didn't answer.

Vivian said, "I don't know what to say."

"What about our children?" Gertrude asked.

"Yes. What about them?" Vivian said.

Mary muttered in Polish and crossed herself.

"Santa Maria Goretti," Berneta Cellini said.

"I don't understand," Mrs. Sullivan said.

Vivian turned to her. "At age twelve Saint Maria Goretti was stabbed to death, defending her virginity. Mrs. Cellini's concerned about her daughter's ... purity at Sleeder High."

"Oh, gross," Mrs. Sullivan said. "Dying that way is not an art form."

The Siamese twins gasped.

Mrs. Sullivan hurried to say, "I mean religion is no protection when it comes to the urge to merge. Kids need to be taught about safe se—" She stopped, reddened.

Vivian felt sorry for her. Getting the unconverted talking was always the first step. From there conversion was a slow, patient process; there would be no time for that now. She gathered from the way the women lowered their eyes and shook their heads, that the situation was hopeless.

"Mrs. Sullivan," Vivian said, clearing her throat, "we're glad you're here." She let a moment go by, trying to set an example of an acceptance she did not feel. "If God intends the children to go on without ... us," she had almost said *without me*, "well." She swallowed hard. "God knows how all of you have sacrificed to send your children here. I think we can be confident—" Her voice trailed. "We should count on their moral fiber."

That said, a sense of devastation descended on her. She wanted to cry, to lean on these women who were leaning on her, expecting wisdom and comfort. *Why am I always supposed to be the strong one?* No matter what she said or did, they always agreed with her and when she didn't know what to say or do, they still expected her to lead. If only she could reach out, ask for hugs. But she wasn't one of them; she had taken vows for life, a life that now lay in Reverend Mother's hands.

A burst of the kind of piano music that belonged anywhere but in a convent startled them.

"Oh. My," Vivian said, half-rising.

The women froze like children spun and flung out in a game of Statue.

"What a terrible way to start the New Year," Vivian said, referring to the closing. "Terrible. Excuse me. I'll be right back."

She closed the parlor door and tapped to no avail on the music room door then opened it. The culprit of the saloon music proved to be a slender, bittersweet chocolate-colored man, fingers moving so fast Vivian could hardly see them. Mary Ruth sat beside him on a chair, her expression one of fulfillment. Mary Ruth looked up, saw Vivian, quickly uncrossed her legs, and extended her hand over the keys to stop the music, and stood.

"Vivian, this is Mr. Johnson. Clyde Johnson. Vivian Tiamet, my ... our principal."

He raised his finger in a salute. "How do. Happy, Happy New Year. Hope you dig Joplin."

Vivian pressed her lips against a smile. Obviously the man wasn't Catholic. Mr. Johnson was about five-eight with upper arms so muscular he must lift weights. His strong, chiseled forehead suggested strength, his mellow open eyes hinted merriment. His unmistakable attitude dominated: In a forest of oaks, this man stood as serene, sure, and stunning as a redwood.

"Mr. Johnson, I'm sure Mary Ruth is delighted with your expertise. But I, uh, I'm meeting with a group in the next room." She indicated the wall. "If you could reduce the ragtime to a shuffle for a few minutes? Until we're finished?"

"Oh. Sure." He beamed his smile at her. "Copasetic."

She closed the door and pulled her thumb and forefinger together in a pinch over the bridge of her nose and smiled. The man showed a strong sense of self mixed with a strong sense of fun. *Holy Mother Mary.* It had been awhile since she had smiled and it felt good, but she couldn't reenter the parlor smiling.

The women had donned their coats.

Mrs. Lucky said, "We just wanted to pay respects."

"Respects," echoed Leila.

"Keep us in your prayers," Vivian said, wanting to hug every single one of them. She called after them, "Look for your utensils in the vestibule on Sunday by the baptismal font."

Once they departed, Vivian's loneliness and emptiness returned. She found herself staring at a pile of potatoes, asking, *Do I still have a will of my own? And if I do, when was the last time I used it?*

Vivian ferried the gifts to the kitchen and with forced cheer addressed Sister Dominic. "Agnes Pzsinski brought Kolachies. Want one?"

Sister shook her head. "Getting powdered sugar off this habit is devil's work."

Mr. Johnson executed a klutzy scale, then Vivian heard Mary Ruth's muffled voice instructing him. It must be as difficult for a man so accomplished to start at the beginning as it was going to be for her. She must tell the other sisters. Kimberly had visited so many families over the holidays, it was a miracle she didn't know. Or did she?

CHAPTER TWENTY-THREE

As soon as Mr. Johnson left, Vivian summoned the sisters to the kitchen.

"Did you hear those ivories sing!" exclaimed Mary Ruth. "That's what Clyde, Mr. Johnson, calls them, ivories."

Kimberly said, "I need to interrupt. Before I forget, the red light's blinking on the upstairs smoke detector."

"It needs a new battery," Vivian said, "or it will start beeping. I have extras in the school supply room. I'll take care of it. Thank you."

"Clyde composes as well. I'm going to ask his opinion of 'Baby Divine Sleep.' "

Mary Ruth's enthusiasm disconcerted Vivian, who wanted to tell them the bad news and be done with it, yet she didn't want to spoil Mary Ruth's optimism. She turned to Sister Dominic, who, she could tell, had guessed because of the food. Without looking up, Sister Dominic raised a trembling index finger and pushed her glasses up.

Suddenly Vivian wanted to cry rather than obey. What dismal duty. She heard the old woman ask, "Can he play, 'When the Saints Come Marching In'?" Vaguely Vivian realized Sister Dominic was buying her time to compose herself.

Mary Ruth hummed a few bars of "Saints." "I'm sure he can."

"Where did all this food come from?" asked Kimberly.

Vivian's ring finger was swollen; the band wouldn't twist. She wanted to take it off. A deep knife-like pain like severe heartburn radiated from her solar plexus and made her sit down. As it dissipated slowly, she decided how she would tell them; she would call their weekly chapter of faults, which would move them into solemnity. Then she would tell them. That way acceptance might be easier.

Vivian steeled herself and answered Kimberly. "The ladies of the parish came calling. Now, because of certain ... circumstances, we'll hold chapter."

The three stared at her for a moment, then Mary Ruth stood and pulled her little black chap from her blazer pocket, set it on the table in front of her, and folded her hands. Kimberly rummaged through her pockets. "Oh, pooh," she said. "Mine's upstairs."

One was supposed to keep her chap with her at all times.

When Kimberly returned they bowed their heads.

"Hail Mary, full of grace," Vivian began and they joined her. When the prayer ended, Vivian nodded to Sister Dominic.

Sister Dominic recited the preamble from memory. "I confess my faults before God, the Holy Virgin, the Communion of Saints, and my sisters in Christ." Then Sister Dominic picked up her chap, but without looking in it, said haltingly, "I accuse myself of indulgence in ice cream. I accuse myself of being continuously distracted from the presence of God, I—" Sister pressed the back of her trembling fingers against her lips. "I accuse myself of dreading being without the joy of children ... of being without you, my family. But mostly," she reached her index finger beneath her glasses and wiped away a tear. "I accuse myself of dreading life in the infirmary... where one can be consumed with the body's demise."

Oh God! Help her, prayed Vivian.

"Because of this preoccupation," continued Sister Dominic, "I have failed to say how much I appreciate ... all that you do for me,

141

with what loving charity each of you cares for me. Before God and the Holy Virgin and the Communion of Saints, and my sisters in Christ, these are my faults as I know them. With their correction, I seek the most patient help of my sisters."

No one spoke. Vivian didn't want to tell them. Jesus must have felt as depressed as she during his agony in the garden. *Will this cup not pass from me?* She nodded to Mary Ruth.

Mary Ruth stood, moved behind her chair and slid it silently in to the table. She faced her superior, knelt, and kissed the floor, and opened her chap and read. "I confess my faults before God, the Holy Virgin, and the Communion of Saints, and my sisters in Christ. I accuse myself of humming while I work, of ... humming ... to avoid what's unpleasant. I accuse myself of lack of detachment, of overenthusiasm regarding the talents of a gifted student."

Vivian's mind strayed while Mary Ruth recounted lesser faults. Mr. Johnson's lesson had ended, not with Chopsticks, but with a vigorous Gospel duet.

"Before God, the Holy Virgin, and the Communion of Saints, and my sisters in Christ, these are my faults as I know them. With their correction, I seek the most patient help of my sisters."

No one took the opportunity to speak. Mary Ruth kissed the floor and sat.

Vivian nodded to Kimberly. The young woman scraped her chair, thudded to her knees, and pretended to brush the floor with her lips. They waited as she tugged her skirt free.

"I-confess-my-faults-before-God—"

"Please," Vivian said, "it's not a race."

Kimberly resumed speaking so slowly that it took willpower not to scream at her.

"I accuse myself of forgetting to move silently. Of squelching happiness. Of avoiding fun. Sometimes only sound tells me I'm *here!*" Kimberly looked at Vivian, ignored her chiding glare. The novice said, "I just don't understand how increasing my capacity for suffering will redeem either me or the world."

I will not take this bait, will not, will not.

The girl made it sound like a battle plea. "Submission is not commitment; commitment is not submission."Jennifer possessed the kind of bravery Vivian wished she had and would never have, a fact that routinely wounded her pride.

Silence filled the air.

"What others call faults, I don't," Kimberly said.

"Exactly!"

With nothing more forthcoming, Kimberly grumbled, "I'll try to do better. before God and the Holy Virgin—"

Keeping custody of the eyes, Mary Ruth spoke softly. "I accuse Kimberly of vanity, of applying and reapplying makeup."

"Thank you," Kimberly said, expecting this reprimand which she had heard before.

"I accuse you," Vivian said, "of keeping bubble bath beads. Please dispose of them."

"Th-thank you."

Hearing no further comments, the girl touched the floor with her lips and sat.

Vivian moved her chair silently, knelt, and kissed the floor. "I accuse myself ... of striking out at Father Rupert in a most unseemly fashion, of thoughtlessly making long distance calls during the wrong hours. I accuse myself of ... intense resentment." Percussion reverberated in her head. "Worse, I accuse myself of making a serious promise, which I may not now be able to keep." Her heart burned.

Sister Dominic said, "I accuse you of complaining about your vows, of forgetting you are to set our example."

Vivian rocked back as if she had sustained a blow, though she held custody of the eyes. She swallowed and said, "Thank you, Sister."

"Instead of throwing away that bubble bath," continued the old woman, "I suggest, courtesy of Kimberly, that you use them. Vivian, indulge yourself until they're gone."

Vivian snapped a glance. The old woman meant it! Vivian abruptly lowered her gaze. Steeped now in guilt, it occurred to her that she should have accused herself of complicity against Mrs. Suges. *No, that would betray Jennifer's confidence.* Despite all that had transpired, Sister Dominic intended to teach her a lesson. Humility made Vivian feel hot. She would reek from the unpleasant scent of jasmine. She turned to Kimberly and said, "Your sister in Christ asks—" The words clutched her throat.

Barely above a whisper, Kimberly said, "You may have my bubble bath beads."

Vivian kissed the floor and resumed her seat, confused, wondering why Sister Dominic had turned on her. Why? "Hail Mary," she began and they joined in the prayer.

Discernment was getting harder and harder. God knew one merely strove toward impossible perfection. Sister Dominic hadn't turned on her; it just felt like it, that's what she told herself. Vivian tapped her ring, prepared herself by stifling all sense of emotion.

"Sisters," she said, straightening, drawing a deep breath, feigning composure. *Lord, help me do this right.* "I have news. News ... which I wish I didn't have to tell you." She hesitated. "There's no way to soften this." She drew a shaky breath. "On Monday when school resumes St. Anthony children will attend public schools."

"Bad joke," quipped Kimberly.

"Angel of God!" Mary Ruth turned ashen.

Sister Dominic fingered the rosary beads at her side.

"It's not true!" Kimberly said looking from one to another of them, then blanching as she realized that it was.

Vivian gripped the edge of the table with one hand. She said, "It seems the men of the parish have decided against the wishes of

many of the women. That's why they, the mothers, came calling."
She gestured toward the food, reached up and moved her hair back,
blinking back tears. "They wanted to show their appreciation.
Father says the decision is final. While I think it's a wrong
decision, there seems nothing I can do."

"Why?" Kimberly asked, looking astounded.

"Tuition's no longer affordable. Our families are losing land.
The convent needs a new furnace. The school needs a new roof.
Dwindling resources. I could go on and on." Still, the dilemma
besotted Vivian. *We're not in the roofing business; we're in the
saving souls business.*

Mary Ruth sounded incredulous. "In the middle of the school
year?"

"What can we do?" Kimberly asked. "There must be something
we can do."

"We wait until we hear from Reverend Mother. I'm still hoping
something will change this decision, but have no rational reason to
think so."

"If it's money, why don't we just go out and earn some?"

"Kimberly, that would be taking matters into our own hands.
Reverend Mother makes assignments; we accept them.

"That's not taking responsibility!"

Vivian looked at the girl, thinking, *Sister Dominic said you
were aligned with God's will!* In the old days she would have
tapped the young woman into silence, but the old days were gone.
She would turn to prayer. Sister Dominic would rally. Mary Ruth
would turn to music. Children would come for lessons as long as
they were in Sleeder. Kimberly was the one who would have time
on her hands.

Vivian said, "Our vow is obedience. After Sunday masses,
parents and children will be picking up their school belongings. On
Monday please be in school to take phone calls regarding the
transfer of records. Kimberly, if you find yourself idle, perhaps

145

you could starch and iron the altar cloths. Otherwise, Sisters, beyond daily *ménages* and saying your office, do as you will."

Sounding distant, Sister Dominic said, "The Blessed Virgin's appearing in Yugoslavia, in Medugorje, not far from where my parents once lived." She seemed in a trance. "My mother spent hours rolling strudel dough so thin you could see through it. It draped over our porcelain table like an altar cloth. She said if I talked while she rolled, it would put holes in her dough. All these years, rolling, rolling."

Mary Ruth hummed.

Kimberly moved to Sister Dominic and stroked her arm, her back.

Vivian was as surprised by Sister Dominic's moving into herself as she was by Kimberly's moving out of herself.

Not knowing what else to do, Vivian went up to the chapel to pray.

CHAPTER TWENTY-FOUR

A lamentable cheer repeated in Kim's mind: Gimme a V, Gimme an I, Gimme a C, Gimme a T, Gimme an I, Gimme an M. Victim. Victim. Victim. Yea, yea, yea. She couldn't believe they were in this despicable fix. She phoned Brenda several times and finally left two messages before remembering that the Sullivans were attending a Rose Bowl party. Because Vivian had announced she would leave early the next day and be gone perhaps even into early evening, Kim wanted to seize the opportunity to lunch with Brenda. Later, after the others were asleep, she tiptoed to the phone and scheduled their lunch the next day.

As planned Vivian left early. Clyde Johnson picked up Mary Ruth shortly before ten to shop for music books. Kimberly remained in the kitchen with Sister Dominic.

"Sister, how do you feel about ... the upheaval?"

Before answering the old woman considered. She said, "It must be part of God's plan."

"I wasn't looking for a pat answer. How do you really feel?"

Sister Dominic stuck her needle onto the embroidery hoop and let go of it. "Sad," she said. "Very, very sad. Getting old is hard enough, but it's a reminder that I'm only putting in time before the grim reaper claims me." She looked into Kimberly's eyes. "I didn't know I would feel this way, but I do and I'm ashamed."

"Oh, Sister, it's only natural to feel that way."

Sister's eyes widened.

Kim said, "I think this fiasco could have been avoided."

147

Sister Dominic seemed to calculate her next words. She picked up her needle and wrapped thread around it three times making a French knot and inserted it. "The rift between Father and Vivian is a long-standing one, but it is the same rift that priests and sisters engage in everywhere."

"When we're priests, that will change."

"I doubt it. Even in farm animals I saw differences between males and females. It's the same with humans, only more complicated because we have intelligence. Intelligence outwits us more than we know."

"We can't undo that!"

"No, but there are ways around it."

Kimberly had not known Sister Dominic could be so philosophical. "What ways?"

"The heart. The spirit."

"You think men are of a different heart, a different spirit?"

"No. When it comes to heart—ow, I stuck my finger—I think we're on the same footing when it comes to heart and spirit."

"So we shouldn't compete with words. We should fight with heart and spirit?"

Sister dropped her hoop into her lap. "Never! Heart and spirit don't fight. Either heart and spirit prevail over evil intentions, or, if you must fight, be better at the game."

Vivian didn't know how to be better at the game. Vivian didn't know when to stand her ground, when to the bend rules. Rigidity tripped up their superior every time.

"Sister, do you believe this could have been avoided? Your real opinion, the truth."

"Seems there's something in Father Rupert that insists on failure."

Sister Dominic was right. Everything that man touched ended in some degree of ruin. "Sister, how did you get so smart?"

The old woman's wan smile acknowledged the compliment and betrayed her weariness. She said, "I have a bit more time for contemplation than the rest of you. It's surprising what one learns listening to God in solitude."

Kimberly smiled and said, "I love you. You know that, don't you? I love you."

Sister blinked several times in what Kimberly took to mean surprise until she saw the woman's moist eyes. She said, "Sister, I'd like to bottle your spirit and carry it in my pocket. What you said makes me feel better. Like ... we didn't fail one hundred percent." *We just failed our fair share.*

"Dear, don't be too hard on Vivian. We all fight inner demons of our own making and are very much in earnest as we go about it. Until truce is at hand, we go at it."

This lay beyond Kimberly's comprehension. When Sister had noted Father Rupert's pattern, Kimberly saw it and also how Vivian failed to draw the line. She didn't know what Mary Ruth's flaw might be, unless you counted overenthusiasm for music. Sister Dominic seemed beyond reproach, but then she had made that truce, hadn't she?

"Dare I ask about me, Sister Dominic? What do you see?"

A wave of the pleasure of intimacy crossed Sister's face. She puzzled for what seemed a long a time. "When Father Damien was here, he smoked. We kept ashtrays for him. On one, a scriptor had started to write a word. There was this big 'T-H,' then the writer calculated a shortage of space and made the 'I' smaller, followed by an even smaller 'n.' The last letter fell over the edge with enough of a hint to know it would have been a 'k.'"

What a dumb story. Given the toxicity of passive smoke, the sisters should have forbidden smoking in the convent. Fidgeting with discomfort now, Kimberly glanced at her watch, said, "I need to leave soon. Is there anything I can do for you?"

Sister Dominic fetched for eye contact. When Kim avoided it, she said, "Go. I can manage quite well. Enjoy."

The weather proved briskly cold and overcast. Unsettled and slightly off kilter, Kim boarded the bus. Because of the closing, she expected she might lose her cool, so hoped to lunch where she wouldn't be recognized. Once at the bank she and Brenda decided on The Roadster, a truckstop on the eastern edge of town. There, they took a red vinyl booth in the no smoking section. Grease spots soiled the extensive menu. Brenda ordered a Greek salad, and Kim, the hoagie with extra pickles. As soon as the waitress left, Kim accused Brenda.

"You must have known. Why didn't you tell me?"

"I didn't, not for certain. Mike was sporadically involved. I stayed out of it."

"Sherry's not out of it."

Brenda rearranged the flatware.

Why, she wants Sherry in public school! Hurt mixed with Kim's anger. "Are you saying Father Rupert didn't decide by himself?"

"I'm sure he prefers to share the blame."

The man had the manipulative skills of a bird in search of a worm. He played "Wolf, Wolf" until Vivian cut corners beyond reason, beyond poverty. *That's why she was nervous and out of sorts! A part of Vivian knew!*

"Now you understand why I was confused by your I-want-a-job visit."

"You could have warned me."

"I didn't know, didn't want to know. It was ... upsetting."

You and Mike were fighting about where Sherry should go to school.

"What about you?" Brenda asked.

"Vivian's been on the phone so much her ear's going to fall off. Mary Ruth's become a 'musaholic.' " Kim tried to extract a paper napkin from the overfull metal dispenser. "Sister Dominic's in a daze." The napkin shredded. "Hold this thing, will you?" She wriggled two napkins free, one for each of them. "Mom warned me about the Sanctuary Movement. Dad warned me about Guillermo. He said, " 'Kimmie, there are no live martyrs.' Why do we ignore the obvious?"

"Did you ... want to hear them?"

"Of course not."

Sister Dominic hadn't told her anything about herself she didn't already know. She heard Guillermo say *No hay amor mas grande que este: dar la vida por sus amigos.* There is no greater love than this: to lay down one's life for his friends, and that's exactly what Guillermo had done, died a martyr's death. She never wanted to commit herself to someone like that again, not face such pain. Guillermo's voice said: *From a new heart peace is born.*

Kim picked up the hoagie she hadn't noticed the waitress set in front of her. She squeezed the bun; mayo dripped onto her plate. She would have followed Guillermo to Mars, Pluto, beyond the universe, and here she was on earth stuck without him. She said, watching the bleeding mayo, "What I need is a new heart."

Brenda asked, "Where will you go? What will you do? What happens now?"

"If I knew what I wanted— I was gradually working my way through the maze of my own ... *folly.*"

"Sometimes," Brenda said, sounding overly cautious, "when you don't know what direction to take, it's best to sit still."

Her parents had warned her about entering the convent; they said it was too soon after Guillermo's death for her to know what she wanted, but she saw convent life as a way to heal past grief. She had blamed Vivian for her misery until talking with Sister Dominic; now she wasn't so sure. She didn't want to think about any of this.

Kim said, "It's happening to a lot of our schools. Trouble is, I think it could have been prevented. Freedom of conscience ought to be an inalienable right."

Brenda rolled a Greek olive between her fingers. "Why is the Holy Father not helping? The Church seems so—" Brenda fetched for the right word.

"Fickle? That's the million dollar question. I'd say money. Specifically, American money. Polls show American Catholics now think individually. If those who divorce believe they're still 'in,' they are; if they believe they're 'out,' they are. The clearest example for me is how some marriages are annulled as quickly as Clairol changes hair color," Kim snapped her fingers. "If your name is something like Kennedy. Never mind that annulment makes the kids illegitimate."

"Aren't you avoiding the issue?"

"Polls also tell us that Catholics are now socially and economically more upwardly mobile than people of other denominations. And, surprise, surprise, more tolerant and politically active. Catholics hold a lot of Congressional seats and despite school closings, our kids are better educated than most with parents committed to their higher education."

"Really? You're escaping into your head. I didn't know that."

"Some orders advertise for public school kids and get them by claiming: No knives, no guns, no drugs, only disciplined scholarship. Cloning may be our only answer to survival. God help us. We lie down then wonder why we got run over."

"Hey, I'm in the choir."

No you're not. You want Sherry in public school. In all fairness in Brenda's shoes, she might feel exactly the same way. *Brenda's right. I am avoiding the issue. By entering the convent, did I cop out? Shut down and drop out?* Vivian took her cues from a Church that moved so slowly any shakeup amounted to a tiny rumble that could never threaten to become an earthquake.

152

Kim said, "What makes me the maddest is how the Church insists on compulsory pregnancy, sentencing an unborn child to a life of poverty in goods and spirit. It's a double standard, isn't it? If the Church insists on compulsory pregnancy, it ought to guarantee the child's quality of life, offer a solution to the problem it has mandated."

Brenda pulled back. Her expression suggested that she was seeing a side of Kim she hadn't seen before.

"Sorry. I'm dumping on you. Disenchantment does that to me."

Kim's mind and mouth continued to avoid whatever it was she should be focusing on. "The Church once taught that education damaged the female brain." Religious orders still believed one bad apple might spoil the whole barrel. *And I am one bad apple.*

Kim wet the tip of her index finger on her tongue, touched a crumb on the table, and flicked it onto her plate. Freedom didn't fall out of the sky and grab you; you had to take a hold of freedom, use it responsibly. More women were burned at the stake for having intuition than the number of Jews murdered during the Holocaust. Kim glimpsed a mental image of the ashtray Sister Dominic had described.

She took a deep breath and exhaled slowly. "Brenda, I'm a bit disillusioned, that's all. I value many things about the convent and the Church. I do. It's just that ... the Church loses a lot of Catholics due to its stand on birth control. The pope has a loophole through which he can reverse the ban on it, yet he doesn't. Sooner or later some pope will or there will be no more Church. History can help. As early as the twelfth century canon law claimed embryos were *un*formed at conception, that boy embryos took on life after forty days, girl embryos after eighty days. Truth is, until the twentieth century, abortion wasn't even an issue."

"Is this about the Church or about you?"

Kim didn't want to hear Brenda's words. "For centuries people used abortion as the primary means of birth control. Some countries still do. In China they drown newborns like unwanted kittens, especially females. Throughout time, women used the safest means of birth control available, however crude. Sumatran women pierced the uterus with bamboo slivers. Zambezi women drank papaw juice. Eskimo women inserted a mini-harpoon rib. During the Industrial Revolution, women drank iron filings or copper sulfate crystals dissolved in water."

An unshaven trucker passed their booth and crossed to the jukebox. Kim paused and watched him insert coins. These were facts she had learned when she worked at Planned Parenthood. Madonna's seductive voice filled the air.

"Abortion used to be an everyday occurrence, a simple extension of English law when our Constitution was written. By the time women got the vote in 1920, men had taken control over our lives."

Keyword, control. Kim's mind flashed an image of men on the other side of the communion rail wearing bandannas over their faces in the dim church, women with their shawls pulled low over their foreheads. Listening to each of them share a painful, personal trauma of torture, rape, cruelty, her heart had gone out to them. That's when and why she had elected to help Guillermo. The only hope those poor people had was the Sanctuary Movement and it failed them the same way Guillermo had failed her. Kim drew a deep breath and released it along with tension.

Madonna's seduction bypassed heart and went straight to lust.

Kim said, "I feel better, which means you must feel worse.

"I'm sorry."

"Believe me when I say I didn't know enough to say anything."

Kim regretted having vented. "I guess we each do what we must. I'm wired by the bad news." *Sister Dominic's right. If I don't feel free, it's not because of Vivian or Brenda or Guillermo; if I don't feel free it's because I'm not choosing freedom.* She said,

"Please. Forget everything I said. I love the kids and feel like the loser in a custody suit. I've been pulled away from them."

Kim looked around avoiding her friend's eyes.

"At least you don't need a job."

Not true. The convent needs money more than ever; God helps those who help themselves. She needed to know. "I know how hard you and Mike wanted to have Sherry. Do you ... would you like another child?"

"We're happy and grateful for Sherry and have decided to let other infertile couples have a chance."

"What if *in vitro* hadn't worked?"

"I really don't know, Kim. The gynecologist didn't think I produced enough eggs for *in vitro* to work. We had discussed surrogates. In desperation we may have returned to options we had ruled out." Brenda shrugged. "We wanted a child."

Kim felt determination. She knew now what she would do. She drew a shaky breath and slowly exhaled it. "Time to go," she said, picking up her check. She led the way to the cash register.

No matter where I am, there's a biological baby or two or three in my future, my sacred gift to some lucky couples.

CHAPTER TWENTY-FIVE

If Vivian hadn't said she'd be gone for the whole day without leaving a number where she could be reached, Mary Ruth probably would not have accompanied Clyde Johnson. With Vivian gone, she decided she didn't need to ask permission.

Clyde's Porsche hugged the road, the bumps of which she could feel under her; the ride made her feel insecure. He said his car was ancient, that he liked to tinker with old cars. He parked next to a meter in front of a line of red brick stores on Main Street and got out and skipped around the front of the vehicle and opened her door. He offered his dark hand to assist her from the low seat. She hesitated at first, then acknowledged his courtesy with a smile. He took her hand with confidence and warmth and lifted it in a way she experienced as electrifying.

"I'll plug the parking meter," he said, releasing her hand.

The white paint on the car looked shiny new. Clyde wore no hat and hunkered down into the fleece collar of his sheepskin jacket. His nostrils flared against the cold. They walked toward the music store.

"Your school made the front page," Clyde said, blowing on his cold fingers. He hummed a few bars.

"What's that you're humming?"

" 'Human Nature.' It's one of Madonna's. The *front* page."

She certainly didn't want to talk about the likes of Madonna. Mary Ruth let a moment pass.

The announcement of the closing had rendered Clyde's lessons the only bright spot in her life. They had just begun his lessons and already she dreaded the day they would stop. *What if he decides he doesn't want to continue, that there's no point?*

She said, "We might be here for months. We just don't know."

The last part was true; they *didn't* know.

His solemn expression affected her the same way his male energy did, energy that drew her into what felt like soft sweet music as sure as a line of melody. Despite the cold she felt her cheeks flush with heat and turned away from him. She experienced an urgency to make conversation, to minimize her awareness of so much high energy buzzing about inside her. She became aware of Clyde's bouncy, spirited gait.

"How long have you lived in Sleeder?" she asked. "Where's home?"

"Wherever I roam. This is my premier year." He grinned his crooked whimsical smile. "May I ... say something?"

"Of course."

"I don't like thinking of you as a sister because that term means something else to me."

"Mary Ruth is just fine." Since they would be leaving soon, how could it matter?

He said, "I am partial to dual names. Southern."

"You grew up in the south?"

"If you count southern Indiana. Boonville. Isn't that a terrible name?"

She smiled. It wasn't exactly refined.

"East of Evansville," he said.

She asked, "Do you have a dual name?"

He closed one eye, narrowed the other, and squinted at her. "Clyde Hawkins Johnson. Pirate, first mate."

She laughed. When Clyde teased her like this, his eyes, the color of her father's dark European ale, seemed to dance into her soul. She had known few adult African-American men, none to really talk to, not like this. What she admired most about Clyde was his attitude: I'm black and proud of it.

"Hawkins goes back to slave days on my mother's side."

Mary Ruth flinched. They had arrived at the green and gray striped awning of Schmitt's Music Store. She didn't like to think of Clyde as a descendant of slaves. She should have worn boots, not given in to vanity and worn her patent leather pumps. Her toes were freezing. She was glad for the escape from the subject of slavery.

"Mr. Schmitt," she greeted the white-haired owner, who stood near the cash register checking a stack of audiocassettes against a list.

"Nice to see you, Mary Ruth. Hello, Clyde. I have some new selections you'd like."

"Thanks. Today, I'm with my teacher."

Mary Ruth led him to the classical section. "This," she said, giving him Hanon's book of scale exercises. "And Czerny for fingering and control, a nice repertoire with classical underpinnings, not too juvenile. It'll tone down your jazzy spirit."

"Nothing will tone down my spirit," he said, mimicking her inflection.

Mary Ruth giggled. Teasing was not a typical part of her life; she liked it.

"It wasn't *that* funny."

Clyde crinkled his nose at her and held her eyes with his for a moment. She could hardly pull her gaze away, felt near to giddy. Quickly she opened the score and pretended to study it. He peered over her shoulder at the page. She felt the warmth of his aura blending with hers, how the heat of them mixed.

"It looks tricky," he said, lightly. "Are you sure?"

"You've strayed far," she said, looking up at him then setting down the sheet music. She knew how well he responded to a challenge. "Maybe you're incapable of learning the basics," she said, adding Agary on top of the other books he held.

"Yes, ma'am."

For a moment she saw his long, dark tapered fingers ripping out Bach's "Three Part Inventions" and shivered with pleasure. His energy caused her to be aware that they might be taken for a couple. She hadn't considered that and should have because a sister shouldn't be seen alone with a man, especially not a single man. She glanced in the direction of Mr. Schmitt. He kept matching audiocassettes to the list.

"I guess that's enough," she said, hurrying toward the front of the store.

Clyde stayed on her heels. "Hey, wait up. Don't drill out the thrill. When I get the fingering right, my talent shows up." Clyde addressed Mr. Schmitt, "I'll be old before she finishes with me."

"You can count on that, son. Time to play today?"

Clyde shook his head. "*She's* punching my time clock."

"Sometimes he plays that Steinway over there, makes my day."

"Does he now?" Mary Ruth peered up at Clyde with appreciation. Why, he was blushing! "I've got time to listen," she said.

"No," Clyde muttered, taking his change, then her elbow, moving her to the door. "Some other time," he said, saluting Mr. Schmitt with one finger. Clyde moved between her and the street, as if they *were* a couple. Suddenly Mary Ruth felt self-conscious and shy.

"I can exercise my digits anytime," he said, "but I seldom have an opportunity for intelligent conversation. Any day I'd rather talk with you than play Smitty's Steinway."

She stopped and turned and peered into a store window. A dramatically bent mannequin showed off a bright, smart, flattering dress cut on the bias, a dress Kimberly would like.

"M'Ruth, let's warm up these bones. How about a cup of coffee? A burger?" She shook her head. "Okay, that's cool," he said, sounding disappointed. "Lots of folks here aren't comfortable being seen with—" His mouth curled to one side.

"Oh, no! Never for a moment. How could you even think such a thing?"

She knew what it felt like to be singled out as ... different ... how sisters wearing habits were so often treated like germ carriers.

Clyde bobbed up and down, stomped his feet. His teeth chattered. "Well, if you don't mind being seen with a cold African-American, let's move on."

She considered his offer. No one at home would ask questions; no one knew where Vivian was. She hadn't thought about how a black man in Sleeder could feel very alone.

"Cocoa would be nice."

"Great! Gracie's," Clyde said, touching her arm lightly and pointing to the café. The "i" and the "s" were missing in the yellow lettering outlined in red on the window. It said: Grac e' Cafe.

He said, "You just saved my soul."

"You have more soul than a body can hold."

The heat of the café proved more welcome than she had expected. Her toes hurt.

"Hello, Mr. Johnson," the pony-tailed waitress said with a bright smile.

"Ellie," he said. "How ya doin'? This here's Mary Ruth."

"How do you do?"

Ellie looked through Mary Ruth, then led them to a booth. She waited with her pencil poised.

"Cocoa, please," Mary Ruth said.

"Whipped cream on it?"

"Sure," Clyde said, answering for her.

"For me, Ellie Sweet, a giant Coke." The timber of his voice, higher than a white man's, mellow. He didn't appear lonely, not with Ellie Sweet.

"Would you like a sandwich, Mary Ruth?" Clyde spotted a couple he knew and waved to them. "Fries? Something more?"

"No. No, thank you."

The girl left. Mary Ruth leaned forward and asked *sotte voce*, "Everyone knows you?"

He shrugged. "I'm at all the games, not to mention I monitor kids' detention, Jesus help me, twice a week. And, I teach required Health. None of that makes for good company. I'm what you call visible. Ellie Sweet, what took you so long?"

"Give me an A, Mr. Johnson."

"No bribes."

Ellie cast Mary Ruth a look that could melt a candle and walked away. *Why, the girl's jealous!*

"Let me guess," Clyde said, using his straw to stir his Coke, then removing it. "Home for you is somewhere in the East. Connecticut? New Hampshire?"

She smiled and relaxed. They would stick to safe subjects. Good.

"Between the ages of four and nine I lived on the outskirts of London. That's probably what you detect in my speech. There, children teased me so much about my American accent that I worked hard to sound more like them. Guess some of it took hold."

"What were you doing in London?"

She mustn't reveal too much. "My father ... worked for the government, ours, not theirs. When I was nine we moved to South Africa. Flowers everywhere, bougainvillea, mauve jacaranda, fig trees, ferns, incredible sunsets. It's a beautiful country."

"Apartheid," he said.

Yes. Ever present apartheid. "That was most unpleasant. Sad." She swallowed, knowing how he must feel about apartheid. She said, "There's much to respect about rearing children in England. Quality children's drama, concerts! Every week my father and I attended concerts at St. Martin-in-the-Fields." She was talking too fast, sounded speeded up. *Whatever is the matter with me?* She took slow, deep breaths to calm herself, sipped her cocoa.

"Where did you study music?"

"Mostly private tutors. Father wanted me to apply to Juilliard, but I knew I wasn't good enough. Cousins' camps in summers. That's what we called Americans, cousins. Sometimes Yanks."

He pointed to his nose, then to hers, and chuckled. "Whipped cream," he said. "May I?" He reached out and took her chin lightly in one hand and dabbed at her nose with the corner of a paper napkin.

At his touch her heart began to beat hard like pelting rain.

"Summers," he said, reminding her. "Music camps."

Her face, warm as her cocoa, her chin, electric. "Oh. Yes. Brevard, North Carolina," she said, sounding breathless. "That was my favorite camp. It's in the Blue Ridge Mountains. Simply beautiful. Once I spent a whole summer with my mother in Kentucky." *You're saying too much.*

"Your parents were divorced?"

"Catholics don't divorce."

"They don't?"

She looked around, shouldn't be here, not alone with him in public. She should have thought of that sooner—

"My father met my mother when he was stationed outside Louisville. Later when he was assigned to England, she chose not to come along." At least that's what her father had said back when he and her mother were vying for her affection so much she feared she would break in two. "How many hours a day do you practice?"

"Four. More if I can spare the time."

"Really? That much?"

"It shortens long evenings, know what I'm saying? My social life is nil. Unless you count being in crowds at games. I usually eat here or at Mario's, sometimes out at the Roadhouse Truckstop. Music's my main high."

Her heart unfolded and opened with welcome like one of her origami mangers.

She knew that kind of aloneness. "I understand," she said.

"I promised myself that when I could afford lessons, I'd take them. Now, " he said, teasing her, "I'm not so sure."

She peered into her cup. There was a bubbly residue on the bottom. "Why Sleeder? Why not—"

"A black school?"

She pressed her lips, nodded.

"M'Ruth, like you say about music, first you learn the rules, then you decide which ones to keep. Same with sports." He shrugged. "Life, I guess. Sometimes white folks take the long way around. When I know which of the rules I want to keep, maybe I'll move over to the other side of the tracks and teach the brothers."

In America blacks lived on the wrong side of the tracks; in South Africa, on the wrong side of the veld. Mary Ruth imagined dancers doing the *toyi-toyi* in protest.

Clyde said, "Some rules are just never spelled out."

She slipped her arms into the sleeves of her coat, said, "I must get back."

Clyde looked up with surprise, then stood and took out his wallet. "Whatever you say," he said, setting down a dollar tip.

Ellie Sweet was right there picking it up, focusing her big, bright smile on him.

CHAPTER TWENTY-SIX

Jennifer sat beside Vivian in the car, cradling a monkey made of discarded nylon stockings. It was missing one bright button eye, had a downturned, mournful red mouth. She asked, "Isn't Horowitz a Jewish name? I thought we were only supposed to go to Catholic doctors."

Vivian peered into the rearview mirror, looked over her shoulder and pulled into the passing lane. Nothing seemed to be working right. Parts of the US government were shut down for lack of funding. Even aides from the White House were on leave. The day had begun overcast with the promise of bitter windchill. She glanced at the girl.

If Jennifer held her baby like that, it would smother. *Guilt is making me overcritical.* Why had she at the last minute switched from Dr. Kaczmarek to Dr. Horowitz? She said, as if to convince herself, "Doctors are pledged to honor a patient's religious belief."

Jennifer didn't comment.

Perhaps, Vivian thought, she should be driving Sister Dominic to the doctor instead. Each day when the mail arrived and with it no letter from Reverend Mother, the old woman grew more cantankerous, intolerant of plinking music lessons that, she said, invaded her contemplation. She told Mary Ruth in no uncertain terms that discordance disturbed her prayer. Fortunately for them, parishioners had increased lessons, their way of helping them out during this stressful period.

Vivian said, "When the Home makes a referral it means the doctor is a good doctor, which includes discretion. They know." She wondered if Jennifer needed to know what to expect. "Have you ever had this kind of examination?" she asked in a lighter tone.

The girl lowered her head and shook it.

Vivian turned the car north. "What helped me the first time was to remind myself that a doctor does dozens of exams, that, for him, mine was merely routine."

"I didn't know sisters got PG!"

The car veered off the shoulder.

"Sister," Jennifer said, grabbing the dash.

"Sorry. I didn't mean to scare you. I wasn't talking about pregnancy. I was talking about getting a physical, a Pap smear."

Today's kids knew more about Pap smears, herpes, AIDS, birth control, and do-it-yourself pregnancy tests, than they knew about dental hygiene. In Vivian's high school family course, Father Cyprian had said, "In marriage any body part of one partner may touch any body part of the other without sin." Someone snitched because suddenly, Father Cyprian didn't teach their class anymore. Still, that didn't keep her and her classmates from fantasizing how that vital bit of information might be applied.

"Jennifer, what do they teach you in school about … you know."

The girl looked away, mumbled, "That at Planned Parenthood we can find out what teachers aren't allowed to tell us, that we're welcome there."

If you had heeded that advice, you wouldn't be pregnant.

The girl poked at the missing eyespot on the monkey, said, "I know what's a sin."

Vivian raised her chin. Road conditions were awful.

"S'ster, I've made lists and lists of the cost of baby food, the cost of diapers, of bottles. I thought a lot about this, about everything."

165

You've ruined your whole life. Did you consider medical and immunization costs? Ending your education? Sooner or later your parents will find out and hate me for helping you. Mary, mother of God, keep this secret.

The office clerk at the clinic assumed Vivian was

Jennifer's *mother*. Because of anxiety, neither Vivian nor the girl corrected the error or even thought much of it.

Dr. Horowitz proved a dark complexioned man in his late forties with hair enough to suggest he would never go bald. "Take deep breaths. Breathe through your mouth."

Vivian squeezed the girl's hand. Jennifer's eyes closed and scrunched. A single tear escaped and clung to her eyeliner.

Mary. Please, please, please, prayed Vivian.

"All right," the doctor said, pushing back the rolling stool and snapping off his gloves. He patted Jennifer's ankle. "Get dressed. We'll talk."

The nurse handed Jennifer tissues and followed him out. Silence ensued, the kind of earthshaking silence that followed watching an acorn disappear beneath snow, leaving an invisible exit that would melt into nothingness. What could anyone say? Vivian turned her back to give Jennifer privacy. She took out her rosary and moved the beads through her fingers.

When the doctor tapped on the door, Vivian dropped the rosary into her pocket. She reached up and moved hair back from her eye, as if that would make her hear better. His tone was serious but gentle, as he got to the point.

"The baby's due in mid-July."

Jennifer's eyes seemed to turn in on themselves. Vivian feared the girl would faint. Her own hand moved to her throat.

"Have you considered your options? I can refer you to counselors," he said.

There are no options.

Jennifer mumbled, "I know abortion is an option."

Vivian petted her throat against verbal eruption. Jennifer and the doctor exchanged a few more words she didn't hear, then he was gone.

"Is there anything I can do for you?" the nurse asked Vivian.

Hug me.

"No. No, thank you."

As Vivian and Jennifer passed through the waiting room, the pregnant women appeared to be trying not to look at them.

Vivian turned the key in the ignition and waited for the engine to warm up. Jennifer was pulling on the monkey's good eye as if she hoped to blind it. *Say something. She needs you. I'm a failure as a confidante, as a friend, as a ... woman.*

"Jennifer?" Vivian rested her hand on the girl's sleeve. "Maybe while we're here we should visit the Florence Crittendon Home."

Jennifer shook her head.

"Oh, child, dear, you really should get your name on the waiting list; otherwise you may not be able to get in. Listen. When I promised to stand by you, I didn't know the school would close. I'll try, Jennifer. I'll really try, but it's no longer up to me to say where I'll be."

Jennifer raised the monkey over her head and thumped it on the dash, yelling, "I don't want to be pregnant." *Thump thump.* "I don't want to be pregnant. You promised." *Thump. Thump.* "You promised." *Thump thump thump.*

Vivian pulled the girl to her and squeezed. Jennifer buried her face in her shoulder.

Vivian said, "I promised. I did. I know I did. We'll find a way."

Vivian dropped off the girl a half block from her home. She felt drained, spent. It had been rash to renew her promise when she didn't know how she could possibly keep it. Yet she fully knew how alone and desperate Jennifer felt. The girl could crack and that would only make matters worse, even jeopardize her secret.

As soon as Vivian entered the kitchen and saw Sister Dominic's embroidery on the table with no sign of supper preparation, she knew something was amiss. She knocked on the outside of the bathroom door. Getting no reply, she opened it and knocked on the inner door. "Sister Dominic? Are you all right?"

The room, empty.

Alert now, Vivian heard the persistent *beep-beep-beep* of ... the smoke detector!

"Sister Dominic! Sister Dominic!" Vivian leaped the stairs, spotted the broom handle on the floor, saw Sister Dominic lying beside it, eyes closed, one arm across her body, the other flung over her head.

"Dear God!" Vivian put her ear on the old woman's chest, groped for a pulse on her wrist. Faint, but beating. She stumbled down to the phone, calling, "Mary Ruth, Kimberly! Sisters!"

The woman who answered 911 said, "Don't move her. Someone's on the way."

Vivian returned to Sister Dominic, moved her finger inside the old woman's mouth to make sure her tongue wasn't obstructing her breathing. The *beeping* persisted. She removed the old woman's guimpe and untied her coif. *Please, please, please.*

Vivian waited for what seemed an eternity in the emergency room waiting section.

"I'm Sister Gloria," said the nursing Sister of Mercy, a slight young woman with blond hair, wearing a zip-up white polyester jacket with patch pockets, and matching slacks. "Everyone calls me 'Glory.' Come. You'll be more comfortable in the sisters' lounge. We admitted Sister Dominic. Considering the circumstances, she's doing well."

"She's conscious?"

"Barely, and miserable." Glory took a chair. "She said she was trying to stop some noise when her knee buckled. Dr. Milde and Dr. Levler, the radiologist, are with her. They'll need some time."

Time. That's all anyone had, time. Except for candles burning on either side of the crucifix and a *prie-dieu,* the room could be any waiting room. Glory seemed imbued with an aura of compassion, the kind that made Vivian feel any secret would be safe with her. Glory untied one shoe and put her foot up on her knee and massaged it.

"Flat feet," she said. "Dr. Milde wondered why Sister Dominic didn't have knee replacement surgery when he recommended it. The cartilage of one knee is completely gone."

"He recommended it? When?" Vivian's hand moved to her throat. "Sister Dominic knew? She *knew*!"

"You didn't?"

Vivian shook her head. So that was why Sister Dominic had insisted on seeing him alone. Glory's eyes had turned to kindness.

Glory said, "She may have a concussion. They don't make us like that anymore."

This news was hard to absorb. Sister Dominic hadn't trusted Vivian enough to— "Isn't she too old for an operation?"

"Knee operations are almost always performed on older people," Glory said.

"It was my fault."

Glory flexed her stockinged toes once, twice. "These dogs are barking," she said, picking up her shoe and inserting her foot. "I doubt Sister Dominic blames you or anyone. You weren't even home," she said, smiling warmly. "She is a bit confused, though. Dr. Milde won't prescribe anything until he's sure of the problem. We need a signature on the release form, hers or yours."

Vivian thought of the worst possibility. Sister Dominic could be stubborn. "What if she refuses?"

Glory said softly, "That would not be good. Wheelchair. Enough painkillers to affect lucidity. I think she's hurting enough to want to cooperate."

Vivian eyes landed on the suffering Christ on the crucifix. She was responsible for two lives now. And her conscience. She had said she would change the batteries and she hadn't; now her friend lay steeped in pain, facing an operation she clearly had wanted to avoid.

Glory washed her hands in a small corner lavatory Vivian hadn't noticed. Glory said, "The question isn't whether or not to operate. It's whether to do one or both knees." The nurse dried her hands and came and sat beside Vivian on the narrow sofa and took Vivian's hand.

"Most patients who have this operation say they wished they had done it sooner. If Sister Dominic does her physical therapy, really does it, she'll walk better than she has in years and without pain."

"Really?"

Glory exuded empathy. Vivian wanted to throw herself into Glory's arms and beg forgiveness.

The nurse stood. "I have to get back on the floor. The exercises hurt and require a lot of assistance. In the beginning someone will have to lift her legs for her. She'll want to quit. Sister Dominic doesn't strike me as the dependent type. You'll have to insist she keep on or she won't regain good use of her muscles."

Vivian understood. "I will persist." She drew a fragile breath, said, "I keep wondering how long she lay there."

"Losing consciousness was a blessing. I'll get you some water."

"I-I'll be all right," Vivian said, not nearly so sure as she sounded. She inhaled deeply trying to calm herself. "She'll exercise. Whatever it takes. I'll insist."

God forgive me.

* * *

170

Dr. Milde saw them in the hall outside Sister Dominic's room and came out to them.

"I didn't know," Vivian said.

"I'm not surprised." He was a slight man in his sixties, mild mannered as his name, and judging from the way his shoulders slumped, fatigued. "She's got spunk and is in enough pain to want it over with. I assume Glory filled you in. Any questions?"

Only one: Why didn't she tell me? "Not now. Maybe later."

"She's prepped," he said to Glory. "The anesthesiologist is in transit. Start the IV as soon as the release is signed." They watched him recede down the hall, then went into the room.

The old woman's thin, gray hair splayed across the pillow. Her scalp was pink as a newborn's, her face pale. Vivian took her blue-veined hand in hers.

"Sorry," Sister Dominic whispered.

"I'm sorry, too. I should've changed those batteries. Where were the others?"

"Practicing the organ in church. Library."

No doubt Mary Ruth was trying to honor Sister Dominic's new priority for quiet.

The old woman turned her eyes to Glory, raised two fingers.

"You've decided on both knees?"

Sister Dominic closed her eyes and nodded slightly.

Glory lost no time writing on the form.

"Dear lady," Glory said, "it's a good decision. You'll walk like you're thirty years younger." She handed the paper and pen to Vivian.

Vivian read it. She looked at the frail, old woman. "This is permission for the doctors to do both knees. Will you initial it?"

Vivian aided her, then signed her own name and handed it back to Glory. Glory turned and opened the clip on the IV. Their eyes followed the flow of liquid as it descended. Vivian dipped the corner of a washcloth into the glass of water and touched it to

Sister Dominic's lips. "I love you," she said. "I want you to know. I love you."

"She's drifting."

Vivian reached out and moved her thumb in the sign of the cross on Sister Dominic's forehead, then bent and kissed the old woman's cheek. There was so much more she wanted to say. She walked beside the gurney until it disappeared through the swinging doors, then went back to the sister's lounge and knelt on the *prie-dieu* and prayed.

After a long time Glory came in and said, "It's going well. I've called your convent. One of the sisters is coming for you. Go home. Rest. It'll take at least seven hours. After that she'll be in recovery for another two."

"You'll call?"

"In the middle of the night, whenever."

"Thank you."

CHAPTER TWENTY-SEVEN

Gregorian chant played softly in the background. The three women sat in the kitchen. Mary Ruth and Kimberly were trying to comfort Vivian. Mary Ruth said, "Sister Dominic wouldn't blame you, Vivian. Not for one minute."

Kimberly asked, "Wouldn't you like something to eat? Let me make you a sandwich."

"I can't eat."

"You're shivering," Mary Ruth said. "I'll get your robe."

"You really should eat," Kimberly said, sounding concerned. "I'll get you a cup of tea."

Why had she not noticed the girl's compassion before? Kimberly had been the first one to pick up on Sister Dominic's depression after news of the closing and had responded with warmth, same as now.

Kimberly set a cup of tea in front of her. "Is ... Sister in any danger of—"

"They say not."

Kimberly was making a sandwich.

"I'll draw a bath for you," Mary Ruth said, draping Vivian's robe around her shoulders.

"Without bubbles," Kimberly said, trying to make light of it.

"Th-thank you," Vivian said. Her vision blurred. She had no idea they would be so thoughtful. Kimberly set a peanut butter and jelly sandwich cut into quarters in front of her. She *was* hungry. It tasted good. They made small talk as she ate, trying to lighten her burden. When she finished eating and moved up the stairs, wires hung like torn ligaments from the wall where the smoke detector had been. Vivian slid into the warm water thinking that when you lost parts of yourself, you were never again the same.

Somewhere in the distance bells tolled death, one bong for each year of life. Vivian reached out and touched Sister Dominic's twisted knee. It *craaacked* loud as a gunshot and gave way. Blood gushed from it like afterbirth and became a red river flowing uphill. At the top of the hill, a soldier wearing a Roman crest on his helmet marched toward Vivian. Golgotha, that's where she was, climbing crucifixion hill.

The soldier asked, "Shall I break his bones?"

Three bells. *Bong, bong, bong.*

Vivian bolted upright. The phone, the phone was ringing. She fairly tumbled down the stairs.

"I'm glad you could sleep," Glory said. "Everything's fine. It went well."

Slippers *swish-swished* on the stairs.

"Thank God, thank God," Vivian said, thrusting a thumb up to the others.

"The cartilage was gone. They replaced one kneecap. She's in recovery now. Dr. Milde said it couldn't have gone better."

Vivian felt so cold, buried in snow. Blinking away lingering, gory dream images, she asked, "When will we know more?"

"No way to tell. Older people heal slowly. Let's take it a day at a time. She'll be sedated, so rest. There'll be plenty to do later. If anything changes, I'll call. We'll know more when we know more."

"Thank you. Thank you."

Mary Ruth and Kimberly stood on the stairs waiting to hear. Vivian said, "Dr. Milde said it couldn't have gone better."

"Thank God," Mary Ruth said.

174

"She's lucky," Kimberly said.

Vivian put one hand on her chest to still her heart.

Mary Ruth touched Kimberly's hand and tilted her head in the direction of their rooms.

Vivian moved to the chapel and knelt at the communion rail and recited an Act of Contrition for the failure that had hurt Sister Dominic, for all the failures of her life. *Oh, Lord, I am not worthy, I am not worthy.* Words came to her from the Office of the Dead, which she endured each month like a miserable period: *When my body will be but food for worms.*

CHAPTER TWENTY-EIGHT

As if the Protestants had won some final victory in a game of Rover, Red Rover, send Mary, or James, or Frederick on over, on the next day, the day school was supposed to resume, Vivian's office phone rang and rang. The public school administrators asked questions, expected answers. Each call reminded Vivian of some family conference where she and parents grappled for a particular solution to model a moral ideal the child needed to learn. What would life be like for children without such an example? How would they ever find their way?

Mary Ruth and Kimberly and the lay teachers graded papers and entered notes in student files and cleaned their classrooms. They assisted parents who came to retrieve their children's belongings. As required, Vivian called various teachers to the phone.

In Mary Ruth's classroom Arvid Allan and Betty Lou shared a box of crayons, twittering about skipping school. For some reason Mrs. Wesley hadn't gotten the word. After checking on Sister Dominic, who was holding her own, Vivian tried to reach Mrs. Wesley. There was no Mr. Wesley. Vivian called the backup numbers in the Wesley file. One had been disconnected. A woman at another said Mrs. Wesley did daywork, but today she thought Mrs. Wesley might be tendin' with Mrs. Melrose, whatever that meant.

No answer at the Melroses.

Calls subsided around two in the afternoon. Vivian gathered the lay teachers in her office, except for the two who hadn't shown up: Cyrus Kephart called in to say he had a job interview; Berneice Jacquoit said she was too stressed. First, of course, they inquired about Sister Dominic. Once reassured, young Miss Frank, always a delayed reactor, Catholic and controlled to the core, sat stoic in the front row. One never knew what Miss Frank was thinking. Twittering Mrs. Flanagan, however, as if striking some compensating balance, usually made up for her.

"What's going to happen to us?" asked Mrs. Flanagan. "We had a contract. This is unfair."

Mr. Meriwether raised his fist to pound on Vivian's desk, but missed it. "Severance? What kind of severance? Work's not easy to come by," he said, slurring his words. The man had been drinking. The image of John the Baptist's head on a platter came to Vivian. She slid the box of tissues closer to Mrs. Flanagan. "I truly regret the way this happened."

Mr. Meriwether raised his bloodshot eyes to her and waved his hand in a gesture meant to accompany words that did not come. She had known about the man's predilection and had given him a chance; now, thanks to Father Rupert, the man had returned to drink.

Mrs. Flanagan said wistfully, "Daughters need so much more," no doubt thinking about the loss of free tuition for her four daughters which comprised most of her salary. "Do you know what it costs to buy clothes for girls?"

Vivian said, "A lot I'm sure."

Mrs. Flanagan had quit college because she was pregnant with her fourth daughter, lacked only two courses for her degree. Without a degree, Mrs. Flanagan would have to take employment other than teaching. If only Father had considered these facts.

Vivian had thought of herself as one of the most responsible people in the world until Kimberly's remark about taking responsibility.

Turning to Mr. Meriwether, she said, "I'm sorry. Father Rupert didn't mention anything about severance. I don't know his intentions."

Miss Frank *harrumphed*. Mrs. Flanagan emitted a little squeal and blew her nose. Mr. Meriwether's fist hit the desk. "When a man can't count on his church—"

A sick feeling rose inside Vivian. How, when, had her teacher standards slid so low? Compared to bishops and priests, sisters were far better educated; sixty-five percent of sisters had master's degrees, twenty-five percent, Ph.D.s, yet in recent years Catholic schools had settled for less and less.

Mrs. Flanagan said, "I want everyone to know my husband d-didn't vote for this ... this dismemberment. I want everyone to know that."

"Molly, of course, he didn't," Vivian said.

Miss Frank said, "Had I known, I would have said something."

Damn right," said Mr. Meriwether. "Damn right."

The church clock chimed. The man looked at the doorway wistfully. Vivian waited for the chimes to finish so she could be heard, thinking that only a couple of days ago she had been their principal; now life itself spun out of control and she didn't have a job.

"Severance," she said, thinking our loud. She was in charge through the month of December. Father Rupert would be furious. She said, "I can backdate your checks to include severance through December." She pulled open her lower drawer and took out the checkbook. "I suggest you cash them as soon as possible."

Mr. Meriwether was not too inebriated to miss the point. "You bet. Cash," he said.

"I want to close out the books," she said, giving an unnecessary rationalization as to why they should immediately cash their checks. Everyone knew Rupert. Relishing rebellion, she wrote, giving them what was rightfully theirs. She folded each check in half and sealed it in an envelope. She would mail checks to those absent. "Feel free to take school supplies," she said. "And, I would appreciate your coming in the next couple of days or at least call in for messages."

Now they sat mollified. Vivian expected Mr. Meriwether to stop at the first bar he passed. Briefly she considered mailing his check to his wife; legally it was his.

Miss Frank said, "I can't believe the conspiracy."

"I won't in a million years," Vivian said.

The phone rang, an unwelcome intruder when honesty had just arrived. On the third ring, Vivian reached for it saying to the teachers, "Thank you for coming in. I'll write each of you a letter of reference. If there's anything more I can do—" She cleared her throat. "St. Anthony School, principal's office. This is Miss Tiamet."

"Vivi?"

"Mom?"

The teachers closed her door.

"How did you know?"

"Know what?"

"You didn't call because you heard?"

"Heard what?"

"Sister Dominic's in the hospital. She had a tragic fall. I feel responsible."

"Why? What did you do?"

"It's what I didn't do. I said I'd fix— It doesn't matter now. I failed to do something I said I would and as a result, Sister Dominic had this accident."

"How is she?"

179

"She's doing well for now. It's too early to tell."

"I'm glad to hear that."

"There's more. St. Anthony School is closing."

"Oh. Oh, my. How awful. Everything at once. Why, you built that school from ... nothing!"

Vivian lowered her voice. "A dreadful way to start the New Year, dreadful. I'd like to strangle that priest!"

"You love every child as if it were your own!"

More than you know. "I did. I do, still do."

After a bit of silence, her mother said, "I'm sorry about Sister Dominic. I'll send her a card and pray for her. As for the priest, I've still got your father's hunting rifle."

Now Vivian smiled. "Keep it handy," she said. "And clean. I wouldn't want to miss. How does that man sleep at night? Today the kids start public school. I've been on the phone all morning, records, haven't had time to think."

"What will happen to you? Where will you go?"

Vivian bit down on her lower lip. "Who knows? We're waiting to hear from Reverend Mother."

"I wish I could be there for you."

"Me, too." Vivian took a deep breath. "Frankly, I'm awful to live with, persnickety, bitchy. Mary Ruth plays incessantly on her electronic keyboard. Unatural sounds. Sister Dominic's pining. Kimberly's always on her computer." *Take responsibility. The girl has little patience for me.* "I'd like to throw dishes, crash cars."

"Oh, sweetheart. Vivi. God love you. You can't turn back the clock. It'll work out. It always does."

So her father used to say. Her mother's words washed over her soul. "Guess I needed to talk with someone more than I realized," Vivian said.

"I wish there were something I could do."

"There's nothing anyone can do. Not now anyway." She sighed feeling the weight of it all. "Thank you for the airline ticket. The holidays were really nice, until— Everything's crazy. I haven't had time to write thank-you notes." Odd, her mother phoning during school hours. "Mom? I'm so wrapped up in this. You must have had a reason to call." When her mother didn't answer, Vivian said, "You're scaring me."

"Vivi, sending you a ticket wasn't all gratuitous; this certainly isn't a good time."

"What's wrong?"

"Dr. Kreppit wants to do a biopsy on a lump in my breast."

"Oh, God, Mom!" Vivian pressed her hand to her forehead, felt dizzy.

"I insisted on waiting until after the holidays. He didn't want me to. I had ... important things to take care of. I didn't want to spoil the holidays for any of you; I haven't told Christine. Now I think maybe I should have because she babysits those grandkids while Loey works and won't be able to get a sitter on such short notice. Vivi, I couldn't imagine being sick with her here and those four kids running amok. Wears me out just to think of it. Larry can't come all the way from Chicago. Maeve has her job. I just—"

"I'll come."

"You've got your hands full."

"Mom, if you need me, I'll come. I'll be there. I will."

She heard her mother's shallow breathing.

"Dr. Kreppit said it may be just fibrous tissue. I can tell he's humoring me. What if they can't get it all?"

You could die!

"Mom, I'm not teaching now. Listen, I—" Jennifer. *Oh, God, Jennifer.*

"Vivi, I'd really like for you to be with me."

Vivian's throat felt hot and sticky. *Mom could die without ever really knowing me.* She swallowed, felt panic. *If she knew, could she forgive me? Would she still love me?* "Mom, I love you, I love you."

CHAPTER TWENTY-NINE

Sister Dominic heard a distant moan that sounded like her own voice. Her body hovered up near one corner of the ceiling. Her body was healthy and young because she knew it could still play kick ball.

She saw herself and Sister Yvette kicking the ball in the motherhouse gym. She crossed one leg over Yvette's, blocked, and scored. Sister Yvette laughed. Then Sister Dominic's hovering self saw her chilled and shivering body in the bed, pillows propped under her bandaged knees. She lay without dignity. When would the operation begin? Over and over she repeated, *Hail Mary, full of grace—*

If she were her dog, Scooter, they would put her to sleep; if she were *Cerna*, Blackie, her horse, they'd shoot her; if she were a trout taken from the brook behind the barn, they'd drown her in air. All around her, cherubs curled up like babies with their eyes closed, floating, their pink knees up against dimpled chins, little hands kneading the air in search of—

Mama? I hurt. Mama.

She had given her mother no grandchildren. Maybe in another life.

Female silhouettes appeared against a twilight horizon. A baby beside a young girl with sprouting breasts, beside a woman with firm breasts, beside a line of women whose breasts sagged, sagged, sagged. A white arc, an albino rainbow, drew itself over the heads from infant up over the woman in her prime, down to the oldest, stooped woman, who seemed as dependent as the infant. The old woman hobbled over and took the baby's hand. The figures formed a circle and danced the game that started at sight of the death rash during the Great Plague: *Ashes, ashes, all fall down.*

They fell and their bodies erupted into disconnected buoyant parts defying gravity as if air were water. Elbows, arms, knees. Sister Dominic didn't want any new parts, only old ones that worked as good as new. Ropes hung from Dr. Milde's grotesque, misshapen ears, and fastened on a cold spot over her heart. She saw him lift the ends of her ankle-to-thigh incisions, opening her legs to the insides, easy as zippers.

How cold she was. She must be dying.

"Good," the nebulous image said.

Holy Mary, Mother of God, pray for us now and at the hour of our death.

CHAPTER THIRTY

In the morning after calling the hospital nothing had changed. Vivian phoned Jennifer hoping to catch the girl before she left for school.

"Did you send in the form?"

"I'm not going to."

Vivian's head throbbed. "I see," she said, not wanting to argue. She understood, but that wasn't enough. She explained about Sister Dominic, that if Jennifer didn't hear from her, it wasn't for lack of interest, that she'd be at the hospital. She said they must make a plan soon and hung up. Sister Dominic was alive. Three feet of snow had fallen in New England and killed over one hundred people. She removed her copy of the Florence Crittendon Home application from her desk drawer and filled it out, using the convent address, then signed it "Clara Suges." She mailed it on the way to the hospital.

A machine on wheels hissed incessant cold air onto Sister Dominic's bulkily bandaged knees. The old woman's lips were blue; her forehead, cold as a marble statue. Umbilical-like cords gave her nourishment, air, medicine, and drained away her waste. It was all Vivian could do to see her friend like this. She kept her coat on and located a blanket in the closet and lay it over Sister Dominic.

Glory came in carrying a steaming mug.

"Is she really all right?" Vivian asked. The mug warmed her fingers. "Thank you."

"The cold will keep down the swelling."

"If she doesn't die of pneumonia."

"I know." Glory pressed her fingers to Sister Dominic's wrist. "Tonight we'll get her up."

"That doesn't seem possible."

"I waited for you. I'm off duty."

Vivian felt deeply moved by her thoughtfulness. "Thank you," she said. "For everything."

"Just doing a job I love. Sister's attitude will count most. The weight of that blanket may be too much. She'll let you know. Take care of yourself," she said, and left.

Vivian couldn't remember the last time she thought about loving *her* job. She moved around to the other side of the bed out of the stream of the cold. She moistened a cloth and touched it to Sister Dominic's parched lips. "Sleep with the angels," she said softly and took out her rosary.

Advent dictated Vivian should name each of the five Joyful Mysteries at the beginning of each of the five decades of Hail Mary's. But when she came to the first mystery: Thou hast conceived a Son, she stopped and instead named the first Sorrowful Mystery—the Agony in the Garden.

CHAPTER THIRTY-ONE

At great length Mary Ruth explained to her mum how Sister Dominic's accident had happened.

"She's so pale. The doctor says he thinks she lacks the will to get well. Members of the Rosary Sodality are helping us by taking turns with her. She doesn't qualify for Medicare because we don't earn salaries and did not contribute to Social Security. At a time like this, that seems so unfair. My music lesson money is hardly enough to meet such high medical expenses. Of course, the motherhouse will pay them, but their coffers are as low as ours, just in a different way. I pray Sister Dominic's guardian angel will urge her to wellness. We don't know how long we'll be here, but we must stay until she can comfortably travel.

"Inconveniences that seemed major yesterday are minor now, like the stop on the organ that sticks. I miss the Wesley twins. I miss routine. I find my eyes clinging to the antique chandelier in the parlor with longing. I keep praying the child's prayer, 'Angel of God, my guardian dear, to whom God's love commits me here, Ever this night be at my side, to light and guard, to rule and guide.' I wish none of this were happening.

"Vivian looks wretched. Unfortunately, she may have to go to Texas to be with her mother, who has a

suspicious breast lump. If she goes, we'll hold the fort. At night I hear her pacing. Kimberly just goes her own way, showing independence in some ways I wish I had. Maybe it would help if I knew where I will be assigned next year, but I am not sure about that. I'm trying to focus on the full half of the glass.

"Clyde's finally stopped riding the pedal and is making remarkable progress. My goals for him before I leave may be ambitious. What a joy to have a student who actually practices. He says he regrets that just when he has found someone from whom he can really learn—"

Mary Ruth stopped. She felt more sadness than she thought she could tolerate.

"I have never spent time with an African-American man, not as an adult, so I guess I am intrigued. His dark, perceptive eyes disclose what I suppose you would call his spiritual legacy. The man has a mystical ability to grasp the intent of a composer. I envy that. Clyde has generously offered to take me grocery shopping tomorrow. Vivian's occupied at the hospital and we're low on staples. More soon.

"Your loving daughter, Mary Ruth."

CHAPTER THIRTY-TWO

If Vivian had asked her to scrub the basement floor, Kimberly would have done it. She did not, however, have idle hands, nor did she intend to reward the priest's despicable behavior by starching and ironing his altar cloths. She supposed Vivian wanted to speak with her in the chapel to ask why she hadn't done them. Once they were gone the priest would realize how much they did for him.

Vivian sat waiting in the front pew.

Kimberly knelt beside her and said a short prayer, then sat, expectant. Vivian bent and turned up the kneeler to make room for their feet. The way she wrung her hands and failed to make eye contact relayed her great discomfort.

Vivian said, "Everything's been so emotionally charged, it's been awhile since we've discussed your spiritual progress."

Kim straightened. *What does she know?*

"I ... need you to know I'm not neglecting you."

That'll be the day! "I didn't think you forgot."

"Well," Vivian said. "You're probably not any more prepared for the future than I am."

Vivian appeared dyspeptic, like someone enduring Montezuma's revenge. *Where is this conversation headed?* Cautious, Kim said, "Had I known we were meeting—"

"It's okay." As if praying for strength, Vivian looked toward the tabernacle on the altar where the consecrated host resided, then turned back to Kimberly and said, "I owe you an apology. You were right about Father Rupert. I ... shortchanged you. It would have helped if I had listened."

Kim found herself speechless in the presence of this miracle!

Vivian made eye contact. "You were right about computers, too. I did request them. He—" Vivian waved her hand the same way the priest waved aside her requests. "I did my best. Clearly, it wasn't good enough. My inability has hurt all of us."

Kim said, "We don't blame you," though she had. "It's hard, really hard going up against such a sexist." She had stuck her foot in her mouth. She stopped, swallowed. "I mean—"

"I know what you mean and you're right."

Kim couldn't believe what she was hearing.

"You were right about another thing, too."

Kim's defenses crumbled; she didn't want to be defenseless. Curious, dubious, she waited.

Vivian blinked, lowered her gaze, nibbling on crow. She said, "You were right about the small, simple pleasure of a bubble bath. While I would have chosen a different scent, it is relaxing and invigorating."

Kimberly wanted to smile, but dared not. She pressed her lips tight.

"I know that I ... misdirected my anger towards you. You didn't deserve it. It's a wonder you're still here."

Now Kimberly felt unhinged, confused. She had built up distrust over time, couldn't transform in an instant, not like a chameleon. If they were going to discuss her spiritual progress, she wasn't sure she had made any and had even more to hide.

Vivian folded her hands, said, "I'm very sorry."

"I don't know what to say. I mean, thank you. I think it took a lot of courage for you to say this." For the first time Kimberly saw her superior as a vulnerable human being. Kimberly said, "I do a lot of things without understanding why. It's only later that I discover a reason and might gain some insight. That happens. Sometimes."

Vivian sighed and appeared relieved. She swallowed. "If you'd like more bubble bath—I'm obligated to finish yours—but feel free to enjoy your own and thank you for the grace of understanding. I'm in no frame of mind to give anyone spiritual direction."

Kim reached out and touched Vivian's hand lightly. "Thank you," she said. "Things will get better."

Knowing Vivian's apology to be genuine, a small spot in Kimberly's heart softened toward her superior. Still, she cautioned herself, Vivian had not become a leopard of different spots overnight; Kim remained on guard. She didn't tell Brenda about the apology, rather chose to wait and see. Besides, if Vivian learned what she intended to do—

Sister Dominic wouldn't be able to travel for several weeks and Mother had agreed that all of them were needed to assist in her recovery. So Kim continued to gather the information necessary for her application as an egg donor. Saying she might take an Internet course, she requested a copy of her IQ and test scores from the motherhouse. She requested LifeSpring to send her application in a plain envelope, which they said they did anyway. She scheduled a consultation with Dr. Lovejoy.

Kim thought long and hard about how to ask her father's help then phoned him at his office where, of necessity, he would be in a hurry. She explained she needed an extensive and detailed medical history of the family. Before she could share the explanation she had concocted he said he had the information stored somewhere in a carton, that it would take him a bit of time to find the particular box. Once he located it, someone on his staff would copy it for her. Kim thanked him profusely for the computer. It made taking the course and so many other heretofore unimaginable things easy. "Thank you, thank you, thank you, to both you and Mom."

"Kimmie," he said, his tone suggesting: I hope you come to your senses soon and leave that place.

"I love you," she said.

She intended to read whatever she could find about donors and recipients and had to decide how she would handle her convent status in an interview—reveal the whole truth or nothing. There would be no middle ground.

CHAPTER THIRTY-THREE

"Vivi, just a minute. I'll get a pencil."

Vivian could hear conversation and laughter in the background. "My bridge club is here."

Vivian had hoped for a heart to heart. She felt her shoulders sag with disappointment.

"Honey, I haven't told anyone," her mother whispered. "I can't talk."

"I understand." Vivian read possible flight times and waited as her mother recorded each one.

Her mother said, "Something's bothering you."

Suddenly Vivian felt unable to breathe, like she was thrust into high altitude much too fast.

"If it's me, honey, I intend to be all right. I do."

"I hope so." No one could keep promises about what lay in the future. "Listen." Vivian brought her mother up to date on Sister Dominic, then taking a big risk, ventured, "A former student of mine is ... with child. She's asked my help in telling her mother. She's still in high school."

"How sad."

"Awful for the girl."

"I suppose. Vivi, Just a minute."

Vivian's mind shouted. *I am trying to tell you something important, something you should know. Listen! Please, listen.*

"Vivi, honey, they're waiting for me. I'm sorry. I'm sure the girl will do the right thing."

The right thing. A child with child didn't sleep, tossed all night fearing flutters of life and life itself. A child with child pined for redemption, prayed for salvation from God, from her mother. "Adoption?" asked Vivian.

"What else?"

"She, the girl, mentioned ... abortion."

"Oh, Vivi, a girl who's had you for a teacher wouldn't consider such a thing. I know you. You'll do right by her."

What if you're wrong? Vivian closed her eyes. It felt like the lining around her heart were ripped away. Jennifer would endure the shame of strangers watching her give birth and be sentenced to a life of not knowing where her baby was, whether or not her child was safe or happy. She would wonder if it looked like her, what games it played, what foods it liked, if it ever got lost.

"Vivi, I have a room full of company."

"Yes. Yes, of course."

Vivian's heart ached. Jennifer's mother had to stand by the girl, she *had* to.

Vivian met Jennifer at McDonald's and followed the girl around a small tent board on the floor that said: Caution. Wet Floor in English and Spanish.

Vivian said, "We should sit in the no smoking section."

Jennifer shrugged and selected a booth that faced Playland. They transferred food from the tray to the table.

Jennifer used her teeth to tear open the plastic ketchup packet.

"What's that for?"

"The hash browns."

Jennifer squeezed sweet 'n' sour sauce onto her pancakes.

"I thought you couldn't tolerate food."

"That was before. Now I can't wear a bra and I'm hungry all the time. If you were ever PG, you'd know what I mean."

Vivian raised her Styrofoam cup and sipped coffee, which was all she had ordered, and shivered, remembering how tender her nipples had been.

"Are you cold?"

Vivian recovered quickly. "Only when the door opens."

Ketchup clung at the corners of the girl's mouth. Jennifer said, "I want to graduate with my class."

Vivian wanted to reach out and shake her, just shake her.

"Of course you want to graduate." Did the girl know nothing about nutrition? Did she take prenatal vitamins? Any attempt to instruct her would be handily dismissed as a lecture.

"Jennifer—"

"Sister, a child deserves two parents. Not half of one. I like to pretend I'm grownup, but I know I'm not. God wouldn't expect me to spend the rest of my life paying for ten stupid minutes!"

Ten. Stupid. Minutes? Vivian stared at the girl. Why, Rob had given her pleasure that still gave her pleasure! Enough to last a lifetime.

Jennifer said, "God's not mean! S'ster, I have dreams. God's not mean."

"You don't have to give up your dreams; you just may have to rearrange the order of them. Soon you'll look like you're carrying a basketball under that sweatshirt." Jennifer's hash browns stood in ketchup, a testament to her lost childhood. "We *must* tell your mom."

"Aren't there exceptions? What if I had been raped at gunpoint by a serial killer? What if the man had AIDS? What about my parents? They don't deserve this. They work hard to make ends meet. What about me and my life? Doesn't what I want even count? Why should a baby be born into such, such—"

Inadequacy.

"Dear, you *must* plan. Get on a waiting list for a home, a waiting list for couples who want a baby. Your baby and its future parents deserve time to prepare. Catholic Charities will find good parents."

"S'ster, that's what you would do! You want me to do what *you* would do! It's not what I want."

Vivian looked away. When she turned back Jennifer had closed her eyes and was folding gum into her mouth as if it were ribbon candy. Tears flowed down her cheeks.

"Jennifer, I don't know how you can do this without your mother."

Jennifer swiped at her eyes with a paper napkin, smudging eyeliner across her cheek. "Do you know a way to tell her so, for sure, she won't tell my dad?"

"I can't know that."

"We'll know. I can tell what she'll do," Jennifer said, sounding bitter. The girl's pained expression told of her misery. She said, "When my mother doesn't want to hear something, she gets this beady-eyed look. Like this." Jennifer squinted. Her shoulders drooped in defeat. "Cross your heart. You have to cross your heart," Jennifer said, sounding resigned.

Vivian crossed her heart.

"Okay. Maybe we can try to tell her, but if she goes beady-eyed, she's going to throw me out or tell my father, or both. If that happens, we don't tell her. That's it, that's the deal. Wait! Excuse me. I have to throw up."

Jennifer headed for the Women's Room. Vivian stared at the rest room door through which the girl had passed, feeling her own nausea. *I am helplessly mired in this pregnancy as if it were my own!*

CHAPTER THIRTY-FOUR

"M'Ruth, you like black-eyed peas?" Clyde held up a tin of them.

"Not particularly," she said, turning to Vivian's penmanship of precise ovals on the grocery list.

"Black-eyed peas with raw onions and tomatoes chopped fresh from the vine, daubed with vinegar. Umm-um." His eyes twinkled. His smile beamed like a bright sun in a dark sky. She felt her cheeks burn and pushed the grocery cart to get away from him, but the right front wheel jammed.

"I'll get it," he said.

The way his narrow behind rose high to the small of his back, the way his dark fingers curved around the wheel *So this is what it's like marketing with a husband.*

"That should do it," he said.

"Thank you. I'm looking for instant oatmeal. And oat bran."

"Grits man myself," he said, following her. "Do you like Elton John's music? 'I Believe?' You don't do this much, do you?"

She bristled, straightened. "Why would you say that? I don't listen to pop music."

He shrugged. "You bop about the store like a water bug. Why not just hoove the groove?"

She looked down at the list. Knowing Vivian, the items were probably in the order in which they appeared in the store. She felt dumb knowing little about music that was obviously well known. She raised her chin, strode away at a clip.

196

"Hey, wait up! Did I say something wrong?"

"Of course not."

"Coulda fooled me."

Produce smelled of onions and cabbage and dew. They were back at the beginning of the store. She had thought getting the fresh items last would be smart. She selected tomatoes that looked like wax, grapefruit, bananas. Being with Clyde brought out the worst in her. Why?

She reached for a bag of popcorn kernels, then, as if she had been caught wrong, returned it to the shelf. Clyde sent her one of his what-for looks, the kind he gave her when she demonstrated difficult fingering. He reached out and plucked the bag from the shelf and dropped it into the cart, saying, "I insist."

Mary Ruth's lips parted.

"Not a word," he said.

Wasn't it enough that she would have to explain that he had driven her here out of kindness without her also having to explain this gift? There were fine points to vows that Clyde did not comprehend. Still, she could tell her objection would accomplish nothing. She simply said, "Thank you," and tried to relax.

"You people," he said, shaking his head. "Vivian's no superior. Not to you."

Peanut butter, she needed to find peanut butter. "You're a self-appointed judge?"

"No. Entitled to my opinion."

Mary Ruth tightened her lips against retaliation.

After a beat, he asked, "When do you leave?"

Clyde dissolved into a wavy figure. She took a step back and fumbled in her purse for her handkerchief, felt his presence beside her. When she looked up his eyes were full of compassion.

"We don't know," she said. She stepped aside to let a mother with an infant in her cart pass. She said, "Right now is not a good time to ask Vivian anything. She's nervous as a fugue. What we do know is that it'll be at least six weeks before Sister Dominic is able to travel."

"That's goooood," he said, following on her heels. "Maybe I can help. I've helped lots of athletes with injuries."

Mary Ruth imagined the old woman wearing nightclothes, Clyde exercising her legs like scissors, and couldn't help but smile.

"I mean it. I'm available," he said. "And *willing*. You don't have any idea the kind of strength and stamina it takes."

"Kind of you to offer." Mary Ruth stopped and looked at him. His eyes glowed like a saint's on a holy card. If healing flowed through him the way music did— She shivered. Clyde was a kind man; he didn't even mention her unexpected weep. "I'll remember your offer," she said, pushing on. "Thank you."

No way in Johannesburg could she market with a black man unless he were her servant. She returned to the facial tissue aisle. When the tissue she wanted proved beyond her reach, Clyde stretched his arm beside her. Her breath caught at his nearness. The energy between them intensified. She saw ... fondness in his eyes, resisted what she felt. She accepted the box, nodded a quick thank you, and tossed it into the cart, and pushed away, imploring St. Cecilia, patron saint of music, to inspire her as his teacher. She wouldn't tell Vivian he had offered help even if they were in overwhelming circumstances. She told herself she must remember that she was this man's teacher, nothing more.

CHAPTER THIRTY-FIVE

Unable to sleep peacefully the previous night—once again Vivian's unborn child had taken center stage in her dreams—Vivian rehearsed how she, they, would tell Clara Suges. They must do it today because tomorrow she would be leaving for Texas. She sat at the kitchen table checking off items Sister Dominic needed for exercises: stop watch, rubbing alcohol (to mix with water to make slush to shape to her legs to keep down swelling), large freezer bags, two extra pillows, a volleyball, two small tote bags with handles, two large cans of baked beans, another night-light. Bananas, ice cream(s), cherries, whipped cream, nuts. Glory had requested that they meet before Vivian left. The matter had to be important because the nurse would stay after her night shift to meet with her.

Father Rupert had left her a message to phone him. She did not want to. He asked, "Is there anything I can do for you?"

She responded crisply. "No, Father. Thank you."

He would not let it go. Finally she explained. "Mary Ruth's found an experienced person to help when Sister Dominic comes home. Kimberly is occupied with a project. We'll get on fine."

"Tell the sisters they may call on me."

"I will."

Both were exceedingly polite. A silence followed. What else was on his mind?

"Brandenburg?" he asked.

"I haven't heard."

"You're dealing with so much. I hate to ask you."

Vivian stiffened, braced herself. *Ask me what?*

"The city has leased the school."

"Oh." The word escaped against her will. The seal of finality.

"For a homeless shelter."

Mary Ruth was playing "Onward Christian Soldiers," a Protestant hymn. Vivian pictured strangers in tattered clothes shuffling through her beloved halls, absent the sounds of children. Her mouth felt dry as chalk dust. Rupert talked very fast. She squelched all feeling, heard vaguely. The bishop supported the lease. It was a good purpose. The school should be emptied, ASAP. So many memories.

"Yes," she heard herself say. She wanted, needed more time for emotional closure. "Father, it will have to wait until I can do it."

"But—"

"When I return."

She could tell he was taken aback by her insistence.

Rather reluctantly, he said, "I'll say a mass for your mother," and hung up.

That he had backed down so readily made Vivian wonder if the school would have closed if she had been firmer sooner. She had little time to analyze her part in failure for their state of affairs. Until this moment, she hadn't thought she had played a role in it at all.

Glory sat in the nurses' lounge with her shoes off and her legs up. She looked tired and bobbed a tea bag in a steaming cup. "Sister Dominic's asking about a living will. I get the impression that this is not an okay request."

Vivian's lips parted. This was so unlike Sister Dominic.

"It's natural enough," Glory said. "Does your order have a policy on the subject?"

"Not that I know of." *Does Mom have a living will?* "Does the hospital have a policy?"

"If a patient's terminal and we've extended ourselves and the family agrees *and* the patient has a living will, we relieve pain, provide comfort, let life take its course."

"You're saying you honor individual conscience?"

Glory seemed to draw into herself. "Are you asking for the position of my order or for my own opinion?"

Are they not the same?

Without waiting for an answer, Glory said, "You may or may not know, we Mercies take a fourth vow: To serve the poor. It colors our thinking. Rome's more explicit about the beginning of life, conception, abortion, sterilization, than about the end of life. When the poor face death, everything is on the line—emotional, spiritual, financial. In that context dying becomes, we believe, a matter of individual conscience."

What about Jennifer's context? "Abortion?" Vivian asked, refuting the guilt snaking up her spine.

"That's harder," Glory said, rubbing one eye. "Closer to questions about birth control." She sighed and crossed her ankles and said, "About a month ago, a Catholic man came to the emergency room and was diagnosed with transmittable VD. He said he didn't want his wife to know about it. Squirming, he said he and his wife still very much 'wanted each other,' that she was sterile, so wouldn't it be all right for him to use a condom?"

Vivian's heart constricted. She knew the answer. Forget VD or how he had contracted it; even though he might infect his wife, the cruel, ludicrous answer was: No.

"The stories," Glory said, shaking her head. "We're supposed to tell HIV positives it's not all right to use condoms to prevent AIDS. Who knows what possibilities technology will bring? Negate *in vitro* fertilization, surrogate motherhood, egg or sperm donation."

Vivian hadn't thought about these issues, nor about the circumstance she now faced with Sister Dominic. Her head hurt. All the mind-boggling ethics to sort through. She knew that doctors serving in a Catholic hospital signed an oath to uphold hospital policy. She knew that one-third of Catholic hospitals provided the only health care in their communities. *If you don't believe*— Heat amassed at the base of her skull and flared upward.

Glory said, "I'm not qualified to play God." She took her cup to the sink and rinsed it.

Emboldened by the rush of heady heat that Vivian now named anger, she asked, "What is the hospital's policy on abortion?"

"We no longer perform them, not in name anyway."

No longer? Not in name?

Glory leaned her back against the sink. "I think it's ironic that in all of western Europe, abortion is legal in Poland and in Italy, in John Paul's two countries. Those countries also have the highest abortion rates. John Paul seems blind to reality. He continues to dictate policies we're supposed to follow."

Vivian froze. She had no idea Catholics, let alone any sister, felt this way. At least she had never heard one. Kimberly she discounted.

Glory continued. Vivian appreciated and was surprised by her trust.

"Once the holy father threatened to disenfranchise our order if we continued doing therapeutic abortions. You can't imagine our grief. We practically memorize the encyclical *casti conubii*—that calls any procedure, or any part of any procedure, with *any* potential that might prevent a life from starting, mutilation. This mutilation includes a D & C following rape or incest. It includes sterilization performed for safety or to save a life. Never mind history—all those Sistine choir sopranos who qualified to sing by way of castration."

Vivian pressed her hand against a low, sharp cramp.

202

"I shouldn't be talking like this."

"It's okay. I ... had no idea how troublesome these matters were for nursing sisters. I'm ... learning. I appreciate your trust, your respect."

Glory said, "Some women choose abortion over poverty. The choice is never easy. I see women commiserate, know from personal experience that either choice takes great courage."

"I don't know what SIHM's policy is on living wills, but will find out." Vivian no longer felt like visiting Sister Dominic with whom she had expected to share that she had apologized to Kimberly and how gracious Kimberly had been.

Glory said, "When I'm this tired and discouraged, I talk too much. Afterwards, I think differently."

Vivian said, "That happens to me, too. Thank you for staying up for me. I'll visit Sister Dominic tomorrow on my way to the airport."

Vivian drove home in a mental fog which she kept at bay by what she had yet to call denial. Upon her arrival at the convent, she found a letter from Reverend Mother, no doubt the one they had been waiting for, the one with their assignments. She just couldn't cope with more upsetting news, not before meeting with Jennifer and Clara Suges. She took the envelope upstairs and slipped it unopened into her top dresser drawer.

CHAPTER THIRTY-SIX

While Clyde Johnson played heavy-handed descending chords in the adjoining room, Vivian showed the Sugeses into the parlor. Clara Suges folded her coat across her lap. Rhinestones snaked across Jennifer's yellow sweat suit. Like a neon sign, the girl's expression flashed: *Don't blow this.* Jennifer stretched her bubble gum to the breaking point.

Clara Suges said, "Jennifer got a C in geometry."

"I'm pleased," Vivian said. "I hope you are." She hoped her nerves didn't betray her apprehension. She told students God always answered prayer; sometimes God simply said no. She had rehearsed what she would say.

"In geometry," repeated Mrs. Suges.

Jennifer's toe traced the border of the Tabriz.

"She's really trying," Vivian said, her eyes catching Mother Mary Gertrude's stern expression.

"Tell me, Mrs. Suges—Clara," Vivian said, feeling her false smile, thinking, *My child is dead. God is giving me this chance to save another child,* "what hopes do you have for Jennifer?" She saw the innocent face of her unborn baby girl in the ashes in the fireplace; its virgin-blue eyes accused her. Vivian shuddered and quickly repeated, "What do you expect?"

"I suppose," Clara's brow wrinkled in thought, "get an education, not to have to work so hard as us. Marry a farmer. Be a good wife and mother."

Jennifer pulled her sweatshirt out and touched the rhinestones one after another as if counting them.

Vivian drew a nervous breath, glanced at the girl, risked saying, "Jennifer's capable of college work."

The woman gripped her purse so tightly her knuckles whitened. "My husband, Sister, he says the boys go. But if Jennifer wants to—then I'll see to it."

"Certainly you would want her to complete her education, even if something interrupted it."

"No interruptions, Sister." Mrs. Suges raised and lowered her purse. "Jennifer goes. That's it."

To Mrs. Suges education equaled insurance against the death or disability of Jennifer's future husband, education the girl was not supposed to use unless forced to. Jennifer hunkered down. Mrs. Suges' fingers tapped her purse.

Vivian folded her hands to keep from twisting her ring, a habit, she now decided, that must be as annoying as gum popping.

"In a way," Vivian said, treading lightly, "in a sense, education continues throughout one's life. For instance, we sisters return—"

Mrs. Suges said, "College is all. After that, Jennifer does for her own children."

Vivian counted backwards slowly from ten, asked, "You'd like grandchildren?"

"That's a long way off, Sister. I'll baby-sit grandchildren, but not too much. Already my body's tired."

They sat so still Vivian became aware of how her bone structure supported her body. How did you get through to someone who didn't want to hear you? Vivian exchanged a look with the girl who appeared wizened, old.

She turned back to the mother. "I-I've been thinking a lot about my students, all my former students, because we'll be leaving soon I suppose. Inasmuch as you and I, we, have recently talked—" Vivian steadied her gaze as if they were two women making special, but surreptitious, plans. "I thought I'd seek your advice, that maybe you could help."

Mrs. Suges' eyes narrowed, suggesting that what she had just heard lay slightly beyond her mental reach.

Feeling like she was about to fall off a cliff, Vivian said, "I've been intellectually ... exploring."

Mrs. Suges' frown tightened into intense interest. Jennifer's fear was palpable.

Vivian said, "Now that St. Anthony children will go to public school—"

Mrs. Suges seemed to be trying on Vivian's words like a new hat, this way and that.

"I was trying to guess which parents would ... stand by their ... sons no matter what, when we sisters aren't here to help. Which parents? And what kind of limits they might set?"

"Stand by? Limits? What do you mean?"

Vivian's heart *thump-thumped, thump-thumped*. Maybe Jennifer had been right. This wasn't going the way she had mentally rehearsed it.

"Let me put it another way. Might you stand by your sons differently from, say, the way you would stand by Jennifer?"

Mr. Suges' eyes narrowed to slits, surely a look that could be described as beady-eyed. The woman turned to her daughter.

Jennifer squealed. "Ma, I got a C! If I work hard, Ma, Miss Tiamet says it can be a C+, maybe even a B-."

"The thing is," Vivian said, clasping her hands so tightly her ring bit into her flesh, "I need to know just how hard to push Jennifer. She can be—"

"Stubborn," said Mrs. Suges.

"I was going to say resistant."

"Like her father. Sister, if you had a husband, you wouldn't ask such a question. Men, they think in straight lines, aim at a target, hit it, and miss noticing everything else around it. Stop with the gum. Straight lines. From here to there." The woman's finger planted two points in the air. "Plow, fertilize, plant. Get it over with. Get it over with. Shopping. Know what you want. Drive to the store. Ask someone where it is. Pay. Go home. In the forest, men got to name each tree's bark. While they do that, Sister, we women are harvesting trees, feeding the children, and planting next year's crop. That's the way it is. My husband fights for the farm. I put money aside for Jennifer for college."

The girl wouldn't look at her. Vivian perceived how miserably she was failing. She lacked practice in deception. Befuddled, she backtracked. "Jennifer's a worthy student and a good girl. I believe in Jennifer."

"Go ahead, Sister. Push all you want. No study, I give her this." Mrs. Suges mimed spanking and smiled complicity. "So push." The mother turned to her daughter. Jennifer lowered her gaze. Clara opened her purse, took out a tissue and held it under Jennifer's mouth.

Jennifer spat her gum into it.

Mrs. Suges shook her head and tucked the tissue into her purse. "That mouth, always busy," she said, snapping her purse closed. "Eats too much, too."

Jennifer straightened her back, pulled in her tummy.

"Chopin," Mrs. Suges said, looking at the wall. "The only good Polish composer." She turned back, took Vivian's hand, and patted it. "It's so like you to be leaving and still interested in our children."

Suddenly the music changed to a honky-tonk duet. For a moment the three stared at the wall.

Vivian drew a deep breath. She had hoped for so much more from this meeting. All of them had come to the end of the lesson. One thing was sure: a new baby was coming and she had to find a way to keep her promise. Maybe adoptive parents would pay for Jennifer's lying in.

After the Sugeses left, Vivian remained numb and alone in the living room for a long time. Then she went to her room and took out the letter from Reverend Mother and read it. The combination of the failed meeting plus the zap in the letter, upset her. She found herself a trapped prodigal daughter with no one to turn to, on the cusp of moving backwards faster than she could stop herself. Zombie-like, she climbed the stairs to the attic and cautiously crossed the rafters for her suitcase.

CHAPTER THIRTY-SEVEN

Just when Vivian thought things couldn't get worse, they did. Vivian wished she didn't have to read Reverend Mother's letter to the others. Sister Dominic's chair stood empty, a specter of her presence. Her own packed suitcase waited beside the front door. Mary Ruth appeared with a comb stuck in a tangle of her wet hair, towel over her shoulders.

"Kimberly, would you help me, please? Ow."

Vivian and Kimberly chuckled as the comb came free.

"That smile felt good," Vivian said. "There's not been much cheer around here lately."

"Thanks a lot," Mary Ruth said.

"Anytime," Kimberly said, pulling cotton balls from a plastic bag.

Vivian wanted this task over with. She started on a lighter note, said, "Sister Dominic says we've done a good job of balancing visitors with her need for quiet time."

Mary Ruth hurried to say, "We'll take good care of her while you're gone."

Must be my imagination, thought Vivian, *or my own guilt about leaving.* She said, "Guess we're just going to learn what our lives would be like if we were nursing sisters."

Kimberly blew on her pinkie nail. "Your mother needs you. We'll be fine."

I have been so wrong about you.

"I appreciate your saying that," Vivian said, suddenly feeling unnecessary. She hoped they would accept their assignments better than she had hers. "I have ... a couple of announcements. Sleeder has leased the school and plans to turn it into a homeless shelter."

"Oh, that makes me sad," Mary Ruth said.

"Me, too."

Kimberly said, "At least it's for a sacred purpose."

She's making a spiritual connection I didn't!

After a bit of quiet Vivian said, "If you have spare moments, which I doubt, gather boxes and start packing up the stuff in the school because the city wants to start remodeling. Under no circumstances, however, let Father Rupert pressure you into doing more than you can. When Sister Dominic comes home, her needs are your first priority. Save your energy for her."

They took that in, nodded. Kimberly asked, "Does SIHMs have a mission to the homeless?"

Vivian recognized the veiled question, *Is there a way we may stay?* "I don't think so. When our charter was written I doubt there even were homeless, not in the sense that we know them now."

Kimberly possessed the kind of tenacity and bravado that serving the homeless required. Vivian doubted she could develop such skills. The notion of Kimberly aligned with God's will had caused her no end of discomfort. She exhaled long and slow, held up the envelope.

"This is the other announcement."

"Oh, God," Kimberly said.

Mary Ruth folded and refolded her towel.

Vivian opened Reverend Mother's letter, made the effort to keep her voice even.

"I'll just read it." She flipped her head to remove hair from her view and lowered her chin to prevent showing the sadness she felt in her eyes.

" 'Dear Sisters in Christ, We have been learning how other orders are taking on the challenge of the upcoming millennium. Among them are signs of constant change and the kind of progress we seem to lack. While we all wish to continue God's ongoing work, we must first address immediate needs.' " The letter fluttered in her hand. Vivian looked up. "There's a ... long preamble," *designed to soften the blow.* "Unless either of you objects, I'll skip right to the assignments and then later you may read the entire letter for yourselves."

Vivian steeled herself in the grip of tension. " 'St. Therese de Lisieux in Bogalusa, Louisiana, welcomes Sister Mary Ruth—' " This seemed a breach of the promise Reverend Mother had made to Mr. Vangaard. She swallowed, continued, " 'to teach catechism classes and conduct music affairs.' "

"Louisiana?" Mary Ruth said, sounding weak.

"There's more. 'St. Therese de Lisieux boasts more than seven hundred youth in catechism and an even greater number of adults. Sister Mary Ruth will assist incumbent Sister Concepta.' "

"Oh, my."

Concern filled Vivian. Sister Concepta was feebler than Sister Dominic had been before her accident. *What will this do to Mary Ruth?*

Kimberly, missing the full meaning, still waited with anticipation. Vivian nodded to the young woman, willed her voice steady.

" 'Sister Kimberly McCall will matriculate a doctor's program in September, selecting from our greatest needs, theology of spiritual discernment or gerontology.' "

"Back to school! I don't want to go to school! My experience is with young children!"

Vivian's energy dropped to below zero. She had questioned both assignments, didn't know what to say or do, wasn't the least bit inclined toward giving a homily on obedience. Mary Ruth slumped as if she had sustained a blow. Vivian drew a shuddering breath and read on. " 'Until then, Sister Kimberly will serve in the motherhouse infirmary.' "

"This is a joke!" Kimberly flushed red, stood.

Vivian wanted to cry, forced herself to detach. That's what she needed detachment. She mustn't think or judge, not now. She lowered her gaze.

Kimberly said, "Custody of the eyes and hands and feet and mind only puts us out of touch with reality. No priest is going to turn me into a sheep with wool over my eyes! If I'm going to get mugged or swindled I want to be able to identify who did it. St. Therese," she said, turning to Mary Ruth, "before you agree, ask questions. Maybe it's sweatsville. Maybe they don't even speak English, just French. I'm ready for God's work, for action, not school."

"Action?" Vivian felt a residue of her former self. *Reduced to sheep?* She moved her hands to her lap to hide their tremors.

"What's spiritual discernment anyway? According to whom? Aquinas? Augustine? My own authority? Does personal discernment count?"

Does what I want even count? Jennifer's words.

"Will I even teach piano?"

Keep it together, remain detached. St. Therese is a poverty-stricken parish. Probably no piano. Whatever made me believe they would follow in blind obedience? Vivian, strung out, said, "Please."

"Gerontology." Kimberly twisted the cap on her nail polish with finality.

"Louisiana has a strong musical tradition," Mary Ruth said weakly. "Parents might—"

"They wear masks, binge on sin, and parade in front of TV cameras." Kimberly turned to Vivian. "What about you, Vivian? What's your sentence?"

Vivian bent to the letter, read haltingly, " 'Sister Dominic Ozretich will be comfortable in the infirmary. Sister Vivian Louise Tiamet is called into retreat—' " She reread the sentence silently. *Sister Vivian Louise Tiamet is called into retreat at the motherhouse for an indefinite period,* the kind of assignment a priest guilty of sexual transgression would get. When he proved sufficiently contrite, he would be sent to some remote, tiny parish that negated indiscretion. The paper fell from her hand. Words were only black marks on white paper. Mary Ruth *huuuuummmmmed,* fingers playing the piano on the surface of the table.

"We're not emotional cripples! Why can't we protest, *do* something?"

Vivian's tears flowed down her cheeks.

Kimberly left the room.

CHAPTER THIRTY-EIGHT

The next morning, as if hung over from having taken a sleeping pill, Vivian moved slowly. She drove to the hospital feeling thickheaded and emotionally numb. First and foremost, she didn't want to upset Sister Dominic. From the hospital she would take a taxi to the airport. Mr. Johnson would bring Kimberly to pick up their car, saving them from having to ask Father Rupert from whom they wanted nothing.

In response to Vivian's inquiry, the old woman said, "I've had better days." She pushed her nightcap back from her forehead. Her arm was bruised, discolored from IV needles.

"I'm sure you have."

Wrinkles scrunched the bridge of Sister Dominic's nose, revealing how troubled she was. "Food's terrible."

"I'm sure you could teach the chefs a thing or two. Would you like to sit up?"

Sister Dominic fumbled for the button and partially raised the pillow portion of her bed. "Off-brand, canned tomato soup mixed with water. Uninspired."

"Maybe you're just feeling better."

"That's not it." The old woman sounded bitter. Vivian knew the signs; now she was going to find out what was really bothering Sister.

"Once I saw them bathe Sister Yvette. They strapped her naked into a metal chair with holes in it and cranked her up over a canister whirlpool and dunked her in like a donut."

214

Vivian's hand moved to her chest. It was a heart-wrenching image.

"Then they patted her down with a towel like sorry lettuce, didn't dry behind her ears or between her toes or—not *there* at all. Indignity akin to murder. She wasn't conscious." Sister Dominic slapped the blanket, looked into Vivian's eyes directly and said, "I want to sign a paper that says not one tube will go into me whose purpose is to pretend to keep me alive."

"Oh, Sister, you're doing well. That's not necessary. Maybe you won't dance a jig again, but—"

As if Vivian were deaf, Sister Dominic said, "I want my name on that dotted line."

"I just don't know Reverend Mother's attitude about— I hear you. I do."

"Dear lady," Glory said, poking her head in the room, "I can hear you mean as a spider all the way down the hall. Can we sweeten you with some juice? Cranberry? Orange?"

"Cranberry!" Sister Dominic and Vivian said in unison. They looked at each other and the old woman's lips softened into a hint of a smile.

"Grape," Sister Dominic said. "I want grape."

"Yes, ma'am."

As soon as Glory left, the old woman said, "I'm the one's got to live through it, and I don't intend to." She breathed with effort. "Have we heard from the motherhouse?"

Vivian hadn't intended to tell her. The others wouldn't; it was her place to do so. She reached out and touched the old woman's cheek with the back of her hand as light as touching a cherry to whipped cream. She said, "Kimberly will help in the infirmary until September."

"No comfort whatsoever."

But she can care for you. "Kimberly's not exactly enthusiastic either. Come fall, she goes back to school. Mary Ruth ... will assist Sister Concepta."

Sister Dominic's eyes magnified behind her lenses. Certainly she was asking, Why is it okay for Sister Concepta to keep on and not me? Surely she wondered why Mother was breaking the devil's bargain she had made with Mary Ruth's father.

The wrinkles at the corners of Sister Dominic's mouth twitched. "And you? What about you?" she asked.

Vivian busily smoothed the blanket. "I'm afraid I'll miss my plane," she said.

Sister Dominic pressed the button that lowered her head. Sounding defeated, she said, "I wish your mother Godspeed."

"Sister, if only—" Vivian glanced at her watch. She did need to go. "I don't want to leave you like this."

"Like a hole in a donut? I'll pray for both of you."

Sister Dominic had pulled seniority and dismissed Vivian. She felt—on the outside—excommunicated. The woman had erected an impassable wall between them. She hesitated, pressed her thumb in a blessing on Sister Dominic's forehead when she wanted to bend down and kiss the old woman's cheek.

Vivian took the woman's hand and peered into her eyes. "I'll be back as soon as I can. I will. And I will pray, too. You're not alone."

As Vivian moved down the hall, Sister Dominic called out for everyone to hear, "If you won't help, I'll find some Protestant who will."

CHAPTER THIRTY-NINE

When Clyde drove Kimberly to the hospital parking lot to pick up their car, he said he would drop in on Sister Dominic. Kim thanked him and took the car to a service station and filled up the gas tank and headed for Peoria, hoping Vivian wouldn't check the odometer.

Dr. Lovejoy proved a maternal woman. She deemed Kim in excellent health, said LifeSpring's waiting list was long, but no doubt the agency would contact Kim soon after accepting her application. Kimberly left carrying reading material and a prescription for birth control pills. Excited now, she wanted to share her good news with Brenda, yet if Brenda told Mike— She couldn't tell Brenda. Keeping her secret dampened her joy.

As soon as she saw the bank's executive cafeteria, Kim pictured scarlet-robed cardinals there clinking crystal wine glasses, making rules for: The Flock. On the sixth floor, it was the highest spot in downtown Sleeder with windows on three sides.

"I didn't suspect there was a place like this in Sleeder," Kim said, walking behind Brenda, who followed the *maître d'*. Heads turned to them; the energy in the room charged with what felt like resentment.

Kim whispered, "I feel like an exhibit."

Even before the *maître d'* left, the busboy had filled their water glasses. A waiter, clean-cut as a seminarian, set down a tray of raw vegetables around a dill-flecked, creamy dip and a basket of croissants and recited the specials *du jour*.

Brenda said, "I don't recommend the chicken salad. The Veal Oscar's good. I'm going to have it," she said turning to the waiter, then back to Kim. "Most people here know the menu. Maybe you would like more time?"

Sister Dominic would be impressed. "The grilled salmon with blueberry sauce."

"A good choice," the waiter said, taking the menu before Kim had a chance to check out the desserts. The way he snatched it made her think, *Men practice a theology of acquisition, women one of acceptance.*

"What's up?" Brenda asked.

Kim didn't want to burn her friend's ears the way she had at The Roadster. "Remodelers are hammering in the school night and day. My life's supposed to be a rare blossom in the desert. I get to go back to school in the fall, yuk. Before that, bedpans in the motherhouse infirmary. At least Sister Dominic will be there, though she's not happy about it. Mary Ruth and I are doing the cooking. I try not to throw anything out, but sometimes I mess up and have to start over." *And, I'm going to have a baby.*

Brenda laughed. "It's good to see you undone in the middle of things."

"Muddle's more like it." Kim smiled, picked up the bud vase and smelled the single yellow rose; the scent had been all but bred out of it. She set it down, sighed. "I just wanted to be with a friend."

"It must be hard."

Kim helped herself to black olives, strips of green pepper, carrot sticks. She didn't want to discuss the closing.

"Thanks. We're coping. Does Sherry like her new school?"

"Loves it, but misses you, says her new teacher doesn't know how to have fun. She seems freer."

I wish I felt freer.
"How's Sister Dominic doing?"
"Better than any of us expected. Without Vivian, it'll be tough."
"How is she?"
Kim hesitated. "She seems to have had a change of heart toward me. Actually she complimented me and apologized for her attitude."
"Really? Isn't that good?"
Change the subject. "Learning to trust her would be good." *If it's merited.* "She made me feel vulnerable, defenseless. I'm trying to give her the benefit of the doubt." Kim swallowed. "Do you always get the cold shoulder when you enter this restaurant?"
Brenda's cocked her head as if to say, Yes, but it's nothing. "I'm the only female executive. I don't eat here unless it's business or, like today, when I can't spare the time to go elsewhere. I should do it more often, invite a woman friend. Makes me feel supported."
"Does that happen in meetings, too?"
Brenda set down a piece of croissant, clearly feeling uncomfortable.
"How can you function?"
"It's like a dance. Meetings are choreographed to divide and conquer. Sometimes I remain neutral, sometimes I take sides, but I try always to stay in the wings. I don't solo until I'm sure of what I want. First I usually mediate by providing something to every ego in the room; then I ask for what I want, hoping I've stroked them enough for us to end up with what's best for the team. And, I never take credit."
Kim tried to imagine herself in Brenda's situation. She lacked the necessary tact, the grace, the will. She had neither the patience nor the stomach for such endurance, exactly what Vivian was up against with Rupert. Seemed like what men called power, women experienced as responsibility.
"Will there be anything else, Mrs. Sullivan?"

"Some wine?" Brenda asked Kim.

"No. No, thank you."

Crisp green asparagus flecked with toasted almonds lay beside the salmon glistening with blueberry sauce. "It's beautiful," Kim said.

The waiter said, "It tastes even better than it looks."

"You're right."

He smiled.

"That's it then."

"Very good, Mrs. Sullivan." He took the vegetable tray.

"This sauce is to die for. Who would think to put blueberries on salmon? Sister Dominic would love it."

"Next time I visit, I'll bring some."

Kim had been thinking. "You must be good at solos or they wouldn't keep you, Brenda. I always think of you as having a strong sense of personal power and admire that in you. Obviously the strategy works."

"I don't feel like I have any power. Often I feel like a token presence."

I know what that feels like.

Kim reflected a minute. "You know, there's a bit of research that indicates that as early as age ten, boys and girls process what they consider to be right, differently: Boys set rules. Keep the rules, you're acting morally. Break them, you deserve punishment. Girls decide what's right or wrong depending on the situation. They take circumstances into account, then work hard to minimize hurt, to strengthen relationships. That's what you do."

Brenda frowned, deliberating.

Women worked at creating some sort of communion of saints while men set down rules and reinforced them with ever-increasing defenses. *No wonder I don't connect with Vivian! She believes in the Church's male rules!*

220

Brenda said, "I don't spend much time thinking about power. Mostly I just feel guilty."

"Guilty?"

"When I'm home I feel guilty because I'm not working; when I'm at the bank, I feel guilty because I'm not getting things done at home." She brushed croissant flakes from her fingers onto the bread plate. "I suppose I do have a rule I live by. It's a hymn I learned as a child. 'Brighten the Corner Where You Are.'"

"That sounds like painting yourself into a corner."

"I don't think so. My little corner is the only turf I can affect so that's what I try to do. I can't change or fix everything, though," Brenda chortled, "that doesn't keep me from trying."

Kim's parents had taken on and fought for any and every social cause. Given that, she failed to understand why they had not accepted her taking on Guillermo's cause. Guillermo opened himself to vulnerability in a way most men wouldn't; he said it made him feel free. Her father said freedom resulted from setting limits in the same way darkness limited light.

Brenda said, "I stopped worrying long ago about what I can't fix or change. It's hard enough trying to be a decent wife, a good mother, and an honest employee."

Rather a simple rule. *Just brighten a corner.* The corner could be a pontiff's throne or a seat on the ground with your back up against a cold adobe church, waiting for Juan to appear or *this* chair in this restaurant whose waiters didn't like serving women. Beauty lay in such simplicity.

"Coffee?" Brenda asked.

"Please. Decaf," Kim said.

Light, dark. Freedom, vulnerability. Power, discipline. Did everything boil down to balance, to finding balance? Did one not exist without the other?

Brenda declined dessert with the kind of discipline Catholics said Protestants didn't have. A man seated at a window table was trying to cut a Napoleon. Every time he applied the fork, the paper doily on which the Napoleon lay, slid. Kim wanted a more solid philosophy to hold onto, not something slippery like a Napoleon on a doily.

"No, thank you," she said.

The waiter left.

"Are there women on the Church's board of directors?" Brenda asked.

"Very funny." One day the Church would be forced to deal appropriately with women, give womanpower its due. Free and open exchange in cyberspace would erase secrets and lies.

"Brenda, may I ask a personal question?"

"Ha! Has that ever stopped you? You know if I don't want to answer, I won't."

"Few Protestants who signed the marriage promise to rear their children as Catholics, do. What made you take it seriously?"

Brenda tapped the handle of her coffee cup with her index fingertip. "No one's ever asked me that." She considered a moment, nodded, sighed, made fleeting eye contact, and said, "You may not like hearing this. Sherry knows I signed that promise. She knows I expect her to value and to keep promises. If she sees me keep mine, I believe she'll keep hers. Well," Brenda said, peering into Kim's eyes, "Mike holds forth about going to mass, except he goes only when he's in the mood, which, after we've been out late on a Saturday night, isn't often. When Sherry grows up I'm confident she'll keep her word, but I wouldn't be a bit surprised if she's lukewarm about getting to mass."

Bingo.

"May I ask one?"

"Shoot."

"Kim, I worry about you. When are you going to get out of your head and get on with your life?"

"Ouch!" She didn't know exactly what Brenda meant, but the question hurt, which meant Brenda knew something. Kim made light of the question and changed the subject.

CHAPTER FORTY

"Curve your fingers," Mary Ruth told Clyde, pressing the record button. Later, when he accomplished the lesson, she would play his performance back to convince him of the improvement correct finger posture made. "Round. Like holding an orange." If she had talent as natural as Clyde's, she'd be on her knees from Matins to Compline thanking God for it. Why was this so difficult for him? She wanted to motivate him yet found it difficult to think about anything except Bogalusa. "If you're going to excel, you must learn 'round.' " She waved her hand for him to proceed.

Clyde gnarled his fingers in the air in a stranglehold near her throat, crossed his eyes, and growled, "Slave driver."

She realized she was taking out her displeasure about Bogalusa on him and pulled in a short breath and tried to refocus, said, "I know the feeling. Maybe if you think of it like a sport you learned the wrong way, and now, in order to be competitive, you must learn the right way."

She watched his ego dissolve as he rounded his fingers and tried again and again. "Damn, M'Ruth, this way cramps my digits."

"Only because your muscles are not used to it."

Instead of another *arpeggio*, Clyde rippled out a stirring phrase of soul that startled her. The bass *v-rumphed* under his unrounded fingers, driving the intricate melody forward. After sixty-four bars, he stopped abruptly and turned to her with self-satisfaction. His dark eyes dared her to top what he had just played.

She accepted the challenge, motioned him to move over, and slid onto the bench beside him. She raised her chin, rounded her fingers, and trilled an *allegro* passage from among Rachmaninoff's most brilliant.

"Lord," he said.

Mary Ruth repeated the musical phrase slowly so he could observe technique, then again *a tempo*.

Clyde tried, failed, banged the keys.

"Your obstinate black soul's getting in the way," she said, hearing her inflection sound just like her mother speaking to her uncle. "I mean," she said, backtracking, contrite, "exercise will set you free."

"Listen," Clyde said, giving her one of his what-for looks and executing clean thirds, fifths, sevenths, then played a country-dance, his favorite from Anna Magdalena Bach's "Notebook." He lifted his hands from the piano and turned to her. "I can't spend my black soul on prissy ... white stuff!" He launched into a passionate twelve bars that *crescendo-ed* like flames fanned by a wind to blaze everything in its path. He bent thirds, fifths, sevenths in different octaves, mocking everything she had been trying to teach him, while underneath the melody crept a sultry, shaded blues.

Fascinated by how he divided the line of melody into so many seemingly unrelated parts that still flowed in and out of each other, she wondered how Clyde could possibly resolve their tensions.

Bass drove the main theme forward; bits of it frolicked off, taunting, not wanting to be caught. Just when Mary Ruth thought he couldn't possibly split the phrases again, Clyde did, snatching stray bits here and there, knotting and loosing them, quick as strobe lights flashing in darkness.

Magic. This was magic. Her adrenaline rushed. Themes of his people of her mother's people split and resplit, then unfolded like blooming time-lapse flowers. This music produced by instinct lay beyond anything Mary Ruth hoped ever to be able to achieve. Clyde's mystical legacy.

He began resolving tensions in brilliant sparks, weaving errant strands as only a master could, while instilling new musical ideas with insightful hilarity, transforming his unique vision into some unfolding, universal truth. He commanded the final chord, sustained it with his foot on the pedal, letting it resonate beyond silence. Mary Ruth sat awestruck, no longer able to objectify any of it into theory.

"Okay, Sister Smarts, that's what I have to say. Now, you. Make like Savion Glover. Tap out on the keys what you have to say."

Savion who?

She felt something akin to terror, shook her head.

"What we've got here is goose and gander," he said. "I've been working on your terms. Now try mine," he said.

If I fail?

"From here," he said, touching his heart. "Shoes on the horse. Barn door's open."

Mary Ruth feared losing his respect, felt she had no choice but to try. "You're too close," she said, an excuse to gain time.

Clyde picked up the chair she usually sat in and took it to the corner of the room, turned it around, and sat on it. He folded his arms across its back and rested his chin on them.

Unsure, she fidgeted, refusing to look at him.

"It's not easy, but you can do it," he said softly. "Quiet down inside. Breathe and listen. You're not the only one in this room with religion," he said, not unkindly. "Breathe and listen."

If ever Mary Ruth wanted to run away— She breathed.

"Notice the space between your breaths. That's where the insights are. That's where the energy, the real you, is. Watch for it, listen, give it life."

Mary Ruth determined to try. Before long, she heard her mother's voice singing the familiar lullaby. Unsure, eyes closed, she played the opening phrase, was even surprised that she had not played it before. She stayed out of its way, *followed it*. Images flowed energizing her fingers.

Mary Ruth opened her eyes. Excited, she played, saw herself as a little girl on Granny Mae's lap rocking in the cane chair near the fireplace. She smelled fresh tuckpoint between the cabin's logs, the mild scent of wild flowers in the clay vase on the pine table, ham hocks cooking. Her mother, quilting nearby, looked up and smiled at her. Granny Mae crooned their oral story in a chant: *The tall black man, he beat the drum, beat the drum; the strong black peoples, they crossed de water, crossed de water; those big dark arms, they oared de ship, oared de ship, oared de ship.*

Sound beat that drum, pulled the ship that rolled and rocked. People on deck fell. Down in the hole women bled, children cried, men fought. The dead, dumped into the sea. When the ship docked, kin shuffled in chains, one by one clinking onto: The Block.

A current of pain pulled Mary Ruth through the story passed down from mum to mum to Granny Mae, to her mum, to her, from the first woman in this country fettered upside down on a horse, moving *hobblety-hobblety-bob-bob* to York, South Carolina, where the young, strapping woman plucked cotton until her fingers pricked and bled and her body withered up like an empty cotton pod. Strains revealed how little Mae, sold before the age of five to a Kentucky rancher, was inspired to keep their story alive.

Little Mae grew up with horses and worked in the stable. Later she was free only to discover herself enslaved by poverty. Mae Ruth, Mae's freeborn chile, Mary Ruth's mama defiled the family by marrying a white soldier. Hellfire Baptist rantings punctuated and fought counterpoint silent rests, melodies so at odds that Mary Ruth couldn't resolve them—one, a romantic folk strain, tried to be a march, while the other rattled an unsettled, very present score.

Mary Ruth's fingers searched for a way out of the conundrum. Aware of her confusion and keen to override the stalemate, she introduced an above-it-all English air that took root, not from some quiet inner place, but from a more pretentious origin. Just as Mary Ruth tended to remove herself from unpleasantness by humming, the melody dallied across a saccharine refusal to realize itself.

From all the way across the room, she could feel Clyde's judgment. She looked up, measured his disapproval, set her lips firmly, and forced authenticity by moving the ditty to an earlier, primitive rhythm, hoping to find her way back to the lullaby and somehow end this ... this charade. A fetching, plaintive strain, one she didn't summon, one with its own identity, crept into the drumming bass. Its audacity astonished her. Almost against her will, Mary Ruth's fingers played out of control as if her guardian angel had taken command of her fingers.

She pounded out her fury at apartheid, at bullets, at her father's order: Stay away from *them*. The bitter taste of acid rose in her mouth. To her own father she was as despicable as any Zulu stealing food from a garbage can!

How can I not be who I am?

She felt lightheaded and faint as her fingers fell into soothing, repetitive Gregorian chant. Relief. Survival. Acceptance. Hearing it this way shocked her. She raised her fingers from the keyboard and looked down at them as if they were not hers. Lost, seeking explanation, she turned to Clyde. His eyes were ablaze, a mystic seeing God. As in a mist Mary Ruth saw him rise and move to her in slow motion and take her hands in his. They breathed as one. She felt the pressure of his thumb on her ring.

"Pl-please," she said, trying to withdraw her hand.

"M'Ruth," he said, his voice sounding raspy and distant. "You may think you know where you're going, but—" he whistled long and low, "your soul be taking you someplace else."

228

CHAPTER FORTY-ONE

Vivian saw infant faces crying, sleeping, staring blankly in the clouds outside the airplane window, unborn, unbaptized babies unable to enter heaven.

"Are you finished?" asked the stewardess.

Vivian's ice cubes had melted a clear island in her tomato juice. *Blood is thicker than water.* "Yes, thank you."

Were public sins any worse than hers or Jennifer's? The Oklahoma bombing? The assassination of Yitzak Rabin? Newt Gingrich violating House rules? Couples now, including Catholic ones, cohabited without marrying and conspicuously produced no children. Some Catholics declared themselves pro-choice and ran for public office. The pope forced sisters like Glory to choose between vows and providing the kind of health care they believed in. *Can anyone renounce bridal vows taken for life? Isn't a marriage to Christ until death do us part, too?* The plane banked, turned, and began its descent. Vivian felt the force of resistance followed by the jolt of landing.

Vivian's mother smelled of makeup, fresh perm, and a delicate rose fragrance. She had lost weight and appeared fragile sitting up against the pillows in her hospital bed.

Vivian reached out and touched a soft gray ringlet. "You look pretty," she said.

"Vivi, I'm so glad you could come. You look ... tired."

"The school. Sister Dominic."

229

"How is she?"

"Considering everything, she's doing well. Even a bit grouchy."

"That's good to hear. Look, the nurse made me remove my nail polish. Something about needing to see the color under my fingernails. Chris gave me this." She fingered the pink lace trim of her bed jacket. Fear glistened in her mother's sad, glazed eyes.

"If only Daddy were here to comfort you. It's lovely."

"Gone seven years. Can't believe it's been that long. After awhile one remembers only moments of love."

Or moments of sin.

"Did you know that when I first met your father he was shy about dancing? Boys used to line up for a place on my dance card. He wouldn't pay attention to the beat, and that's all it took. Once, I bought tickets to the Policemen's Ball for us and Dad insisted on staying on the sidelines while I cut a rug out there. Then he got jealous and insisted on taking me home before 'Good Night, Sweetheart.' " Her mother smiled to herself. "How special that made me feel."

Special?

"Soon after that he had me all to himself."

Outside the window, a pair of cardinals, colorless female and pompously bright male, perched on the pine tree. *If Dad were here, Chris wouldn't have given you so frivolous a bed jacket; Larry wouldn't have bought that plush, rose-colored robe.* Her mother had given up so much to be a wife. Vivian took her mother's hand. "You're pretty," she said, "and kind."

"Why, Vivi, th-thank you." Her mother's smile made her seem young again, momentarily pink and blissful.

It occurred to Vivian that her relationship with Father Rupert resembled that of her parents—constant critical disapproval and few compliments. Her father usually started with disapproval: *Little girls don't do that.* When that didn't work, he turned to distraction: *Lookie here, Vivi, your baby doll's crying.* He expected each of them to be strong, stalwart, stoic. Like him.

Her mother turned the name on the plastic wristband on top: Lillian Louise Tiamet. "What about the girl, Vivi, the one you said you were helping?"

Vivian felt her pulse beating in her temples, said, "We ... couldn't tell her mother." The cardinals flew away.

"For the best."

"Why?"

"Who needs to feel like a bad parent?"

Dust coated the bed rail.

"When I was pregnant with Larry," her mother said, "I didn't believe it."

Fear and dread filled their home around that time. Vivian had even asked her father about it. "Nothing's wrong. Your imagination's working overtime," he had said.

"I called my morning sickness flu until one day I looked down when my stomach was out to here and I had to believe it. Are you cold?"

"A little. Wasn't Dr. Zelasny Catholic?"

"Of course, he was." Her mother looked down at her folded hands. "When I found myself pregnant, I was so ashamed." She sniffed. "I never told this story to anyone."

Ashamed! Vivian's heart went out to her mother. Married couples who didn't want to conceive were expected to live as brother and sister, to abstain from sex. She tried to comprehend what kind of toll such a marital decision would take. Vivian touched a tissue to her mother's eyes. "Mom, how awful for you and Dad."

"Dr. Zelasny told us to ask Father Henry for permission to tie my tubes. Oh, Vivi, that was so ... personal. I couldn't ask that to a priest's face. So your father did. The man said, 'Never.' I didn't want to, Vivi. I didn't, but—" Her mother sobbed with guilt. "Oh Mom." Vivian embraced and rocked her.

How insensitive, how devastating. Her students had been right to question the way the Church changed teaching. Back then, given a choice between the mother's life and the baby's, the baby lived. That had changed. Her mother's experience now sounded ... unbelievable, as if this had happened yesterday.

"Shhh," Vivian said, stroking her mother's back.

"I w-was s-scared, confused. I didn't know what to do."

"Your father shouted at me like I became pregnant all by myself. I w-went along with his decision. He s-s-said, 'If I go to hell for this, Lillian, God will forgive me.' I had to go to the Protestant hospital. The way they looked at me—"

Vivian felt the rejection. "Mom, Larry's here. You're here."

"Afterwards, Father Henry looked at me like I was scum. I couldn't live with myself."

That was why we switched to St. Columba's! "How dare he judge you! We make mistakes. We're human. We do. We all do. God knows I've made mine." This was the perfect opening. *Tell her.*

Her mother said, "I h-h-hated m-my body. Your father wouldn't touch me. Now, they're going to cut off my breasts."

"No! It's not punishment! It's not!"

Her mother looked up, clearly wanting to believe her.

"Don't do this to yourself." A knot of anger loosed inside Vivian. "Daddy made decisions for you because back then husbands—and wives—believed men were supposed to make the decisions. We both know behind all that Billy Goat Gruff, Dad was a kind man. Surely he wanted the best for you, for us. We know he did. Today, it would be different. Mom, it would."

"You really think so?"

"I know so. Now a couple goes from priest to priest until they get the permission they want, or they don't ask." *They make up their own minds in good conscience. Like Kimberly.*

"But how can it be okay?" Her mother blew her nose.

The devastation! The confusion. The destruction. How can it not be okay? Vivian's mind presented an unwelcome image of Father Rupert holding forth in the pulpit.

"Listen, Mom. Forget what that stupid priest said. Daddy's not here now and you're capable of making your own decisions." She reached out and took her mother's hand and pressed it to her cheek. "You deserve happiness. In your heart of hearts, your intention was always pure, wasn't it? You know it was; so do I."

Mine was far from pure. Her mother's words echoed in her mind: *Who wants to feel like a bad parent?* Vivian shivered, froze out all feeling as if she were in the tundra, thinking, *I'm guilty of having spouted dogma like a parrot who swallowed the catechism.*

"Vivi, you have no idea how good it feels to tell you and still have your love. I didn't think I could ever tell anyone."

Their eyes connected in a rare moment of bonding. Vivian bathed in the warmth that entered her soul. She smiled softly, welcoming this intimate gift, one greater than she could ever return. Knowing now that she must keep her secret, she tried to resign herself, even joked in an effort to brighten her mother's spirits. "Who knows? Maybe you'll get to wear falsies."

"Oh, come now." Her mother chuckled.

Insight dropped on Vivian with a drum-beating headache: *Parrot regurgitates catechism.* Unwelcome self-knowledge drenched her with pain. *How much harm have I caused?*

Back when her father had insisted that her imagination was working overtime, that's when she learned not to question, not to trust her own perceptions, to actually deny truth. Vivian swallowed and leaned back and fought against the visceral invasion of truth: Her mother, her father, their whole family, had lived one big lie.

CHAPTER FORTY-TWO

Vivian first paced the small hospital chapel, then the waiting room, waiting to learn the outcome of her mother's operation. Her thoughts tossed about what she had learned, arranging and rearranging so-called truth, so much so she couldn't pray her rosary.

Dr. Kreppit finally arrived, said, "We're cautiously hopeful."

"Her lymph nodes?"

"Clear."

"Thank God," Vivian said. *Thank you, God. Thank you.*

"We'll start chemo as soon as we can," he said and stopped.

"What? What!"

"Vivian, I don't know quite how to say this."

Vivian moved her fingertip along the line of her hair, pushing it back.

"Your mother needs—well, a positive attitude can make all the difference."

"Yes," she said. "We're ... working on it."

"Good," he said, sounding relieved. "I'm glad you could come. She was anxious for you to be the one at her side."

"It means a lot to me, too."

"We'll talk again," he said.

"Thank you. Thank you so much."

Vivian watched him move down the hall and into a room. Last night, after almost taking a jasmine-scented bath, Vivian flushed the remaining three beads down her mother's toilet, an overt act of disobedience for which she felt no remorse.

She phoned her brother. Larry said, "That's better than I had hoped. Give her my love."

Vivian was tempted to tell him the price they had all paid for his life but, of course, she couldn't. She would keep her mother's confidence. "I will," she said. "I will."

Christine said, "Thank God. It's always something, isn't it? Come, keep me company. Play aunt. Get to know the kids."

"I will. In a little while."

The two women Vivian loved most in the world, her mom and Sister Dominic, were hurting; there was little or nothing more she could do for either of them. She dialed the convent.

"Straightaway that's great news. We're getting on just fine, thank you. Sister Dominic had a good night. Charlene Melrose visited. We'll keep praying. Praised be Jesus Christ—"

"Forever and ever. Amen."

Vivian found herself standing at the phone wondering if Chris had ever known Rob, if her sister knew if Rob were married, if he had a family, what he did for a living.

"You remember your Aunt Vivi."

"Congratulations on your new baby brother," Vivian said at Cory's eye level.

"His name's Andrew," three-year-old Cory said. He sang, "A-b-c-d-e-f-g."

Not to be outdone, four-year-old Timmy chanted, "1-2-3-4-5-6-7-8-9-10."

"You're both very smart."

"I can whistle," Cory said.

"But he can't wink," Timmy said. "See."

Vivian smiled, tweaked the boy's nose. "Where's Annie?" she asked, looking around.

"Behind the sofa," Chris said, bouncing the baby. "Takes her awhile to warm up. Something to drink?" Christine wore slacks with elasticized waistlines and oversized Mickey Mouse T-tee shirts. Christine had let herself go.

"Is beer allowed?"

"Is the holy father Catholic? Out on the patio, Kids. Aunt Vivi will play with you later. "I'll get your beer."

Vivian stepped gingerly over toys on the floor—blocks, trucks, dolls. How did anyone live with such chaos? Five-year-old Annie peeked around the end of the sofa. "Oh, don't look at me, don't look at me," Vivian said, covering her eyes with her hands. Annie giggled and came running to her and jumped onto her lap. Vivian cuddled the child, feeling the warmth of her, the roundness of her, the radiant innocence. They were beautiful children, all towheads.

"Hope you don't mind drinking from the bottle," Chris said, setting Andrew beside her on the sofa.

Vivian took a swig. "At least you don't have pets."

"Yes, we do," Annie said.

"You do?"

Annie nodded. "A gerbil. Boffy. I named her."

"That's a nice name."

"Annie, take this truck to Timmy. He wants it."

Reluctantly Annie moved with it toward the patio, turning around to confirm that they were watching her.

"They're precious."

"Only if you're not with them all day." Chris put her feet up on the ottoman.

"Mom's doing okay," Vivian said. "The time with her last night was good." *Very good.* The baby gripped Vivian's finger. She had no idea a baby's grip could be so strong. "How old is Andrew?"

"Three-and-a-half months."

Andrew peered into Vivian's eyes.

"It's hard thinking about— Annie, back out on the patio. Go. Now. Sorry. Once Mom knew about the lump, she kept putting off going to the doctor like it would go away. She didn't tell me.

Excuse me. Perpetual motion." Chris took Annie by the hand and walked the girl to the patio, then closed and locked the screen door. "I'm too old for this," she said.

"Don't you have a playpen? A gate?"

"If Lois had them all day, I guarantee she'd have one. Loey reads too many child-rearing books. Careful, he'll slobber on you. Put this on your shoulder. Larry doesn't go to church anymore. Did you know that?"

No, she didn't. Vivian shook her head. It felt comforting to hold a baby.

"If the subject comes up, Mom gets this stone-washed expression as if she'll be the one who'll go straight to hell instead of him, so don't bring it up."

Women suffer guilt. Men lust. Vivian suffered both.

Chris said, "Auntie Vivi and I want to talk. Be good and you can have a cookie for dessert. Too bad you missed out on all this."

Vivian kissed the baby, stroked its downy hair. She bounced him lightly on his feet. She asked, "Do you remember Daddy seeming different around the time Larry was born?"

"I remember I lost a boyfriend because Daddy yelled at him. I remember Mom being sick and us having to take care of 'our little miracle.' Look at me. I'm still doing it."

"Which boyfriend?"

"Jimmy Geckle. Imagine. Christine 'Geckle.' " She crinkled her nose.

"I had a crush on Rob. Rob Runion."

"Earl's younger brother?"

Vivian nodded. "Whatever happened to him?"

"Oh," Chris said, "he fusses like that all the time. Let me take him. It's too early to feed you, Andrew. C'mon, give us a smile. He really smiles," she said, looking up.

Is there no end to constant interruption? How could this day after day without adult companionship, without respite? *When does she pray, take quiet time?*

"Where were we? Oh, yes. Earl went into the military. I think Rob became ... some sort of sales rep, medical supplies, pharmaceuticals, something like that. Atlanta I think. The south anyway. They used to say he could charm the pants off anyone."

Vivian lowered her gaze. *That's not true! It can't be true!*

"Stop that!" Chris yelled, moving to the kids who were throwing toys at the patio screen.

Vivian had been the one responsible for their indiscretion. She had flirted and teased Rob until he succumbed. When Rob mentioned contraception, she, like so many foolish Catholic teenagers, had refused to discuss it because contraception was a sin.

"You okay?"

"I didn't sleep well. After Sleeder, this is the tropics."

"Never affected me that way. Do you know where you'll be assigned?"

To hell. "Reverend Mother hasn't decided yet where I'm needed. Until then, it's Brandenburg."

The baby had fallen asleep. "Vivi, do you ever regret entering the convent? Not having children?"

Every day. "Either way there are advantages."

"Privacy's not one of them," Chris said, handing the baby to her. "Never fails." She headed for the patio.

"Now be nice. I'm taking this toy away. Be nice. Show your Aunt Vivi you can be nice. He threw up on you," Chris said, returning.

"Is it always like this?" Vivian asked as Chris rubbed cold water on the spot on her shoulder.

Vivian appreciated Kimberly's extraordinary patience with children in a new way. This hadn't been her idea of motherhood.

She was naive about day-to-day events, about how children manipulated adults. She tipped her beer up and finished it. "Okay. I'll play with them now."

Chris appeared grateful.

No matter which child Vivian focused on, the others fought for her attention. She hadn't realized how unrelenting caring for toddlers could be. She would never have freely chosen such a life for herself, not one without time for prayer, reflection, contemplation. By the time Chris returned from the kitchen, Vivian was physically, emotionally, and spiritually drained.

"They're on their best behavior because you're here. Lucky for us, they'll go down early. We can play poker."

"Shouldn't we go see Mom?"

"Vivi, she'll be zonked, out. Tomorrow she'll be glad you're there."

"O-okay. It's been years since I've played. Do you have chips or do I need a roll of pennies?"

"I suppose you'll insist on a two-cent limit?"

Vivian nodded. "Dealer's choice, two raises."

Chris rolled her eyes upward and said, "Chips."

By the time they sat down to play Vivian was sufficiently fatigued to lose herself in the game. The beer helped, too.

"Baseball," she announced, dealing. "Threes and nines wild. Extra card for a down-four costs you five."

John, Loey's husband, asked, "How do you remember all these games?" He was a slight, soft-spoken man, not like anyone else in their family.

She laughed, said, "High IQ." Her parents started a nightly poker game when the kids entered junior high, their way of knowing, they later confessed, where their children were and with whom. Even after they left for college, neighborhood kids still came to play.

"Possible straight," Vivian said. "Pair. That'll cost you five. No help. A three."

Fred, Chris's husband, folded and said, "At least this isn't the army; I won't get cleaned out."

"No fair teasing," Vivian said. "I'm a guest. You should let me win. Four nines." She squealed with delight and raked in the chips and passed the deal to Fred, who had gained a paunch since she had last seen him. "Ante up," she said, pushing two chips into the middle of the table. "Play low spade."

"Spit in the ocean," Fred said.

"Oh," groaned Vivian, "I always lose that one."

"That's why we're playing it."

Everyone laughed

Vivian held her four cards close. The wild spit card in the center was a four. She had a four, trips, which in this game, could win.

"Spit," Loey said.

Fred threw a seven on top of the four.

"Ouch. Dead in the water," Vivian said.

Loey giggled, signaling she expected to win.

"You play in the convent?" John asked.

"Not on your life."

"Call," Fred said. "Vivian saves this threat for our family."

Loey showed her hand.

"Deuces, a pair of deuces?" John exclaimed. "You call that a good hand? I dropped with better than that," he said with disbelief.

"Good for you," Vivian said, pushing the pot toward Loey.

"Up and down the river," Chris said.

"Doesn't anyone play five-card draw, seven-card stud?" John asked.

"Bor-ing," giggled Vivian, alert for her next card. She hadn't had this much fun since the last time she was home.

"I'm out," Loey said. "Anyone want anything?"

"Another beer," Vivian said, downing the last of hers.

"Good," Fred and John said in unison.

"Boo-hoo," Vivian said and they laughed.

At eleven, when Vivian wanted to call the hospital, Chris volunteered to do it.

Their mom was sleeping.

"Time for me to go home," Vivian said, fishing for her rental car keys.

"No way," Fred said, taking them.

"What?" Vivian asked.

"I'm the designated driver."

"I don't think I'm tipsy."

Chris smiled, said, "I'll bring your car in the morning."

"But the rental agreement," protested Vivian. "I'm the only one who's supposed to drive."

Chris said, "Sometimes rules have to be broken."

"I've heard that before. An echo." Vivian chattered all the way to her mother's house. "Ta-ta," she said, waving goodnight.

John pushed his head out of the car window, said, not too loudly, "Moneybags, I want another chance before you go home."

Vivian giggled, waved, remembered to lock the door once she was inside. Her head felt like a load of bricks was on top of it. She dropped her purse, stumbled over it, and fell onto the bed.

In the morning, head throbbing, Vivian sat holding her mother's hand, trying to imagine Jennifer showing the kind of patience an infant or a toddler required. She tried to imagine Jennifer with a child, with children, and couldn't. She thought of Sister Dominic who, in many ways, had acted maternally toward her. Vivian prayed for all of them. Her mother, Jennifer, Sister Dominic, herself.

CHAPTER FORTY-THREE

Clyde's Porsche had no boot, not even a back seat.

"Where will we put Kimberly?" Mary Ruth asked. "Where will she sit?" Clyde had taken her grocery shopping and they were picking up Kimberly, who had dropped their car off to replace the muffler.

"On your lap." Clyde grinned.

Ever since she had unwittingly played his stupid improvisation game, tension expanded and contracted between them like bellows puffing danger into the air. She rubbed her neck; celery leaves were tickling it.

"There she is," he said, touching Mary Ruth's thigh and pointing toward the service station.

Kimberly waved, and made her way to the curb. Clyde pulled up.

"I don't know what to do," Mary Ruth said, getting out, trying not to think about Clyde's touch on her thigh. She had been too embarrassed to buy toilet paper and now one of them was going to have to ride on the other's lap.

"Hi, Mr. Johnson," Kimberly said, kneeling on the passenger seat, wedging her purse in between the grocery bags in back. A bus pulled in behind them; its brakes *hiss-hiss-hissed.*

The driver caught Mary Ruth's eye and poked his middle finger up in the air at her. She slid onto Kimberly's lap and closed the door, braced one hand on the dash, raised her chin, and reluctantly wrapped her arm around Kimberly's shoulders. "We're in the bus's way," she said.

Kimberly said, "I didn't know you cared."

Clyde laughed. He shifted, bumped Kimberly's knee, leaned forward and addressed Mary Ruth. "You're like a doll on a shelf. When will the car be ready?" he asked Kimberly.

"Tomorrow afternoon."

"I get out of class at three," he said. He downshifted and turned the corner tightly. Mary Ruth's head hit the top of the car. "If you'd like a ride."

"We could ask Father Rupert."

"We could," Kimberly said.

"Whatever," Clyde said. "I have nothing better to do."

"Okay then," Kimberly said. "Mary Ruth's paying. She's our breadwinner."

"That true?"

"In a manner of speaking. Just now."

"Idle hands," giggled Kimberly.

"Bet you make that devil run," he said.

Mary Ruth stared straight ahead at oncoming headlights. She could pummel both of them.

"You ladies want to go to the hospital tonight?" he asked, pulling into their driveway.

"Sister Dominic's worn out from company," Mary Ruth said. She got out and smoothed her skirt, her hair, tucked in her blouse. "Sister knows the car is being serviced."

Kimberly was retrieving her purse.

"I'll get the groceries," Clyde said.

The show-off hefted three bags at once. Mary Ruth carried the plastic milk gallon and, key in hand, led them to the back door. Next time, Kimberly could take the bus.

Clyde returned with the remaining bags.

"Will you stay for supper?" Kimberly asked him.

"He can't!"

"Don't speak for me," Clyde said, peering at Mary Ruth with dismay.

If Kimberly had asked her first, which she should have, Mary Ruth would not have permitted it. Being around Clyde felt like testing a freshly sharpened, double-edged knife, beautiful when you admired it, dangerous when you touched it. Increasingly, that's what being around him felt like. A sharp edge.

Kimberly muttered to Mary Ruth, "After all he's done for us, it's only good manners." Kim turned and addressed Clyde as she donned her apron. "It's my turn to cook. The chili's already made."

"Love chili," he said. "Especially if it's spicy."

Kimberly knew how to make one *gauche* dish and here she was acting like chef for the pope's Swiss guards. Mary Ruth plunked cans onto the counter.

Kimberly said, "You'll like it."

Mary Ruth remembered how Clyde hated eating alone and softened. There would, after all, be three of them.

"Please," Mary Ruth said. "Stay."

He grinned, slid his palms against each other and said, "Don't mind if I do."

Kimberly poured cranberry juice into two glasses. "Here," she said. "You two go into the parlor. I've been sitting all of the day and it's my kitchen duty. This won't take long."

Mary Ruth tried to protest.

Kim said, "Go. While the chili's heating, I'll put stuff away, toss a salad. She took the Dutch oven from the refrigerator and butted the door closed with her hip.

Mary Ruth moved past Clyde, telling herself to remind the novice that with the other sisters absent, *she* was the senior sister, the one who gave orders, the one who made decisions. She feared Clyde would ask about the improvisation that had flowed from her fingertips like Mary's immaculate conception, conceived without the stain of original sin. She could not explain the improvisation, then or now.

Clyde took in the parlor. A tuft of hair, not unlike pubic hair, curled at his open collar. Mary Ruth lowered her gaze, thought of Father Joseph in fourth form, explaining that a man's private parts were external which made a man more naturally prone to sexuality; therefore, a male required greater understanding, quick forgiveness. Her cheeks burned.

"Who's this?" Clyde asked, gesturing with his glass toward the portrait.

"Our founder, Reverend Mother Mary Gertrude."

Jesus must've had hair as dark as Clyde's.

"Fierce eyes."

Mary Ruth wanted to reach out and touch him. "They say the artist didn't much like her. Cataracts."

"I'll remember that when I commission my portrait." He smiled and sat beside her.

She shivered and sipped her juice. "How's Mozart?"

"Bastard thinks my digits can jump double-Dutch." He stopped, blushed, muttered, "Sorry."

She laughed, mimicked the hint of southern drawl he tended to take on when frustrated. "No worse, I'm sure, than a coach drivin' his players."

"You do that well."

She pretended to pick lint from her skirt. "So," she said lightly. "What do you do for fun? Movies? Football?"

"Fun? M'Ruth, I spend most of my free time here. What do *you* do for fun? I hardly know anything about you."

Teaching him was more than fun. Joy. "Kimberly knows all about football. I don't." Compared to soccer, football seemed a vulgar game. "The Mercy sisters have a VCR and a swimming pool. Vivian swims a lot. We have a pool at the motherhouse. We also use the gym which is part of our girl's boarding high school there, Brandenburg Academy." His eyes were fastened on her face. "The piano," she said, looking down at her hands. "The keyboard, the organ. That's what I do for fun." From what she had learned, there would be little of that in Bogalusa. Suddenly she heard her mother's low-timbered voice, telling her on the phone, "Stay in Sleeder, baby. Or come home. You always welcome. That woman won't take my phone calls."

"Reverend Mother's busy, Mum."

"Like a rooster on the roof, she's busy. To skin a catfish, nail it to a tree."

Her mother had a way of taking up white people's rules like a clump of backyard clay that would neither perk nor breathe, and trying to reshape it. When Mary Ruth appealed to Reverend Mother regarding Bogalusa, Mother had remained firm. "We are trying to correct our mistake," she said, which only confused Mary Ruth.

Her mum improvised words the way musicians did jazz, taking on how the words fell onto a listeners' ears. However, Mary Ruth's emotions vibrated closer to her father's military directness, a violin with strings about to break.

"Anybody home?" Clyde rolled his glass between his palms near her face. "H-e-l-l-oo. South Africa, is your soul still in there?"

"No!"

"Okay." Clyde held one hand up as if she had aimed a gun at him. He wore one of his what-for looks.

"M'Ruth, I'm telling you, it was honest and won't go away. Whatever inspired your musical honesty came from your soul. It put you in touch with the source of your passion. Revel in it."

Honest? Source of passion? Revel in it? Whatever does he mean?

She remembered how her mother always left her free to act while her father acted on her behalf without ever consulting her. Hearing about Bogalusa, her father said, "We put you in that veil and we damn well can take you out of it!" Her parents still used her like a pawn. Resentment built up inside her.

"I'd like approval," she said softly.

"Who wouldn't? Maybe you should've eaten greens for good luck on New Year's Day."

That sounded like something her mother would say.

Trying to placate her father and protect her mother at the same time, Mary Ruth had twisted herself into knots so tight, they could never be undone. Whenever she had done something that reminded her father of her mother, he said if she didn't behave he wouldn't send money to Kentucky. Mary Ruth straightened, looked at the doorway. "I wonder what is taking so long?" She turned to Clyde. "Forgive the delay. Kimberly's still a novice."

"Hey, everything's hunky-dory. She's natural, unpretentious. I like that."

She was anything but natural. A man not a priest shouldn't be here. "I had better find out," Mary Ruth said, needing to get away from Clyde's aura.

He followed her.

Kimberly was ladling chili into bowls. Glasses of ice water stood on the table, and salad and chopped onion and grated cheddar. Mary Ruth took Clyde's empty juice glass and gestured him toward Vivian's chair, which would put him between the two of them, and keep him from having to look at salad remnants. Inasmuch as Kimberly had invited him, she could have at least cleaned up the mess.

Clyde looked around, sounded awkward, "I'd like—"

"Over there," Kimberly said, nodding at the closed bathroom doors, which *phuffed* and rattled after him.

The toilet seat hit the back of the tank.

The women looked at each other. Mary Ruth went to the kitchen sink and squirted soft soap into her hands. They heard

Clyde's powerful stream. Mortified, Mary Ruth turned the faucet on full force to cover the sound.

"Wish we had crusty bread," Kimberly said.

"Corn bread," Mary Ruth said. "With chili, he'd like corn bread."

The toilet flushed. The seat dropped. Clyde came out, did a double take at the doors.

Please, please, don't ask.

"Clyde," Kimberly said, taking off her apron. "Will you say grace?"

Mary Ruth wanted to stamp her foot. Why did everyone forget Clyde wasn't Catholic?

"Honored," he said.

They sat. He reached out and took each of their hands. Feeling her hand firmly in his took Mary Ruth's breath away. Clyde closed his eyes, took forever to begin, while her hand in his grew warmer and warmer.

"Jesus," he said, "bless this house and these ladies. Bless the ones who aren't here and bless those they love with good health. Bless us with honesty as true and as natural as music. And, bless this cook, and this food, man, because if it tastes as good as it smells—amen." Clyde squeezed Mary Ruth's hand.

Mary Ruth found herself holding onto Clyde after he had let go.

"That was very nice," she said, withdrawing her hand. *If a bit unorthodox.* She passed the cheese, the onions, the crackers.

Kimberly smiled at Clyde and moved the chili pepper shaker closer to him. She said, "I heard one of Mary Ruth's kids teaching a grace to one of mine on the playground: 'Father, Son, and Holy Ghost, I hope to hell to eat the most. Bless the meat and damn the skin. Open your mouth and shovel it in.'"

Clyde threw his head back and howled.

Mary Ruth could throttle Kimberly, just throttle her. *It wasn't that funny.*

Kimberly shrugged at her as if to say: Well, *he* liked it. If ever anything deserved to be recorded in Kimberly's chapter book—

"My, oh my," he said. "Been a long time since I had chili good as this. Uh—is it true? You brought Latinos across the border?"

Kimberly looked at Mary Ruth and hesitated before she turned back to him. "Yes. It's true. However, Vivian prefers I not talk about it."

"She's not here and I'm curious," he said, snapping crackers apart.

A man certainly introduced another dimension. There would be no stopping Clyde now. Mary Ruth should never have mentioned Kimberly's activity.

Kimberly said, "It's neither complicated nor mysterious. I couldn't help but get involved after the INS, the Immigration Naturalization Service, arrested people, many of whom were clergy and sisters assisting refugees. They, the refugees, were entitled under international law and our own, to safety. A just cause."

Clyde listened with raised eyebrows, clearly impressed.

"Most were found guilty of espionage and put on probation for years."

"How did all that affect you?"

Kimberly thought a moment. "I suppose what remains indelible is going with Guillermo, another Sanctuary Movement worker, to Guatemala where he hoped to locate and bring back his brother, who was caught behind fighting lines. We ran into more danger than we expected."

Now Mary Ruth was curious too; this was more than Kimberly had ever revealed.

"M'Ruth, can you believe it? Guns? War?"

"The trip was not without its humorous moments. My accent was bad and my Spanish poor so I had to keep my mouth shut."

"That's hard to imagine."

They ignored Mary Ruth.

"We, Guillermo and I, decided I should act loco." Kimberly drew circles with her index finger at her temple. "And dumb, literally dumb." She pressed her lips together tightly, mimed locking them, and throwing away the key.

"International intrigue!" Clyde said, eyes afire.

"A regular Marcel Marceau."

"Guillermo sent word on the grapevine for his brother to catch up with us at any one of a number of checkpoints. When we got to one, Guillermo bought food that we'd eat in the open where Juan could see us together. He didn't know me. Guillermo wanted him to get that I was a friend. When we finished eating, we'd select a spot where I would sit. I'd put my head on my knees and pull the serape over my head and hang out my crossed wrists, pretending to siesta, the signal for Juan to approach. Guillermo stood watch nearby, usually at the well or water source. He chatted with people as they came, tried to learn what he could about the fighting.

"I sat that way outside Acayucan, Teziutlan, Panuco. Our money, papers, and credit cards lay inside the hobo's bundle that lay beside me on the ground. To pass time, sometimes I'd move rosary beads between my fingers. That's when Guillermo started calling me Sor Rosario, Sister Rosary," Kimberly said, laughing.

"South Africa wasn't exactly boring," Mary Ruth said. "More?" She picked up Clyde's bowl.

"Please," he said, turning right back to Kimberly.

"We got to the Texas border; no Juan. We had selected that particular spot because we thought it would be out of the way and deserted. Except the area had become a thoroughfare, complete with flea market. Vendors hawked food, baskets, purses, velvet paintings. So many people clamoring to get across made any border spot doubly dangerous."

Clyde said, "What fright!"

"I sat with my back up against the adobe church, telling God that if I got home safely, I'd devote my life to changing the world. I hedged, meaning changing it in a way that didn't invite death. It was late in the day and I was hot and thirsty when two nearby men started shouting.

"I clung like dung against the church. A boot nudged my leg and a deep voice addressed me, 'Senorita,' and demanded something in Spanish. When I didn't respond he kicked me hard.

"Even though we had rehearsed for such a moment, I was frightened beyond belief. I washed dullness over my face, crossed my eyes, and raised my head. The man pointed to the hobo bundle. I couldn't keep my eyes crossed forever, my tongue drooped like this."

"Oh, for pity sake."

"I prayed, 'Guillermo, where's Guillermo?' "

"M'Ruth, isn't this fantastic?"

"Guillermo arrived and explained too rapidly for me to follow. He was supposed to say, My poor dullard sister, she's not right in the head. She means no disrespect, can't talk, can't help the way she is. Someone saddled this poor girl with an infant, imagine that? Guillermo stooped and moved the bundle over to the man's feet and backed away, bowing deference.

" 'Ah-ha,' " the man said, looking around at the crowd, all-macho now. He stooped and untied the knot in the bundle. Out rolled two plums, tortilla crumbs. I could feel his excitement as he selected the small inner bundle wrapped in a big leaf. He held it high for all to see. People mumbled and moved forward, curious.

"The man set the bundle down in the dirt and unrolled the leaf. When he felt the dampness and saw the brown-stained diaper, he jumped back, yelling, 'Ayyyyy!' "

"Angel of God!" Mary Ruth half stood in protest. They paid her no attention.

"People jeered and pointed, laughed and slapped each other on the back."

How could Clyde be fooled by such clever dramatics?

"The shoe polish looked real enough. Guillermo explained to the man that whenever his dullard sister had to leave her infant, she insisted on taking a soiled diaper with her. What could he do? She wasn't right in the head."

Clyde's eyes filled with admiration.

Kimberly said, "It worked."

"Did Juan show up?"

"Only later when we thought we were being kidnapped."

Mary Ruth said, "Let's clean up." She stacked their bowls and salad plates and plopped them into the sink. Her life, dull compared to Kimberly's.

"I'm interested," Clyde said, casting her the oddest look.

Mary Ruth stared at Kimberly.

Kimberly shrugged. "Just thought—" She turned to Clyde. "Did you know Mary Ruth plays a mean game of soccer? That she's an accomplished equestrienne and a pretty good sailor?"

"Say what?"

She'd box the girl's ears until the Angelus rang in her head all night. Hadn't enough American beans been spilled? "What's for dessert?" Mary Ruth asked.

"Ice cream. Fruit cake."

"Just ice cream," he said. "You're full of surprises, M'Ruth."

"Surely," she said, opening the freezer, "you're ten times better at any sport than I. We better discuss how to get Sister Dominic home; her legs won't bend."

Kimberly kept silent as they worked out the details.

Mary Ruth glimpsed the younger woman looking oddly from her to Clyde and back again.

CHAPTER FORTY-FOUR

"Welcome home, Sister Dominic. Welcome home," Mary Ruth said, opening the hospital van's door. Sister Dominic sat in the second seat, veil askew, coat open revealing her nightgown.

Clyde reached in and took the old woman's hand and said, "It's good to see you."

"Just a minute, just a minute," called a male voice. Mary Ruth turned to see Father Rupert rushing across the street, zipping his jacket. "Sisters," Father said, greeting Mary Ruth and Glory. He extended his hand to Clyde. "I'm Father Rupert."

"Johnson. Clyde Johnson."

"Fish bowl," muttered Sister Dominic.

Mary Ruth took the old woman's ankles. Glory nudged Sister Dominic's hips from behind, walked them across the seat.

Clyde brought the wheelchair around from the back of the van, set its brakes, and stood beside Mary Ruth assessing the situation. "Hey, Rupert, come help," he said. Clyde bent his knees and crossed his arms forming a half seat.

"Oh, my," Sister Dominic said.

"Easy," Glory said. "Easy."

"Hup, two three," the priest said.

Sister Dominic flung her arms around the men's shoulders and latched onto Clyde's Adam's apple. They moved her up the steps and deposited her on the bed. Lying there rumpled, she appeared mortified.

"Glad to help," Father Rupert said, wiping his brow with his handkerchief.

"Well, dear lady, that part's done and you're no worse off," Glory said.

"I'm not so sure."

"I'll get the wheelchair," Clyde said.

Mary Ruth said, "Let me help you with your coat." She removed pins from Sister Dominic's veil and set them on Glory's waiting palm.

"Where do you want this?" the priest asked, referring to the walker.

Glory said, "Rest it against the wall."

Mary Ruth caught Clyde's eye as he set the wheelchair at the door of the room. She tilted her head in the direction of the music room. He finger saluted and started toward the music room.

"Glad to meet you, Hanson," Father Rupert said.

"Johnson. Name's Johnson."

"That's right. Johnson. Sister, I'll be by with communion. Take care now."

Sister Dominic said, "I'm plum tuckered."

Clyde ripped into "When the Saints Come Marching In."

"What?" Glory asked.

"He knows what perks me up. Where's my nightcap?"

They found it for her and Mary Ruth held the propped pillows while Glory eased Sister Dominic against them.

"For all your grumbling," Glory said, putting pillows under the old woman's knees, "you'll miss that hospital bed. You have to go up and down on your own now."

"Tired." Sister Dominic closed her eyes.

Mary Ruth pulled up the blanket.

"Pain pills," Glory said, setting the bottle on the bedside table. "She's been taking one only at bedtime, but may want one now."

"No."

"God bless," Glory said, and to Mary Ruth, "Call if you need anything."

Mary Ruth walked her to the door and thanked her. She returned to the room and folded Sister Dominic's veil and slipped it into the drawer. She unpacked the small suitcase. It was pleasant working and listening to Clyde's music. She went to the kitchen for a pitcher of ice water.

Sister Dominic said, "I best go to the bathroom."

"I'll get the wheelchair." Mary Ruth pushed it to the doorway. "It won't fit!"

Flustered, Mary Ruth tapped her ring on the open music room door. Clyde stopped.

"I thought you'd forgotten me," he said.

"The wheelchair won't fit through the doorway. Sister Dom—" Embarrassed, Mary Ruth gestured toward the kitchen.

"We'll manage," he said, moving ahead of her.

Clyde hooked his arms under Sister Dominic's armpits and they moved her to the end of the bed. "M'Ruth, take her ankles. Okay, Sister D. Easy now."

"Such a bother," Sister Dominic said, face crumpling with pain.

This proved a lot harder than Mary Ruth had expected. At night it would require both her and Kimberly. They settled her in the wheelchair.

Clyde patted the old woman's shoulder. "It'll be easier next time. M'Ruth, bring some towels. Be brave now," he said, bending over Sister Dominic's shoulder.

Mary Ruth returned from the upstairs bathroom out of breath. Sister Dominic had her eyes closed, one finger across her moving lips.

Clyde took one towel and folded it in three lengthwise, then rolled it up. "Do this with the others," he instructed. He pushed the wheelchair to the bathroom. "We'll back you in, Sister. It'll be your job to hitch ... to keep anything from getting in the way.

255

M'Ruth, when I lower her, ease those rolled up towels under her ankles to minimize the pressure to her knees."

How in the world are we going to do this?

"Trust me," Clyde said. "Put the towels there close by. Take her ankles, M'Ruth. Don't jerk. Glide easy. Ready, Sister D? One-two-three."

Sister Dominic gasped as they lifted her, Clyde under her armpits, backing in, lowering her gently. Once down, he edged forward in the small space and held the old woman's ankles while Mary Ruth moved the rolled towels under them.

"Are you okay?"

"I th-think so."

"Do you want me to stay?" *How mortifying.*

"N-no."

The doors *phuffed*.

"Lucky I was here," he said. Ignoring the tinkling sound, he moved one finger down the side of the door to the hinge. "If I take these off maybe the chair will go through. I'll measure. Or," he said, teasing, "I can bring my sleeping bag over."

Mary Ruth raised her chin and pointed to the basement door. "Tools are downstairs," she said.

They resettled a very pale Sister Dominic. "Sure glad you were here," she said to Clyde, her wan smile betraying a hint of mirth.

"With practice, we'll learn. You're a trooper." He wedged pillows under her knees.

"Like zippers, these scars," Sister Dominic said. "Not like the nice, old-fashioned metal ones that work, more like the new-fangled plastic ones that don't."

As Mary Ruth and Clyde simultaneously reached for the blanket, their hands touched. They looked into each other's eyes.

"Well," he said, smiling, "we broke that ice fast enough."

Clyde let go of the blanket and touched the tip of Sister Dominic's nose and said, "I knew you'd see the humor in this. Those zippers on those gorgeous legs, Sister D? They'll fade."

"Oh," Sister Dominic said, waving one hand at him and blushing. "Go away."

At sight of their intimacy Mary Ruth lowered her gaze. Embarrassed, she kept custody of the eyes.

Clyde tapped out the door hinges and whistled as the old woman lay lightly snoring and Mary Ruth handed him tools. The process reminded her of helping Uncle Wilbur, the warm comfort of handing tools to a dark man who was proud of himself and whistled as he worked.

CHAPTER FORTY-FIVE

The pain pill coerced Sister Dominic's dream images into ethereal shapes. Fog. Dim forest. Musty. Child, girl child, Jella, Helen, the child she once was. White dress. Embroidered yoke. Arms extended. Wobbly legs. One tentative foot moving in front of the other on ... a tightrope? Path? Air? Heat undulating on one side, COLD on the other. Like a hot fudge sundae.

St. Joseph, lily between feet. Flash of comet light from its center. Streaks overhead, down, and around the other side of her. Light carries her as gentle as an egg. Keeps her from stepping on a nest of writhing snakes. Afraid to take a step in any direction, entangled tree roots, treacherous. May fall, break bones. Distant *bells*. Bed of hemlock sprouts over snakes. *Bells*. Gather poison hemlock in skirt. *Bells*.

"Wake up, wake up."

Sister Dominic blinked, raised up on an elbow.

Mary Ruth's hand cool on her forehead. "Are you all right?"

"Bad dream," Sister Dominic said, lying back. "Dream." Perspiring. Clammy sheets.

"It's the middle of the night. I feared you had a fever." Mary Ruth wrung a cloth in a basin of water. "I'll wash you then change your sheets."

"That pain pill," Sister Dominic said. "I'll cut it in half." She moved the cloth over her face, across the back of her neck, asking God, *Why won't you call Sister Yvette home?*

Dr. Kevorkian was on trial again for assisting someone with a fatal illness who wanted to die. She had thought the man foolish, deranged even, until Sister Yvette's prolonged situation made her reconsider the man's point of view.

Why, oh why, must Yvette suffer so? Behind that thought was one she refused to think about: *What if that happens to me?* That's when it came to her. *Clyde. Maybe Clyde is the one to ask for help.*

CHAPTER FORTY-SIX

After changing Sister Dominic's sheets, Mary Ruth returned to her room and tossed for over an hour. Finally she inserted Mendelssohn's violin concerto into the tape player and put on her earphones. She danced, swayed and twirled in her soft-soled slippers to its rising elegance, expecting it would tire her. Instead, the improvisation she had exchanged with Clyde intruded its forceful chords over those of Mendelssohn. She stopped the tape and inserted the one she had made that day, the one with her improvisation.

Listening, she felt stunned at how much anger she had expressed and how, toward the end, her conflicted emotions came through. What had Clyde known that she had not? Feeling brittle, she pulled the earphones from her head thinking she must destroy this tape. She looked around for a way to accomplish that, which, of course, was ridiculous because her brain had recorded the lesson; it would play on inside her until she found a way to still it.

She put both the tape and the recorder in the drawer in her bedside table and turned off the light and pulled up the covers. For some reason she remembered that her mother had suggested that her father had taken her out on their first date in response to some sort of dare, a bet perhaps. He liked to take her dancing, liked the way she expressed herself physically, enjoyed others watching them.

From the beginning of their relationship her mother said she saw how the rebel in him mixed possessiveness and contempt, how crossing the racial line and getting away with it somehow pleased him. Later, when the prejudicial heat became too hot to bear, he requested a transfer into the US Information Service, which was part of the CIA. Soon after that they left for England.

When Mary Ruth and her father arrived, he explained that her mother had refused to leave Kentucky. He could not, he said, leave Mary Ruth in the hands of a woman who would not provide the kind of Catholic upbringing his belief required. Her mother had caused the forbidden divorce by refusing to come along.

Shaken by this newer version of what had happened, sure that it was the truer one, Mary Ruth fell asleep and dreamed that her body was covered with an itchy rash. Fitful, she tossed and tossed until the doorbell and Sister Dominic's bedside bell woke her. She stumbled to the bedroom window and knocked on it to let Clyde know that she heard him. Quickly she dressed.

Clyde stood bouquet in hand, eyes still swollen from sleep. "It's cold out here," he said. "Here, M'Ruth, hold these."

She closed the door, took the bouquet. Baby's breath, daisies, small freckled lily-like blooms that spiraled up their stems. Seeing him this way, boyish and vulnerable, with flowers, made her feel shy.

"She up?" he asked.

"I am," called Sister Dominic.

He took the flowers. Mary Ruth's eyes followed them as he moved into the bedroom.

"Sorry," Clyde said to Sister Dominic, "birds-of-paradise aren't in season."

"You," the old woman said, waving one hand at him and sniffing them.

"The purple and pink ones are—I practiced this— A-stro-mer-i-a." He smiled with such replete affection.

"You shouldn't have," the old woman said, clearly pleased that he had. Sister Dominic looked every bit the night-capped

Rembrandt lady. Mary Ruth helped her into the snap-front model's coat of pastel sprays and swirls that the sodality ladies had given her.

"I'll get a vase," she said.

"Beauty turns my head. What can I say?" he said.

"You're a devil you are."

Mary Ruth watched Clyde's dark fingers circle Sister Dominic's swollen ankles, watched him gently raise each leg, urging her on with just the right mix of gentleness and firmness. "One more time, Sister D. Just one more. You can do it," until one more time became, five, six, seven. Clyde anticipated her pain, knew when to push, when to hold back. Mary Ruth hated herself for envying his attention, for feeling so much petty jealousy. He must be a skillful teacher.

"My leg took no vow of obedience. God will get you for this," panted Sister Dominic.

Clyde did the heavy leg lifting as Mary Ruth held and moved the modesty towel, clicked the stopwatch, made hatch marks counting the number of times Sister Dominic did each exercise.

"I'm going to die."

Clyde smiled at Mary Ruth, said, "Not lucky enough."

Mary Ruth inhaled his spicy rum aftershave, never would have guessed Clyde could be so attentive and loving. The stopwatch on her palm grew hazy.

Sister Dominic grumbled, "People are entitled to mercy same as a horse or a dog."

"You'll be kicking up your heels in no time."

"I'd just as soon kick the bucket."

"Sister Dominic, don't say that!"

The old woman's arm searched for the cardigan sleeve Mary Ruth held behind her. She said, "Wait and see how you feel at my age. I've applied for sainthood."

"I'll get the ice, Methuselah."

Mary Ruth eased pillows under the old woman's knees and folded the blanket down to the foot of the bed. She took Sister Dominic's hands and looked into her pain-filled eyes. "We, Vivian, Kimberly, Clyde and I, are one hundred percent here for you. You *will* walk."

"That's true," Clyde said, setting down the tray with bags of slush on it. He placed his hands over Mary Ruth's. "We love you. We all love you."

Mary Ruth filled with a feeling she couldn't identify and shivered.

"I know, I know," Sister Dominic said, trying to hide her pleasure. "Let's get this bundle of joy over with."

They shaped the slush to her knees. Mary Ruth's eyes met Clyde's. Tenderness. So much tenderness.

"Might as well be chilled inside as out. Dear," she said, addressing Mary Ruth, "bring us some ice cream."

"Clyde?"

"A little chocolate, dab of marshmallow."

The spot where Clyde had touched Mary Ruth's hand buzzed with a kind of electricity.

As soon as she thought Mary Ruth was out of hearing range, Sister Dominic said to Clyde, "Spare me from becoming a cabbage. Get me one of those living wills."

"I thought you Catholics liked suffering."

Back in her novice days when she requested toothpaste, she had hoped and prayed to receive a brand she liked, not some odd-tasting one like Vademecum. Back then she had believed it was not her place to question; now, she intended to take matters into her own hands.

"I'm serious," she said. "Serious. Will you do it?"

"Why?"

"I want a living will." Reassuring him, she said, "I'm not intending anything foolish. Vivian won't get me one of those forms. Will you?"

"Okay."

"Good." She covered her heart with her hand, crossed her lips with her finger, said, "Shhhhh."

He winked at her. "Got it." After a moment, he said, "I'd better see if M'Ruth needs help."

Clyde took the jar of marshmallow cream Mary Ruth was trying to force open and twisted it easily. "Sometimes it works if you run hot water over the lid."

"I'll remember. Thank you. She seems depressed."

"I don't think she is, not in the serious sense. I'll bring my portable TV. Let her watch soap operas, learn about real hardship. I'll teach her to play chess."

"She loves card games." The brightness of his smile caught Mary Ruth by surprise. Certainly he had a lady friend. Not Ellie Sweet, someone closer to his own age. She felt a rush. "You're a miracle worker. Here, take yours. I'll carry hers and mine."

They enjoyed banter and ice cream. Mary Ruth found herself hoping Vivian would be gone a long, long time.

CHAPTER FORTY-SEVEN

Vivian's mother's condition continued to improve and her old spirit returned. While Vivian felt a bit of shame for allowing herself to over imbibe, she knew her family recognized the event as an exception, and had actually enjoyed seeing her that way. Nevertheless, she resisted the pain of what she was deeply feeling.

Still, while her mother was pulling herself together, *she* was falling apart. Hoping for forgiveness, Vivian had arrived in Texas as a prodigal daughter only to discover her prodigal mother. Now she hoped routine and solitude would mend her soul. She rescheduled to a midnight flight as if returning earlier to Sleeder would hasten resolution. Vivian expected to silently slither back into safety, forgetting that neither routine nor solitude existed at home.

The morning Angelus tolled Vivian awake. She rolled onto the floor and kissed it. She said her morning prayers, dressed. While descending the stairs, she thought she heard a man's voice coming from Sister Dominic's room. She glanced at her watch; it was barely 6:30.

"Good morning," Sister Dominic said, spotting her.

"How do?" Mr. Johnson said, pulling one of Sister Dominic's legs out to one side.

Beside him, Mary Ruth dropped the towel she was holding.

"You're back," Mary Ruth said. "I, we didn't know." She brushed Vivian's cheek with hers, first one, then the other offering the kiss of peace. "Peace be with you," she said.

"And with you," Vivian answered. *What on earth is going on here?*

"I thought you weren't d-due until later today," Mary Ruth said, flubbing.

"I wasn't," Vivian said. She looked from one to the other of them.

"God's answered our prayers," Sister Dominic said, hitching her thumb toward Mr. Johnson.

Vivian blinked, bent, and extended the kiss of peace to Sister Dominic. They were all in violation of the Grand Silence. "How are *you*?" she asked.

Sister Dominic said, "Thanks be to God for your mom's health, for your safe return." She tilted her head in Mr. Johnson's direction. "He's a hard taskmaster." The twinkle was back in the old woman's eyes.

Mary Ruth stood with her eyes downcast.

Vivian was still half-asleep, jolted from precious quiet to face whatever this was. "Mr. Johnson, you're early enough."

"We're working on it."

Mary Ruth hastily said, "He's helped many athletes."

"None as stubborn as this one," Clyde said, tweaking Sister Dominic's toe.

"Stop that!" Sister Dominic moved her toes away from him, pointed. "Clyde's TV."

"I see." On top of the TV stood a deck of cards, a bowl of nickels. Mary Ruth looked guilty, knowing full well she should have identified her "helper." Vivian collected herself.

"So, it's Clyde now, is it?" she asked. "It's kind and generous of you to help, especially at this hour."

"They're turning me into an inch worm," Sister Dominic said, touching the walker.

"She's walking faster than that," Mary Ruth said, clearly hoping for some sign of approval.

Vivian closed her eyes. She set her thumb and forefinger on the outer corners of her eyes and brought them together at the bridge of her nose. Obviously, they had managed.

"Well," she said.

"H-how is your mother?" Mary Ruth asked.

Vivian made eye contact. "Not as chipper as Sister Dominic, but coming along. She's doing physical therapy, too. Time. We're ... hopeful." Vivian looked toward the hall. "Kimberly?"

"She left already," Clyde said. "She's one dedicated, hard-working woman."

The library wasn't open at this hour! Vivian's gaze landed on the bowl of nickels.

"Sister D plays a mean game of poker."

Vivian turned to the old woman. "She does?"

"Can teach you," Sister Dominic said, grinning.

"I'll bet you can. Carry on," Vivian said, waving her hand. "I'll do breakfast."

"We have already eaten," Mary Ruth said.

Vivian felt more disposable than she wanted to admit. Had they given up silence altogether?

"Okay, Sister D, torture time."

Vivian left them, turned on the flame under the kettle, turned around to see Mary Ruth.

"About Clyde," Mary Ruth said, shifting her weight, nervously cupping her hands back and forth.

It was natural to feel left out. What they had done had worked. "Sister Dominic looks rejuvenated," she said. "I'm pleased."

"Thank you," whispered Mary Ruth, not one to tempt fate, disappearing as quietly as she had arrived.

Vivian dropped bread slices into the toaster, wondered how St. Anthony children were faring in public school, and what possibly called Kimberly away so early in the day. She heard Mary Ruth and Clyde bantering with Sister Dominic. They were good for her. At 7:15 Vivian rinsed her dishes and crossed the playground to call Jennifer before the girl left for school.

Wires and iron reinforcements protruded from the school walls. Capped plumbing pipes stuck out. Window shades, blackboards, even toilets and sinks gone. The sisters had stockpiled boxes. Except for a layer of plaster dust, only the gym remained unchanged. Vivian stepped over a bundle of chalk ledges and picked up an empty box and took it to her office. When she found the phone line dead, she panicked. *How will I contact Jennifer? How will I have privacy?*

She pulled out her top desk drawer and dumped its contents into the box. She turned the drawer upside down, removed the key, and slipped it into her pocket. She tossed items indiscriminately into the box. Chaos like this summed up her life. She finished what she could in the time she had, wrote her name boldly in blue felt tip pen on the boxes, and pushed them against the wall. She made her way through the school peering into each office.

The lay teachers had done a more thorough cleaning of their rooms than either Mary Ruth or Kimberly. In Kimberly's room a pile of children's drawings lay on top of an unsealed box. The artwork of small children always tugged at her heartstrings.

She crossed to the drawings, remembering the ones Cory and Annie and Tim had sent her for Christmas. She deciphered a child kicking a ball, sun over flowers, ill-placed limbs, upturned and downturned mouths. She shook her head in wonder, reached into the box to see if there were more. Kimberly no doubt intended either to preserve or return the drawings.

Vivian's fingers landed on what felt like a compact. Curious, she opened it and saw a circle of pills. She was sure she had seen a photo of this compact in a magazine ad. She dropped it and quickly covered it with innocent drawings, stifling a shrill, sound. Was nothing as it seemed?

Get a grip, she told herself, wondering if Kimberly, like Sister Dominic, had kept some medical condition from her. Was the young woman ill? Dare she ask? Feeling brittle to the breaking point—perhaps she had failed miserably and their novice— She remembered the appointment she had made before leaving for Texas. Now she crossed the street to keep it with the last person she wanted to see.

Atypically Father Rupert wore faded jeans and a dark plaid flannel shirt. Dark half moons under his bloodshot eyes suggested he hadn't been sleeping. After inquiring about her mother, he said, "I know you have a lot to do, but I need the books completed through the end of the year."

"I'll get to them as soon as I can."

Is Kimberly sleeping with you? Vivian considered, then discounted the priest. Kimberly disliked him as much as she did. *Still, it was a priest just like you who turned my parents' lives into a moral hell.*

"The parish," he said, "it's changing."

She remained silent.

"I no longer know who my boss is: Father Abbot, the bishop, the city commissioner?"

I know the feeling. The pope? Reverend Mother? You? Priests took, if not the frosting, the whole cake. *I answer to God.* Uncomfortably she realized that Kimberly did, too.

He said, "This isn't why I was ordained. I presumed saving mankind."

Life would be difficult for him without students snapping to attention, saying, "Yes, Father. No, Father." *I presumed saving myself. The Church promised to take care of me, too.*

She ventured, "We're an endangered species, Father." With an act of will, she set aside her mental distraction, asked, "Do you know what's going to happen to the convent?"

"I told them they couldn't go in until you leave. Administration offices."

"Thank you."

In the awkward silence that followed she noticed the calendars on his wall indicated a lot of free time.

"Vivian, you are the one who made everything click around here."

Oh, you know that, do you?

"You kept us going when I couldn't. Now it'll be ... different."

Vivian was surprised at what appeared to be sincerity. She had taken no more effort to understand him than he had to understand her, no more time than she had taken to befriend her own mother. She softened. It was too late to change anything between them.

"I appreciate your saying so," she said. "I'll do the school's bookkeeping as I can."

"That'll do." Without bothering to stand, he raised his hand and blessed her. "*In nomine Patrie, et Filii et Spiritu Sanctu. Amen.*"

That he used the old Latin moved her immeasurably. Still, it was a gesture motivated by control, wasn't it?

CHAPTER FORTY-EIGHT

On the day of Vivian's return from Texas, Kimberly left the convent before dawn and took the bus downtown, rented a car, and drove three-and-a-half hours to Springfield. Her efforts toward egg donation had moved unbelievably fast and smoothly. Not only had her father sent a complete family medical history accompanied by the added benefit of his medical knowledge, but also photos of family members he thought would interest her. To these Kim added some of herself at different ages and forwarded everything to LifeSpring along with a copy of her test scores.

Given her tendency to say too much, she felt apprehensive about today's interview. Brenda's prodding bothered her: *When are you going to get out of your head and on with your life? Isn't that what I'm doing?*

The young receptionist greeted her warmly and took her coat. Kim wore a light teal silk blouse that brought out the hazel color of her eyes, an expensive suit of Italian textured fabric, taupe with a pink cast that made her skin glow. Shoes, purse, and gloves, all a teal/charcoal hue. She anticipated this outfit which she had owned prior to convent life, would suggest a motive other than financial. The receptionist escorted her to an office where a desk and computer took up only a corner of the room. More noticeable was the living room setting, a sofa and chairs, lamp tables, soft lighting.

"I'm Judy Whitlock," the slightly overweight woman said, coming forward, extending her hand. "I've been looking forward to meeting you." The woman's maternal smile put Kim instantly at home. In her mid-forties, Mrs. Whitlock was the kind of woman anyone wanted to hug.

"Call me Judy," she said.

"I'm glad to be here. Call me Kim."

Judy wore a white blouse with a small offside ruffle at the neckline and a dark skirt. Her suit jacket hung on the back of the computer chair.

"The sofa's comfortable. Would you like tea, coffee?"

"Maybe later. Your map was excellent. I had no difficulty."

"Good. The information you sent arrived quickly and complete. We're all impressed. Everything's there. Usually some pieces are missing."

"Thank you. I wish I could take all the credit. My father who's a doctor—you know that—has been gathering family history for a long time. When he was still in medical school he researched a branch of my mother's family as a gift to her." She was saying too much. "That started what became his lifelong interest. I was lucky to be able to call upon him."

"Your parents approve of your application then?"

"No. Yes. I don't know. I mean I didn't mention it. I'm sure they would approve."

The woman smiled.

"It just—well, this seemed like a private matter. At least until it's a *fait accompli*." *Relax.*

Judy smiled warmly. "Confidentiality is important, more so to some couples than to others. Not all our recipients are married. Would that make a difference to you?"

Kim hadn't considered the idea. "Do you mean I have a say?"

"To some extent. Do you have any restrictions in mind? Religion, for instance."

Sticky subject. Kim felt panic, didn't know what to say.

Judy must have picked up on her discomfort, because she reassured her. "Many terms can be negotiated and included in the contract. For instance, some recipients and donors agree to continue involvement; others don't. An example might help. In a recent agreement, the two parties agreed that at least once a year around the time of the child's birthday, the recipient would write a letter and send a photo of the child to the donor. They agreed that at a time chosen by the recipient, the child would be told of the nature of its conception, and that if the child when grown wanted to meet the donor, the recipient would agree to such a meeting." Judy paused to let the information sink in. "If you were a donor child, would you want to know?"

Kim felt scrutinized. *Don't go hyper.* "I don't know. I might. Roots are important, aren't they?" She squirmed. "Surely the child would be—well. They say adopted children often experience something as missing. I expect it could be the same for a donor child. My emotional bond, my attachment, would be to the parents raising me, wouldn't it? Once I knew about coming from a donor, naturally I suppose I would be curious. Meeting the donor would fill in that missing piece, wouldn't it? I also think I would be concerned about hurting my parents. If they were comfortable with me meeting the donor, that would relieve my concern, wouldn't it? Otherwise, I probably wouldn't pursue it and continue experiencing something as missing."

Judy nodded, smiling softly. "I noticed you didn't name a religion. Would you object to a recipient of any particular religion?"

"The reason I wrote in 'moral, ethical, concerned about the human condition,' is that I didn't want to rule out any particular religion. I am a Christian who regularly goes to church and am aware that most people in the world are not Christian. They're Buddhist or Hindu or Taoist or Muslim. It depends on where one lives, doesn't it? I think we're all seeking God—goodness—by whatever name one prefers."

"To what might you object?"

"I suppose ... well, I think my one objection would be ... intolerance. Quakers are tolerant. Unitarians, Bahais." Kim stopped abruptly, feeling embarrassed, and she knew it showed. "I think accepting others who think differently, at least honoring their right to think differently, is important."

"Do I hear a 'but'?"

Careful. "To me, anyone who claims to know the only right way to God or goodness is suspect. By that definition some fundamentalists on the far right might fall into the intolerant category. I mean no one holds an exclusive right to God's ear!" Kim experienced panic. *What if Judy's a fundamentalist!*

Judy made a check mark on a small slip of paper that she held under her thumb over the folder in her hand. Kim hadn't noticed it before. Kim told herself to slow down, to think before she answered, and drew deep breaths and tried to exhale slowly to steady herself. She tried to see herself as Judy's did.

"Dr. Lovejoy says you couldn't be healthier. Let's see. Yes. You included your childhood diseases. What were you like as a child?"

"Curious. Definitely curious. An only child with parents who devoted a lot of time to me as well as to social causes. Spoiled, I guess."

Judy smiled. "Causes?"

"Christmas for the needy. Shelters for the homeless. Dad volunteered one afternoon a week at different schools seeing children whose parents couldn't afford medical care, and he was always on call at shelters. If there was an outbreak of some contagious disease, he'd go. Or if he was doing inoculations he often took me with him. Sometimes Mom, too."

"Tell me about your father."

"Incredibly patient and thorough. Kind. He expected directions to be followed."

"Your mom?"

"A fighter. She didn't hesitate to take on the city fathers. If they were, say, backing down on opening a halfway house for the mentally ill because neighbors objected, she would advocate for it. Mom was a professional volunteer. She gathered data and challenged objections. She knew that only a very small percentage of the mentally ill fell into violence or perversion and that those kinds of patients wouldn't be placed in a neighborhood anyway."

"Are you a professional volunteer?"

"Well, I ... tend to ... pull for the underdog. Maybe underdog's a poor choice of word. For example, I have a soft spot for new immigrants. Coming from Arizona I saw firsthand how difficult the transition could be—loss of friends and family, having to learn English idioms, new customs. I think we take the best from everyone who comes. The melting pot made this country strong, didn't it? The earlier children understand this, the healthier their relationships are apt to be with those they might consider different from themselves."

She was talking passionately, saying too much, couldn't seem to stop.

"I empathize with any woman seeking an abortion. For the right reasons, of course. I mean, if she/they can't afford to bring up a child, the child could be shortchanged, couldn't it? I mean life's hard enough without starting out unwanted. It's not for me to judge. I mean, it's enough to say I believe in a woman's right to choose."

A few beats of silence.

"Have you ever had an abortion?"

"No."

"You have strong opinions."

"I'm not wishy-washy." *God! Shut up!*

"Might I have that cup of coffee now? Please."

Judy crossed to the roll-in cart near her desk. She poured and handed Kim the cup and sat again. She said, "I wasn't going to get into this until later, but this seems like the right time. You mentioned accepting people who some might call different. What is your attitude toward a nontraditional recipient?"

Kim frowned. "You mean a single parent?"

"That or a same sex couple."

Kim set down her cup. "I haven't reflected about that possibility. Thinking aloud, I assume LifeSpring doesn't accept everyone who applies, that you screen carefully and expect certain qualifications—financial stability, psychological stability—which is more than a lot of children are lucky enough to be born into." Kim breathed quietly. "I doubt I would object to anyone you've scrutinized and accepted."

Judy smiled openly. "I didn't think you would. Now. Why is a pretty, intelligent young woman like you not married?"

Kim's coffee cup tilted. She should have anticipated this question. She held the cup with both hands now, put her elbows on her knees to steady it.

"The most honest answer is, I was engaged. He ... died."

Judy appeared stricken. "Oh. I'm so sorry."

"Thank you. It was awhile back. We expected to marry, have a family—" *Unnecessary.* Kim swallowed. "He was a good man. W-we had friends with whom we double-dated, Brenda and Mike. When Brenda and Mike tried to have a child, they couldn't. Firsthand over many months I experienced their frustration and anxiety and longing. When they finally had a daughter by *in vitro*, they were ecstatic. It was from their experience that I learned how much wanting a child can hurt. That's how I came to believe it would be a loving and generous gift to help someone who couldn't have a child."

"It is," Judy said. "No boyfriend since then?"

"Not one to mention."

"No one now?"

As if Guillermo were alive Kim felt his love stir and amplify inside her. She said, "My fiancé was an American of Mexican descent. Five feet eight, dark-complexioned, mustache, handsome, brave, a good human being. He cared about helping others. We laughed a lot." Kim rested her hand over her heart. "He's here." *Don't ask how he died!* "Almost four years ago."

"And no current boyfriend?"

I have to give her something. "If anything's going to come of it, it's a couple of years away."

"Why so?"

"I'm, uh, thinking about going back to school for my doctorate. You know how much time and focus that takes."

"In?"

"Something in the humanities."

"What university?

"Don't know yet."

"Tell me about this young man."

Kim sipped her cup empty, swallowed, thought. "He's very good with people, learned in a maverick sort of a way. A carpenter. I mean he speaks his own mind."

"How is he like your fiancé?"

"Well, my current friend is Jewish, so they have ethnicity in common. Both tend, tended—I'm having trouble with tenses—to fight, for what they believe, respectfully, of course, and were, are, leaders, who are good with people."

"How are they different from each other?"

"My fiancé would overrisk. Sometimes it was hard watching him." That last terrible picture of Guillermo came to her. She blinked it away. "This friend's less easily fooled, people perceptive in a deeper way,"

"My guess is you aren't easily fooled either."

"I like to think I'm not, but pride goes before the fall, doesn't it? Narrow is the gate," Kim said, referring to a Matthew *Bible* passage.

They smiled.

Judy glanced at her watch. "You're scheduled to take the Multiphasic in ten minutes. I'll show you where the ladies' room is. After the Multiphasic, you're welcome to join some of us for lunch or, if you prefer, go on your own."

The Minnesota Multiphasic Personality Inventory posed problems like: I would rather be a forest ranger than a ballet dancer. I prefer adding numbers by hand to using a calculator. It is all right to lie if it prevents hurting someone's feelings. I would like a career in precision mechanics. As a child I was frequently constipated. I like to keep opinions to myself. When I am angry I hold my urine. I follow authority to the strict letter of the law. By the time Kim finished, her brain felt wrung out and her body ached for lack of movement. The same question had been asked so many different ways, no one could fool such a test. There was too much at stake for her to say the wrong thing. She elected to lunch on her own, during which she hoped to regroup.

Once outside, she walked briskly for the first half-hour. She couldn't get Brenda's words to go away. *What did Brenda mean— spending too much time in my head, get on with my life?* She stopped and ate a light salad, then walked back to Holy Family Church, which she had passed earlier, and went inside and prayed.

All this is happening so fast. This must be in keeping with your will. Once the process starts I need to be able to finish it. It would be cruel to raise a couple's hopes, then not fulfill them by moving away. Give me your blessing. Guide me to appropriate, truthful answers. Don't let me trip up. I want to offer the gift of life and happiness to a family who badly wants a child. I am yours.

* * *

As cozy and warm as Judy's office had been, Dr. Jeffrey Payne's proved stark as a cell, emotionally cold. When he moved, the fluorescent reflection on his shaved head roved a shiny beam across it. The man was formidably large-boned. Kim couldn't tell where the sleeve of his burnished brown suit ended and his hand began. An open manila folder on the desk before him seemed the size of a recipe card. The psychologist's presence absorbed all the space.

He said, "You teach in a Catholic school."

"Yes."

"Are you Catholic?"

She didn't want to discuss her particular views of Catholicism, which some, including Protestants, considered overflexible. "Yes."

"You hedged your answer."

She fidgeted.

"I answered as truthfully as I knew how."

"Are we playing a game? You didn't say you were Catholic."

You are. "I'm not."

"Explain what you meant."

She said, "There is Catholic and what some people think it means to be Catholic. I wouldn't want to confuse the issue."

"I am confused."

Don't let him make you angry. "All right. I consider my religion, my relationship with God, to be individual and personal. Given limitations, my own and those by virtue of being human, faith can be seen only in action. That's why I answered 'moral, ethical, concerned about the human condition.' "

"You're ashamed of your religion."

"No."

"I think you are."

"Doctor, if you are as firm in that belief as you sound, nothing I say will dissuade you. I am comfortable with Catholicism. If I were not, I would seek another path of worship."

"Which one?"

"That's a moot question, like asking me if I weren't married to this man, which other one would I choose? I'm comfortable with and committed to my relationship to God. If I become uncomfortable with it, I will consider other options. At the moment none are open."

He tapped the crease of her folder on his desk. "If you are happy teaching in a Catholic school, why are you thinking about getting more education? Why not continue doing what you're content with?"

I'd like the answer to that one! "The matter's under consideration. No decision is made."

"Oh, it's only a dream, like going to the moon or becoming a motorcyclist."

Or murdering a psychologist!

Kim counted backward from ten, said, "I usually make decisions based on goals. Currently I am setting new goals, one of which may be earning a Ph.D." *Is this how Vivian feels when Father Rupert plinks her like an old banjo? You will not rob me of my power.* "Technology is changing so fast, it will be hard for any of us to keep up. My ultimate goal is to improve my earning skills."

He made eye contact. "You have a high opinion of yourself."

"Would you prefer low self-esteem?" She smiled.

One corner of his lipline raised, granting her the point. "You don't think you're being adequately compensated."

"Doctor, it's no secret that Catholic schools pay less than public schools."

"Why?"

"We— Catholic schools are experiencing teacher shortage. Traditionally convents staffed Catholic schools and convents are now short of applicants. Because the sisters worked for little or no pay salaries weren't part of the budget."

"So I understand. Foolish women. Then Catholics value education less than others do?"

Bastard. One one-thousand, two one-thousand. Take no bait. "That might be one perception. Another might be that education plus moral teaching is so valued by Catholics that parents are willing to pay tuition in lieu of accepting public school education which they already support with taxes. In that scenario, faith and values take priority." She held eye contact until he looked away.

Without looking at her, he asked, "Are you not concerned about the Church's attitude toward egg donation?"

"I am unaware of the Church's attitude, though I have my own. Helping a childless couple conceive seems like a remarkable gift to give." Her lips parted. She closed them.

He smiled more to himself than to her, asked, "What makes you angry?"

Narrow-minded people. "Rigidity."

"How does that apply to your school situation?"

Careful. "Sometimes I feel angry toward the principal. Sometimes her goals seem at odds with mine. After all, I teach first grade."

"What do you mean?"

Damn, I said too much. "Teaching first-graders includes a lot of play; running a school is not play."

"An example is—" He studied her.

Kim pondered what she had meant. She said, "There's a game I play with the kids called choo-choo. I invented it in a way that makes it flexible enough for me to cover many subjects simultaneously, to draw little bees into the sweetness of learning. I include material that connects boxcars to other material, along with teaching how to follow rules, how to share responsibility, whatever skills makes sense in the moment."

"For instance?"

"For instance, I combined singing, 'We Are the World' and having each child, each boxcar, share a custom from his or her heritage. The kids interviewed their grandparents beforehand and came in prepared to tell their story." Kim launched into the respective roles of the engine, the coal car, the boxcars, the caboose. As she shared the kids' stories, acted them out, *woo-wooed,* her enthusiasm rose and she quoted nearly verbatim. "The lesson goal was to teach that we are simultaneously, fundamentally all the same *and* different. Difference is an individual strength. Recognizing our own individuality helps us accept people who, like us, are different." Breathless, she said, "I didn't mean to run on."

He smiled. "I enjoyed it. How would what you just explained be at odds with your principal's goals?"

Kim bit on her lip. "She thinks it unseemly for me to get down on the floor with the kids."

"Ah," he said. That's all he said, ah.

"Does she/he not teach?"

"She. Eighth grade."

"How old is she?"

Beyond her years. "Between forty-five and fifty."

Dr. Payne nodded as if he understood. Then he peered at her with eyes that seemed to bore through her.

"Why did you choose LifeSpring?"

"Once I decided donation was what I wanted to do, I consulted resources on the Internet. Everything I needed to know was in your information. After that, geographical convenience."

His expression softened. A twinkle appeared in his eye. He seemed to resist smiling. The man stood and extended his hand and said, "Thank you, Miss McCall."

Firm grip. Kim found herself out in the hall, back up against the wall, knees shaking. *God,* she prayed, *spare me from another interview like that one*

There followed more casual conversation with two interviewers and Judy in Judy's living room setting. They asked her feelings about disconnecting from her genetic heritage, what her psychological needs might be in the event of donating her eggs, how she felt about knowing or not knowing a recipient. They raised issues Kim had not thought of. She acknowledged that and said she would deliberate.

When only Judy remained, Judy smiled and said, "Dr. Payne's never been wrong about an applicant."

Kim pressed her lips together.

Judy laughed. "A royal pain. Pun intended. Anyway, I'm so sure you'll pass our tests that I'm going to suggest you pose for photos while you're here. You said it was hard for you to get away; it would save you a return trip. Once approved, LifeSpring puts photos on the Web and contacts recipients on the waiting list who seem appropriate."

Kim wanted to jump and yell *woo-woo*. Instead she pretended to be Vivian and said, "I appreciate your thoughtfulness. Thank you."

She posed until the photographer was satisfied, then drove home paradoxically weary and ebullient.

CHAPTER FORTY-NINE

Vivian wondered what had happened to the sisters during her absence. Sister Dominic fairly glowed with youthful spunk, Mary Ruth had taken up cooking with enthusiasm, and effusive, birth control-taking Kimberly wore sedate like a garment. The young woman spent long periods at the library, at least that's where she said she was. Vivian didn't know whether to confront the celibacy issue or leave it alone.

Mary Ruth reported they had shifted their main meal to a late dinnertime because of Clyde's schedule. When Vivian asked how she might help, Mary Ruth recited the menu: meatloaf, twice-baked russets, scalloped cabbage with green peppers, brown 'n' serve rolls, more time-consuming than what Mary Ruth usually cooked. Vivian sat before the food feeling more like a guest than the superior in charge. She felt like an extra tooth in a comb.

Sister Dominic said, "Dr. Milde said I should go slow, not push too hard. He said whatever I do I should not travel too soon, better later than sooner."

"What's too soon?" asked Kimberly.

"March, maybe April."

April! "Oh," Vivian said, "we might have finished the school year."

Sister Dominic paid no attention to her, announced proudly, "I'm lifting two ounces of sand on each ankle. Clyde got it from the Melroses. He says the first two ounces are the hardest, that in no time I'll be up to nine or ten. That doesn't sound possible.

When I reach what he calls my max, then I graduate to canes." She smiled at Mary Ruth. "I'll tap-tap like a metronome."

"Clyde cajoles her," Mary Ruth said.

"It hurts. It hurts a lot."

"Of course it does," Vivian said.

Sister Dominic said, "I go as fast as I dare."

"I'm sure you do," Vivian agreed, gesturing for her to pass the sour cream. "When you're ready, you're ready, not one second sooner."

"Thank you."

Apparently sin had taken Kimberly's tongue.

Sister Dominic looked around at them and announced with pride, "I cheat at cards."

"You don't!" Kimberly said.

"Clyde knows but pretends he doesn't. That makes it all right." The old woman brimmed with pleasure.

"I don't believe it," Vivian said. "I leave a saintly woman and come home to a cheating card shark!" She couldn't help but smile.

"Clyde plays her favorite tunes, too."

"And brings flowers," Kimberly said. "Not to mention his TV and VCR. Looks like romance to me."

Mary Ruth sent Kimberly the oddest look.

Sister Dominic turned to Kimberly. "*You* don't mind watching those videotapes."

"Someone has to check out what you watch. Ask if it's on after bedtime," Kimberly said, teasing, addressing Vivian.

"I don't watch after bedtime."

"Do, too."

"Only if I'm in pain and can't sleep."

Clyde is the center of their lives! Vivian's stomach felt queasy. The floor seemed to tilt. Being with her mother had overextended her. She was experiencing fallout, that's all. She must hold it together for Jennifer, who would be her priority. Jennifer needed her.

Rising, Mary Ruth said, "I saved the last of the baklava for tonight."

"Is everything else gone?" asked Vivian.

"Except for the store-bought fruit cake. Clyde doesn't like it."

He eats here?

Kimberly said, "Tell us about your mom."

Despite Vivian's ongoing confusion about what to do about Kimberly, she appreciated the question because it forced her to focus. She relayed how her mother's condition had progressed from the day of the operation until the end of her stay. She said she saw her mother in a new light now, that she owed all of them her gratitude, including Clyde, for being able to be with her mother. They inquired about Chris and the rest of her family. Vivian admitted she had gained a keen awareness of how daunting the care of young children could be. "I never dreamed what a toll it takes," she said to Kimberly.

"Guess it's a good thing you're not a mother."

Vivian gaze hardened sharply, but saw only innocence and quickly lowered it. *How dare I judge? Kimberly's sin, if there is sin, is certainly less than mine was.* Compassion, that's what the young woman needed, deserved.

Mary Ruth volunteered, "Maybe you already know, Vivian, the convent is going to become offices."

"Father told me. The man's ... despondent." Her tone suggested she might have been less than fair to him.

"What? Rain isn't wet?"

"When one person's muddle gets mixed up in another's muddle," said Sister Dominic, "things get difficult to sort."

For some reason, Vivian's mind turned to the notion of priests and nuns flogging themselves to demonstrate their love for God. Over time, the Church had boiled down its interpretation of family, religious or otherwise, to a dysfunctional residue. Flogging belonged neither in liturgy nor in life; flogging, plain and simple, equaled self-abuse.

Sister Dominic, who rarely complained, said, "I can't make peace with my new mission."

Vivian too quickly said, "That's my fault."

Mary Ruth said, "My mother has often invited me to live with her. I never have, you know, lived with her, not since I was four. I really don't know my own mother."

Vivian winced.

"Mum told my father about Bogalusa and he phoned Reverend Mother. Reverend Mother will no longer accept his calls."

Kimberly asked, "Am I missing something?"

Vivian and Sister Dominic exchanged a glance, then lowered their eyes.

"T-tell her," muttered Mary Ruth.

"Tell me what? What!"

Vivian moved hair from her view and pressed her index knuckle against her temple because she felt a headache coming on. "When Mary Ruth joined SIHMs," she said, "Mr. Vangaard and Reverend Mother ... arrived at an agreement."

"More like he extracted a contract from her," Mary Ruth said. "Some people would characterize my father as a white, self-righteous, militaristic, Catholic, Dutch Boer."

Oh, my! Vivian's hand went to her chest. "I'm sure he thought it was for your own good," she said, sounding breathless. "Not that I agree," she hastened to add.

"My mother is southern, Baptist, and black."

Kimberly looked from one to the other of them. "Am I the only one here who didn't know?" Receiving no answer, she said, "We're supposed to be family!"

Vivian hadn't noticed much evidence lately of shame distorting Mary Ruth's self-image. In fact, now that she thought about it, Mary Ruth seemed rather self-assured.

Kimberly said, "Roots are a birthright, something to be proud of. How could Mother agree to such a thing? That's ghastly. Like asking me to pretend I'm not half-Irish."

"You don't know my father."

When everyone in a family guards a secret, too much is missed. Vivian gripped the edge of the table. Sounding weak—feeling like the sky could crack open if she questioned authority— Vivian said, "It isn't like Mother to break a promise."

"African-American is not Irish."

Vivian felt faint, thinking, *Birth control is not celibate.* She pulled rote text from her brain, said, sounding wimpy, "It's not our place to question."

"Why would Reverend Mother send me back to school when we're short of help?"

Three assignments, three objections. Four. Vivian drew a deep breath, summoned courage. "I don't know why I'm being sent into retreat either, but I will obey."

Loud silence charged the air.

Vivian's faith divided into bits that seemed to float in the air like confetti.

"Even I know what that means." Kimberly, Kimberly.

"I d-don't want to talk about it."

The girl's tone changed to compassion. "In Guatemala we depended on strangers because we had to. Without language we formed a sacred trust, and the more we trusted, the safer we felt, and were."

Vivian recognized the invitation to open up. She couldn't.

Sister Dominic said, "That must sting."

You don't know the half of it.

288

Kimberly asked, "Is there any chance Mother might have mixed us up with some other St. Anthony?"

"I-I'm sorry," Vivian said, searching her pockets for a handkerchief. Not finding one, she pressed her napkin to her nose, did not want to cry in front of them.

Kimberly came and stooped in front of her and put her hands over Vivian's. "You're a great principal and a good superior," she said. "We all love you. It's unbelievable. If only you— If only you wouldn't be ... so hard on yourself."

Striving for perfection is an impossible goal. The floor of Vivian's soul melted with vulnerability. "Th-thank you," she muttered.

Kimberly reached up and moved Vivian's hair back and peered searchingly into her eyes. "Everyone knows you ran the parish and that Father took full credit for that. It's not ... cricket. Mary Ruth has her music, Sister Dominic, her cooking."

"And you?" Vivian asked. "What do you have?"

Kimberly let a beat pass. "The children. Still, I didn't feel like I belonged."

Vivian tried hard to imagine what it would feel like to grow up after Vatican II, to not know the Church's solid tradition as a cultural part of yourself. The young woman belonged to contemporary times and, in some ways Vivian had to admit, Kimberly was ahead of the rest of them. *Maybe Mother's right to call me into retreat.* She patted Kimberly's hand. "Thank you."

The novice returned to her chair and said softly, "I'm considering a project that might bring in some income. I'm not sure yet. I'd like to contribute if I can."

"Clyde increased his music schedule so he can learn as much as possible before we leave. I assumed that was all right." Mary Ruth tentatively touched a fingertip to the edge of her plate.

Mary Ruth had made Vivian's job easier. In the name of obedience she had kept silent about Mary Ruth's heritage and now she experienced that silence as complicity.

Sister Dominic said, "I would like to pose a question. None of us, thank you, is going to blow out our candles on the cake forever. I want a living will and I need to say who will speak for me if I am unable to speak for myself." She addressed Vivian. "If the order has an opinion on this, I don't want to hear it."

Whatever is happening to us?

Indeed Sister Dominic breathed shallowly as if her life depended on the answer—as it did.

"You're recovering," Vivian said.

Extended silence.

"Not one of you will give me this gift?"

"Oh, Sister, I'll stamp my feet, bang heads, and raise such a ruckus, they'll listen if only to shut me up. I'll do it. It's not like she's asked to have an abortion," Kimberly said to Vivian.

"We probably won't be around," muttered Mary Ruth.

Vivian felt tottery, like one of those inflated, weighted-at-the-bottom figures kids sometimes punched on the playground.

"My, my," Sister Dominic said, dropping her shoulders. "Only one out of three." She said to Kimberly, "Dear, don't ever let anyone dampen your old-fashioned pluck and determination."

The woman might as well have slapped Vivian. Vivian could not breathe. She felt spacey, disconnected. *How can I lead if no one will follow?*

"I'm tired of trying to act like a walking sermon," Mary Ruth said.

Kimberly, never one to shut up when she should, said, "I agree with the sisters who signed that *New York Times* ad."

That ad called for open dialogue on abortion; it called for plurality of conscience. In response, Rome prosecuted each of its twenty-four signers for being in contempt of canon law. The male signers caved in immediately. In the end, only two sisters held to their convictions.

Kimberly continued. "All they wanted was discussion. A sincere effort at communication."

Yes, and for that their orders dismissed them. The young woman was right about too many things which made Vivian wrong about too many.

Kimberly said, "I agree with Sister Marie Augusta, who's backed up by scholarship. Quote: 'The Church's major sexual problem is the human rights of women as they exist *in the consciousness of men.*' "

Vivian suddenly felt extremely tired, her spirit down-spiraling toward depression.

Kimberly said, "Someday, Sister Dominic, I hope to be as elegant and as wise as you."

"Why, thank you." The old woman fairly glowed.

Vivian caved in, said, "I think I need to lie down."

CHAPTER FIFTY

Riddled with guilt, Kimberly washed dishes. How could she challenge the others about keeping Mary Ruth's secret when she was keeping such a big one of her own? Still, when authority exceeded moral bounds, Christian soldiers, like any soldiers, should question authority. How could a woman as smart as Vivian bumble so, continue to accept anything and everything? Why could Vivian not acknowledge such obvious skeletons? Convents and monasteries had facilitated Nazi escapes. The Church had decanonized its own saints and failed to acknowledge its many HIV priests, failed to ordain women. Would the Church ever speak out against battering and sexual abuse?

Kimberly pulled out the sprayer and rinsed the dishes. Would the Church ever acknowledge women? Had Reverend Mother read the newsletter that she had anonymously subscribed to for her? *Will I get caught trying to brighten the corner of some loving couple's nursery?*

"Here you are," Vivian said.

Caught unaware, Kimberly startled. "I hope you feel better. You looked so pale when you went to lie down. Yes. I'm slow tonight."

"I do."

Kimberly squirted lotion on her hands, smoothed it in. She could hear Mary Ruth reading to Sister Dominic in the bedroom.

Vivian patted the chair next to the one she sat in, said, "Sit a minute. I'm concerned about you spending so much time at the library."

"I'm not shirking any duty. Mary Ruth and I discussed it. With Sister's exercises, I would only be in the way. Clyde knows what he's doing. When Sister Dominic gets up at night, I'm right there. I do my share of housework and am slowly, but steadily, packing up my classroom."

"I don't doubt you're helping. But why the library?"

"You can't believe the noise here. Sister Dominic moans and groans. They joke and laugh. And then there's the TV. I need quiet. What I knew about using a computer is coming back, though a laptop's harder to use. The keys are too close together, like using a calculator that's too small. I'm doing research."

"Research."

"Checking out universities, different aspects of ... gerontology, that sort of thing."

"Uh-huh. What have you concluded?"

"That gerontology is not for me."

"I'm not surprised."

Vivian twisted her ring nervously and seemed to be working at patience. Tending her mother had surely exhausted her. Going into retreat must be more than she could bear.

Vivian smiled falsely. "What about spiritual discernment?"

"That would be interesting for my own edification or entertaining if it would move me toward ordination."

"That's not likely."

Kimberly looked at Vivian. "I don't want to teach comparative religion. I don't see how discernment would earn a salary."

"Maybe after John Paul if there are any Catholics left," Vivian said, clearly referring to ordination. I agree. It is ... a sorry state of affairs."

How unlike Vivian!

"Would you say you've grown spiritually since we last talked? How?"

293

Kimberly picked at a cuticle. Soft from lotion, it resisted. "I've been too upset to notice. I wish we had time to get used to the idea of closing. I mean I, we, could have taken part-time work." She admitted, "I miss the children, their joy, their innocence, playing with them. I'll miss Brenda."

Brenda. "Yes, I thought you might be lonely."

"Not really. There's plenty to do. I saw Brenda a couple of times, but she's busy. Tax time's approaching."

"Mike, will you miss Mike?"

"I seldom see him, only when I'm invited to dinner. Only relative to Brenda."

Relative to Guillermo, too.

This upheaval had been hard on all of them. "Is there anything you ... wish to share?"

Kimberly frowned and thought, finally said," When I figure out what I want to do, I would welcome your support in convincing Reverend Mother."

"Nothing's troubling you? Nothing at all?" Vivian seemed so intense.

She can't possibly know. "Besides the forced move, besides Sister's accident, besides being assigned to the infirmary and heading back to school when I'd rather not?"

Vivian's index finger pressed against her lips as if trying to keep from saying something. Finally she sighed and said, "I guess it's a trying time for all of us." She hesitated then said, "When we give God a chance, he is loving and forgiving. I mean, when *I* give him a chance."

Kimberly smiled. The woman *did* listen. She was taking responsibility.

"Clyde seems to be here at all hours. How do you feel about his presence?"

"Super. What he's done for Sister Dominic is just super. He's upbeat. He was here the day she came home and in no time she needed to go to the bathroom. That's when they discovered that the wheelchair was too wide for the door. Mary Ruth said if it hadn't been for Clyde, she didn't know what she would have done."

Vivian thought a long time about what Kimberly had said. "You weren't here?"

"Glory was. And Father Rupert. And Clyde. And Mary Ruth. Too many chiefs. Mary Ruth said I wouldn't be needed."

"Father Rupert? Why was he here?"

Kimberly shrugged. "He seemed genuinely concerned."

Vivian deliberated a moment, shook her head mumbling to herself.

"Have you noticed how wretched he looks?"

"Yes." Vivian frowned, said, "I know how much you loved Guillermo. Having been ... so close ... I wonder if, well, if that makes celibacy ... overly difficult?"

"Actually I think it makes it easier because the mystery's gone. I think each of us might create a good life with any number of ... partners, though really Guillermo was one of a kind. I could never settle for less. Not that he was a saint," Kimberly hurried to say.

A dark shroud crossed Vivian's expression, a wave of what looked like pain.

Kimberly added, "I will always love him. He's gone." *Yes, but I haven't let him go. I measure a lot by what Guillermo thinks ... thought.* Anxious to move away from this subject, she said, "I'm glad your mother will be fine. How much you must love her, how relieved you must feel."

Vivian swallowed and seemed somehow disappointed. "Yes. I do. Thank you. I need to ask. Do ... you have a medical condition I should know about?"

The question surprised Kimberly. Then she remembered that Sister Dominic should not have kept her condition to herself.

"No. Nothing."

"If anything comes up, anything, you will feel free to tell me? You will do that?"

"Well ... sure."

"Anything. Anything at all."

"Okay."

After awhile Vivian got up and left.

Kimberly sat there still holding onto Guillermo, expecting him to take her in his arms. She realized something she hadn't known about herself. *I'm afraid to commit to anyone or anything that might disappear and leave me in unbelievable pain. I want to be Joan of Arc without getting burned!*

CHAPTER FIFTY-ONE

Sister Dominic watched as Mary Ruth punched her knee pillows like they were enemies. The poor hummingbird had no idea of the strength of the forces she faced. With all that had happened Mary Ruth had yet to break her father's hold on her.

"Dear, you're fond of Clyde, aren't you?"

"What's all this irrational business about dying? After all we're doing for you? You're not dying."

"It's inevitable. I intend to be ready." Sister Dominic considered a moment, said, "A father can only keep what his child refuses to claim."

Mary Ruth momentarily stopped fussing, then busily overreacted. She set out a pain pill, checked to see that the nightlight was on, pulled her covers higher, set her rosary nearby.

Watching, Sister Dominic couldn't help but wonder if God might want something different for this dear young woman than what she had claimed for herself? What if God intended her to be with Clyde? Sister Dominic rather enjoyed him. In fact, as she progressed, she fully expected her recovery to slow down. Why go to the infirmary sooner than she had to? Maybe she could help Mary Ruth. Kindly, she tried again. "Your father doesn't own you."

Mary Ruth turned pale, extinguished the light, and said, "Good night."

FIFTY-TWO

Time moved slowly as Kim waited to hear from LifeSpring, as slowly as the days after she had learned of Guillermo's death. That last image of him haunted her anew—her lover lying dead at the side of the road, his body covered with dust, his bloody crotch. This image clung to her as she thought about giving new life.

Vivian handed Kimberly a jar of jam from the basement shelf. "You seem preoccupied."

"No more than anyone else." Kim rolled the jar in unprinted newspaper and set it in the box. They were sorting through what to pack, what to sell, what to give away, what to discard. Kim had not seen Vivian in slacks before, slacks that belonged to another era. Kim did not understand the penetrating look Vivian gave her. Mornings, Vivian helped with Sister Dominic's exercises and, following cookbook directions, prepared a casserole for later in the day.

Vivian said, "Your hand is shaking,"

True. The jar of zucchini jelly betrayed her nervousness. Judy had e-mailed LifeSpring's approval of her application and said hard copy confirmation would arrive via snail mail. Vivian was keeping closer tally on her whereabouts, making scheduling interviews difficult. Fortunately not all couples wanted an interview.

A second e-mail from Judy said they were inundated with requests for more information about her. Kim e-mailed back requesting that interviews take a half day or less and be located within a two-hour radius of Sleeder. Keeping this endeavor secret ran contrary to her nature. She wanted to celebrate, not hide her news.

Vivian let the damp dust cloth she was using droop over the edge of the box and sat on the kitchen stool they used for reaching high into cupboards.

Vivian said, "Something is definitely bothering you."

Kim set the jelly jar back on the shelf. "Nothing. Everything. You were right. Guillermo's presence is still with me when I thought I had let go of him. I can't get used to— I don't like the idea of someone else deciding what's ... right for me." The raw lightbulb overhead lit only Vivian's head and neck; her superior appeared disembodied.

"It is never easy," Vivian said, "to lose someone you love. Whatever you're struggling with, I can try to help. I'm here to help."

"Vivian, thank you. This is one God and I have to wrestle through."

Vivian started to say something then stopped herself. Instead she said, "Perhaps you're spending too much time on the computer. I've read it can be addictive."

"No problem," Kim said, dismissingly.

Vivian waited, said sounding resigned, "If you say so."

Kim realized that Vivian needed to help her, that it was Vivian's job, and if she didn't give her something, Vivian would ply her with picayune interrogation.

Kim relaxed her guard and found herself crying. "Packing, leaving, somehow reminds me of Guillermo's death. The last time I saw him was ... awful. I know that part of my life is over. I'm not trying to get it back. I know Guillermo's gone. Th-the last terrible image of him lying there in the dust murdered by God knows who, with his ... his—"

Vivian stroked her hair. "You can say it. Whatever it is, say it."

"His penis stuffed forever in his mouth."

Vivian gasped and pulled back.

Kim shuddered full of deep pain and the shock of seeing him. She felt Vivian's hand on her shoulder. "I try to remember him alive, his smile, the sparkle in his dark eyes but that image—"

"So barbarian."

"It's—the Latin way. Exactly what's intended. Unforgettable."

Vivian grew agitated, became a big blur as she got up and brought a child-size chair for Kim.

Kim sobbed. "Severing a man from any p-possibility of regenerating himself. Cut from the source of his own children, the cruelty, the finality. Jesus Christ, how could anyone *do* such a thing?" Kim flailed. "What kind of God—"

Vivian hugged and rocked her. "You're safe now. Safe."

"No one's safe! No one's ever safe!"

"You are," Vivian said. "You *are*."

Kim released a torrent of pain. Vivian held her through all of it. She remained silent and wiped away Kim's tears with the tail of her blouse. Kim had expected some textbook instruction. She felt naked and vulnerable, exposed in the presence of such respectful silence.

That's what Brenda meant. Get out of your head. Let heart do its work.

Kim hiccuped sobs. "I don't want to be s-stuck. I want my life to have m-meaning, significance. That's what I want."

"It will happen for you."

Kim looked up. "Is this just a selfish wish of a spoiled child?"

"Kim, we all like to think we're unique when we're not. We all want our lives to be meaningful and significant." She stroked Kim's hair. "God gives us gifts and expects us to use them. You've compensated for this terrible grief for a long time. I don't know how you could function."

Kimberly didn't know what to say. While she had fought words against describing that image out loud, it felt good to finally tell someone.

"Can you remember him the way you loved him?"

Kim closed her eyes. *Mi vida*, Guillermo said, smiling and bending and kissing her eyelids softly.

"Are you doubting your vocation, thinking of leaving the convent?"

No. More like making the convent a better place.

"Not really." She felt too drained for a heady philosophical discussion. Some people escaped into their heads, others into music, or prayer, or duty.

"But if I chose to leave, I would hope to be the one to make that choice. Oh boy, my head hurts." Kim blew her nose. She picked up the jar she had set aside. "Who but Sister Dominic would make zucchini jelly?"

"It's surprisingly good. If you haven't tried it, do."

"I will," Kim said, standing and stretching her neck to one side then the other in an effort to relieve muscle tension. Vivian hoped for something more when Kimberly had already given more than she ever suspected she would. Vivian had been kind. Nevertheless, Vivian would not appreciate what she intended to do. Kimberly inhaled deeply, asking herself. *What is the worst that can happen?* The swift answer: *That I leave Sleeder before donation takes place.*

If that happened, she could reapply because LifeSpring belonged to The American Society for Reproductive Medicine. Her paperwork would simply go to another agency.

"Thank you, for listening, Vivian. I appreciate your kindness. Where were we before I drew out the best in you?"

CHAPTER FIFTY-THREE

"M'Ruth, you got something on you Ajax won't wash off!"

The more they were together the more they bickered. Something in her body buzzed like a fly locked inside a car; whatever it was, it wanted out. "You're riding the pedal!"

"This music's like a dog chasing its tail."

"Preferable to ragin' Cajun that starts in the middle, goes nowhere, and just stops." She hated to admit that Clyde's description of Bach was apt.

His eyes turned into lasers that burned through her. "M'Ruth, I can cotton to just about anything except— I'd like to shake some sense into you." He looked away, cracked his knuckles, said, "Sorry."

One thing Mary Ruth had decided for certain was that never again would she be without someone in her life to whom music was important, someone who might teach her a thing or two— NOT improvisation. She didn't want to think about that improv, refused to think about it. There were other things she could learn— like jazz. Even if he didn't know it, when she was with Clyde her life became like a coda, where every time she arrived at the choice of Repeat or End, memory failed her and she was forced to choose Repeat. She was stuck in a loop that kept her from completion. Why had she spilled so many secrets?

She stared at his beautifully tapered dark musician's fingers. "Stress," she said, "so much stress." She softened. "I'm sorry, too."

He stared at the piano keys with a strained expression.

One thing Mary Ruth knew, whenever Clyde was due to arrive, her heart fairly skipped with anticipation. As soon as he did though, she put an invisible shield between them, like the veiled grate through which cloistered nuns talked to visitors.

Mary Ruth counted the silence she and Clyde shared now in four-four time; she was afraid to speak, afraid not to. Between lessons he phoned and she would explain *ma non tanto* or *di molto* or *assai*, or other musical notations *ad infinitum,* words that sounded like mulatto. When she wasn't talking to Clyde on the phone or instructing him in person, she played selections from Bach's "Preludes and Fugues" which she hoped he would one day play and love as much as she did. She became overly aware of each moment *tick-tocking* them toward separation. Sister Dominic's walker *tap-tap, tap-tapped* out in the hall.

Clyde turned to her. Mary Ruth looked up into his eyes. What she saw made her soul somersault. "Please," she said, lowering her gaze, sounding out of breath, "continue."

Reluctantly Clyde did. His controlled fingering, his feverish silent counting prompted an image of the twin clocks on the twin spires, four hands ticking away at Roman numerals, one hundred-twenty times an hour, parsing life by the numbers, creating a void that insisted some absolute essence absent from her life.

Clyde's foot rested on the pedal; sound reverberated. He raised his lovely dark hand and softly asked, "M'Ruth, if you could take anything with you, what would it be?"

You! Her breath caught. *Where did that come from?*

Why, even if she knew the answer to his question, she wouldn't tell him.

"Play," she said.

He plunked without grace or enthusiasm, *chop-chop-chop.* The phrasing, made Bach sound even more repetitive than he was. No longer would she be able to help Clyde advance. Sister Dominic's query had duly warned her, had signaled knowing more than she herself knew, or wanted to know. She must shape and rehearse a cordial, formal good-bye.

Her foot lightly tapped in counterpoint to Sister Dominic's *tapping* in the hall. She thought of a first grade lesson Kimberly had shared: Kimberly had passed around a piece of chalk and discussed white as the absence of all color; then she passed around a lump of ebony and they discussed black as the presence of all color.

Is that all pigment was, the absence or presence of color?

Clyde's temple pulsed with concentration. Loneliness flooded her so intensely that she felt separated from herself, a loneliness remarkably different from the aloneness to which she had grown accustomed.

CHAPTER FIFTY-FOUR

LifeSpring had arranged an interview with a couple in a motel suite in Joliet, Illinois. While the organization usually sent a representative to such interviews, the Milcheks, who lived in Evanston on the northside of Chicago, insisted on meeting with Kim alone. They would, of course, pay expenses. Fortunately for Kim, Vivian had ceased questioning her. Because Kim didn't want to risk more questions, she didn't ask to use the convent car. Instead she borrowed Brenda's.

She drove. Nerves addled her. She wore forest green woolen slacks with a matching cardigan and a short-sleeved mint green silk blouse, black pumps, stud pearl earrings. She felt a constant urgency to urinate, though she didn't really need to. Before arriving at the motel Kim stopped at a McDonald's anyway to use the rest room and arrived on time at 10:30 a.m.

The desk clerk directed her. With trepidation she took a deep breath, let it out, and knocked. The woman who opened the door stood a little taller than she, had soft brown curls and peaceful, light brown eyes.

"Kim?" she said, breathlessly.

"Yes."

"I'm Sharon." She wore a dark brown, nubby-textured slacks suit with flecks of green and tan in it, loafers over nylons.

"Come in, come in. I'm Bill," her husband said, resting his hands on his wife's shoulders.

They shook hands. Kim felt immediately embraced in an aura of sincerity. Bill stood taller than six feet, lean, not particularly muscular. She noted his intensely interested hazel eyes. Sharon twiddled her fingers; her words came out in near whispers.

"Coffee? Tea? A soft drink?"

"Thank you. I'll wait a bit," Kim said. "I appreciate your meeting me halfway." She took a navy blue chair that didn't appear too deep and sat sideways so she could rest her back against the arm and sit erect, stay alert.

"We would do anything to meet a suitable candidate," Bill said. "Was it a smooth trip?"

"Yes, thank you."

He sat at one end of the sofa. Sharon handed him a cup of coffee, her eyes awash with the kind of love that belongs to new love. She perched on the arm of the sofa beside him, rested her hand lightly on his shoulder. They looked at Kim intently, as if trying to memorize her features.

"You teach at Northwestern," Kim said, addressing Bill. "I've heard its right on the lake."

"It is," Sharon said. "Lovely. You teach, too?"

"First grade."

"Do you like it?"

"I love the kids. They're so—" Kimberly, aware that this was a sensitive subject, stopped and swallowed. "Animated," she said. To hurry past the mention of children so soon, she said, "Teaching may be a stepping stone to something else."

The couple glanced at each other. Bill said, "We understand you may go for your doctorate. In what?" he asked.

"I've been thinking about gerontology. Heaven knows there's a need. However, whatever the field, I would like to use my organizational skills. I've successfully organized and supervised volunteers. I like the satisfaction that comes from watching the whole thing come together. Gives me a real high."

"I can identify with that," Sharon said. "I'm a social worker for the physically challenged."

Kim said, "You have extraordinary patience then."

"It takes ingenuity. Sometimes laws pass without provision for realistic expectations, like a client may qualify in more than one area."

Sharon could be flexible and had her client's interest at heart. That was good.

Bill said, "It's easy to miscast oneself in the wrong field. I learned that one the hard way. I'm teaching undergrad statistics, which is hardly my strong suit, not at all."

"Somebody has to do it," Kim said, rolling her eyes upward.

They laughed, melting the ice.

Kim asked him, "What is your favorite class?"

Sharon answered. "Not teaching at all. Bill has his heart set on opening a psychology practice. He, we—"

"We're in a bit of a Catch-22," he said. "Frieda—Sharon's mother—is ill."

"Alzheimer's," Sharon said, brushing his cheek with the back of her hand.

"I have excellent health insurance," he said. "If I leave teaching it would mean a temporary dip in income."

"And no health insurance," added Sharon. "Mother doesn't qualify for Medicare yet."

Sharon is at risk for Alzheimer's.

Bill said, "I use summer and holiday breaks to spell Sharon. Still, we like to think that when our kids graduate from college, we will still be young and healthy enough to do some of the things we can't do now. We don't want to delay having children much longer."

"Everything considered," Sharon said, "we're managing well."

Bill said, "To start a practice at the same time we're starting a family—"

And taking care of Mom. Kim reminded herself that the agency had approved them. They were putting both having a child and Sharon's mother's needs ahead of their own personal goals. Kim liked that.

Kim said, "Sounds like you're really thinking it through, like you agree on priorities."

"We do," they said in unison.

Kim smiled and relaxed.

Sharon said, "Everyday my work is about priorities." She gave a couple of examples, proving her both dogged and clever in meeting clients' needs.

Bill revealed two instances where students showed up his shortcomings in statistics. "It's almost like teaching numbers by the numbers," he said. "No one is seriously shortchanged, though. I share my biases and weaknesses and students have Internet resources now. I stay ahead of them most of the time."

"He spends hours on the Net to do it."

"Isn't it fun?" Kim asked. "I've logged on recently. That's how I found LifeSpring."

Sharon moved her hand to cover Bill's mouth. "Don't get him started on the Net," she said.

They laughed.

Bill went to the stove and refilled his cup. "Kim?"

"Please," she said. "Black."

"Tell us little things," Sharon said. "Like your favorite color. Your favorite game. Your favorite food."

"Good. Questions I can answer. I'm bold with color. Wouldn't dream of decorating in black or neutrals. One of my dreams is to take up oil painting so I can splash color about. I like interior decorating though I've not done much. I like acting games like charades. When it comes to food, I like everything as long as it's not boring."

Bill said, "You're a sensual person."

Kim lowered her gaze, felt found out, embarrassed. "You could say that."

"And creative," Sharon said.

Vivian didn't like that about her. "I think so." Everyone had creativity, even Vivian, who, if she let go of control, might discover it.

The couple seemed to communicate silently and to come to some sort of agreement. Sharon moved to sit on the sofa beside Bill. She asked, "Would you say that you have a spiritual life?"

"Oh. Definitely. I do. Yes."

Bill said, "Maybe you can describe how you experience it."

Kim looked at him. "Hm. Describe it. I like how you phrased that. Spiritual life is a practice, isn't it?" She thought a bit. "I start and end each day with a prayer, not a formal one, but one of my own creation. I believe in people, in the human family. Given a chance, I think each of us lets the best come out. I feel very much a part of creation, I mean I feel one with it and not more or less important than any other part of creation." *Am I talking too much?* "I like to think I give what I can, take what I need, a symbiotic thing. Energy is constantly changing and exchanging, re-energizing itself, buzzing about in glory. I'd say energy's at the heart of my spiritual life. I try to bring the best out in myself, though my ... friends might not interpret it that way."

"Do you believe in God?" Sharon asked.

"I suppose I define God as life energy and believe in putting that energy into action."

"You're an environmentalist?" Bill asked.

"Yes. There's the energy of ecology and the energy of psychology. We all experience people's vibes. Watch kids and you'll see how they respond to them." Maybe she shouldn't have suggested watching children, but they didn't seem to mind. "Vibes are powerful."

"Or," Bill said, "you mean they think the vibes they pick up are their own."

Kim thought about that. Little psyches had no boundaries, were easily invaded.

"Yes," she said.

A lull in conversation occurred as they thought.

Finally Sharon asked, "Is anyone besides me hungry?"

"I am," Bill said.

Kim had eaten early and was starved. "Sure," she said.

Bill said, "We brought stuff for a stir fry or we could go out."

"I'm having too much fun to break the mood," Sharon said.

"I agree," Kim said. "May I use the bathroom?"

When she returned the smell of sesame oil filled the air. Bill shuttled carrot slices around a wok. Sharon peeled shells from shrimp.

"Bill's the best cook," Sharon said.

They worked like an experienced team.

"I'm impressed," Kim said. "What can I do?"

"Nothing. Sharon's a great cook. Don't let her fool you. Just enjoy."

Sharon said, "Sometimes I'm in court or chasing an emergency at the end of the day and I stop and check on Mom before going home. Bill has regular hours so he usually starts the meal."

"She has real talent," Bill said, winking at his wife. "Doesn't get home until the food's prepared."

"And who washes the cars?" Sharon asked.

Kim asked, "Would you mind if I kick off my shoes?"

"Kim, I thought you'd never ask," Sharon said, slipping off her loafers. "You have a choice. Chicken, beef, or shrimp."

They're were trying to please her as much as she was trying to please them.

"Shrimp," Kim said, peeling beside Sharon.

"Like this," Sharon said. "If you peel toward the tail, the tail meat stays intact. Well, most of the time."

Kim tried and lost the tail meat. She and Sharon laughed. Kim tried again and succeeded.

Bill said, "We brought a bottle of wine to celebrate. Would that be all right?"

Kim nodded, said, "It sure feels like a celebration." She liked this couple and they seemed to like her. *What if I'm gone before we can proceed?*

Sharon leaned close and peered at Kim's hair. "It's naturally curly. No perm?"

"I can't stand the smell of perm."

"Me either," Sharon said, smiling.

"Ready for shrimp."

"You know your way around that wok," Kim said, amazed at how vegetables lay stacked along its sides, while the well cooked the shrimp.

"Oh, the rice!" Sharon said. "I need to microwave the rice. It's already cooked. Brown rice," she said to Kim.

Kim felt quite at home. Clearly this couple loved and respected each other. She had the feeling they didn't keep much from each other either, that a new child would feel as welcome as she did.

"This isn't my idea of china," Sharon said, setting out glossy blue paper plates. She struck a match to light the candle as Bill poured stir-fry into a bowl.

"When in Rome," he said

"Eat Chinese," finished Kim.

They laughed. Bill uncorked the wine. They sat on either side of her.

"Do the honors," Bill said to Kim.

Kim closed her eyes and trusted the right prayer to come. "This new relationship is already blessed with the pregnancy of love, with the pregnancy of life, with the pregnancy of all that is good now and in the future, whatever is decided. Amen."

Kim lingered after she should have left. After lunch, Bill suggested they read awhile to let their food settle. They had brought a tote bag of books and magazines from which to choose. Kim read an article Bill had published in a professional journal about children becoming parents to their parents.

They took a leisurely walk and discussed his article and politics and a range of ideas. When they returned Kim wanted to leave, but Bill convinced her to play a short game of charades, one turn each. Bill, with accurate irony, acted out his interview with Dr. Payne.

They laughed a lot.

"I must leave," Kim said, breathless after her mimed version of "From Here to Eternity." "I've overstayed. I'm due back."

Bill and Sharon looked at each other. Bill took Kim's hand and held it. "Thank you for coming," he said.

Sharon said, "You're the answer to our dreams.'

"I hope so," Kim said.

Sharon walked Kim to her car, hesitated, said, "May I ask a question? Not waiting, she asked, Your period, where are you in your cycle?"

It was a fair, if embarrassing, question with more to come. Kim poked in her purse for her calendar.

Sharon exclaimed, "We're only three days apart!

They embraced. It was a feeling like no other Kim had experienced, an instant bond.

"I-I'm in awe," Kim said. "I don't know any other way to describe what I'm feeling."

"Me too," Sharon said. "Bless you. We'll be in touch. Drive safely."

Kim smiled and waved and accelerated the car. It had been a most satisfying day.

CHAPTER FIFTY-FIVE

Other couples interviewed Kim, without hesitancy, she favored the Milcheks. They were her kind of people and she believed their marriage could withstand whatever fate dealt it. When they would leave remained unknown. Kim hoped the timing would work out. Sister Dominic's recovery had slowed.

LifeSpring finally approached Kim to broker the arrangement Kim felt she had to tell Judy about moving. Judy asked a few questions, was quick to say, "I'll check the participating physicians' list. Surely there's someone within driving distance, probably in the nearest metropolitan area."

"Indianapolis," Kim said. "Or Cincinnati."

Kim felt relieved. No longer would she have to finesse Vivian's curiosity. When she moved, Judy would work it out. If necessary, Kim would find some excuse to fly or drive to Chicago.

The agreement was brokered by phone.

Since neither Kim nor the Milcheks were prepared to decide whether or not the child could meet its biological parent, the question remained open and at the discretion of the Milcheks. Kim could not risk faxing the document anywhere in Sleeder, so it would come to her via regular mail. The women's respective doctors conferred and relayed instructions to each of them.

CHAPTER FIFTY-SIX

"It doesn't feel right, S'ster, talking in church like this."
They sat in the last pew. Their words echoed. A bead of holy water
clung to the middle of Jennifer's forehead.

"Don't worry. No one comes at this time of day."

"What does it mean 'Courtesy of Mr. Clyde Johnson'?" which
was what Vivian had written on the outside of the envelope Clyde
had given the girl at school.

Another outmoded nicety. "It's a way of acknowledging his
helpfulness."

Jennifer followed Vivian's gaze to the detectable mound
beneath her loose-fitting shirt. "S'ster, I don't need help anymore."
The girl pinched and pulled the yellow angora of her mittens into
tufts then smoothed them.

"You've told your mother?"

Jennifer shook her head.

"Someone else then?"

Jennifer shook her head.

"I said I'd stand by you."

"You don't mean it."

"I do. I do!"

Jennifer mumbled.

"I didn't hear what you said."

"I said I'm going to Mrs. Melrose."

Vivian made a sound like a bird expiring. *Charlene's mother?*
Mrs. Melrose does abortions? No wonder Charlene won't look

314

anyone in the eye. Jennifer's dark hair roots showed. A tear fell on her mitten. Vivian reached out and tipped up the girl's chin and looked into her sad eyes.

"It's natural to think about abortion. It is. You're not a bad person, Jennifer. I understand. I do." Vivian embraced her. "You don't want to add a second foolish decision on top of the first one." She took Jennifer's shoulders and made eye contact. "Abortion can be risky. Especially when not done by a doctor. You could lose the ability of ever becoming a mother."

Jennifer's face scrunched up like an infant about to cry. "S'ster, I d-don't want to b-be a mother. It would be unfair to the baby."

Vivian exuded the love and compassion she felt. "Sweetheart, one day you'll meet Mr. Irresistible and fall in love and get married and want a family." She dabbed at the girl's eyes with her handkerchief. "It'll be different then. You'll be proud. Believe me."

"You don't get it, S'ster! You don't!" Jennifer wrenched free. "I've fallen down and I'm trying to get up and it's like you keep kicking me while saying you want to help. No matter what I do I'm going to regret it forever. No matter what. Forever. Some days I can't keep track of my classes. I'd be an awful mother. I can't do this to a helpless baby. I'm trying to be responsible." The girl swung her arms hysterically. "I want to die, to die."

Vivian ducked and caught and held onto Jennifer. Men made fulfilling their rules sound so easy. They divined solutions like abstinence while women and children paid dearly for such failures.

"Stop. Don't do this to yourself. Don't. Jennifer, listen. I know what you're going through. I really do. I do because I had an abortion once."

Jennifer stopped and stared at her in disbelief.

Vivian hadn't intended to go this far. "I-it's true," she said, feeling color drain from her face. She took the girl's hands in hers.

"I was sixteen. Jennifer, I remember it on every anniversary of that day, and in between it haunts me."

The girl seemed to take in each word and examine it like a puzzle piece.

"When one of my students celebrates a birthday, I see my little girl—it's always a little girl—blowing out candles on her cake. I wonder what kind of cake she likes, white, chocolate? I wonder how smart she is, if her eyes are gray or blue, what she looks like. And on holidays—" Vivian stopped. She shouldn't be sharing any of this. Her guilt, her failure would only confuse Jennifer. This was more than she had revealed to anyone. "Oh," she said, "I do understand."

Jennifer buried her face in Vivian's lap and sobbed. Vivian stroked her back, her hair, cooed softly, giving what she had wanted and needed when she had been in the same predicament. Who would be Jennifer's special friend after she left Sleeder? Would there be anyone?

"Dear, you're right. Your life won't ever be the way it was before. You will have to become your own best friend. You will have to live with the decision you make for the rest of your life. Think about that, about what you can live with." *You will endure. You will persevere.*

Vivian rested her hand on Jennifer's hair, remembered the obstetrician's hair close to her as he bent to inject the saline solution. Once again she smelled his oversweet jasmine aftershave, the coppery smell of blood. Sickened, she shuddered and closed her eyes and let Jennifer sob her heart out.

By the time Jennifer's eyes were swollen red and her sobs gave way to gulps for air, Vivian had eased her own queasiness with deep breathing. She said, "Back then I acted against everything I had ever believed and been taught. No matter how often I have forgiven myself, I'm still tormented. I regret my decision."

Jennifer sniffed. "I won't tell anyone. I won't."

"I know you won't."

Vivian's mind presented a dreamlike image of the door to her parent's bedroom opening. Inside was a long, narrow hall flanked by many closed doors, each a choice, each hiding sad consequences yet to be discovered.

CHAPTER FIFTY-SEVEN

"This isn't the way to the market!"
"I'm taking you to my place."
"I can't go to your flat!"
Clyde shifted, bumped Mary Ruth's knee. She jerked it away.
"Sorry."
Everything about Clyde registered nobility, the way his long, tapered fingers held the wheel, the way his hands hinged from his wrists, the way his profile exuded the strength of Caesar's image on a coin. Mary Ruth liked that about him. By the time they arrived, curiosity had taken hold of her and quelled her protests.

She stepped out of his Porsche into what could have been a Norman Rockwell still life—an ax stuck in a tree stump in front of a neatly stacked cord of firewood, a log cabin that reminded her of Granny Mae's, except this one was larger and better cared for.

The hinges on the door squeaked.

"That's something I've been meaning to fix."

Mary Ruth spotted the upright piano, a camel-colored sofa. In front of the sofa stood a table with a thick glasstop and a lacquered tree trunk base.

Clyde bent and ignited crumpled newspapers in the fireplace. "I keep this kindled," he said. "It'll heat up quickly. I'll take your coat."

She was wearing a cream-colored suit over a peach-colored blouse, Kimberly's pearl pin.

Sports and news magazines and a couple of picture books lay on the glass-top table. Over the back of the sofa hung a brightly-hued, hand-crocheted afghan. Someone must come in to clean; everything was tidy. Clyde hung their coats on wall pegs near the front door and moved around the counter into the kitchen. "Put on some music if you like." He nodded toward the stereo.

She pilfered through his collection of tapes and compact discs— Hootie & the Blowfish, Michael Jackson, Whitney Houston, Barbra Streisand, Madonna, Madonna, Madonna.

She said, "I love the smell of a fire."

She didn't know how to choose, so didn't put on anything. On the wall beside the fireplace hung three African gourd rattles. Above them hung an oak-framed sepia portrait of a slender African couple. The woman wore a high-necked lace dress with a bustle, had one hand on the chair beside her. In the chair sat a poker-faced, mustached gentleman with a top hat perched on one knee.

"Family?"

Clyde was setting biscuits—cookies—on a plate on a tray.

"Only generically speaking. I come from down-to-earth folk. Bathroom's through the bedroom."

She saw the crocheted bedspread on the brass bed. A quilt, stitched ever so proud, as her mother would say, lay folded at the foot of the spread.

"This table's lovely."

"I made it."

"You did! It must've taken months. It's beautiful."

She sat on the edge of the sofa and picked up one of the picture books on the table and flipped pages past Hattie McDaniels and Sidney Poitier accepting Oscars. The other book's title was: *African-Americans: Architects of the New World.*

"Have you read Cornel West?" he asked, rattling utensils in a drawer. Without waiting for her answer, Clyde said, "He's one articulate brother. Tells African-American history like it is, without hate. Most of us carry too much black pain around to be able to do that."

Whatever was black pain? Mary Ruth frowned. They should discuss what Clyde wanted and leave.

"I also made these," he said, holding up two mugs, then putting them in the microwave above the stove. "There's a tad of rum in this. Hope that's okay."

"A tad?"

"Absolutely."

She smiled.

"Music," he said, crossing in front of her to the stereo.

Even though he was several feet away from her, Mary Ruth could feel his aura.

"Excuse me," she said, both to get away from him and to satisfy her curiosity.

On the wall over the headboard of the bed African warriors danced on an unframed welt of homemade paper. Barbells and an exercise bike stood in one corner next to a cedar chest with a saxophone on top of it. Clyde's spicy scent tinged the air. She moved into the bathroom and leaned her back against the wall and closed her eyes, picturing him pedaling the bike, sleek with sweat, playing the sax. She opened her eyes and saw an excited stranger in the lead-spotted mirror.

Clyde had added a log to the fire and put on some music. He seemed larger than life rocking in the chair by the fire. Sultry sax shimmied up her spine, the primal pleasure of rhythm and blues.

"I mustn't be long," she said. Then, "Your place isn't anything like I imagined it to be. I mean your home isn't what I would have guessed a bachelor's would be like."

"Family recipe," he said, raising his mug. "For ... special occasions. To happiness," he said, toasting. "To us."

She looked down quickly at the creamy liquid, made no comment, picked up the cup and sipped.

"Uh, Sister Dominic would like this! It's ... rich."

"Sinfully."

Mary Ruth felt his eyes on her.

"Rock candy soaked in rum mixed with softened ice cream, butter, brown sugar, and refrozen." His rocker *swish-swished.* "M'Ruth?" Clyde leaned forward. "M'Ruth, I want to say something."

Suddenly she was dying of heat.

"M'Ruth, I don't pretend to understand your religion. Or your sister thing. I, uh, know you're a kind and caring woman, a truly gifted woman. Maybe a little stuffy," he smiled uneasily, "but kind and caring."

No one had taken her to task for discipline before.

Peering into Clyde's dark, piercing eyes produced a kind of push/pull sensation, the oddest mixture of assertion and resistance, offering and withholding.

"I ... admire you," he said.

Mary Ruth experienced a rush of emotion. "Th-thank you."

Embers formed a row of bright beads, a rosary, along a curved splinter. Silently, she recited the bride's prayer she had said aloud at investiture:

> *He has placed his seal upon me that I may prefer no love to Him.*
>
> *The winter has passed; the turtledove sings; the vineyards burst into blossom.*
>
> *With his own ring my Lord Jesus Christ has wed me, and crowned me with a crown as his bride.*
>
> *The robe with which the Lord has clothed me is a robe of splendor with gold interwove, and the necklace with which he has adorned me is beyond all price.*

She said, "In England, without central heat, it seem cold even with a fire."

His rocker *swish-swished.*

She sipped.

"M'Ruth. This may be our only chance."

Clyde's crooked half-smile disclosed anguish.

"My mother wasn't Catholic," she said, saying the first thing that came into her head. "I wasn't allowed to visit any other church, not even high Anglican."

Her father had so many complaints about Baptists: Granny Mae's fervor, her and her mother's ignorance, her mother's drawl, her family's poverty. Once when she was about nine and in a snit, she asked him why he was complaining about her mother, that if he disliked her mother so much, why had he married her?

He said, "To make her an honest woman."

Mary Ruth straightened because now, right here, for the first time, she understood what that meant. Her emotions tumbled. *But they had to produce a marriage certificate to prove my legitimacy before I could enter the convent!* Clyde had said something and was waiting for her response. *That's* what his contract with Reverend Mother had been about!

"Financially," she said, forgetting about Clyde, "my father supported my mother, but I don't think he ever intended to share his life with her, certainly didn't intend to share my life with her." Why her father had snatched her away from her mother the same way a slavemaster took a child from its mother.

"Dear God."

"What's the matter? M'Ruth, are you all right?" Clyde set his mug down and came over to her.

Something inside her chest avalanched like the force of a rushing waterfall.

"You're pale! Are you ill?"

Mary Ruth looked at him.

322

"What's wrong? Did I say something? Tell me anything. You can. When I'm with you, I feel so ... accepted," he said.

She let his compliment seep in and warm her, a kind, concerned man.

Her father had promised she would be safe in the convent. *Safe from what? Safe from him having dark-skinned grandchildren!* "Bloody, bloody, hell," she said, flattening her hands, pressing on her knees.

"What is it? What!"

"I'm blood," she said, looking into his eyes. "Blood. My black Baptist mother lives in Kentucky."

Confusion riffled in his eyes, his expression stunned. He leaned forward as if trying to hear better.

She hurried to say, "That's why you catch me staring at you. I've known so few African-Americans, none as an adult. I'm ... intrigued. I-I'm sorry." Her father had strongly suggested that African-American men would contaminate her. "I shouldn't have blurted that out. It's just that, just ... in that instant I realized something ... painful that I should have known long ago."

"Wait a minute," he said, frowning, cracking his knuckles. "Did I hear right? You blood?"

"I am, but I needn't have mentioned that."

His eyes widened. He reached out and lifted a strand of her hair and moved it between his thumb and forefinger and peered at it in the light of the fire. "I never suspected."

"There's no reason you should have. I'm sorry."

"For what? For joining the human race? For being blood?" He seemed angry now, stood and circled, a caged lion. He said, "This changes things."

"Nothing," she said. "It changes nothing."

"M'Ruth, I know about such things. This won't be gone tomorrow, M'Ruth. No, ma'am, it won't. You can't just snuff out who you are!"

323

"Actually," she said, sliding into the corner of the sofa, "I'm ashamed for having had so much when Mum and Granny Mae had so little. On religious grounds, Father wouldn't divorce Mum. Nor was he keen on helping her. When I was little he'd often threaten that if I weren't good, he wouldn't send Mum her money."

"What a terrible burden for a kid! Don't put your hand up to try to stop me. I'm not going to chill out. No, Mary Ruth, I am not."

What was he so angry about? This didn't affect Clyde. Yes, her father had used her. Tears burned her eyes as pain filled her.

Next thing she knew, Clyde was holding her, consoling her, kissing her temple, stroking her back. "Why didn't you tell me? Woman, I want to comfort you and I want to shake you. I don't know what to do."

"Oh," she said, resting her head on his shoulder with her face turned away from his. "Just let me rest. I wanted to tell you," she closed her eyes, "only because I wanted you to know that I understood some things about you that you did not think I did." This confession felt like closing a wound. How nice to be held, to trust.

Clyde stroked her hair. "No wonder. M'Ruth, I don't want to be ... inappropriate. I-I can't hedge. There's something I must say. Don't get mad at me, okay?"

Flames danced behind him.

He took her by the shoulders and forced her to look at him. "Whenever I'm with you, I'm happy. My heart overflows like a, I don't know, a wonderful cadence. I'm flabbergasted that you're blood. Can't believe it. Delighted. It ... frees me. I have to know. Is there any way for you, for me, I mean is there any way ... for us?"

Oh. She pulled back. He mustn't do this.

"You must know that I ... care very much for you."

She didn't know any such thing, was shaking her head.

"Tell me that you feel some of the same, that we have a small chance. Tell me it's possible."

Her weeping must've affected her hearing because she kept hearing words Clyde had no right to say, would never say, could not say. In profound bewilderment she shook her head. When she finally stopped, the tenderness in his eyes washed over her. She saw how his hands trembled, how vulnerable he was, how very much in earnest.

"I'll stop riding the pedal, master any music, do anything. Name it."

Mary Ruth heard the plea in his voice, the fear of disappointment creaking in his tone. She searched his eyes, thinking about her vow of celibacy. Before she realized what was happening, he was kissing her, and she found herself responding in an unknown way. Inside her resounded a resplendent organ fugue, all stops open.

"Please," she said, breathless, gently pushing him. "Please." She eased distance from him, swallowed, met the blaze in his eyes, knowing that in this moment she truly felt what he did. They must never be alone again, not like this.

"Woman," he said, "you are black and beautiful and your heart beats one with mine. I know it does. It does."

"Please," she said. "I've laughed with you, learned from you, even ... improvised with you. You bring me joy. Great joy. But—" Her fingers moved involuntarily to her lips where she still felt the pressure of his. It had happened so fast. "I admire and respect you, Clyde, but, in the eyes of the Church, I'm already married." Seeing the pain in his eyes and needing to hide her own, she took custody of the eyes, instinctively interlaced her fingers, and bowed her head. She said, "We mustn't speak of this again. We mustn't. We won't."

CHAPTER FIFTY-EIGHT

Vivian followed distant taillights in the blinding snow and kept the car at thirty miles per hour. The windshield wipers fought against heavy, wet clumps. The tires *slush-slushed.* Jennifer clutched her monkey. The last time they had gone to Peoria Vivian had lied by default when the staff person assumed she was Jennifer's mother. This time— Jennifer reached out to turn on the radio.

"No," Vivian said. "It's hard to concentrate. I'm sorry." The girl's muffler was wrapped around her neck. "Are you warm enough?"

"Y-yes."

Vivian eased the car into the tire tracks ahead of her and pushed the defroster lever. Given the grace of time, she would have canceled Jennifer's appointment and scheduled another. Urgency, however, had become the order of the day. Like Sister Dominic she felt compulsion to cross some invisible moral line. The air in the car felt pressurized with guilt.

How can I willingly lie? How can I not?

Once Sister Dominic had secured her advocate, once she had accomplished her goal, the old woman glowed with peace and radiance.

"We can turn back," Vivian said, pushing the girl, convinced that what Jennifer wanted to do would rob her of all measure of peace.

"I don't want to turn back."

"Are you okay?"

The girl popped her gum. "I'm here."

What about me? How can I live with this? The Church offered only clichés: The end never justifies the means; two wrongs don't make a right. Where were the clichés that supported thinking for oneself? Jennifer could change her mind, tell her mother she wasn't going to spend the night with her girlfriend after all. Clara Suges would let it pass the same way Vivian had passed Kimberly when, deep in her bones, she knew something was amiss. *Why did I do that? Because I didn't know what else to do, I really didn't want to know—* Vivian didn't want to think about Clara Suges, not about how she was failing her.

"Jennifer! Don't snap."

"Sorry. Before this—" Jennifer patted her tummy, "I didn't chew gum."

"You didn't?" Vivian glanced at the girl, seeing her differently.

Not once had Vivian been permitted to act on her own recognizance. Early on she learned that someone else was supposed to think for her: her parents, the Church, the pope. *When do I get to think for myself?* She swallowed, had not quite thought of it that way before.

"Jennifer," she said, squinting at the road as if this would improve her insight, "you know I don't agree with your decision, but I do respect your making it. I want you to know that."

Jennifer's owl-like eyes met hers briefly. "S'ster," she said, breathing in quickly, pushing aside her muffler and biting her lower lip.

The right decision shouldn't bring on shame, but then Vivian wasn't sure that what she saw in the girl was shame. For generations women had been willing victims to those insecure enough to need to believe they were in control.

Jennifer poked her finger at the monkey's absent eye.

The kind of decision Jennifer made took more guts than Vivian or her own mother had shown. Someone sometime must take the initiative to break the imaginary chain. Someone must squelch fear and challenge so-called authority and act on her own belief.

But to blatantly lie?

Jennifer wrapped the monkey in her muffler. The tender way she held it made Vivian realize how the girl must have wrestled, and continued to wrestle, with her conscience. Their tires slid off the shoulder. Close to tears, Vivian eased the car back into the tracks.

Even Kimberly seemed to be successfully wrestling down demons. In the time Vivian had known her, the novice had become surer of herself than Vivian had thought possible and less accident prone, even contemplative. Vivian's mind heard her mother's indictment: *After that your father wouldn't touch me.* Authentic love required letting go of control. One held on by letting go.

"What's duress?" Jennifer asked the woman who cleverly posed the same question many different ways. The monkey lay limp on Jennifer's lap.

"Are you *sure*?" the woman asked.

Jennifer fumbled for Vivian's hand and squeezed.

"I'm sure."

"Good," the woman said with finality, then turned to Vivian. "Insurance?"

"Yes," Vivian said. "I mean, No. No insurance."

"You're going to make a donation then?" the woman asked, all business. Vivian nervously counted out twenty-five ten-dollar bills. The woman stared at the money as if cash were something she hadn't seen before. Then she opened a desk drawer and poked around in it until she produced a paper clip.

"Sign where the X is," she said, handing the pen to Vivian. "Please."

A wave of heat washed over Vivian, a steaming coat of armor. The type on the paper blurred. *This means damnation.* Every nerve in her body ached. Her memory triggered how much she had wanted someone to do for her what she was doing now for Jennifer. The girl held her breath, face crumpled in a tortured plea, waiting for Vivian's signature. Vivian turned to the paper. Full of misgivings, she detached a part of herself from another part of herself, and signed: Clara Suges. Guilt dropped like a hot lead ball into her solar plexus. She rested the pen. Dare she ever ask God's forgiveness for this willful act?

The woman slid the signed form inside the folder. "We'll need a specimen and a blood sample," she said. "There may be a wait. We're shorthanded because of the weather. Usually there are few or no complications, but it's good to be informed of what could happen. The mandatory video's seventeen minutes long." She led them to a small, private viewing room and left them sitting beside each other on a green, vinyl-padded bench. The sign said: TO START press here. It wasn't too late for the girl to change her mind.

The monkey lay on its stomach across Jennifer's lap.

"Jennifer?"

"S'ster, I've thought and prayed about all the consequences."

Guilt pumped in Vivian's bloodstream. She remembered Jennifer's questions: *What if I were raped at gunpoint by a serial killer with AIDS? By an uncle or my brother? Is there never an exception?* Abortion was never to be taken lightly. She remembered her conversations with Glory. She remembered her mother's plight and what it had done to their family. Her final decision came down to whether or not there could be one possible exception when she could name several. The bigger stumbling block had been whether or not a woman had a right to her own conscience, to make her own choice. Vivian shuddered. She had counseled Jennifer: You will have to be able to live with yourself.

As if reading her mind, Jennifer said, "I can live with this, S'ster," and started the video.

Lawyers must have prepared the narration because complex sentences full of incomprehensible medical terms supported visuals so explicit, they could be called savage in their illustration of potential mishaps. Vivian smelled blood and experienced cramps.

"S'ster," Jennifer said, muting the sound and closing her eyes.

We could say we changed our minds and just walk out. On the way home, the car will skid on ice, slide off the road, and we'll both be killed. Stop this, she told herself. *You're wallowing in old brainwashing which is the worst kind of rape, invading another's conscience, interfering between God and—* She turned to Jennifer, who beyond a doubt had prayed and reflected. *Is she responsible enough to make this decision?*

If God intended Jennifer to think for herself then God intended *her* to think for herself; if nothing else her mother's experience had confirmed that it was wise to take responsibility.

Jennifer lay on the examining table. Vivian sat on a metal folding chair near Jennifer's right shoulder, one hand on the girl's arm.

Dr. Horowitz asked, "Do you have any questions?"

Jennifer's steady gaze indicated the girl's resolve. Jennifer shook her head. Vivian did, too.

"Okay," he said, rolling the stool forward and positioning himself between Jennifer's legs.

The nurse, whose nametag said Peggy, was a middle-aged woman. She said, "Jennifer, the doctor's going to insert a local anesthetic. Take a deep breath now and breathe through your mouth. Don't move. Breathe. Breathe."

Vivian turned her face away. Her gaze landed on the small sink. Her brain spouted text memorized long ago: If no priest is present, anyone may baptize. Pour the water, say the words. If she believed she were guilty of killing, of murder, she wouldn't be here; neither would Jennifer. The words were pabulum spoon-fed in the name of control. How many lies, told by someone playing God, had she and so many other women swallowed whole?

Dr. Horowitz snapped off his gloves and patted Jennifer's shin. "I'll be back when that takes effect."

Peggy pumped the blood pressure gauge. "Honey, remember," she said, "don't move if it hurts. You could cause harm to yourself. Good," she said, leaving the band wrapped around Jennifer's arm. She pulled the IV stand closer. "This is Valium just in case," Peggy said, tapping on a vein. She inserted the needle and checked to be sure the clip on the hose was closed. "We won't start this unless it's necessary. It makes the doctor's work harder, and, believe me, the aftereffects aren't worth it. However, if you're in too much pain—"

Vivian and Jennifer exchanged looks. There had been no way to adequately prepare the girl for the steps of the procedure. None. Peggy rolled a machine close to Jennifer's feet, then a table with a tray of cloth-covered instruments. She lifted the cloth and silently counted the row of silver-handled, wedge-shaped instruments whose ends graduated from small to large.

Peggy stopped and turned back to them with one hand on the doorknob. "Don't be concerned about that horrible video. Dr. Horowitz is very gentle. I'm sure everything will go well." She hesitated, then said, "You know, I see lots of mothers and daughters. You two have a special relationship. It's nice to see." She smiled and left.

Vivian turned to Jennifer, hoping she still might change her mind.

Jennifer said softly, "I love you."

Tears turned the girl into a blurry image. "I love you, too." In this moment Vivian felt known and loved, held in Jennifer's heart, the bond mothers must feel.

"I feel strange," Jennifer said. Fear had turned her ashen.

"Me, too." Vivian stroked the girl's forehead. The hardest part of parenthood must be allowing a child to make her own decisions, her own mistakes. Unconditional love required it. In theology, intention was everything; in relationship, Vivian now knew, love was primary.

"I'm s-scared."

Vivian pulled a tissue from the box Peggy had set beside Jennifer and moved it across the girl's forehead. "You have every right to be."

"I'll never forget this."

Vivian heard her father's voice say: *If I go to hell for this, God will forgive me.* A spasm convulsed deep in her abdomen. "Neither will I," she said, squeezing Jennifer's hand. She moved a wisp of Jennifer's hair back from the girl's face. "Maybe we should pray," she said, resorting to the familiar. "Hail Mary, full of grace—

"You're doing fine. Only a couple of centimeters more."

The machine sounded like a lightweight vacuum. Vivian's memory produced smells—alcohol, blood, and jasmine-scented aftershave. Peggy alternated padding instruments onto Dr. Horowitz's palm with pumping the blood pressure gauge. Pale Jennifer crumpled into expressions of pain and fear. She squeezed Vivian's hand so hard that Vivian's ring bit into her flesh.

"No more! No ... more!"

The air brimmed with tension.

The doctor pressed low on Jennifer's torso.

The girl whimpered.

Vivian snatched the crescent-shaped metal bowl and held it under the girl's mouth. Jennifer dryheaved. Vivian looked at

Peggy. Peggy's eyes shifted to the IV. Vivian looked at Jennifer then shook her head to Peggy.

"We're almost done. I'm going as fast as I dare."

The *whir*.

"I wa-wanna die."

Vivian had wanted to die, too. She wiped streaks of black eyeliner from Jennifer's cheeks. "Honey, you're doing well," she said, "fine."

"Don't move!" the doctor and Peggy said as one.

Emotionally braced against pain, Vivian stood and pressed on the girl's hipbones with her hands.

The sound stopped. Dr. Horowitz pressed Jennifer's abdomen. Vivian wiped the girl tears.

"Done," he said, removing his gloves.

Jennifer breathed relief. Vivian squeezed her hand.

"Take it easy for at least twenty-four hours," he said. "Pay attention. Your body will tell you what it needs. If she runs a fever or has excessive bleeding, call," he said to Vivian. "Peggy will give you written instructions. No regrets now," he said, turning to Jennifer. "Not many moms have the courage to stand by their daughters the way yours has." He touched Jennifer's cheek fondly, said, "Be well."

"Doctor, thank you," Vivian said.

Peggy removed Jennifer's feet from the stirrups. "You're going to be okay," she said. She handed Jennifer two pills and a paper cup with water in it. "This is for pain. How do you feel?"

"D-dizzy."

Vivian's eyes fixed on the covered basin. A rush of what felt like white heat moved into her face. Some sisters had chosen to return to secular life for defending the right to choice.

"That went well," Peggy said. "I'll remove the IV."

Vivian saw an image of herself wearing a priest's white stole, holding a cruet of holy water in her hand. She could sprinkle the

333

water, say the words. She glimpsed Kimberly's countenance ingenuous as Mona Lisa's, watching to see what she would do. Vivian drew a quivering breath. Either she had already acted according to her conviction or she hadn't. Jennifer knew that, too.

Peggy picked up the basin, said, "I'll be back with orange juice and toast. Stay here as long as you like, then go into recovery room two. It's clearly labeled. Coffee? Tea?"

"Black," Vivian said, swallowing and staying right where she was. "Black."

CHAPTER FIFTY-NINE

Vivian had been kneeling in the chapel for what seemed like hours. She wanted to feel redeemed, saved. Jennifer lay sleeping in one of the convent's spare bedrooms. Dazed and numb, that's what Vivian felt. Regardless of what Kimberly had tried to get away with, it would not compare with what she had done. On the holy card in her hand, King Solomon sat on his throne pointing to the swaddled baby lying near his feet. *Cut the child in half,* he ordered.

Vivian had lied outright and, in doing so, robbed Clara Suges of a mother's right; at the same time her deed had given Jennifer a new life. The girl had rights, too, didn't she?

Mom lived a lie. Dad lived a lie. Ergo, I must live a lie?

She was tired of living a lie, of keeping secrets, of guilt and shame. What had all her self-denial achieved? *Nothing.*

She had allowed Jennifer to decide and the girl's relationships and life had remained intact. The girl's life remained intact. Didn't she, Jennifer, anyone, deserve joy, laughter, happiness as well as blame and shame? Didn't everyone deserve the right to decide, to choose, and accept the consequences that resulted? Would Jennifer come to resent her assistance? Would the girl eventually hate her because she *knew*? How would Jennifer feel about herself?

A part of Vivian knew she could never, never repeat this act, not put herself between a girl and her mother again. What if the truth came out? What about judgment day?

She heard Jennifer saying: *God is not mean!*

CHAPTER SIXTY

Mary Ruth knelt on the wooden floor in the parlor beside her open trunk, one of four in the room. She sorted sheet music into four stacks: Processionals. Recessionals. Mass/benediction. Miscellaneous. As much as she tried to focus on the task, all she could think of was Clyde, how she felt when she was with him, how she missed him when she wasn't. His dark face and twinkling eyes had taken up residence inside her. She tried to stay busy and not think.

What little furniture was left after their sale had been pushed under Mother Mary Gertrude's portrait against the rolled-up Tabriz. Only their founder's image remained on the wall; ghostly rectangles testified to the removal of other pictures. Bending over, Mary Ruth became aware of her breasts, how small they were, how her nipples raised like antennae whenever Clyde entered her mind. She smelled his spicy aftershave, felt his body next to hers, tasted his lips on hers, and moisture secreted between her legs. She straightened, forcing her attention back, not allowing herself to ponder—not for one second more—Clyde's improbable, impossible suggestion. Order, she must reestablish order.

Everything will go back to normal in Louisiana when I do not see him, do not hear his mellifluous tones, do not smell his unique presence. She would say, *It has been interesting working with you and good-bye.* Or, *You have progressed much more than I would have guessed.* Or, *I have learned from you, too, Clyde.*

Nothing she rehearsed satisfied her.

336

Nettled, provoked, she set her neatly folded habit on the floor beside the Gregorian Chant pages she intended, once and for all, to dispose of. Why had she kept them anyway?

"Temptation, that's all Clyde is," she muttered. *I wouldn't know passion if it struck me like lightning.* How could one discern temptation from passion? If Vivian had held chapter as she was supposed to, this bloody interior blaze might never have ignited. Could temptation and passion ever be one and the same? If so, would her heart ever stop aching?

She would no longer share Clyde's contagious laughter or banter with his African sense of humor, or spark at the brush of his hand inadvertently touching hers. When the glow had been but a pilot light, Vivian could have snuffed it out easy as wet fingertips touching a taper flame. Mary Ruth straightened her spine, raised her chin. *I should give her bloody hell. Letting that gum-snapping girl spend the weekend here without one iota of explanation.* Rules applied to Vivian, too, and in this instance Vivian had blatantly disregarded them. That girl, Jennifer, had talked Sister Dominic to death.

Muddled, she didn't know in which stack to put "Baby Divine, Sleep."

No matter what had transpired, no matter how she had been tempted, she had kept her intentions pure. *Pure, pure, pure, pure.*

Out in the hall, Sister Dominic's canes *thumped.* Mary Ruth looked at the closed door. Dare she ask the wise woman for spiritual counsel? Not when Sister Dominic competed with her for Clyde's attention. The old woman loved him, too. Asking Kimberly would be less than prudent and Vivian was the last one she would consult. In or out of the confessional Father Rupert was a confirmed sexist. *Dear God, I'm going mad like those English cows buckling over from mad cow disease.*

She bent again to her task, resolving to simply say good-bye to Clyde in a way that demonstrated her genuine fondness without betraying her deeper feelings. She straightened and stopped what she was doing. The solution was so obvious she had almost missed it. She would speak directly to Clyde. That was exactly what she would do. No go-between.

Now feeling a tinge of rebellion despite Mother Mary Gertrude's staring down on her, she sorted more quickly. She could share what she valued about him, tell him what she wanted to remember, how much she appreciated his dedication toward Sister Dominic's recovery. Already, she felt renewed, proving this decision the truly right and best one.

"M'Ruth." Clyde slid his hands under his thighs on the piano bench like a child told not to touch anything.

"Clyde," she said, summoning bravery, but sounding short of breath. "I want you to know how much I've appreciated your friendship, your dedication—"

"Don't do me any favors."

Disarmed, she peered at him, felt a surge of admiration at the conviction in his tone. Unlike her father, Clyde expected honesty. She hungered for it, too, along with a new, heretofore inexperienced— *Stop. Don't even think these thoughts. You know what you have to do.* Afraid to utter a word, Mary Ruth sat with one hand over the other in her lap like a penitent. She listened to their breathing. Sometimes he read her thoughts before she even knew them. He seemed to be able to read her very soul.

Clyde reached inside the V-neck of his sweater and extracted an envelope from his shirt pocket. His free hand reached out and picked up her right hand and slapped the envelope into it.

"Take this," he said. "It's taxi fare and an address. I'm asking you to meet me in Chicago on your layover to Boga-boga. Maybe on neutral turf we can be honest. Don't ... hum."

Madness. This is madness. She turned the envelope over. Blank on both sides. She traced the seal with the tip of her index finger, as if inside were a music stipend so generous she dare not accept it. But once in her hand, how could she possibly return it? Apprehension and anxiety mixed with another daring emotion she couldn't identify. It moved up her spine.

She whispered, "I don't know."

"Hey." He stuck his hands up in the air. "No gun at your back. Not a finger will touch you. No siree. Not without what you call permission. I'm offering only honest talk."

He made permission sound like a dirty word. She met his gaze, felt both challenged and reassured. How dare he mock the way she had chosen to live her life?

"I'll pray on it," she said, raising her chin.

"You do that," he said, getting up and pacing with his hands in his back pockets. "So," he said, "I asked you once before. If you took a souvenir from this place, what would it be?"

"The chandelier," she said, not needing to think more about it. Sometimes instead of going to the chapel to meditate, she sat in the parlor watching the sun create rainbows in its crystals.

"Well," he said, rubbing his hands together, sliding back onto the bench. "Tasteful choice. M'Ruth, may I respectfully say that you light up a room without benefit of any chandelier. Bless that woman's illness," he said, putting his fingers on the keys.

The saints marched in.

On the other side of the closed door the others must have taken "Saints" as a signal to join them. Their eyes fastened on Clyde's dark fingers, watching him fill the room like a joyful procession, like a litany come to life. Mary Ruth joined her sisters knowing full well that all of them would not be together as a family again. She belonged with the sisters.

Clyde played the last repeat twice and when he finally stopped, he glanced at Mary Ruth and removed his foot promptly from the pedal. Then, much too quickly, he stood and took hold of Vivian's hand. "I hate good-byes," he said, giving her the kiss of peace.

"You've been such a lifesaver," Vivian said, pushing her hair aside, blinking back tears. "Are you sure we can't sprinkle a little holy water on you?"

"I'm already saved," he said. "At least I hope so." He peeked at Mary Ruth with such significance that she lowered her eyes lest she betray herself.

"Sister D, I'll sure miss you," he said, cuffing her chin, then embracing her. "Keep on thumping."

"Oh, you," she said, turning pink and waving at him. "I'm taking you with me," she said, tapping the middle of her forehead. "I'll keep you in my prayers. God bless."

"Keep the faith," he said to Kimberly, brushing each of her cheeks with his.

For once Kimberly didn't try to be clever. She merely smiled and said, "You, too."

Clyde came to Mary Ruth and immediately turned glassy-eyed. He took her hands, squeezing tightly as he touched her cheeks with his. "Make 'em sing like angels," he said. Mary Ruth's eyelashes fluttered as she looked into his eyes. "Every day," he said. He squeezed her hands again, let go, and stepped back.

"All of you," Clyde said, "let me know how you're doing now, hear?"

They stood in the cold draught and watched him descend the steps until he moved out of sight. They waited until the sound of his Porsche faded before closing the door.

"A prince," Sister Dominic said.

"Unforgettable soul," Vivian said.

"Charmer," Kimberly said.

"H-has anyone seen my breviary?"

CHAPTER SIXTY-ONE

The three sisters bid Mary Ruth good-bye at O'Hare Airport and boarded their plane to Cincinnati, where a sister from Brandenburg would pick them up. Kimberly and Sister Dominic sat beside each other near the back, while Vivian sat in a bulkhead seat.

As soon as they were airborne, Kimberly found herself listening to Sister Dominic listing instructions she had heard too many times: Sister Dominic wanted medication for pain even if it hastened her death. She did *not* want to be fed intravenously. She expected, per custom, to be interred in her habit *sans* casket in the convent cemetery. Because she had heard it before and because she was apprehensive about her session later in the day with Reverend Mother, Kimberly found herself only half-listening. What could she possibly say? *I don't think I belong here. I want to do something dramatically meaningful.*

"And, what is that?"

"I don't have a clue." She could hardly tell the woman that in a matter of weeks or a couple of months she'd know whether or not she was going to be a mother.

Kimberly said, "I'm looking for my little corner of the world."

"It's not a corner," Sister Dominic said. "Inside you where the answers are is not a corner. It's a place more like being inside the quiet eye of a tornado. You have to work through a lot of conflicting currents to find that spot, but it's always right there waiting to be discovered."

Kimberly must've appeared baffled because Sister Dominic expounded. "If your light's under a bushel, you have to burn your way out. If you entertain straight lines, angles, squares, corners, then you're following the rules of doing when you mean to be following the rules of being."

"Say more."

"Dear, I thought you would never ask. I'm prepared to answer. Think of life as a seesaw on a swivel base. The ends of the plank go up and down and the whole plank also goes 'round and 'round. If you limit your action to up and down, your life will jolt bumpety-bump-bump with awful mood swings. If your action goes only 'round and 'round, you're apt to get dizzy, disoriented, confused. Trick is, to put yourself in the center of that stillpoint. From there, you can observe all the action and choose when and where to venture into it. There, life is serene and easy, safe from falling off the edge, or taking into fancy flight. That's where God's power resides in you."

Even if she didn't grasp their full meaning Kimberly recognized how profound these words were. She studied the old woman's face.

Sister Dominic patted her hand. "You young ones are blessed with so much physical energy when your life's work is to search for and find your source of spiritual energy. Oh, my, I've talked myself out," she said, sighing, She closed her eyes and reclined her seat.

Kimberly stared ahead. Baffled, that's what she was, baffled.

Jolly Sister Bonaventure, supervisor of the infirmary, met them. Sensing Sister Dominic's downheartedness, Sister Bonaventure told them a joke about an Irish golfer who kept trading off increasing amounts of his sex drive to a leprechaun, who promised, and delivered, increasing tournament wins. Finally the leprechaun asked, "Sir, why are you so willing to give up so much of your sex drive?"

"That's easy," the golfer answered. "I'm a Catholic priest."

That was just the beginning of Sister Bonaventure's repertoire. By the time Kimberly left, Sister Dominic could've been nicknamed Chuckles.

Kimberly, however, was not merry. She descended stairs, passed through two sets of locked doors on each landing that separated the convent side from the girls' academy, and made her way to the chapel.

I can't out and out lie. I'm done for. The intense silence in the halls overwhelmed her. When she approached a set of double doors, she could hear the voices of the high school girls on the other side. Outside, the *thudding* of a ball. The sound reminded her of the *thud* the Arizona clay made when she had dropped it on Guillermo's casket. Sometimes she thought she smelled it on her hand.

A lone postulant knelt praying at the communion rail. The vast dome made Kimberly feel miniscule, like a mere mite. She slipped into the last pew-for-two and knelt on the unpadded, wooden kneeler. She had forgotten how hard these kneelers were. She buried her face in her hands. By now, no doubt, Vivian had reported to Reverend Mother how willful and disobedient she could be. Reverend Mother would set her to scrubbing floors. Or worse. Why hadn't she chosen to stay in Sleeder? There, she would have Brenda's friendship. And the Milcheks.

When in doubt, leave it out, her father always said.
She had stayed and not left convent life because that didn't feel right either. Some place, somewhere she would find her corner, well, *her spot*, to brighten. Her own dilemma seemed like kid stuff, compared with Vivian's loss of face, compared with Sister

343

Dominic's struggle for health, compared with Mary Ruth's decision, which was transparent to Kim even if no one spoke about it. Why did everyone keep referring to the folly of her youth? What about the passion and verve of youth?

I can't keep running from one sanctuary to another. It's time for me to put up or shut up. Guillermo, let me rest in peace. It's time I got on with life. Let me rest in peace.

Brightness from the four large windows behind Reverend Mother cast the woman's face in shadow. Mother had lost considerable weight and no longer wore her habit. Kimberly focused on the woman's pectoral cross, which rose and fell on her white blouse. She knelt and kissed Mother's ring.

"We are pleased you are here. Be seated."

Reverend Mother smoothed her bangs, touched the half-veil she wore here, there. "I can't make myself go without it," she said, touching the veil lightly, as if Kimberly deserved an explanation.

On her desk sat stacks of papers, books, and a ream of holy cards held together by a metal strip, a product of the convent print shop. Also an open copy of the "Newsletter of Leadership Conference of Women Religious." Kimberly's eyes widened when she spotted it. Had she been found out?

"Dear, you've been crying."

So much for hiding.

"Farewells are difficult, Reverend Mother."

"I didn't mean to pry."

Bookcases flanked the windows.

"How was your trip? How is Sister Dominic?"

"Sister Dominic's weary and ... concerned. Reverend Mother, she ... she needs to know she's contributing. Sometimes all she talks about is dying." *Stupid, stupid, stupid.*

Reverend Mother's hand moved to the Christ figure on her cross. "It may comfort you to know," she said, "that once Sister Dominic settles in, she may choose her own tasks."

"Th-thank you."

After meeting Sister Bonaventure Kimberly felt a lot better.

The light behind Mother had moved, bringing a bit more visibility to her face. The woman seemed older than Kim remembered and wore lines of worry. Perhaps that resulted from her loss of weight. Mother's index finger tapped absentmindedly on the newsletter. "Are you aware that sick persons who are prayed for improve disproportionately to those for whom no prayers are said?"

"No, Mother."

"That's what I read in this newsletter. There were studies. Does that excite you?"

Kimberly hadn't thought about it. She said, "I pray for Sister Dominic." *And for myself. I pray for myself.*

Moments passed. Reverend Mother shifted uneasily, as if she, too, were uncomfortable.

"Forty-two pounds," she finally said. "I've lost forty-two pounds."

"You look great!"

"I do, don't I?"

The woman touched a fingertip to the corner of one eye. "Contacts," she said.

"I *knew* something was different!"

The exchange happened so rapidly.

Reverend Mother drew circles on the desk with the tip of her thumb. Why was the woman nervous? So far there had been no indication that Vivian had snitched, but something was on the woman's mind. What? Mother moved her thumb along the metal binding holding the holy cards. "Lest vanity take hold," she said.

She looked up, sighed, and folded her hands in her lap, asked, "You've elected to study gerontology?"

Across the street on the second floor porch of the guesthouse, a row of rocking chairs was turned backwards and leaned against the wall. Kimberly wouldn't lie, nor would she tell the whole truth.

"Reverend Mother, I've given that a lot of thought. It just doesn't feel right, not to me."

"I hoped you would say that."

"You did!"

A plaintive involuntary rasp escaped the woman. "That leaves theology," she said.

No. Not theology either. If I knew what she wanted, I wouldn't feel so stupid and foolish.

"Over the recent months," Reverend Mother said, resting her open hand flat on the newsletters, "I have forced myself to explore the possibilities suggested by Vatican II. At first I'm ashamed to admit, this approach was an attempt to peek into the enemy camp, so to speak, to learn their tactics."

"How this exploration started doesn't really matter. Sometimes," the woman said, smiling uncomfortably, "God sends angels where we fear to tread. I guess you could say I converted." She took hold of her pectoral cross.

Converted? Kimberly didn't breathe. Not sure of what Mother was saying, she squirmed and for once kept quiet. Where was this heading?

"I've come to believe that our traditions— I hope this won't disturb you." The woman appeared tormented as she searched for the right word. "I've come to understand," Reverend Mother said, "how the old ways made us emotionally dependent and robbed us of depth."

Kimberly leaned forward eager to listen closely now.

"Dear, I've come to believe that each sister's inclinations and talents are part of God's plan for *her* life. Our desire to send you back to school when we need sisters in the field so badly is a much contemplated and prayed over sacrifice."

"Reverend Mother, maybe if I—"

"Please," Reverend Mother said, holding up one hand. "Asking what I'm about to ask tries my soul because, well, I'm afraid of your answer. Should you refuse—" The woman's voice trailed off. "First," she said, tapping her breast as if that would still her breathing, "what we're about to ask is a request, not an order."

In this moment Kimberly realized that the tension she felt belonged to Reverend Mother, was not hers! Her lips parted.

"Please, don't say anything, let me finish. Nurturing the mind is as much a duty as nurturing the soul and the body. How else will we transcend human foolishness?" Reverend Mother drew an audible breath. "Aren't we the only one of God's creatures who laughs, who sings?"

Kimberly did not want to disappoint this woman.

Mother paled and crossed her lips with a trembling finger. She said, "The holy father's finally about to own the terrible mistake we made in censuring Galileo. In the fifties, even after the world honored Father Teilhard de Chardin as a leading paleontologist, Rome censored and silenced him. In the sixties, the Church silenced Father Kung for being so liberal. When it comes to us, blindness still prevails. Education is our most precious asset, our greatest investment."

"Reverend Mother, maybe if I—"

The superior raised her hand and stopped Kim. "Kimberly, we hope and pray you need us as much as we need you."

Need me?

"Kimberly, you bring us the kind of energy and intelligence we need a lot more of. Youth and passion for life itself. My request may sound heretical. Indulge me. Catholics make up two-thirds of the world's Christians, four-fifths of all humanity. The doctrine of infallibility, if one can call it that, became part of canon law in

1860. Before that, during the fifteenth century groundwork was laid to give authority to the body of bishops. Technically, therefore, the Church may move toward accepting the moral right of individual conscience." Her expression toughened and Kimberly had the distinct impression that the woman had practiced what she was saying.

"Until the seventies women weren't allowed to study theology in our seminaries. It's taken sheer willpower to pry open those doors." Suddenly Mother appeared drained, as if she had just relinquished whatever it was she was trying to ask into God's hands. "The clergy brewed every bit of the sacred tea we drank.

"Studying at the Jesuit School of Theology at Berkeley may make you feel lonely and as alone as a lost soul. But I assure you, Kimberly, it's time for us to take control, not only of the kettle, but of the ingredients that go into the pot as well. Before brewing we hope to plant and pick our very own tea leaves."

Berkeley? Berkeley!

"With your help we're going to brew a stronger, more palatable theology based on solid scholarship and on personal discernment."

A shiver of excitement moved through Kimberly. Reverend Mother was seeking a way to use theology to challenge teaching and tradition?

"We're convinced God sent you. Please don't disappoint us. We're asking if you will, through scholarship, become the leader that moves us into a new self-definition, one more appropriate to our times. Say yes, Kimberly. We need you."

Knock your socks off and swing the tiger by the tail!

"You're asking *me* if I will go to *Berkeley*?"

"They'll make it hard for you. We'll do our best to help."

Move over Margaret Meade, Ruth Benedict, Betty Friedan, Gloria Steinem. Kimberly reached up and yanked her fist in the air. "Woo-wooooo! I don't have to think about it, Reverend Mother. My answer's yes!"

"I'm an old woman. Take heart, child."

"Reverend Mother, I'll work my buns off. I will."

Reverend Mother dabbed her handkerchief to her brow, her eyes, then fanned herself with it. "I guess I'm right about your enthusiasm," she said.

If only Vivian and Mary Ruth were here. At least she could tell Sister Dominic. She said, "Mother, it's my corner of the world to brighten, my spot, my swivel spot. I just know it. Those Jebbies won't jade me." *Woo-wooooo!*

CHAPTER SIXTY-TWO

"This is it," the taxi driver said.

Mary Ruth looked down at the slip of paper in her hand. The address Clyde had written didn't say it was a Marriott.

"Lady, you gettin' out or what?"

She paid the driver and got out. The sounds of traffic, of airplanes taking off and landing, assaulted her. In case some unforeseen obstacle caused a delay that she didn't want to explain she had scheduled a late departure to New Orleans. Mary Ruth hefted her overnight case in one hand, her purse in the other, and made her way into the lobby where she first located the ladies' room.

She combed and smoothed her hair, freshened her lipstick, appraised her profile in the full-length mirror. Her cream-colored suit complemented her skin color more than she had realized. Her cheeks flushed with exhilaration. Her eyes flashed excitement. Meeting herself on equal terms for the first time, Mary Ruth raised her chin, then threw her coat over her arm, picked up her suitcase, and went to find Clyde.

His instructions hadn't said exactly where they would meet. How like him not to be precise. Twice she strode the perimeter of the lobby, feeling more alarm than she wanted to admit. Humming, she walked in and out of the shops lining the arcade. Clyde wasn't in the newsstand, not in gifts, not in souvenirs. Now with anxiety bordering on panic, she approached the desk.

"Mr. Clyde Johnson. Is he registered?"

The boyish clerk fumbled through slips of paper. "Oh. You must be ... Miss Vangaard. From England?"

Her heart took to racing. She nodded.

"Will you also be staying with us?"

"Oh, no! My flight's later out." *I can't even talk!* "Today. I'm flying. Away." *Good Lord.* "I mean, no thank you."

"Perhaps, next time you'll give us the pleasure," the young man said, smiling.

"Room five-twelve." He pointed. "Take the elevator."

"Th-thank you."

Positive that everyone was watching her, Mary Ruth summoned the lift. She looked right, left, and over her shoulder, then when it opened shrank into herself. She and Clyde must return to the lobby immediately. She knocked *sotte voce*.

"Jesus!" Clyde said, snatching her by the wrists and pulling her in. "I thought you weren't coming."

"Wh-what?"

He closed the door. His eyes were bloodshot with deep, dark circles under them. Everywhere, flowers. All kinds of flowers strewn on both double beds, along the length of the low dresser, in a vase on the table in front of the sheer curtains.

"I didn't know what kind you liked," he said, sounding anxious.

"I thought I had missed you," she said, turning to him. "That maybe you had changed your mind. I mean— They're lovely. Lovely." She envisioned her profile as she had seen it reflected in the mirror downstairs, let herself soften, feel feminine. "So many," she said, looking around. She had never seen him so dressed up— heather gray woolen slacks, a muted gray-and-tan herringbone jacket, a multicolored tie of African design. So handsome. She was afraid to make eye contact.

"I haven't been able to sleep," he said, sounding hoarse.

She was not prepared to defend against flowers, not against such obvious vulnerability. Something akin to terror clouded his eyes.

"M'Ruth," he said, seeming desperate, "a man can't blubber in public; I tried to think of a good public place. I don't know what I would have done if—"

His desperation melted her heart.

"M'Ruth, when you listened with your heart, music came out of you that you didn't even know was there. I know you have to catch a plane. I know you don't have much time. Listen with an open heart now. I'll never forgive myself if— Will you do that?" He swallowed.

She savored every word as if he were Mozart scribbling notes just for her. What did he mean, he would never be able to forgive himself? For what?

He said, "Don't ask me to compete with God. I can't. I hope we want the same thing. I want us to be friends. Cherished friends."

He understood that they were saying farewell! He wanted to remain friends, too. She mellowed and smiled.

His eyes held her smile light as a snowflake. "Thank you," he whispered. He moved as quietly as a contemplative to the dresser and picked up a long-stemmed, dark pink, orchid-like cluster of blossoms and gave it to her. "Cymbidium," he said. "I like to grow them, but I didn't grow this one."

She tipped it to her nose. Growing flowers, that was nice in a man. "I don't know what to say." Looking around, she said, "I'm overwhelmed."

"You deserve more than I can ever give you!" He sat erect now on the edge of the seat, hands on his thighs like a priest waiting at the side of the altar for her to finish playing the organ. Thoughtful and waiting quietly. This is how she would remember him.

His gaze fixed on her, expecting something. What, she didn't know. She slid into the chair across from him.

"What I have to say is simple, M'Ruth. Is your heart open? Are you listening? "I'm about to die," he said.

One of her knees took to bobbing. Her heart thumped the *toyi-toyi*. "I'm listening," she said.

"It would— God," he said, moving his hand across his brow. "I practiced this and now I can't remember."

"Improvise" she said, teasing mildly.

Their eyes locked.

"M'Ruth, if I could pick up that phone and call a priest or a judge, someone certified to— It would make me the happiest man in the world. Don't stop me. I need to get this out. I've never come close to asking anyone before. You have to know that."

He paused and pressed his lips together; they whitened. "I love you." His eyes held hers. "I have loved you for a long time. We're good together. Don't wash this over lightly, M'Ruth, I love you. Marry me. Consider it. Please. That's all I'm asking, that you take time to think about this. Don't shortchange me, yourself, us. If you have any doubts of my sincerity, we can call a preacher up here right now and do it."

A priest wouldn't come; bans had to be published; the sacrament of matrimony usually wasn't performed during Lent.

"I know you couldn't return to Sleeder. I'd have to finish the school year, but then I could take any kind of job, anywhere. I'll play gigs, do anything."

He looked so desperate, she should stop him, but vanity made her want to hear every word. Clyde seemed astonished that he was still talking. Hope crept into his eyes and he talked even faster.

"There's a possibility in the fall that I could teach near my hometown. M'Ruth, I'm dying here. Say something. I can't plan for two by myself. Maybe I could change religions," he said. "I don't know about that. I don't know how we could be together between now and September, where you would live, where you would want to live."

With my mother.

"If only—"

She wanted to hear everything he had to say.

"M'Ruth, I'm offering my heart. Please." His eyes entreated her. "I love you, I love you, I love you. Marry me."

She turned the stem slowly in her hand. Reverend Mother would take it personally. Her sisters would never approve. Her father ... such sweet tender words. Mary Ruth rested the flower on the table, appreciated its beauty. In her peripheral vision she saw Clyde move his handkerchief across his brow. She tried to imagine life without him and sensed a vast emptiness. There would be no turning back. She closed her eyes and breathed and listened to her heart. With him she felt more at home, more fulfilled than even with her own mother or with Granny Mae, anyone. She opened her eyes.

He sat watching her with his elbows on the table, hands together, fingertips touching his lips.

Her vision blurred. "I will," she said. "Yes."

In a flash she felt herself hugged in his arms. He lifted her and spun her around. The room whirled. She clung. For once in her life she felt both happy *and* safe, daring. When he stopped spinning, she held on tight, waiting for the room to still. He kissed her then.

She said, "I do love you."

This time she responded to his kiss. It felt right, good, wonderful. Clyde had saved her from herself.

CHAPTER SIXTY-THREE

"Mum? It's Mary Ruth. I'm in Chicago. I'd like to come home for a visit. May I?"

"Yesterday won't be soon enough, Sugar."

"I knew you'd say that, Mum."

"Is something wrong?"

"No, Mum ... I mean ... Mama. There's just been a ... change. I'd rather tell you in person. I think it will make you happy."

"Door's open."

"I know, Mama. I know. God bless."

CHAPTER SIXTY-FOUR

'Twas the radiant sunset of the first full moon after Easter. Clyde unbuttoned the long row of tiny buttons down the back of Mary Ruth's wedding dress. Her lashes fluttered with shyness as she slid it off her shoulders and stepped out of it. The beauty of the dress was in its simplicity of fabric, cut, and design. It showed off her lovely skin and figure, needed no adornment. No wonder Kimberly liked silk; silk exuded softness and the endurance of femininity. Mary Ruth felt both soft and sure, demure and sensuous, fully a woman-self. She had never suspected all this lay inside her.

"The music," she said, "Mama was so happy."

Clyde paired his shoes and slid them under the bed. Everyday she'd learn new little habits like this about him. She became aware of the sound of the rushing river outside and went over and cranked the window open and peered down at Cumberland Falls. They were on the third floor of the state park lodge outside of Corbin, Kentucky. Fresh, damp coolness promised spring.

Under certain conditions, they said you could view the only moonbow in North America, an ivory rainbow created by the reflection of the moon on the water. Clyde had thought of everything. She looked above the falls to the sky. Streaks of rose, mauve, purple, orange, and gold. Tiny buds graced the trees. Perfect, everything was perfect.

Clyde came up behind her and wrapped his arms around hers and kissed the sides of her neck. She shivered and snuggled into him, feeling his firmness rise against her.

"Your Aunt Mabel's a trip," he said.

"Ummm." She nestled into him. Her father had not come. It was the only note of sadness in an otherwise perfect day. "We're blessed."

Her father would have sneered at Clyde's high-fiving kin decked out in Easter finery, singing full-throated and proud. Perhaps it was better this way. They were her people, not her father's. She saw guests scribbling their phone numbers on the little gold-edged napkins monogrammed "Mary Ruth and Clyde" in Sister Dominic's calligraphy, and exchange them.

Clyde teased a grain of rice from her hair and placed it in her palm. She stroked her husband's tapered fingers, felt the tiny grain in her hand. Small things added up to big things. "By the time I leave my mother's in June," she said, rolling it between her fingers, "we'll have come to know each other." How she had longed to know her mother, not as a child, but as a woman, and now she did. Timing was everything. Mary Ruth placed the grain on the windowsill, an offering. "Thank you," she said, looking up at him. "For persisting. For the moon. For you."

"You're welcome." He pecked her lips lightly. "I have your wedding gift at home."

Home. Come June, they would move into the old Victorian house they were renovating on the outskirts of Vincennes where Clyde had accepted a teaching position. The large bay window of her teaching music room looked out on a huge maple tree.

She said, "My present's there, too."

No longer would the church clocks chime the rhythm of her life. Now her rhythm flowed from within to Clyde and returned energizing her. She had improvised her present to him and written it down, music that expressed her love. Five movements: You entered my life. I resisted. You persisted. I yielded. Love prevailed.

"Hungry?"

"Mama cooked enough for ten weddings!"

He laughed and mimicked her mother. "'Sugar, you put some flesh on that man's bones, hear?'"

Mary Ruth giggled. Clyde took her hand and walked her to the bed, pulled the pillows out from under the cotton spread, and propped them against the heart-shaped headboard.

"If," she said, "you're ... in any way uneasy—" He shrugged, feigned insignificance, added, "That's copasetic."

Mary Ruth picked up the pillow nearest her and hit him with it.

Clyde caught it and pulled her into an embrace with the pillow between them. He said, "Shower's big enough for two."

She kissed him swiftly and moved into the bathroom, saying, "Martyrdom doesn't become you. I get to set the temperature." She slipped out of her undergarments and into the spray to cover her timidity.

He joined her, his dark, sleek body taut with muscle, his manhood raised like a flagpole.

Clyde lathered slippery soap over her back and breasts. They acted silly and shy, laughing until play gave way to an improvisation as ancient as life itself; stirrings giving homage to natural rhythms. Where her body was round and curved, his was long and lean. Where her secret pulse lay hidden in folds, his mystery rose grand and proud.

Clyde bent and suckled one of her nipples. Unexpected pleasure made her gasp and clutch him. He smiled at her, lathered and caressed her like a blind person memorizing every pore.

The warm water, his manhood pressing and teasing between her legs, his fingers finding and calling forth her secret mysteries—she yielded to all of it. Her knees weakened. She heard herself moan. When she thought she could stand no more and wanted fulfillment in the worse way, Clyde turned off the water. She didn't want him to stop. Not now. Not ever.

His penis felt hot to her touch. His eyes, so full of love. Gently he moved the towel across her body. She didn't remember drying him nor him starting the music. Once on the bed, soft, sultry blues surrounded them. She longed for him.

Clyde slithered lotion over the curve of her hips, her breasts, her throat. Mary Ruth shuddered with pleasure beyond anything she could have imagined. He circled the rim of her sensitive nipples, took one in his mouth and pulled so hard, every part of her rejoiced and opened. She arched her back and thought she would die of desire.

Clyde lathered her feet, her ankles, her calves with silky lotion until her whole body felt charged with desire and luxury. Eyes glazed, he guided her hand to his penis and caressed behind her knees, inside her thighs. Again and again his mystery approached, pressed, and retreated from her moist entrance. He touched a hidden spot that made her moan and grip his shoulders. Still, somehow he withheld, titillating, tantalizing her.

Panting in the grip of some powerful primal energy, Clyde's body slid across hers, tenderly making her rise and reach for want of him. He kissed her full and hard and drew her tongue into his mouth. Heat flooded her breasts, her ears, her feet, her body. Desire engulfed her.

Finally, finally she felt him slide inside her.

"Ohhh," she whispered. *Joy. Pure joy.* She abandoned herself to this new wild rhythm, riding higher and higher roughly through waves of heat. She would die for lack of breath. She heard her high screeching sound.

"Yes. Yes," he said, then slowed.

"Please. Please."

Clyde changed his rhythm and rolled them over, easing Mary Ruth astride him. "You know how to do this," he said, his finger a pummel to her sensitivity. "Ride."

She threw her head back and rode gently at first then for dear life, reaching altitudes beyond clouds, beyond heaven, rode into a burst of heat that numbed her feet and rose and rose and rose until it burst inside her and moistened her whole body. She heard Clyde's high-pitched sigh. Together they plunged with full richness a symphony orchestra and chorus.

Every part of Mary Ruth's limp body tingled. She didn't know how long they lay there. The music had ceased. Her mouth felt parched. Deep down inside her, a strong beat pulsed on.

His breath wafted warm pleasure into her ear. She wanted to say something but couldn't. Her body, his body, their bodies. How strange. How wonderful. She looked into his dark eyes. He kissed her forehead.

"Babe, M'Ruth," he said, smiling weakly, closing his eyes. "Before we do this again ... I got to rest."

She watched his dark face on the pillow, his breathing taking on the rhythm of sleep; she smelled scents of their lovemaking. Outside, water rushed, strong and steady as their passion.

Slowly, so as not to disturb him, she slid from the bed and moved to the window and saw the prism of the moonbow arc over the foaming rapids.

CHAPTER SIXTY-FIVE

Vivian stood in front of her Brandenburg Academy class, facilitating a passionate moral debate. Each day she posed a moral issue, insisting that each girl prove her ability to vigorously defend her own viewpoint before graduation. At the sound of the bell, silence ensued. Vivian's breath caught. She counted the tolls of the death knell, each separated by three seconds, one for every year of the deceased sister's life. Four years had passed since she had left Sleeder. Her students knew she had kept vigil with Sister Dominic the night before and remained respectfully silent. Sooner or later all of us had to face the harder decisions in life. Sister Dominic had made all the necessary decisions, including who would prepare her body for burial.

Kimberly said, "I'm so glad I didn't have to advocate for her."

"Straightaway. I feel her presence."

"I do, too," Vivian said, absorbing the grace of their being together again.

"The flowers," Mary Ruth said, checking them in the refrigerator. "Cymbidia."

"And baby's breath," Vivian said, handing each of them a black bibbed apron.

Mary Ruth pulled hers over her white maternity dress. She radiated even in mourning.

"It's super to be together," Kimberly said. She wore a navy blue, raw silk shirtdress.

Sister Dominic's body lay covered with a linen shroud on a narrow white porcelain table, feet extended over the trough. The old woman's habit draped over the back of the chair with her black slip on top, veil on one chair post, starched guimpe on the other, just as it might have waited for her on any morning. Her long, narrow scapular lay accordion-folded on the seat; under it, her pectoral cross, coif, the wooden rosary that would go around her waist, breviary, her rosary.

The previous night, Vivian had pressed a cross on the old woman's forehead with her thumb, saying, "I love you. Godspeed."

This *ménage* of final preparation actually belonged to elderly Sister Joseph, who had laid out what they would need—three basins, washcloths, towels, soap, shampoo, oil, a circular mesh of wire for the crown of flowers.

Kimberly rolled up her sleeves and began filling three basins with water. She said, "Thanks to you, Sister Dominic, I get to delay my oral exams. Some day," she said, turning to them, "when new physics is old physics, we'll be able to prove her presence here."

Vivian needed no proof; Sister Dominic's spirit charged the atmosphere.

Mary Ruth bathed Sister Dominic's face. Then Kimberly held the old woman's head up and washed the back of her neck. They folded the shroud down over Sister Dominic's chest, each woman bathing an arm, while Vivian lathered Sister Dominic's hair.

Vivian asked, "When is the baby due?"

"July. Early July."

Vivian hesitated a moment thinking of Jennifer who was in nursing school now. Jennifer's last letter said she had given up smoking and was dating a Catholic intern whom she hoped to marry. Jennifer's letters offered a daughter-like love, a natural intimacy derived from what they had shared.

"An Independence baby," Vivian said. She addressed Mary Ruth. "Is it true that you and Clyde have the chandelier?"

"Yes. It was his wedding present to me. Piano students comment on it all the time; it also makes a tantalizing baby-sitter. Nicky lies on the floor and watches the sun sparkle on the crystals, or she watches its prisms dancing on the wall."

Her eyes met Vivian's. "We were still at the breakfast table when you called. That night Clyde couldn't sleep. He got up and played 'Saints' over and over. Nicky sat on my lap and we kept vigil with him. She kept asking why Daddy was so sad. Children are so perceptive."

A child was born one with the light; failure lay in losing that light, in not searching for it again.

At the sight of Sister Dominic's faded scars, memories came flooding back. That fateful fall seemed part of another lifetime now. Glimpses of Sister Dominic flitted through her mind: the way the old woman savored that first taste of ice cream; her hand digging deep into her pocket and pulling out a pen knife; fingers pulling gold thread through a vestment held close to her magnifying glass. If ever a woman toiled as the handmaid of the Lord—

Mary Ruth said, "I can't begin to tell you how much I appreciate being here. Did you have to bend Reverend Mother's will for me to join you?"

"Actually," Vivian said, nodding toward Kimberly, "we have the young upstart here to thank. Originally it was her idea. Sister Dominic put the request in writing. Reverend Mother couldn't refuse. Kimberly could have been the one to ask; Reverend Mother agrees to anything Kimberly suggests."

Kimberly blushed.

Vivian said, "Rumor says the bishop's a-skittle about what he calls our new dangerous thinking."

Kimberly chanted, "Look out, the feminists are coming, the feminists are coming," and laughed. "God help us; these feminists think for themselves. Some even have babies without being married."

They chuckled.

Mary Ruth winked at Vivian and bent down and spoke softly into Sister Dominic's ear. "I hear they're going to call her Dr. Kimberly.

"I get no respect." Kimberly crinkled her nose. "Even the pope's apologized for the Church's attitude toward women, though I don't see any action. Dr. McCall has a certain ring, don't you think?"

"One day," Vivian said, setting the comb down and uncovering Sister Dominic's breasts. "One day when I was particularly perplexed with you, Kimberly, Sister Dominic admonished me. She said, 'A pioneer is always alone. Let the girl be.' "

"How lovely," Mary Ruth said.

Clearly pleased, Kimberly said, "That's a real compliment. Pioneer. I don't think of myself that way. I hope I'm never again so out of touch with myself as I was back then. Sister Dominic offered us such a beautiful example. I love her."

Yes. *Love.*

When you were missing part of yourself, you missed love when it was offered, even when it charged all about in high voltage molecules.

Vivian never wanted to be so out of touch with herself again either. After confession and months in spiritual retreat she had figured that much out. She even seriously considered telling the truth to her superiors, but decided that would cause too much harm to too many people. If ever she were asked to help a girl in Jennifer's condition again, she would go about it differently and not lie. What had driven her to lie had more to do with herself than with Jennifer. Owning her part in both episodes had somehow freed her first to forgive herself and to accept forgiveness. She found herself relieved of the need to strive for perfection, was satisfied with her graceful, if flawed, humanity. Her resolution must have showed because Mother Philip Neri called her back into service the following September.

"We all hid," Vivian said, "without knowing from what."

"Nevermore," Kimberly said. "Black ravens have become doves."

Mary Ruth said, "She knew Clyde and I were falling in love even before we did. Sister Dominic tried to warn me, but said to follow my heart because that's where love resided, in the heart."

Sooner or later one has to exchange control for a leap of faith. Maybe that's what growing old is all about.

Kimberly said, "She gave me hope. I was afraid to commit to anything for fear I would suffer the pain of loss all over again. Sister Dominic taught me to trust myself even when I behaved so outlandishly. I'm a lot less rebellious now."

"Thank God," Vivian said, chuckling.

Kimberly stuck her tongue out at Vivian and smiled.

"It took a leap of faith for me to marry Clyde."

Vivian had failed to leap that first time, or, more accurately, had leapt falsely. She said, "Charity was Sister Dominic's greatest gift to me. I could always count on her for the charity of truth."

They grew silent, turned the body over.

Jennifer had leapt successfully without one ounce of regret. Vivian had made the wrong decision for herself, Jennifer, the right one. It had taken Vivian years to realize that God had forgiven her, that it was she who needed to forgive herself. When she finally did her lost child ceased to invade her dreams; peace claimed her soul. Now every breath brought serenity.

Still she grew irritated at the way the Church kept trying to elevate the fetus to the status of personhood when it had yet to give that status to women. God was not inconsistent. God was not mean.

"Nicky's two-and-a-half," Mary Ruth said, answering Kimberly's question. "When she was three months old, I brought her here for a visit. You should have seen Sister Dominic, the proud godmother, waving her pectoral cross over the baby's nose, clucking and cooing, 'Dominique. Look at me, Dominique. Look at me.' "

"I have a godchild," Kimberly said, pulling a photo from her pocket, "close to Nicky's age."

"Is she related?" asked Vivian. "I think she looks like you."

"Only in the sense that I'd like to think so," Kimberly said, passing the photo to Mary Ruth. "Her mother's a friend who lives in Chicago. Her name's Frieda after her grandmother. She calls herself 'Fwee.' "

Clearly Kimberly loved the child. Vivian caught the young woman's eye. Quickly, as if caught doing something wrong, Kimberly changed the subject just the way she used to. She turned to Mary Ruth and said, "I wish Sister Dominic could have embroidered Nicky's baptismal gown." Kimberly pocketed the photo.

"I know," Mary Ruth said softly. She twisted open the bottle of oil and poured some into a small bowl.

Silently they anointed Sister Dominic's body, each lost in her own thoughts. Then, while Kimberly matched makeup samples to Sister Dominic's complexion, Mary Ruth cut stems and began fashioning the crown.

Vivian rolled a black stocking up one leg. She had feared that preparing Sister Dominic's body would repel her. Instead, she found herself rich in the love and joy of belonging.

Kimberly applied a brush of light rouge. "I've learned how to listen to myself," she said, "though I still find teeth marks on my foot."

Vivian couldn't help but smile. Their young novice had come so far.

Kimberly held up the coif and wrinkled her nose at it. "I don't know what to do with this."

"Let me," Vivian said, taking it and trading places with her.

It saddened her that no pockets had been laid out. She pulled the coif tight and tied it in back of Sister Dominic's head, and tucked in stray wisps of her hair. "I wish I had been born later," Vivian said. "Spiritually speaking, these are exciting times."

"Tell me about it," Kimberly said, rolling her eyes upward. "Sometimes it's rough on the front lines."

Vivian wove the black, bead-headed pin into the veil at the middle of the forehead to secure it. "I work at supporting my students in thinking for themselves."

Kimberly fastened the rosary around Sister Dominic's waist, then rolled the black-draped table up alongside her body. She said, "Every day I battle simple-minded seminarians or Church fathers entrenched in the Middle Ages. One, two, three," she said.

They transferred Sister Dominic.

Mary Ruth said, "I spend more time thinking about life's meaning now than I ever did. Motherhood does that to you."

Vivian stopped and stared at her, then pretended to straighten Sister Dominic's pectoral cross. In the beginning of convent life, she had thought of it as punishment, figured she had thrown her life away; in time, however, like a benevolently arranged marriage, she grew into grace surrounded by God's children and the strong sense of God's presence. Truly blessed, that's what she was.

Kimberly laced black rosary beads between Sister Dominic's folded fingers and rested them on her breviary.

Mary Ruth held the crown over Sister Dominic's heart. They touched it and prayed silently, then together placed it on her head.

Sister Dominic would lie in state in the chapel for twenty-four hours.

Kimberly asked tentatively, "Shouldn't we talk about it?"

Vivian stiffened. Sister Yvette's life supports had been mysteriously disconnected and Sister Yvette had died. Discussion would change nothing. She prayed, *Dear God, from whom all mixed blessings flow, I have yet to find comfort with this, even though Sister Dominic always said, when at the crossroads, heed the voice within.*

One went alone to final judgment. Vivian extended her shaking hand and smoothed the folds of Sister Dominic's veil.

"I don't know," Mary Ruth said.

Vivian asked, "What is there to say?"

"I wish," Kimberly said, "I wish that before all the old ones are gone, someone would dedicate a museum to all the American sisters who made so many contributions to our schools, hospitals, and social services. If history's ever to record—

Vivian heard herself say, "Before moths eat all the old habits."

Mary Ruth said, "Super idea."

They looked at Sister Dominic lying there in state so peacefully. The venerable old woman had sought and found moral power. If Vivian lived to be one hundred and ten she would never acquire that kind of strength. She picked up the stack of memorial holy cards and distributed one to each of them. On the face of the holy card stood St. Dominic in priestly white garb, a cheerful saint who focused on beauty and creativity. The back of the card said:

Sister Dominic, Sister of the Immaculate Heart of Mary
née Jella Anna Ozretich,
May 1, 1914—March 15, 1996

Mary Ruth took one of each of their hands and rested them on her baby. Vivian felt an upward thrust, then a downward movement like a somersault. Mary Ruth smiled at them, her eyes brimming with joy. Mary Ruth raised her chin and intoned "*Magni-i-fi-caaat anima mea Dominum.*" They held hands and sang:

> "*My soul doth magnify the Lord.*
> "*Be it done unto me according to thy Word.*
> *For he hath regarded the low estate of his handmaiden.*
> *Henceforth all generations shall call me blessed.*
> *He hath put down the mighty from their seats*
> *And exalted them of low degree.*
> *He hath filled the hungry with good things.*
> *And the rich he hath sent empty away.*"

In the silence that followed, Vivian heard Sister Dominic's voice, as clear as clear could be, say: Your soul is the only compass that points toward meaning. Pay attention.

Sow a Thought, and you reap an Act;
Sow an Act, and you reap a Habit;
Sow a Habit, and you reap a Character;
Sow a Character, and you reap a Destiny.

Anonymous quote from *"Live and Labour,"* 1887.

ABOUT THE AUTHOR

Frankie Schelly has published numerous short stories and articles in magazines and journals. Before turning author she worked both as an Advertising Manager and as Associate Creative Director of an advertising agency. She is mother to three children and lives with her husband in the Blue Ridge Mountains of North Carolina. *At the Crossroads* is her first novel.

A GOOD READ ALWAYS
MAKES A WELCOME GIFT

At the Crossroads is a print on demand book available from: http://www.booklocker.com/crossroads, from the author's website: http://www.firesignexclusives.com, from bookstores via their usual distributor, using the ISBN 1-9313932-7.

9/02

Printed in the United States
5895